I0573878

Woman of the Stone

Modutan Empire, Volume 1

S.V. Farnsworth

Published by Stone Wolfe Press, 2019.

WOMAN OF THE STONE

First edition. October 10, 2019.

Copyright © 2019 S.V. Farnsworth.

ISBN: 978-1733859905

Written by S.V. Farnsworth.

Also by S.V. Farnsworth

Modutan Empire
Woman of the Stone
Monarch in the Flames

Watch for more at https://mailchi.mp/79a2e6d8a775/svfarnsworth-author.

To my dad, Will David Clark, who passed away this year. Thanks for telling me the story of how you read the dictionary for fun as a boy. It made an impression.

Chapter One

Emerald swayed closer to what she wanted yet could never have, a family. Light shone through the wavy glass of a window in an isolated stone cottage. It caught an errant curl of her hair and ignited the fiery highlights. Unwilling to be discovered, she stepped aside and raised the hood of a brown cloak against the winter evening. The peals of children's laughter struck dissonant chords of joy, longing, and crushing sadness within her. Unable to resist, she touched the windowsill and watched.

"All right, little Benny, quit playing and lay down." Amanda plucked her son from his father's shoulders and laid him on the bed. "Husband, they'll never sleep this way."

Benjamin stopped tickling the middle child and set the boy on the floor. "I think your mother is jealous, Sam." He pried a toddler from his leg. "What do you think, Leland? Shall we tickle her?"

The boys giggled and Benny jumped off the bed to join them.

"You'd better not." Amanda laughed as her husband chased her around the room.

The little boys, all under the age of five, swarmed in and reached after her.

"I love your laugh." Benjamin gathered her in his arms.

She stood on tiptoe for a kiss.

Emerald imagined she was the squatter's wife and a certain merchant ship captain's son was her husband. The image didn't last because the shame of her unworthiness pierced the tender feelings. She had fallen in love with Liameo Hume and dreamed of marriage until the purity of her hopes had been dashed by an enemy.

The pain deepened as if to split her chest open to reveal the stone where once a heart had been. Drained, she leaned against the wall and slid to the ground. Of course, she still had a heart, that's why she risked her life coming here tonight. She wasn't here to eavesdrop on these farmers but to protect them.

The cottage door swung open and Benjamin grabbed her upper arms, lifted her, and slammed her against the rocks of the wall. The hood fell back as her head hit the unyielding surface. Feet swinging, she struggled.

"I told you not to come here. You attract flies like manure." He dropped her and cast a wary gaze around the acreage in the darkness.

"I don't stink, Ben, but the flies I draw have fangs." The censure stung. "Take your family to safety in the castle, at least during the full moon." She righted her cloak.

His shoulders hunched as he balled his fists and paced. "My wife believes in you, and we have nowhere else to go." He kicked a tuft of dead grass, visible in the light from the open door. "That's why we're squatting on your land but you're not the ruler of me." He stopped to point a finger. "Besides, there has been a fistful of moons since the Wolf Clan came."

She raised a hand. "Not as many as you think, and the enemy may attack tonight. It's the last night of the full moon."

"If they come, then it will be for you." He charged and shoved her backward to land with a thud. "Go away, thrice-cursed Woman of the Stone." Ben stormed inside and slammed the door.

She stood and dusted off her trousers. Shaking her head to clear the echo of the words, she could not avoid the pain. The epithet had reopened an old wound.

The Wolf Clan sought her life at any cost but with numbers too few to threaten Stone Castle. The fiends lured her out by attacking innocent people. Her compassion would not allow her to let Ben's family die just because he was a fool. Thus, she stayed despite the danger.

Nestled in a river valley, the embrace of winter held the surrounding trees and empty fields in stasis. Fog rolled into the clearing from hot springs that dotted the valley. Like a wave, it flooded the low-lying areas and hemmed in the cottage. Emerald did her best to put away the ache as the moisture thickened on her skin.

The moon had not yet risen. Perhaps, the enemy would not come. She drew the hood of the cloak for warmth and strode to the nearest tree line, determined to guard Amanda and the children throughout the night.

Settled in, she remained alert and watched the hazy halo of the moon appear on the horizon. A wolf howled in the distance. She grappled with a sudden sense of apprehension. There was still a chance it was simply a wolf and no men traveled with it.

The full moon climbed into view to be greeted by a chorus of howls nearby. Her heart raced. How many beasts were there?

The Wolf Clan did not have great numbers. Only two or three men attacked at once, sometimes without wolves at all. This group sounded bigger.

Dread shivered along her spine. Unswerving, she clutched the hilt of an arcane sword on her belt. Malice coiled her arm to sink fangs of power into flesh. She sensed the will of the sword. It craved vengeance.

Six men emerged from the forest to the west, each with a wolf companion. One man opened a lantern to ignite an arrow held by another who launched it. The flaming arrow ruffled the air in a blazing arc until it lodged in the thatch roof of the cottage.

Emerald advanced with grim intent. Like a specter from the grave, she held an ancient power these men could not fathom. She unclasped the cloak. It fell to the ground.

Moonlight reflected on the shaven heads of the enemy to lend them the pallor of death. Clad in furs and covered in nightmarish tattoos of ferocious animals, they brandished weapons and attacked. Their wolves surged ahead of them across the field.

Leather armor offered Emerald protection but not much. She drew the sword, aged green with patina. The sharply honed edges flashed copper in the light of the thatch fire. Young and lithe, she slit throats and spilled red heat into the night. The force of her will matched the force of her blade, fueled by the urge to protect the little boys inside the cottage.

The fog embraced her as if comprised of the ghosts of her dead clan. Savoring every slash, she finished the wolves and engaged the first savage man in death's gruesome dance. With a slice to a carotid artery, she withdrew like a shadow and reappeared like a wraith.

The valiance of her long-dead people made her bold, though fear iced her veins. She'd never faced so many enemies at once. Even as she parried and struck, the men circled. Terror diffused inside her and she felt her wrist for the blade concealed in her sleeve. If these men captured her, then she would slide it between her ribs.

The thought crippled her with a memory.

At fourteen, she had endured an unspeakable assault at the hands of one such a man, the first she had killed. The experience rippled across her skin with horrifying sensation as if it were happening again, but she pushed it away. She preferred death before such torture.

The five remaining men capitalized on her distraction. Throat tight, her composure slipped as they cut off any possible escape. Whooping and growling, they stabbed at her, but she blocked and dodged the blows. The bowmen could have killed her with ease, so why didn't they?

An arrow plunged into the back of the nearest swordsman. The four other men moved to investigate the new threat. Another shaft sank into the eye of an enemy. She slashed the leg of a man and rolled out of sight beneath the waist-high fog.

Two clansmen shouted and charged toward the burning cottage as the farmers fled with their sons. Flames illuminated silhouettes as the savage men engaged them. Ben shot an arrow but missed, and a warrior struck him in the neck with an ax. Amanda stabbed a kitchen knife into the man's bicep as the other dispatched her with a crossbow.

The cries of the couple mingled with those of the children and drove Emerald forward. The little boys returned to the cottage to shelter beneath a bed. Embers fell onto the blankets and wisps of smoke swirled upward.

Horrified, Emerald slammed into the crossbowman and caused him to drop his weapon in the fog. Nothing mattered except defeating these men in order to save the children. The roof crackled and sparks flew as the axe-man pulled Amanda's knife.

Arterial spray filled the air with the smell of copper. Emerald slashed his chest, pleased when the furs offered no protection. Rolling to a squat position, she parried the crossbowman's dagger and stepped behind to draw her blade through his bowels until his spine severed.

The final foe hobbled toward her, dragging a leg due to the wound she had delivered moments ago. She knocked the sword from his hand and struck off his head. With the arcane blade's desire for blood quenched, it released her. Without hesitation, she dropped it to the earth, glad to be rid of it for a time.

SMOKE-FILLED THE COTTAGE and sparks rained as Emerald ran to the children. The tender-aged boys screamed as she pulled them from beneath the bed. Blood dripped into an eye. Realizing how she must look, she wiped her face with the bedding.

"I'm here to help. Climb on my back, Benny."

Hesitant until he saw the flames, the oldest boy clung to her.

Faint, she picked up Sam and Leland and staggered into the fresh air. She gained her bearings and followed an animal trail through the woods as she ascended the foothills of the Impenetrable Mountains. The safety of her home wasn't far away.

Though her muscles burned, she pressed forward until Stone Castle loomed above the tree line. Crossing a meadow, she ducked at the whistle of an unseen arrow. The boys cried, and she gulped air, running until drenched in sweat. Silently, she prayed Benny could hold on. His death grip around her neck simultaneously reassured and strangled her.

Optimism surged as she burst from the forest to behold the silver fields and black moat around the gray granite curtain wall of the castle. Tiny motes of light swirled in her vision and her head wobbled. The narrow drawbridge lay extended, but the gates stood shut.

"Stephan, the enemy pursues." Clear-voiced she hailed the gatehouse.

Her footfalls pounded on the planks of the drawbridge. To her relief, the cumbersome wooden doors opened. Once inside, she collapsed to her knees.

Two adolescent boys pushed the gates closed and secured the crossbar.

"Em, shall we drop the portcullis?" Stephan's fair hair shone in the moonlight.

Breathless, she leaned against the gatehouse masonry. The children in her arms trembled with fright and cold. Stephan took Benny and touched her shoulder.

She caught her breath. "Sound the alarm and take defensive positions."

Stephan set Benny on the cobblestones and hurried after Rick.

"Come with me, Benny." She adjusted her hold on Sam and Leland and lugged the boys toward the keep.

With a whimper, Benny followed. Eager to warm the children, she climbed the steps and pushed open the door with a forearm. Benny shivered violently as he came inside and she booted the door closed.

"Nina?" She set Sam and Leland on the tied-rag rug in front of the fire. Benny joined them.

Outside, the gatehouse bell rang. Everyone across the border in the foreign village of Meadowgren would be alerted. She held no illusions about anyone coming to help, their laws forbade them, but perhaps someone would heed the warning and escape the fate of these boys' parents.

"I'm here, Em."

A plain, slender girl of twelve years unfolded from a cushioned chair beside the fire, dropping a large, leather-bound book to the wood floor with a thud. She picked it up with haste and wrapped a shawl around her patched and mended nightgown.

"The squatters' sons need care, and I must help fend off the Wolf Clan. They're really stirred up this time." Emerald knelt by the children and wiped their tears. "You're safe now. Nina will give you something warm to drink."

"They're filthy, Em." Nina held a stern expression.

"Very well." Emerald ruffled Benny's strawberry-blond curls. "Feed them, bathe them, and put them to bed."

She had watched over the family since last spring. The look of loss in Benny's eyes caused her heart to swell, but she refused to allow those feelings to distract her from the responsibility to protect every orphan in the castle. Intent on her duty at the wall, she crossed the room with purposeful strides.

"Take a cloak." Nina headed downstairs to the kitchen.

Emerald grabbed one from a peg by the door, along with a bow and a quiver of arrows. Advanced skill with the longbow enabled her to strike from the relative safety of the curtain-wall of the castle. If more of the Wolf Clan dared attack, then she would delight in ending their lives.

Once outside the keep, she noted the night sky. It would be hours before the dawn-stars crept into view. Upon the morning, the children would likely be safe for another moon cycle, because the Wolf Clan preferred to move during the height of a full moon.

Perhaps, they viewed it as lucky. However, her people, before they had been wiped out, had called it a death moon. Over the past forty years, there had been no luck in it for the Stone Clan.

She breathed the frosty air and tread in silence on the steps up the castle wall. At the top, she approached Stephan where he crouched behind the snaggletooth crenellations. His attention was focused on the fields.

"Have you seen anything?"

Startled, he dropped a nocked arrow from a bow.

Suppressing a laugh, she took a position from which she could see an enemy should they approach.

He sighed and his posture relaxed. "No, Em. I think you're the lucky one." He pointed a gloved finger at her face. "You have blood smeared on your cheek."

She winced and drew the hood of the short cloak to conceal it. The thought of blood on her skin stirred dark memories of the first man she had killed and the gore on her afterward. She resisted the compulsion to scrub her face with her palms even as her nostrils flared with the remembered stench.

"I thought I wiped it away." She scanned the tree line for the enemy but found none. "In all seriousness, I didn't expect an attack tonight. It's been a long time." She didn't want to frighten him with the fact there had been more of the savages than normal.

"Several moons at least, Em. Nina could say, she keeps track of all your close calls. I suppose she was awake," he said.

"Reading a volume of text by the fire." Emerald shook her head. "I wish she wouldn't worry."

An icy gust took their breath away and caused them to crouch lower. No arrow could reach this height unless the archer stood in the open, but the frozen gales descending the cliffs of the Impenetrable Mountains provided reason enough to take cover. Stephan was bundled in the knitted over-shirt she had made for him and a fur-lined cloak.

"Did the parents survive?" He shifted position to look in her direction.

A young man of sixteen years, slight of build though coming into his strength, he never lacked for courage. It took courage to ask her things. She guarded her secrets well.

"No." The white puff of her breath clouded the air. "They died bravely."

"You mean needlessly." He snorted. "You warned the man last spring not to squat, and what did he do? He shoved you off of land he had the nerve to claim as his own." Stephan scowled. "The stupid squatter should never have talked that way. Your word is law. He should have listened."

"He saved my life," she said.

Stephan's jaw fell open and then clamped shut. "How?"

"An arrow to the back of a clansman and the eye of another."

Stephan shook his head. "No. That farmer couldn't hit what he aimed at for all the apples in an orchard. It was your protector, wasn't it?"

"I sensed nothing."

"I can't explain that, but I've seen someone," Stephan said.

"Who?"

"I don't know, a shadow, and tracks. I've noticed footprints." He shrugged.

"It's possible." She frowned in concentration. "The angle was slightly off for the arrows to have come from the cottage doorway."

"It was him then." Stephan peered at the tree line. "I imagine he's out there right now."

She sighed and knelt, sitting on her heels, confident she had seen nothing like what Stephan described. Born with a talent for sensing the presence of others, she could avoid conflict. On the opposite hand, she could easily ambush an enemy. Within a certain range, she knew who and where a person was.

"If it makes you feel better to think so, then fine." What could it hurt to let him believe it?

In fact, it was possible that the idea comforted Stephan. If she had a protector who ensured she would return home safely, then he wouldn't worry as much when she took these risks. After all, he depended on her, as did all the orphans here. She was the only adult among them, and heir to Danalan. Without her, the Andolin Judge in Meadowgren might send the Militia to oust them.

"George has seen something too. He says it's a man with a dark beard. He almost caught him once." Stephan smiled mischievously. "I think he's a mountain man."

"Ridiculous. Mountain men are invisible." She was only teasing.

"That's what they say, but Timothy was telling me about his brother—"

"He's just a little boy who makes up stories. That's all we have, Stephan. The mountains are sealed." She didn't like to talk about the dead.

Stephan arched an eyebrow. "Then we sure have wasted an excessive amount of time learning their language."

"Point taken." The need to learn languages was politically relevant as well as a tradition.

A ghostly vision clouded her mind as she remembered Ben's words. Had he truly been so callous and ungrateful? The women of Andolin could not own land, so she comprehended the resentment of the laws of Danalan that made her ruler over everything. Surely, he understood that if she had informed the Andolin authorities, then he would have been executed simply for entering Danalan.

It was clear that dire circumstances had driven Ben and Amanda to leave their homeland. That was why she had decided to let them stay. She understood a similar kind of desperation because most of her twenty years had been a struggle for survival.

All of her family had been murdered and now she ruled alone. If not for these foreign orphans, then Danalan culture would die. Unfortunately, she was not permitted under Andolin law to adopt them unless she married. Thus, it was imperative she marry. But she couldn't bring herself to accept any man in that way.

"I didn't care about them squatting." Her voice fell flat.

"I did." Stephan hunched his shoulders against another blast of wind.

"Grandfather once said my family filled Danalan with crops and herds and passels of children, all boys until my birth." She clenched her jaw. "I changed everything."

"He told me the Wolf Clan attacked long before you were born. You're not to blame, Em."

She pressed her lips in a thin line. Stephan was wrong. She couldn't explain why the Wolf Clan had appeared before her birth but she knew they had come because of her. A secret shame told her this. The enemy who had raped her had said as much.

"At least you saved the children." Moonlight refracted off the granite walls to illuminate his face beneath the hood.

"The Stones have always welcomed orphans." She stared across the empty fields. "It's our way."

Would the goodness and generosity of Danalan culture end with her death? She looked at Stephan's youthful face and hope renewed. One day, he would carry on these traditions in the northern land of Frenland, beyond the Impenetrable Mountains, when he took his place as king.

Chapter Two

Sunrise crested the horizon. Because of this, Emerald felt safe to call the older boys from their positions on the watch to the courtyard for morning drills. A few grumbled, but soon everyone sweated through the paces of sword practice. George, Rick, and Gael displayed consummate skills as they wheeled around Stephan in a mock attack.

Stephan's speed allowed him to evade George's longer reach and powerful strokes. Gael and Rick worked well together, but their abilities were no match for the precision of Stephan's movements. He used tactical knowledge to defend a position and defeated them one by one. His skills rivaled her own which gave her a sense of pride.

The welcome smells of ham and porridge wafted with the smoke from the kitchen chimney and caused her stomach to complain of hunger. She rubbed an eye and yawned. No time for breakfast.

"Wash up, eat, and rest," she said.

George, Rick, and Gael rushed to put away the practice swords and leather armor in the gatehouse. Andre hopped off the barrel he'd been sitting on as he watched and ran into the keep.

"Are you coming?" Stephan unbuckled his armor.

"No, I have work to do at the squatter's cottage." Grave work.

Stephan's expression sobered. "And if Liameo comes to check on you?"

"Hide. Have the others tell him I'm fine, accept his gift, and bid him a good day." She had successfully avoided a direct conversation with the man for six years.

"I hope he brings bacon. Anyway, you should have breakfast before you go." He met her gaze.

"There isn't time, but save something for me to eat later."

"I will." He hurried after the others.

Emerald left the castle.

Unafraid of the departed enemy, she strode into the open fields. A steady stride carried her into the forest. She inhaled the bracing air and ran down the valley.

Unencumbered by armor or sword belt, she wore a thin cloak, a white shirt, and brown trousers. She had remembered to tuck a short shovel under one arm. At the clearing by the river, the cottage came into view. The gruesome work would exhaust her, but for now, she enjoyed the sunshine.

A shrill cry of a hawk caused her to slide to a halt in the dry leaves. The redolence of earth filled her nostrils. The bird of prey perched atop one of the dead wolves. Blood covered its beak and its feathers were wet. The hawk's keen eye surveyed her as strong wings bore it aloft.

Emerald swallowed a wave of emotion. Was she like the hawk? She felt bloodied. Stained. The creature's feathers would dry, but what would become of her?

She watched the bird fly out of sight. The brilliant blue-sky pricked tears of regret over things she could not change. Ignoring the remorse, she started the work at hand.

The ground remained unfrozen inside the rock walls of the burned-out cottage. This home had once belonged to Uncle Edwin and his family. She pushed past the grief for everything lost and dug a grave for the slain husband and wife.

Because of his size, Ben proved a challenge to drag into place. Amanda was petite, yet Emerald found it harder to lay her to rest. Perhaps, because she herself would likely have died the same way if she had achieved the dream of marriage and children.

Had she placed her trust in Liameo, he would have failed in a similar way. She had made the right choice not to marry. Sometimes the best a person could do just wasn't ever going to be enough, not with such forces standing in opposition.

It hurt, though, because Amanda had trusted in the Woman of the Stone. Emerald shook her head, blinking back tears. What had Ben meant by mentioning that belief?

Many people in Andolin expected her to one day rule the fractured Modutan Empire. But she had no such intention. Grandfather had explained that it would be enough to reunite the peoples by unsealing the mountains.

He had made it sound simple. It wasn't. The mountains had remained impenetrable for over four hundred years. She had no idea how to fulfill the Legend of the Stone.

With a sigh, she pulled Amanda's body into the grave. The woman's faith had been in vain. How many others had to die before people gave up hope?

Emerald preferred to perform the burial alone. She couldn't sense the spirits of the dead in the presence of the living. She shoveled earth over the bodies and knelt in meditation beside the grave. The stillness of the moment allowed her to feel the couple standing beside her.

The dimly perceived mother smiled. The shadow father extended an open hand. Perhaps, these actions meant they didn't blame her. After all, they had saved her life. She focused her thoughts on them to express her gratitude and vowed to protect their sons.

A shadow crossed the burned-out doorway of the cottage and dispelled the vision.

"Nina told me to bring you breakfast and lend you a hand." Rick extended a cloth filled with what smelled like ham.

Emerald took the appetizing bundle. "Thanks." Her mouth watered and she ate every salty bite.

"Oh, and she said you would need this." He handed her a bar of lye soap.

She put it in her pocket.

Rick sorted through the ashes inside the walls and picked up a pan, a hammerhead, and a cooking pot. When finished, he ran a hand through his hair, leaving streaks of soot on his forehead and through his dark red hair. She concealed a smile.

He was almost grown, but at times like this, she delighted in his innocence.

"I should skin those wolves and wash laundry." She climbed from the ground, tucked the cloth into a pocket, and grabbed the shovel as she walked to the field.

"Where did the bodies go?" Rick followed.

Blood soaked the ground where the men and beasts had died. The animals' carcasses remained, but the men's corpses had vanished. Clothes and weapons littered the field.

"I don't know. It's strange, but that's how it always is." Only one body had ever been left to reproach her and that man's bones lay at the bottom of the well at her grandparent's cottage.

She carried his dagger on her belt and caressed the hilt. A shiver ran along her spine. She kept the secret because the man's body had poisoned more than one well that day.

Time hadn't eased the burden. She ground her teeth and looked at the wolves lying in varied and gruesome attitudes of death. Many bared fangs, yellow eyes open.

Without thinking, she massaged her right shoulder. The scars from the night her parents and younger brothers were murdered no longer pained her, but the memories did.

"What's the matter, Em?" Rick studied her as if to read her mind.

"My Uncle Edwin lived in this cottage. He saved my life when I was six. The ruins of my family's home sit west of here." She pointed to where the Wolf Clansmen had exited the trees.

"He built a fine home." Rick examined the masonry of the cottage. "I see why the squatters chose this place. Even burnt out, it wouldn't take much to rebuild the roof and frame in the door and windows." He grabbed a hand full of soil and sifted it. "This is fertile land."

Emerald's thoughts drifted to that day. Her family had gathered around the hearth before bedtime to enjoy warm milk and buttered bread. Father had come home from tending the bees with flowers for the table and placed one in her hair. He had told a story of the work in the honey fields.

Without warning, the Wolf Clan had attacked and chaos ensued. Flashes of fire filled her mind with remembered terror. Her mother had handed her the baby and told her to run into the woods. Before she reached the trees, a crossbow bolt sank deep into Jebby's side. He died with a terrible cry.

A wolf had charged, its dark body silhouetted by the flames. She still held the boy and tried to shield him from the beast. The animal engulfed her young shoulder in its jaws and shook her like a corn-husk doll in a puppy's mouth.

The pain of the injuries and the shock of Jebby's death numbed her mind. Uncle Edwin had rescued her from the creature, but she could not speak. She didn't talk again for two years.

When Stephan came to live at her grandparents' cottage, he had fixed something. Maybe she had done the same for him. The bond they shared was born of tragedies, but strong with healing.

"Em? What is it?" Rick looked at her with the deep contemplating gaze he did most things.

"Nothing." She shook her head. "I'll skin and you pull teeth."

He nodded.

She handed over a pair of leather-padded pliers and the cloth before setting to the gory work. She saw no beauty in the creatures, not the way the greedy merchants did. The thick, gray pelts retained popularity in Andolin. Though, why Southerners wanted furs she couldn't guess since the ocean provinces stayed warm in winter.

For whatever reason, the furs fetched a good price in the village when tanned. She needed the money to buy food for the children. Heaving a sigh, she wiped a sweaty brow with the back of a bloody hand.

"Gael will love these." Rick held up two long teeth.

"His carved pendants are sought after by traders." She cut the hide from another animal. "One man told me he takes them all the way south to Andoshi. He said men wear them as tokens of bravery." He had confided that men told outrageous lies regarding how they had obtained them, but that seemed too ridiculous.

"They should know the truth." Rick extracted the final tooth and tied the cloth. "You are the brave one."

Emerald walked over to pick up a notched but serviceable sword. She relived the memories of last night and rehearsed the series of moves used to slay the wolves. She would have failed with this dull, bulky thing.

"Sometimes, I think I'm just foolish," she said.

Spotting the slender, copper broadsword, she strode over to take it in her left hand. She compared the blades, ambidextrous. It handled far superior to the steel sword.

The copper weapon looked as peculiar of construction as to have no equal. Two snakes twisted together to form the hilt, with an amber jewel bitten in open mouths at the end and their tails creating the hilt guard. The ancient blade held many secrets. How could copper hold an edge sharper and stronger than steel?

"I don't see how you did it. Six wolves. Six men. Not good odds." Rick picked up a wooden shield from the ground.

"No, indeed." She laughed. "The squatter shot two men with his bow and just in time, too."

"That's lucky." He leaned the shield against his leg, pulled a short length of rope from a pocket, and tied one end to an arm loop.

She dropped the notched sword and rehearsed the moves with the copper weapon. Each beast had hit the blade and died in a shroud of mist. Skill alone had not accomplished that. Not even the power of the sword could explain it. The Creator had blessed her, but why? She sighed and laid the sword on the ground.

"I'll wash the clothes in the river. Will you take everything else back to the castle?" She gathered the filthy furs and clothing from various places around the field where the men had met an end.

"Sure, Em. I'll clean the swords, too. This blade on this one needs to have the nicks filed or it'll split. I know how. I am good with metal." He piled weapons onto the shield and dragged it as he added more.

A glint from an object on the ground caught her attention. She crouched to pick up a pendant. Tin and crude, the token had a worn baby tooth mounted on one side and the etching of a girl with a gap-toothed grin on the other.

Emerald had been this girl's age when the Wolf Clan had murdered her family. Was one of the savage men she'd killed last night a father? She couldn't believe it and thrust the pendant into the dirt.

"Your sword looks fine but I can't touch it without pain." Rick's voice carried across the field.

Surprised, she said, "I didn't know you had tried to handle Dana's sword."

She carried the awkward pile of clothes toward the boy. He was tall for fifteen. She picked up the copper sword and laid it on the makeshift sled.

"Everyone has tried, but only Stephan can." Rick rolled his eyes. "The rest of us get a blazing shock the instant we set a finger on the thing. Whoever Dana the Stonehearted was, I bet no one messed with her."

"I have a feeling you're right, Rick. Thanks for the help." Emerald watched him tug the heavy load up the trail toward the castle.

She made multiple trips to carry the dirty clothes and pelts to the river and tossed the heaps on the bank. Filthy, she hung her somewhat clean cloak on the branch of a tree and removed her bloody boots and coarse wool socks. Nearby hot springs fed the river and offset the frigid temperature. Snowmelt from high in the mountains was the primary source, so it remained cold year-round.

She waded in, gasping and shivering. When the water reached her waist, she placed the pelts on a submerged boulder to soak. She secured each one with rocks so the current wouldn't sweep them away. That done, she squatted and scrubbed the clothing on a rock with a bar of soap. She carried the clean tunics, leggings, and cloaks to hang on the low branches of trees.

The sun climbed high in the sky, causing the air to warm by the time she stripped her clothes for washing. With great efficiency, she completed the task and hung each article to dry. Her naked body crisscrossed with scars. Each mark spoke of her training and struggles against a long succession of enemies.

Not all her scars were visible, but each told a story she didn't care to repeat. She clenched her jaw in anger because she had once been a joyful child. Now, happiness was not something she considered possible, even though this place reminded her of days lost forever.

Adept, she unplaited her luxurious hair from the confining braid and walked onto an outcrop of boulders. The sound of rushing water soothed her and she dove in, allowing the shock to chase away the gloom. She drew smooth, powerful strokes upstream. When satisfied with her exhaustion, she floated back and swam to the river's less turbulent edge.

With what remained of the lye soap, she set to bathing. It didn't take long before the sliver vanished. Impeccable, she hurried out of the water and wrung her hair. Gooseflesh raised on her skin as rivulets flowed off of her. She wrapped in a short cloak and shivered as she walked home barefoot.

Chapter Three

Emerald used her ability to avoid meeting any of the older boys in the courtyard of the castle. The noonday sun shone straight overhead. There was no chance Nina wouldn't spot her as soon as she strode into the keep because of the mid-day meal. Emerald sighed and went inside anyway.

"Em, are you naked?" The girl stopped handing out porridge to a group of children at the enormous table in the main hall, hands on hips.

Emerald flushed but couldn't suppress a grin. "I'm covered." She held the knee-length cloak closed, undressed because she hadn't wanted to put on the wet clothes she'd washed at the river.

Nina huffed and shook her head. Children of various ages clamored around the table for food. The youngest ones still needed help to eat.

"I'll be back. Have the boys come down?" Emerald listened for the answer as she headed upstairs.

"The big boys are doing chores. They haven't slept."

Emerald pulled on threadbare trousers and an often-mended tunic from a chest of clothes. She dressed in the large, sleeping chamber everyone shared. After brushing the dirt from her feet, she slipped on a pair of socks and shoes, enjoying the return of warmth to her toes. She left her hair undone to dry.

Timothy, a year younger than Andre, slept in the bed next to the chest and she reached out to check his sweaty brow. His fever had broken. Good. He was the last to recover from a recent illness that had swept through the castle.

She tiptoed downstairs.

"Have something, Nina. You cooked it. You should eat while it's hot." Emerald took the spoon out of her hand and grabbed a seat by the toddler she had been feeding.

"As you like." Nina picked up a clean bowl.

Emerald nodded and shifted her attention. "Hello, Marta. How are you today?"

She mashed a boiled carrot in the bowl with a spoon and grinned. When Marta smiled back, she shoved the food into the little girl's mouth. Most squished out.

Nina laughed and filled a bowl with vegetable soup.

Emerald glanced at the three small boys she had rescued. They looked wide-eyed and confused about last night. It was a common enough sight around the castle because everyone here was an orphan.

In a flurry, four young men rushed into the keep and hung cloaks on pegs.

"It smells good." Stephan beat the others to the table.

He stood apart from the rest because of the blond hair and brown eyes. That coloring marked him as a Frenlander. Everyone else had hair colors that ranged from strawberry blond to a deep auburn with eyes of various shades of green. These were the typical Andolin coloring and though Emerald and Marta were born in Danalan, they looked the same.

Emerald lifted Marta out of the highchair. She wiped the orphan's face and helped her drink a cup of water. The child's eyelids drooped and Emerald took her to the rocking chair. Steady rocking, humming, and patting put Marta to sleep before the boys finished eating. Emerald rocked out of the chair and carried the toddler to bed.

She kissed Marta's brow and checked on the sick boy. Timothy had awakened, so she helped him downstairs for a meal. By that time, most of the younger children had eaten and gone to play in the courtyard. The older boys sat around the table cleaning and sharpening the weapons Rick had brought from the cottage field.

"Five swords, a crossbow and two short bows, an ax, half a dozen knives, and three nice daggers." Gael whistled. "Good haul, Em. The wolfies really had it in for those farmers."

"Remember," Stephan paused polishing, "this sword is Emerald's."

"How could I forget?" Gael stood by the table looking at the ancient weapon, though he did not touch it.

Stephan held up the unique family heirloom and tilted the blade as he read the etchings along the length. "Dana the Stonehearted."

"I'll take that." Emerald strode by and swept the sword from his hands.

Thanks to Stephan, it was clean and honed. She marveled that the weapon allowed him to handle it. No one had touched it for four hundred years, not until Grandfather had taken her to the shrine in the tombs to retrieve it on her twelfth birthday.

"Looks good." She slid the blade into the scabbard on her belt where it hung on a peg in the entryway.

"It wasn't easy to clean. What did you do?" Stephan chuckled. "Did you leave it stuck in somebody?"

"No, but I was in a hurry." Emerald shrugged.

"What's it like to wield Dana's sword, Stephan?" Gael watched Emerald stride past the table.

"It's hard to describe." Stephan's expression screwed up in thought.

Emerald had not considered how the boys perceived her, but Gael's gaze made the hair on the back of her neck stand straight. Too much admiration. They were children, and she ignored the indelicacies of living with adolescents as long as they behaved. Gael had never acted in any way inappropriate.

Shaking her head, she wanted nothing more than a bowl of something to eat and the last crust of bread before someone ate that too. She scraped the bottom of the pot and shared half with Timothy. It wasn't much, so she hunted around the table for bits of food abandoned by the little ones and then sat next to him.

"It's more than Dana's sword, it's as if it is Dana." Stephan frowned and took a bite of food.

"Is that right, Em?" Rick's eyes narrowed.

"I don't know, never thought of it that way. I've always felt connected to the sword as if it is a part of me." What had Stephan meant?

"No, Em. Dana is different. She's dark, vengeful, set in her hatred." He shuddered.

The description resonated, an echo in a chasm that brought on a chill and stilled her lips.

Into the awkward silence, Gael cleared his throat. "How many wolves did you kill, Em?"

He was a scrawny boy of thirteen with a choppy haircut. Even with a dirty face, she found his smile endearing. Looking him over, she chewed a bite of bread. She had discovered him camped by the river two winters ago and had hoped to fatten him up. But he didn't gain weight. There was never enough to eat at the end of winter, and early spring always proved worse still.

"You tell me." She pointed at the bundle on the shield in the entryway. "Count the teeth."

He jumped up and ran over to retrieve them. Once back at the table, he opened the cloth. Quickly, he divided the teeth into groups and added the piles with his fingers.

"Six."

"Right." She flashed a smile. "I need help to retrieve the clean clothes." She frowned. "I'm half tempted to toss you in the river. What have I told you about cleanliness?"

He blushed and ducked his head. "I'll bathe tonight, promise."

She nodded and looked at the other boys while she finished the meal. "It's time to gather firewood. Stephan, you and the big boys can have a quick nap, but I need everyone to collect wood from the forest. Take the brown mare to pull the cart. Don't quit until every lean-to is full or night falls."

Stephan nodded. "We'll get it done."

He passed a wax sealed letter across the table, and she pocketed it.

Most everyone scattered after they ate.

"Gael, carry the dishes to the kitchen and help Nina wash up, please. I'll sweep the floor." Emerald looked at Timothy. "Back to bed, young man."

"I want to gather wood." The little boy pleaded.

"Not today, but you can help tomorrow."

"Please." He whined.

She knelt and made eye contact as she held up a hand. "I'll arm-wrestle you for it. If you win, then you can collect wood, if you can't, then up to bed."

He giggled and tried but lost.

She smiled and tickled his belly, causing him to laugh even more. "Go now."

With a smile on his face, he padded upstairs.

The room empty, she searched for bits of food on the floor. Hunger never ended. Her ribs showed and her breasts were small, almost as if she were a child. It was no wonder the Andolin villagers treated her with so little respect when she traded there.

She cleaned the floor with a broom that left more straw than it swept dirt. With a sigh, she knelt and unwound the twine, gathered and leveled the straw, and then tied it to the stick. It worked much better.

She collected the debris into a pail and walked over to finish drying her hair before the fireplace. She braided it as she waited for Gael to reemerge from the kitchen. How did hands with this much blood on them stay untouched except by callouses? Thinking better of the decision to linger by the fire, she took the bucket outside to the refuse pile.

The chickens pecked the dirt for the remaining crumbs.

When she returned, Gael waited at the ready. His eyes lit up as she walked into the room. She clapped a hand on his shoulder, and they hurried off to the river.

Emerald sent the laundry home with him for ironing. When he was out of sight, she stripped and waded into the current to retrieve the submerged pelts. She hung them on branches to drip as she dressed and then fetched a wheelbarrow from the outlying tanner's shed. She wheeled them there to scrape and salt. It was exhausting work.

Night found her toiling by candlelight. After a while, she reached a good stopping point. With a yawn, she stretched her arms and back. Hunger gnawed, but she had no way to end it without returning to the castle in the frosty night air. Exhausted, she curled up on a fur she'd finished the previous moon. She drew a cloak over her and tamped out the smelly tallow candle.

Chapter Four

Sunlight filtered through the dusty air in the tanning shed to awaken Emerald. She stretched stiff muscles and her stomach growled. It felt as if she might starve without breakfast.

Wrapped in a cloak, she stepped into the open. The temperature had dropped, and she shivered as a gust of wind swept a loose curl across her face. Apprehensive, she glanced up to see snowfall on the rocky slopes of the mountains. Thick clouds draped the jagged peaks, and she calculated there were only hours before the snow fell at this elevation.

The sound of running water drew her attention toward the river.

"Oh, no." Any abandoned children might have frozen to death in the night.

She secured the shed door and ran across Stone Bridge. A thorough search of the Border Road both eastward and westward produced no one in need. Relieved, she leaned against Stone Bridge and planned her day.

Thirsty, she descended the river bank and scrubbed her dirty hands with sand. Fresh air caused her to realize she stank from tanning the hides. She would bathe tonight in the castle kitchen where she could heat the water.

A fish swam past on the way upstream.

Bemused, she watched it notice and circle an object beneath the water's surface. Her thirst reasserted itself and she cupped her hands to take a drink. Before the water touched her lips, however, she recognized the shape was a burlap sack. The twine that tied it closed wriggled in the current.

She gasped. Water fell from her hands with a splash as she scrambled in and dragged the heavy sack ashore. Rocks clacked as they slid over one another, she set the bundle on the gravel river bank.

Soaked, she trembled as she unknotted the string.

"Please, let it be puppies." She took a breath, opened the burlap, and shut it again, retching until tears coursed her face and sobs overwhelmed her effort to hold them at bay.

Many orphans in the castle had come by way of the Border Road. She had found abandoned little ones in baskets, or hungry, sick children of every age huddled along the east-west track nearest the bridge. On rare occasions, she discovered something like this.

Who could drown a baby? The face looked bloated. Whoever had done this hadn't done it last night.

Heat swelled in her chest. Someone had killed this girl and planned to escape justice. She wouldn't allow that to happen. This was Stone River, and though the child was from Andolin, Emerald had the right to demand the culprit be punished.

Captain Hammond of the Militia would investigate. If he found the person responsible, then Judge Porter would exact justice. At least, she hoped he would.

She reached into the sack and lifted out the rocks before hefting the burden onto her shoulder. Heading south, she slogged toward the village. Meadowgren was poor, but not lawless.

Emerald's grim expression and wet clothes attracted the villagers' attention. Even at this early hour, the streets were busy. A vender paused mid-call to grasp and kiss a talisman hung around his neck, perhaps to ward away bad luck. Several customers followed suit. Emerald trod past, carrying the sack. In the town square, she set it in front of the guard shack.

Two Militiamen came out to meet her.

"What's the matter here?" A pimple-faced soldier spoke.

Emerald recognized him as a local pig farmer's second son. "I found this sack in Stone River. A child was murdered." She held his gaze and calmed her breathing.

"Murdered you say? How do you know?" The shorter soldier stepped forward to take a better look.

Emerald couldn't place him, perhaps a peasant's son. She handed over the sack.

A crowd gathered.

"Whose child is it?" The baker wiped flour on his apron and walked from the doorway of the bakeshop.

"Yes, let's see." The shout came from the rear of the group of onlookers.

The shorter soldier upended the sack. The child landed with a plump, sodden thud on the ground. A chorus of disgust erupted from the crowd.

"Ugh. Sack it back up." The pimple-faced soldier pinched his nose and backed away.

"I'll not touch it." The short soldier nudged the body with the toe of his boot.

"Does anyone recognize it?" The butcher hadn't flinched.

"No." Everyone shook their heads.

"She's not one of ours." The cobbler's wife waved a hand as if to dismiss the issue.

"A girl?"

"Yep, naked as a newborn."

"A year old, I'd guess."

Incensed, Emerald placed the sack over the body. She ground her teeth to keep her mouth shut. Though, she knew full well she couldn't hold her tongue much longer.

"What evil have you brought on us, Emerald Stone?" A peasant woman pointed a dirt-smudged finger. The woman's sleeveless rag of a tunic provided no protection against the elements.

"I?" Emerald balled her fists.

"Aye, Stone maiden, what evil is this you've done?" Hatred marred the carpenter's wife's pretty face. The well-dressed woman carried a basket filled with bread and eggs.

"I've done nothing." Emerald scanned the surrounding faces. "This child was not in my care. You know, I would have sheltered her if given the chance. There was no reason for her to die."

She hadn't expected the need for defense, and the epithet stabbed. Heat burned her cheeks as 'Stone maiden' echoed in her ears. She dreaded the day they found out her virtue had been taken.

"Calm down." The pig farmer's son raised his arms to hush the crowd. "Times are hard. I feel certain this child died of starvation and the family disposed of her as they saw fit. Whoever the dumb dirt grubber was, he should've buried the little thing, but there's no harm done. The Captain will have us dig a hole and all will be well. Now, move about your business." The two soldiers reentered the guard shack and shut the door with a clap.

"I'd prefer my children die than go to the likes of her." The carpenter's wife spoke to the baker's wife as the two walked away with heads held high.

Agape, Emerald stood beside the dead child. The sting of a rock hitting her in the back roused her. She whirled to see a half-dozen boys pick up pebbles from the street.

Without a word, she ran. How could she tolerate this? How could she endure the apathy of these people? Determined, she vowed to inform Judge Porter.

Remembering the letter for the Judge, she checked the pocket to see if she had lost it as she ran. It remained there, though soaked through and likely illegible. She didn't care. She sprinted until she approached the Judge's farm and then slowed to a jog.

Ten Militiamen in brown uniforms milled around the yard of the spacious home. Liameo stood among them, watching her. She had avoided him since her grandparents' deaths and wanted to turn away now. Except, she couldn't allow the baby girl's death go unanswered.

The rest of the men were not strangers. She had grown up with them. Many were cousins or distant relations because women from Meadowgren had married into the Stone Clan for generations. Several young men had a particular history with her since they had proposed marriage or their parents had on their behalf.

As awkward as running into these men was, she knew their presence meant the Judge held a conference with the Militia Captain. She would be interrupting to ask an audience. Her stomach growled as the cook fire wafted the aroma of bacon from the brick chimney.

She noticed Sergeant Liameo Hume's gaze follow her as she walked through the yard. He raised a dark eyebrow as she approached and folded his arms across his broad chest. In the way, he was a massive roadblock.

She continued forward. "Step aside." Gruff. She strode through the crowd.

"You can't go in yet, Em." Liameo stuck out his arm to stop her and brushed her breast with his hand as he reached for her arm.

Awash with indignation, she knocked the hand away. Fury emblazoned her skin, and she grasped her sword. A shock bolted through her body. With a yelp, she released the hilt, her hand completely numbed.

Several men erupted in nervous laughter.

Sweat broke out on her brow, heart racing. Why had the sword refused her use? It had always lent her power before this.

Liameo took a step backward. "Forgive me." He held his hands out to his sides.

Color warmed his dark, mixed-blood complexion. This made him even more attractive and that irritated her. They hadn't been this close since the day Grandfather had sent him away.

She inhaled through her teeth, trying to quash her feelings. He had always been far too handsome to ignore. Truly, she had tried. But he had a hold on her deeper than words could express or explain.

"Now we know what grabs her attention." A snaggle-toothed soldier's words drew chuckles from several of the men.

"Good on you, Islander. She's put you off long enough." An older soldier clapped Liameo on the back.

Emerald kept track of who said what, planning for retribution as impotent rage drove away reason.

"Hush. I meant no disrespect." The Sergeant met her gaze. "I was worried for you, Em. I heard the bell ring last night. Um, I guess you're here with a letter, so someone died. Did I know them?" Liameo stammered a bit.

He was normally articulate, though sparing with words. Emerald's fingers twitched for the sword. She stopped short of touching it for fear of another shock. Though, she had other weapons if need be. Her mood darkened and she tried to go around him.

"Watch out." The snaggle-toothed Militiaman moved to block her. "She's got a rusty sword."

"She might prick you." A white-bearded soldier baited.

Liameo shook his head. "Silence. She's not here to quarrel with me." His brow knitted as he looked her in the eyes.

"No, I'm sure she is not."

Emerald and the Militiamen turned in unison.

"Forgive me, Mrs. Porter." Liameo bowed low.

Elaine Porter, an elegant woman of advanced years, stood in the open doorway of the house.

"I didn't mean to cause a stir, Auntie." Emerald pulled at her clothing to straighten out the damp mess and tossed her braid over a shoulder.

"Come." She stepped back and gestured into the hallway.

Emerald ducked past Liameo to enter the home.

"Sit in the parlor and take tea while the men finish their meeting in the study." She led the way to a splendid room on the right side of the hall.

"I'm sure I would leave a watermark on the furniture, Auntie." The woman was Emerald's great aunt and the sister of her grandmother Estelle.

"Why are you wet, young one?" She handed Emerald a saucer and cup of tea.

Emerald sipped the warm, fragrant liquid, enjoying the warmth as she formulated a response.

"It is a distasteful business and best left to the Captain and the Judge. I should speak to them." She set down the delicate saucer and cup, moving toward the door.

"My sister abandoned the comforts of our homeland. She was enticed by the promise of an education, land, and the chance to vote." Elaine Porter sat in a high-backed chair. "Married to Jacob, all she found was misery and death." She took a sip of tea from her own fine porcelain cup.

Emerald eyed the silver platter and tea service. She could afford to feed the orphans for months with what it must have cost. Silenced by the words, she held her resentment in check, because this woman was blood.

"I had hoped Estelle's sacrifice would yield more favorable results." Elaine met Emerald's gaze.

"Grandmother was a better woman than you realize and she deserves to be remembered well, Auntie." Emerald left the parlor.

On the opposite side of the hallway, she knocked on the study door.

"Come in, Mistress Stone." Judge Porter's voice carried through the polished wood.

She entered the study and retrieved the sealed letter from the pocket.

The Militia Captain bowed where he stood by the window. "I apologize for my men, Mistress. I assure you that you need not fear us. They are decent fellows, Sergeant Hume in particular."

Captain Hammond's steady presence comforted her.

She nodded in acceptance. He had always been fair and had not harbored resentment after she had refused his proposal of marriage a year ago. It was likely that he had only asked because his wife had died and his five young children needed a mother.

"It is fortunate you did not draw that sword, Young Lady. Andolin law would have demanded your life," the Judge leaned back in his leather cushioned chair, "and no one wants that."

Without ceremony, she slapped the soggy letter on the Judge's oak desk. "I apologize for intruding." She shifted her gaze to the Captain. "However, I have another matter of business this morning. Captain, you will discover it at the guard shack in town. I really must go now." She bowed her head, hoping they had not heard the grumble in her stomach. "Inquire at Stone Castle, if need be." She headed for the door.

"What has happened, Em?" Judge Porter's chair scraped on the planks of the floor.

He was a small man around the same age her grandfather would have been had he lived. The two men had once been great friends. But Jared Stone had died angry with Andolin laws that denied him aid against the Wolf Clan's attacks. He had blamed his friend for the deaths of his sons and their families.

Emerald balled her fists and squeezed her eyes shut as she faced her Great Uncle, the Judge. Her distaste at the day's events intensified due to the unpleasantness of this confrontation. Foolishly perhaps, she made no effort to disguise her displeasure.

"Much to my horror, I found a child drowned in the river by Stone Bridge. I took the body to the guard shack on the square. It is my hope that you will find the murderer, Captain Hammond. I trust you will." She met his gaze.

"That must have been difficult, especially for you. I give my word I will investigate the matter, Mistress." Captain Hammond's expression grew grim.

"And this?" Judge Porter held up the limp letter.

Emerald lowered her gaze. "The Wolf Clan attacked a family of squatters. I did my best to defend them. However, the enemy overwhelmed me and the couple died. I rescued three young boys from the cottage as it burned. I have given them shelter within the castle, sir."

The Judge's brows crashed together. "Squatters? Were they Royalists? You know the law forbids the people of Andolin from squatting in Danalan."

She locked eyes with him. "I made an exception. What does it matter why they came?"

He sputtered for a moment. "You did them no favor by doing so. Their deaths are on your head."

"How dare you say such a thing?" She reached for the dagger on her belt.

"Stand back, Emerald. Royalty or not, I will take up arms against you." The Captain stepped in front of the Judge's desk.

She ground her teeth, fighting the terrible feeling in the pit of her stomach. She put her inclination to retaliate in check and bowed instead. "Good day, Captain Hammond, Judge Porter." She spun on a heel and exited the house in a reckless rage, shoving Liameo out of the way as she strode across the yard.

His men roared with laughter.

Liameo followed. "Em, you can't—"

She whirled around, and the giant man came up short. "I can't what? Go home?" She waved a finger in his face. "Yes, I can, and I wish you would do the same." She stalked away. "Return to the sea, Liameo Hume."

His footfalls crunched in the gravel as he followed her past the Judge's outbuildings. To her surprise, he grabbed her by the arm and pushed her behind the barn. She fought, but he held her close and prevented her from reaching a weapon. His face flushed with color, even the ears.

"Go home to the sea?" He smelled of cinnamon. "Apparently, you missed it but the Militia is my home. It has been since I came back for you. I signed a seven-year contract."

Her jaw fell open. "Why would you do that?" Dumbfounded, she went slack, grateful not to be having this confrontation in front of onlookers.

"I did it to prove myself worthy." He released her, though he held her shoulders to keep her steady. "I needed to prove to your grandfather that I wouldn't take you away. If we couldn't wed until you reached the age of majority, then I thought he would reconsider his refusal of the engagement. But I was too late." The muscles in his jaw went slack. "I left dozens of letters at the castle gate. I thought that you not wanting to see me was just your way of waiting until my contract with the Militia was complete."

"I never read the letters." She avoided his gaze. The letters were stowed unopened in her hope chest with the trinkets he'd left for her over the years.

"You made promises to me, Em. I never imagined you were a liar."

She inhaled sharply. "I don't lie." She cocked her arm to slap him.

He caught her wrist.

"You said you loved me."

"Let go." She planted a hand on his chest and shoved.

"Why pretend?" His voice cracked.

Avoiding him had become so ingrained, so visceral, that she did it out of habit. But seeing him this way hit the pit of her stomach like a fist.

"I did love you, Liameo." She swallowed the lump in her throat and glared. "But why is that important now?"

She could not tell him the truth about what had prevented her from honoring her promises. Admitting her lack of virtue was dangerous. Even now, if she was seen with him, then the Wolf Clan would hurt her again. The man she had killed when she was fourteen had said something to that effect.

"It means everything." Liameo leaned closer.

She avoided his gaze, not wanting to encourage him. Intimacy terrified her. She couldn't explain it, though her throat worked to find a way. The man who had killed her grandparents had brutalized her. More than that, he had left her unworthy of love.

"Marry me, Em. You gave me your word." Liameo's voice quavered.

Wide-eyed and agape, heat blossom in her cheeks.

"Grandfather—"

"Can no longer stop us." Liameo took her hands. "I still love you."

She couldn't speak. He meant it. Hot tears scalded her face, but the only thing she could think was, no! She shook her head, striving to quell a rising panic.

Liameo kissed her cheek, his breath on her skin.

Horrors replayed across her flesh and she fought against his advances like an animal.

He grabbed ahold of her, his face scratched and bleeding. "Why, Em?" He pressed her against the barn. "I would never hurt you." He looked her in the eyes. "What aren't you telling me?"

"Sergeant, release her." Captain Hammond's voice broke through the buzzing in her ears.

Several Militiamen rounded the side of the barn.

"No, sir, I need an answer." Liameo captured her gaze.

"I can't..." The sight of his blood caused a rushing sound in her ears and her vision filled with motes of light.

He stopped breathing, the color draining from his face.

"Ten lashes for insubordination." Captain Hammond's pronouncement cast a hush over the men.

Emerald's attention darted to the Captain. "No." The word came out a whisper born of dread.

Liameo released her.

She stumbled away from the men and fell to a knee.

The expressions of the Militiamen hardened as all eyes focused on her. They knew, as she did, that ten lashes could mean Liameo's death. A weight of guilt descended like a millstone to crush her, but she could not take it back.

Braced against the earth, she curled her hands into fists. As her fingers closed, she scraped up handfuls of pebbles in her palms. The small stones steadied her enough that she could stand and sprint away.

Chapter Five

Liameo Hume, the man who had believed he had an arrangement to marry Emerald Stone, ruler of Danalan and heir to a nation, watched her run away. The reason she could not keep her oath of marriage remained unspoken. But he now suspected that she had been raped. The grief of the realization crushed him. To think of the loving, vibrant girl he had admired so tenderly for so long being ravaged body and spirit left him stricken.

"Report to the fort for corporal punishment, Sergeant." Captain Hammond almost sounded sorry, though he must still be angered by the insubordination.

Never having disobeyed an order before, Liameo had surprised himself. But it was done and must be reconciled. He moved, amidst his brothers of the Militia, as one body. They rode together toward the whipping post where he would receive ten lashes.

The number signified the depth of the Captain's regard for Emerald. It was excessive, but he forgave the man without a second thought. Emerald was a noble figure in the community, even if she was feared.

Cursed. Yes, she was, and yet beloved for her perseverance. It was grudging respect, but she had earned it.

Most people kept their distance. All the while the women secretly craved the intimacy of her acquaintance, and the men hoped for the wild luck of catching her interest as a spouse. Reclusive, she rarely visited the village, except when the law required her to report a tragedy or hunger drove her to the marketplace.

Liameo dismounted his chestnut mare in the yard of the fort. Greeted by his blond Wolfhound, Eugenia whose tongue lolled in an affectionate way. He stroked her head.

Lest she see what was about to take place and come to his defense, he locked her in the kennel. A loyal companion, she whined as if she sensed what was to come.

"It'll be all right, Gene."

Her dog brown eyes didn't look convinced.

He removed his greatcoat, shirt, and leather tricorn hat, laying them on top of the kennel crate. Without wasting any more time, he walked to the post and allowed a new recruit to tie his wrists. The man threaded the rope through the loop at the top of the post and then tied the end around his knees so he could not move.

The first lash was a painful shock, but the second tore flesh. Third. Fourth.

Punishment.

Nothing like what Emerald must have endured. He knew when it must have happened. He had returned to her grandparents' cottage six years ago to find no bodies, but a blood-soaked ground as evidence of the violence. He had fallen to his knees, thinking she must be dead.

The only hope had been the castle. However, he had found the gates secured against him. Although he suspected she was near, perhaps even listening on the other side, his pleas had fallen on deaf ears.

Eight. Nine. Ten.

Before they cut him down from the whipping post, Doctor Platt poured alcohol over the stripes on his back and stitched them closed.

"Don't move son. Some of these are deep. It's best to take care of this now and hope to prevent infection. You will heal if we can avoid that."

Had Emerald hurt this much? All alone and grieving for her beloved grandparents, her pain must have known no limits. Stripped of virtue and afraid, how had she endured the loss of everything she cared about?

The girl he had known had lived and breathed for him; she had been so much in love. Finding herself unworthy of the marriage she had planned for, how had she survived? It was all she had wanted.

Heir to a kingdom, she needed to marry and had chosen him. So, when she wouldn't leave the castle or answer his letters, he had hoped it was simply her way of honoring her grandfather's wishes as they both waited out the contract. He never quit bringing baskets of food, jars of honey, and trinkets from the peddlers in the village as signs of his affection.

After many moons without a response from her, he had worried she must have died. Then one day, the villagers were abuzz. Emerald had come to trade the finest wolf pelts ever seen, large, perfect ones, except the stitched together death blows. She had worn trousers and her hair in a tight braid. The light in her eyes had gone out, a woman selling winter squash had lamented.

"Cut him down and haul him to his bunk." The Captain stood beside him, wrapping up the three tailed-whip. His clothes were spattered with red.

Liameo fell, caught by two of his men who carried him into the barracks to lay on his belly in bed. His heart sorrowed as much for Emerald's suffering as for his own. She must have known he would reject her if she had admitted her sin. Yet...was it a sin to have one's virtue ripped away? Could virtue even be taken without surrender?

She had fought the man who had hurt her. His stench had emanated from the well where his bloated corpse had floated. Whatever he had taken, she had exacted the highest penalty for his crimes.

Perhaps, that was as costly to her as anything. The innocent girl he had known would never hurt anyone. She had performed her weapons training with distinction, yet never raised a blade or bow in anger.

She could hit a target at maximum range, yet missed small game up close when hunting. Tender-hearted and almost too kind, she was the only girl he had ever loved. He had remained faithful.

Liameo closed his eyes and feigned sleep, though the pain was far too great for it.

Emerald was changed, scarred by trauma, though...not unlovable. He still wanted her, especially since no one knew what had happened. There was no child, no evidence, no witnesses. He would still marry her and give her posterity for the throne.

His hope burned bright until he realized that Emerald could not endure his touch. She cared, as evidenced by her horrified reaction to the Captain's verdict of ten lashes. However, she could not admit her feelings or accept his hand in marriage.

Hopelessness dragged him under its sway. She was ruined. There was little future for him since she wouldn't have him.

Yet, knowing the nature of her opposition, a spark of hope took root. He devised plans to break through her resistance and regain her trust. He would never hurt her, and somewhere deep inside, she would understand that. She would remember the love she had once felt for him. He would remind her.

Chapter Six

With shaking hands, Emerald hung the damp cloak to dry on a hook on the mantle in the main room of the castle keep. The run home hadn't cleared her conscience of guilt regarding Liameo. He had trusted her to keep her word and fulfill her oath of marriage. Now he suffered because she couldn't go through with it.

Steadying her breathing, she stumbled to the table and collapsed onto a stool. Trembling from head to toe, she reached for a cloth-covered basket in the middle. At the sight of two rolls, tears piqued in her eyes. The presence of a crock of butter overwhelmed her.

Sobs shook her. The man still loved her. How could that be?

She shouldn't get so emotional. The bread and butter would help. Thankful for the food, she savored the first bite. Decorum was of no use, however, and she gobbled the rest. Still unsatisfied, she wiped her tears and headed to the kitchen.

"Hello, Em." Nina washed mushrooms and tubers in a basin. "We missed you last night. Gael said you were tanning. From the smell, I guess that was right." The girl chuckled. "I saved half a dozen rolls from breakfast. Did you find them?"

The comment about the smell caused a deepening feeling of wretchedness to churn in Emerald's tumultuous stomach. Why did Liameo even want a woman like her? A kind of numbness spread inside her.

She steered her thoughts to the mystery of the sword, but that made her head pound in agony. Nothing made sense. Of course, she had no intention of telling Nina any of this. The girl worried far too much already.

Taking a cleansing breath, Emerald raised an eyebrow. "I found two rolls and one had a bite taken out. They were delicious, especially with butter."

Nina scowled. "I told those boys to leave food for you."

"I'm sure they meant to. Don't scold them. Everyone's hungry." Emerald washed her hands and chopped ingredients for the soup. "Did the firewood brigade bring in these?"

Nina nodded.

If the girl had noticed her mood, then at least she had the good sense not to mention it. Nina watched everything she did. In this case, she was probably monitoring the safety of the mushrooms.

"Not to worry, Nina." Her mouth watered at the sight of her favorite food but she resisted the temptation to eat even one. "The mushrooms are safe."

"I wish there were more." Nina shook her head.

"We need meat." Emerald finished chopping and surveyed the pitiful contents of the pot. Her frown deepened. "I will return when I have it. Tell the boys to keep gathering wood. I noticed that one lean-to isn't full." She headed out to hunt.

SWEAT TRICKLED DOWN Emerald's back as she scaled the mountainside. The brisk wind whipped her with a thousand lashes. It reminded her of what Liameo must be going through.

Distracted by such thoughts, she hadn't remembered to change into dry clothes or bring gloves. She lost feeling in her fingers before she reached the snowline. Despite these difficulties, she spotted a mountain goat on a ledge above.

Where she found one, she hoped to find others.

She strung a bow and crouched low, senses as tight as the string. She waited until a large male climbed toward the female. Exercising patience as he came within range, she took aim and dropped him with a single arrow. The other fled, but Emerald grinned until she was forced to clamp her teeth together in order to keep them from chattering.

Grateful for the blessing, she closed her eyes and whispered a prayer of thanksgiving to the Creator. Most hunting trips this winter had been in vain. Without wasting time, she gutted the animal, saving the desirable organs in a leather game pouch on her belt.

Slinging the heavy beast over her shoulders, she descended the rocky slope with care. Fatigue and hunger were enemies now. The frigid air bit her legs as she made her way home. However, the carcass' shaggy fur insulated her enough to prevent her from freezing.

Snow fell in sheets with each gust of wind. Her hands were red with blood, but soon her exposed skin chapped crimson as well. She pressed forward.

Stephan ran out to take the animal as she neared the castle.

"I gathered the children in from the woods long ago, Em. Where have you been?" The lines on his young face illustrated concern.

She didn't have the strength to answer and couldn't remember when her teeth had quit chattering. A worrisome sign. Each step required a terrible effort.

Rick and Gael ran out to take her arms over their shoulders and hurried her inside the keep. They deposited her in the padded chair in front of the fire and Nina brought a mug of broth. Ten-year-old Andre lugged over a bucket of heated water for her feet and a wet cloth to wash her hands.

She sipped the broth but didn't have the strength to pull off her boots and socks, so he did it. The liquid stung her skin but warmed her feet. She finished the soup, hoping for more, though no offer came.

Everyone stared when Stephan carried in a rack of ribs to turn on the spit over the fire. He handed Nina the pouch of organs and she went to the kitchen to add them to the soup. After a while, she brought a steaming pot to the table.

"Soup's done."

In a rush, the little ones crowded onto the benches and stools, holding out bowls.

"Have you thanked Em, yet?" Tears threatened to fall down Nina's young cheeks.

"Thank you, Em." The chorus of young voices sounded enthusiastic.

"You're welcome." She continued to rest in the seat before the fire.

When Nina had served the children, she took Emerald's empty bowl. She brought it back full, along with a piece of hard, blackened bread.

"I'm sorry I burned it." Nina nibbled a lip.

"It's fine. Thank you. Now eat." Emerald waved the girl toward the table.

With the additional food, her strength returned. Empty bowl in hand, she stared into the fire, enjoying the full feeling in her stomach. Before long Stephan offered her a rib to chew. Her hunger reasserted itself and she felt no shame as she ate meat and gristle alike.

"Boys, don't forget to crack the bones and eat the marrow." She hardly needed to remind them.

Gael walked over when she had eaten everything but the marrow. He still looked so hungry. She handed over the bone for him to crack and eat, hoping it would help him achieve his full height.

SNOW FELL FOR THREE days. Emerald consented to the consumption of the entire mountain goat and two of the precious chickens. A final search of the stores produced one basket of redroot tubers for the pot and a few shriveled apples for the table.

If they ate any of the seed stock, there wouldn't be enough crops this summer. That would mean they would starve next winter. To keep out rodents, she ordered the cellars sealed until planting started.

"Make it stretch as long as possible, Nina." Emerald suppressed a sigh and did her best to relax the tension in her shoulders.

The girl took the redroot to the kitchen.

Emerald knew the flour bin sat empty and that meant no more bread. The tubers might last two days. Spring was weeks away.

Little children raced around the main room kicking a rag ball. Their exuberance caught Emerald by surprise. Didn't they understand their peril?

She searched their expressions. Even the adolescent boys had joined the fun with arm-wrestling contests and dart games. There wasn't a shadow of worry on their brows.

Walking toward the fire allowed for a stretch of the legs. She wished she could be so carefree but her mind churned with tasks that needed to be done. She shook her head and exhaled slowly through pursed lips. Coming to rest, she hitched a hip on the arm of the cushioned chair where Stephan sat.

At least they were warm.

He glanced at her.

His expression held a wistful quality, the same he always had when reading books. Aware that he had exhausted the library years ago, she wished she had more to offer. His education was important to his eventual rule in Frenland.

As for herself, she pretended not to feel such yearnings for knowledge. She did feel it though. Grandfather had instilled a love of learning in both of them. It was part of Danalan culture.

Perhaps, there was enough money to make purchases that could not be eaten. She added books to the list compiled in her head for the next trip to the market. It was imperative she go as soon as the weather broke.

Thanks to numerous fallen enemies, she possessed plenty to trade. The purses of the last six Wolf Clansmen had contained few coins, but three had worn gold rings. So, if there was food available in Meadowgren, then she would be able to obtain it.

"What's on your mind, Em?" Stephan's pleasant tenor broke through her thoughts without jarring her nerves.

"I was wondering if you would sing for us." She winked.

"I will if you will." He smiled.

"Very well." She nodded.

Upon hearing this exchange, several children gathered on the rug. Singing was a favorite winter pastime. The culture of Andolin was rich in ballads and oral traditions.

Stephan didn't know many of the local songs, because he had never visited Andolin. His existence needed to remain a secret in order to maintain his safety, but he never complained. Instead, he made up tunes and fashioned lyrics. He sang these songs often and played a stringed instrument he had crafted with Gael's help.

Playful, Emerald alternated between singing counterpoint to Stephan and harmonizing. Adept at sensing the mood and rhythm of the music, she followed even when he improvised. Her vibrant soprano held the children enthralled. Jovial, the singing rotated from one person to the next with improvised lyrics and bursts of laughter.

As the evening wore on, Stephan played and sang softer. He slowed the music until the younger children were snoring on the rug. Emerald carried each little one to bed and tucked them in under the covers. They slept together in the beds and she piled on extra blankets for added warmth.

When she returned downstairs, she noticed Stephan had ceased to play his instrument. He sang a simple ballad of spring in gentle yearning tones. She stooped to kiss his cheek. The other boys and Nina nodded with sleep.

"To bed with each of you."

The night had grown bitter, and she stayed up to feed the fires until morning.

EMERALD STOOD WARMING her hands before the blazing fire when Nina came to start breakfast. The girl bit a lip as she headed to the kitchen. Emerald followed and leaned against the counter as Nina cut a wheel of cheese into thin slices.

"Where did you find this?" Unable to wait, Emerald popped a piece of the fragrant treat into her mouth. "Mm." She chewed with satisfaction.

"I held back." Nina kept slicing. "I wish I had thought to save more."

"I'm going to the village." Emerald dipped water from a bucket by the well and drank. "The snow stopped last night. I'll take the horses and the wagon. It's ready. I'll stop at the tanning shed for the pelts I have finished."

Nina handed over another piece of cheese. "Wear a heavy cloak and don't forget your sword. Double up your socks and wear a pair of hard soled boots. Oh, and put on gloves this time."

"You'll make someone a good wife one day." She grinned at the younger girl and didn't mention what a nag she was becoming. "Do you have an eye on any of the boys?"

Nina's blush made her pretty. "Yes."

Emerald nodded in approval. "Give yourself time to mature. These boys need it as much as you do." Emerald finished the cheese, savoring the sharp flavor. "I hope you have more sense than to set any hopes on Stephan. He can't stay here forever."

"It's not Stephan." The color in Nina's cheeks deepened and she ducked her chin.

"Well, who then?"

"Rick sure is a fine boy." Nina's soft-eyed expression spoke of how fine she thought him.

"He is at that." Emerald gave the girl a hug. "Don't forget to grow up before you think of him too seriously. Promise now." She leveled her gaze on Nina.

"I promise, Em."

With that, Emerald headed to the village. She took all of Nina's advice. By nightfall, she returned to the castle with a barrel of flour, two sides of salt pork, four enormous winter-squash, a bag of beans, a jar of honeyed apples, a cask of lard, and a sack of rolled oats. It wasn't much, and she had paid dearly, but they could survive on it. She had also bought three blankets and accepted three orphans to wrap in them.

Once back at the castle, the older boys unloaded the wagon and tended to the horses.

Emerald ushered the half-frozen and hungry children inside to the fire in the main room of the keep. Listless, they collapsed on the rug. Nina handed them cups of warm broth and slices of cheese. They gobbled the food.

"The boys are bringing in the supplies. I know it's late, but could you prepare a meal?" Emerald knew she was asking more than she had a right to.

"My pleasure. I'll be fast. I have a pot of water boiling." Nina ran to the kitchen where the boys placed the supplies and themselves at her disposal.

Emerald observed the three children. "Are you siblings or did you make that up to gain sympathy?" She made eye contact with the oldest child.

He was a gaunt-faced adolescent male and had wasted away to a greater degree than the two younger females. Glossy eyed, he looked at her from his spot on the rug. Caked with dirt, he stank. If it wasn't too early for vermin to be prevalent, then she would have suspected lice.

"These are my sisters Ari and Loral. We walked all the way from Ando Bay to get here." His face screwed up in a scowl.

Emerald nodded in understanding and shifted her gaze to the girls. "You are safe now."

The sisters huddled closer together. Neither one had spoken a word since she had picked them up in the village. She suspected shock.

"Obey me and you will always have a home. I'm strict about regular bathing." She eyed the boy. "You will be required to do chores and help the little ones. There are many children here and always more coming. I'm sure you will make friends and find time to play but expect to learn to read and write as well as numbers. You may leave whenever you wish. But you are welcome at my castle if you respect others. Can you do that?"

Three pairs of eyes grew wide.

"Yes." The boy nodded.

Emerald knelt on the rug. "I'm glad you're here." The girls rushed into her arms, and she hugged them close.

Loral wiped a runny nose on Emerald's shirt. Taking a handkerchief from a pocket, Emerald finished wiping the girl's face. She handed the cloth to her to keep. Loral clutched it like a gift.

"I hope you feel better soon," Emerald said. "I'll heat water for baths. When Nina brings out the food, don't eat too much or you'll be sick. You can have more after you bathe, I give you my word." She caught each child's eye to assure their understanding before she went downstairs to the curtained-off part of the kitchen and set to work preparing their bath.

It took half the night to feed, bathe, dress, and feed them again. She needed to boil their clothes in lye if she hoped to clean them, but that could wait. She combed their hair free of tangles.

"You look much better." She led the exhausted trio to bed and tucked them in.

With the girls on one side of the room and the boy on the other, she sang a lullaby until the sisters fell asleep.

"You're not what I expected." The boy spoke from across the aisle in a bed with the sleeping Timothy and Andre.

Emerald carried a stool over to sit beside him. "Tell me your name."

He frowned. "Emilio Carter."

"What did you expect, Emilio?"

He shook his head and blinked back tears. "I'm not sure, but you're not it. My parents were hung for following you. They practically worshiped you. I hate you."

Emerald had heard similar stories. Politics in Andolin were worsening. "I don't blame you."

His jaw dropped and his brows rushed together. "I came here to kill you."

"Why didn't you?"

"I'm not a killer." The tension eased from his body and his eyelids fell closed.

Chapter Seven

E merald awakened to look out the windows above her. The sun climbed high in the sky. For the first time in a while, she felt rested. After a deep breath, she let out a yawn and stretched her arms from under the covers.

The sounds of a mid-day meal clamored up the staircase to the dormitory. Hungry, she dressed and descended the stairs two at a stride on the way to the table. The prospect of a change of menu was exciting.

She smiled at the orphans and grabbed a bowl of stew. She ate with alacrity despite the brick hard dumplings. Midway through, she realized the older children were avoiding eye contact. Scanning faces, she didn't see the new boy.

"Where's Emilio?" She looked to George for the answer.

At almost seventeen, he was the oldest and by far the largest. He was painfully shy but behaved responsibly. Because of this, she trusted him with most of the outside work.

"He passed in the night, Em." George broke eye contact and set his spoon in his bowl even though he had eaten but little.

Devastated, the blood drained from her face. She had fostered such high hopes for the gaunt boy in the hours she had known him. She couldn't understand why Emilio should have died. 'Why?' was always a popular question when people passed away, but she had learned to ask, 'why not?'.

She glanced at Emilio's two younger sisters and her throat tightened with emotion. Ari and Loral weren't weeping, probably because they couldn't yet. Her mouth grew dry, though her hands trembled too much to hold a cup of water without spilling.

Blame and recrimination did not help. However, if the villagers had treated the boy better, then he would have stood a chance at survival. He might have deserved the harsh treatment, but she had perceived nothing malicious in him. The inferno of her anger kindled, and it did not bode well for the Judge when she met him regarding Emilio's death.

Silent tears traced Nina's face.

Emerald reached across the table to pat her hand. "We did everything we could." She stood. "I'll prepare his body."

"It's done." George took a bite of stew.

Emerald sat but couldn't bring herself to eat. "Has the fire been lit to thaw the plot in the cemetery?"

"Yes." Stephan handed over a sealed letter.

Distracted by grief, she pocketed the report. "Thank you."

She finished eating without tasting it. Her body needed the nourishment. Death was commonplace in Danalan, perhaps, the only constant.

AFTER THE MIDDAY MEAL, Emerald left the keep, descended the steps, and walked to the stables. She needed to notify the Judge of Emilio's death. Andolin law demanded the investigation of citizen deaths.

The reports she gave the Judge were archived in the Hall of Records in the Capital City, Andoshi. Captain Hammond usually looked the other way on the investigation part. All she had to do was promptly delivered a detailed letter to Judge Porter.

She slid open the door to the stables to find young Andre struggling to lift a saddle onto Dusty's back. The gray gelding nickered and danced as if toying with him. Emerald restrained a smile.

"Dusty, behave." She stroked the horse's nose.

Andre lowered the edge of the saddle to rest on a foot. "I wanted him ready for you, Em."

She cupped Andre's face with both hands and drew him close for a kiss on the forehead. "I appreciate that."

He pulled away, "Yuck," feigning disgust at the affection.

She lifted the saddle onto Dusty's back, cinched and checked it over. "You've done an excellent job mending and maintaining this saddle, Andre. The bridal looks good too." She refrained from smiling at the boy. "However, I'm worried that if you brush this horse any more his coat will blind someone with the shine. You had better stop." She shook her head in mock gravity.

Andre laughed. "Dusty likes it when I brush him."

"He thinks himself quite the stallion to receive such attention, for sure." She chuckled and patted the old horse on the neck.

He had been Grandfather's, and she had brushed him like this as a girl. Looking into his brown eyes, she thought he remembered. She mounted in one fluid motion.

"Don't be too long." Andre's smile slipped away into worry lines.

She chuckled. "It takes as long as it takes. You know that."

She urged Dusty out of the stables, trotted through the castle gates, and crossed the narrow drawbridge that spanned the moat. The wind felt good until the chill set in. The weather had warmed, but she guessed the snow wouldn't melt for days or even weeks.

Covered in white, the beauty of the landscape struck her as flawless.

Judge Porter wasn't at home, so she sought him in town. Several of the village women talked in hushed tones as she rode past. The butcher spat in her direction. Everyone's gaze tracked her ride through the streets. She sensed hostility and avoided making eye contact in an effort not to provoke a scene.

She found the Judge in the village square. It wasn't much more than open space in the center of town but it served as a place where he addressed people, performed ceremonies, and passed judgment on criminals. Right now, he was conducting a wedding.

Dismounting, she held Dusty off to the side of the square in hopes she hadn't disrupted the proceedings. The last thing she needed was to be accused of being an ill omen on the couple's married life. Some of the villagers were superstitious. They viewed the Stones as the epitome of bad luck due to the Wolf Clan wiping them out, and her in particular because that enemy targeted her and anyone around her.

A crowd formed that she suspected had nothing to do with the marriage. Men with angry postures stood between the buildings. They blocked streets from the square.

She had seen these same men lurking in alleyways yesterday when she purchased supplies. The business had taken longer than normal because several merchants had refused to trade. That had been strange since gold was scarce and her furs were coveted.

She ducked her head and kept a tight hold on Dusty's reins. Under her cloak, she loosened the sword in the scabbard. Relief washed over her when it didn't shock her hand.

At that moment, however, a thought struck her and a sick feeling solidified in her stomach. What if Liameo had died? Her mind shied away from the mournful thought.

The Judge pronounced the couple wed. The merriment commenced. The wedding party moved away, enjoying their celebration.

Emerald led Dusty close to the Judge. She needed to deliver the letter. Her great uncle's pleasant expression darkened as she approached.

"Sir, I wanted to ask after Sergeant Hume. Is he all right?" Emerald prayed that Liameo was well.

The Judge's scowl deepened. "He may die."

Like a fist to the belly steals the wind, she couldn't breathe.

"Your silence speaks much." The Judge shook his head. "I expected more from the Woman of the Stone."

"I'm sorry." The burden of guilt threatened to crush her.

"I doubt you came to ask about the Sergeant, so what is the matter?" The Judge squinted.

Emerald gasped at the effrontery, but sadly, he was right.

"The boy, Emilio, the one I picked up in town yesterday, died in the night." She withdrew the letter from a pocket.

The rasp of a sword being drawn attracted her attention. Several paces to the right, the butcher held the weapon. Concerned, she scanned the alleys and streets.

"Leadership involves responsibility, Young Lady." The Judge snatched the letter from her hand.

Emerald snapped around to meet his gaze. "Sir?"

"How well do you care for the children in the castle?" It seemed an accusation rather than a question.

Emerald's blood heated. "I care for them the best I can. They come starved and abused. It is not always possible to undo the harm. Emilio died of starvation; I think. We fed him, but it was too late."

The frown on the Judge's face deepened. "I suspect he stole from you and you killed him for it. Many here believe he was a thief, though no one ever caught him."

Fury blinded her. It took all of her self-control not to release her pent-up anger over past events. The callousness and cruelty of the people in this village, including the man standing before her, was an outrage. Knowing the penalty would be death, she stayed her hand on the hilt of the arcane sword.

"Your suspicion, sir, is in error," she said.

The Judge ripped the letter in half. "Your word is in question, Emerald Stone." He menaced from his lesser height. "I'm sending the Militia to investigate."

Flabbergasted, she stared.

"Don't look surprised. Your actions of late have incensed the populace. To be honest, you have disappointed me too."

She straightened her spine and looked down at the man. "I can't guess what you expected, but I'm not deceiving you, Uncle."

"You have deceived us all. Had I known of your oath to the Sergeant, then I would have—"

"What?" She knew no law but one that could force her to marry against her will. Though she had never met her mother's father, he had not given consent to any of the men who had sought it, at least not yet. "Captain Hammond is welcome to investigate, but his men are not."

The Judge's eyes narrowed. "You show wisdom." He glanced at the onlookers. "Go now and be at peace." The words carried to the crowd.

Emerald mounted and hastened home. Once she reached the courtyard of the castle, she handed Dusty off to Andre and waved Stephan down from the wall.

He hurried to her side. "What's the matter?"

"Captain Hammond is coming to inspect Emilio's body. The Judge suspects me of murder."

"What?" George jogged over from the gatehouse. "That can't be right."

"It's just a misunderstanding. Stephan, stay out of sight." She nudged him toward the keep.

"Sure." He ran inside.

"George, watch the Captain while he's here. We can't trust anyone loyal to Andolin." She leveled her gaze, though she had to look up in order to do so.

He ran to the gatehouse for weapons.

The sound of hooves on the gravel road leading to the drawbridge attracted her attention. Captain Hammond rode through the open gates. He touched the brim of his tricorn hat.

"Captain." She nodded.

He dismounted in the courtyard and bowed at the waist. "Lead me to the boy's body."

Emerald motioned to Andre. He ran over from the stables to take the Captain's horse.

"What have you discovered regarding the drowned baby?"

The Captain sighed and stared at the cobblestones. "Nothing. I've been preoccupied with Sergeant Hume."

She felt the blood drain from her face. "I didn't mean for this to happen."

"He isn't dead, not yet." The Captain shook his head.

"You hate me?"

"No, but everyone else seems to, and for that, I am sorry. I should not have intruded on such a private matter."

Her insides quivered. "Do you think..." She shook her head.

Lost in contemplation, she led the Captain across the courtyard. The mounted the steps of the keep in single file. Traveling through the main room, they went downstairs to the kitchen. Emilio's body lay wrapped in a sheet on the floor behind the curtain. She looked away as the Captain inspected the corpse.

"I see no wounds or bruising and no sign of poison. He's nothing but skin and bones." The Captain's heavy footfalls traversed the room and mounted the kitchen steps.

She followed.

"It is my opinion that no crime was committed." He glanced around the main room at the playful children and smiled. "I will report to the Judge." He walked toward the door.

"I want to pay Doctor Platt." She searched the pouch on her belt for coins, finding not nearly enough.

Captain Hammond stilled her hand. "The Militia takes care of our own. Don't worry. The Doctor is with him."

"He can't die." She hadn't expected to feel so devastated by the thought of losing Liameo.

"Then you will marry him?"

"No." She backed away. "Never."

The Captain nodded. "He is young and strong. I'm optimistic that he'll live." The Captain said.

George stood close by. Armed.

"Thank you, Captain." She was lost in thought.

"Good day, Lady Stone." He departed.

She glanced at George.

"Make sure the Captain finds his way to the gate." She pointed with her chin.

George hurried to obey.

She climbed the stairs to the sleeping chamber and then up another flight to the library. Once inside, she slid the bolt to secure the door and walked to the far wall.

"You may come out," she said.

The bookcase swung on a concealed hinge to reveal a narrow hiding space and Stephan stepped from within.

"It's close in there." He wiped the sweat from his brow. "Is the Captain gone?"

"No, but George will make sure he leaves."

"You look tense. What's wrong?"

She didn't like the scrutiny. "Nothing."

He pumped the front of his shirt to fan himself and walked around the room taking deep breaths. "It felt bigger when I was little."

She couldn't help but crack a smile at the obviousness of the statement.

"There. See? Everything will be fine." He gave her a quick hug.

"I hope so."

Chapter Eight

Late in the day, Emerald and the orphans made their way to the grave-side. Snow blanketed the landscape except for the mound of raw earth beside an open grave. The wind howled down from the Impenetrable Mountains. It caused the children to shiver. They shuffled their feet and fidgeted.

George carried the body. Emerald thought the outline looked frail as he and Stephan lowered it into the hole. Nina hugged Ari and Loral, sobbing with them.

Emerald pulled back the hood of her cloak. It was a sign of respect to uncover one's head at a funeral.

"Emilio could have done many things with his life," she said. "Cruel hunger robbed him." Her throat closed as she fought the emotions that would have her weeping like a child if she weren't careful. "Now, he reminds us of all we have and what life means. His days ended in warmth and comfort, and we will remember him. It is my hope that the Creator will receive and prosper him." She gestured for the boys to fill in the dirt.

With the grave covered, Gael pounded a wooden marker into the ground.

He read aloud, "Emilio Carter, an adolescent boy from Ando Bay, died the third moon, the twenty-third day, of the four-hundred and twenty-fourth year since the mountains closed."

With that said, the children moved off toward the castle.

The words 'Four-hundred and twenty-fourth year since the mountains closed,' echoed through Emerald's mind. She pulled up the hood and hurried to walk the evening trek. She needed to check for children along the Border Road.

Memories of Grandfather filled her thoughts. Jared Stone had taught her about the first Woman of the Stone. He had explained that her name was Dana, the same for whom the sword she carried was named.

Dana had married Prince Krelor of the Mountain Realm and been unfaithful. Her scandalous actions had caused him to seal the mountains and rain death on anyone who approached. It was a terrible story but had happened long ago. She quirked an eyebrow, thinking of the mountain goat she had recently taken in those forbidden, rocky reaches.

When she crossed Stone Bridge, she headed eastward on the Border Road. Grandfather had read the writings on an enormous boulder a day's ride that direction. Rumor had it, the entrance to the ancient passage under the mountains was located close by it. She remembered the gist of what it said but didn't like the message.

An ancient Andolin king had cursed Emerald's ancestor, dubbing her Dana the Stonehearted. He had recorded the proclamation with a hammer and chisel. The words decreed that no daughters would be born to Dana's Clan until the Creator shaped a woman to pass three tests and unseal the mountains.

Adoption was so common among her people, that Grandfather had made sure she realized that she was the first natural-born daughter of the Stone Clan in over four-hundred years. The fact she could wield the Ancient Queen's sword had proved to him that one day she would cause the mountains to open. He had believed in her future and explained that long ago, people had traveled the Modutan Empire without reservation. He had reminded her that the passageways were still in use by a select few.

The Sages knew the secrets of traversing the mountain tunnels, though seldom did they travel between the North and South these days. She had met such a wise woman when she was eight years old. Sarialla, a Royal Counselor to the dead King and Queen of Frenland, had brought Stephan on that visit.

He was four, and she remembered staring at his blond hair and brown eyes in fascination. She had never seen that kind of coloring. Sarialla's hair had been white, though she had been in robust health.

There were only a dozen members of the Stone Clan alive then. But despite the diminished numbers, the Counselor had entrusted the young

Prince to Jared Stone's care. She had declared that, regardless of anything else, he was safer in Danalan.

She had spoken of the war in Frenland where her brother, Salicor, had rallied the nomads of the far North and usurped the throne. Her anger had been keen as she explained how he had murdered the good King and Queen. Saving their heir, Stephan, had been nothing short of a miracle.

Emerald remembered the tears Sarialla had shed while speaking of her brother's betrayal. He had abducted her two young children. Emerald had pitied Sarialla's loss. It was worse than if the twins had died because the poor woman still hoped for a reunion. By now they would be twenty-one, a year older than Emerald. What kind of people had they become?

The snort of a horse on the road ahead brought Emerald out of her contemplations. Glancing up, she caught the flash of a silver bridal in the sunlight. She had traveled farther east than normal and still needed to check the western half of the route.

"Hello, there." The traveler's voice was feminine and elderly.

Emerald narrowed her eyes in concentration, detecting an accent. She bowed without taking her gaze off of the stranger. Her hand rested on the hilt of the arcane sword.

"I seek the Stones." The woman spoke from beneath a fur lined hood.

The white horse snorted at Emerald. The stallion closed the distance with a pack mule in tow. The sound of hooves crunching on the gravel road carried in the evening air.

"You've found all that remain." Emerald did not doubt the accent now. The traveler hailed from Frenland.

The rider leaned forward. "You are the last Stone? I find that unlikely. Reveal yourself."

Emerald laid back the hood and drew her sword to show the foreign woman proof of her heritage. The patina of the ancient workmanship was unmistakable. However, gaging the traveler's reaction proved difficult. The sun was setting and a deep hood obscured the woman's face.

"Emerald?" The woman's voice held recognition and warmth as she spoke in Frenlandish. "Thank the Creator you survived. I would not have known you." She pulled the hood back and smiled. "Child, you come from plain, honest, farmers. Where did you get such beauty?" She laughed in a light-hearted manner. "From your mother, I suppose. Though, the fat of summer will do you good." She stripped a glove and reached forth a weathered hand.

Emerald removed her glove and clasped the older woman's hand. "I welcome you, Sarialla, Royal Counselor." She spoke the Northern language. "Stay as long as you like. I may be the only Stone, but I'm not the only orphan in Danalan. Stephan will let you in. It's a fair walk to the castle and night is falling. You had better ride ahead. I'll be along soon." Emerald slipped the glove on.

"As you wish, I will delay my questions." Sarialla looked westward. "However, take heed, the Border Road holds no good for a Stone."

EMERALD NODDED AT SARIALLA and the old woman rode ahead to Stone Castle. Eager to return home as well, Emerald hurried to search the road for orphans. Nothing could make her shirk the duty.

Shadows deepened pink into purple as the sunset faded on the horizon. Westward bound, she watched the sky transition through the glorious hues. At a rotted tree stump where she often turned around, she noticed movement.

Curious, she scrutinized a misshapen boulder that had not been there yesterday. Upon closer inspection, it wasn't a rock but a group of ragged children huddled in too few blankets. What were they doing here? The hair on the back of her neck raised on end.

"Hello." Not wanting to frighten them, she withdrew her hood. "Are you well?"

"Stop. Leave us alone." A tall adolescent boy stood and held up a hand.

His threadbare cloak obscured lean features, but Emerald recognized starvation in his sunken cheeks and darkened eye sockets. Undaunted, she met his gaze, observing the sheen of sweat on his brow despite the chill in the air. A wind gust swept strands of hair across her face, carrying the smell of earth and ice from the river on her right.

"Do not fear me. I can help. Do you know who I am?" She smiled to show them that she intended no harm.

"You must go." His lower lip trembled, but he squared his shoulders with a hard look in his eyes. "I do not know you. Go now." His arm extended in a warning gesture.

How could she listen?

Among the others, a girl glanced toward a thicket of brush on Emerald's left. Drawing her sword, she rushed headlong into the scrub. In her haste, she tripped over a woman huddled there. Relieved to find no danger, Emerald looked over the winter withered bushes at the children on the road.

"Are these your children?" she asked.

"Yes." The woman's voice quavered. "Please, keep them safe."

"I can only accept orphans in Danalan." Emerald sighed, sheathed the sword, and took a knee in the snow. "I must obey the law." She unclasped her cloak and laid it and her gloves beside the woman. "Take these and the money I have. It isn't much." She pulled one silver and two coppers from the otherwise empty purse on her belt.

A violent flash of metal warned Emerald before the tip of a sword protruded from the chest of the mother. Her blanket parted to reveal that her hands were tied. The coins fell as Emerald reached for a weapon, too late.

A man sprang from the clutch of trees behind the dead mother. He thrust a knife toward Emerald's throat, but she twisted his hand away with wiry strength. Her quick reflexes allowed her to land an elbow to his middle before another attacker clubbed her head.

Sprawled in the snow, she struggled to escape the clawing bramble of the brush she had landed in. Flashes of light and double images distorted the twilight dimness. Desperate, she scrambled through a gap at the base of two bushes and entered the road.

"Run." She warned the children.

An attacker leaped over the scrub. He tried to wrestle a knife from her hand. A second man stomped her wrist. She slashed his calf with a blade from her boot. The smallest man kicked her in the stomach, causing her to vomit the water she had drunk at the river.

He dove onto her and wrenched her hand behind her back until she dropped the blade. An agonizing wave of pain tore through her left shoulder as it dislocated. She cried out before clamping her teeth together.

Furious, she rolled with the pressure he applied and landed a fist to his neck. Free for an instant, she regained her feet. She drew the arcane sword just as the largest man tackled her. The impact caused the weapon to fly away as they slammed into the gravel of the road.

Breathless and dazed she struggled for air.

"Hold her hands, son. This little whore will pay for her oath-breaking." The heavy brute pinned her legs and ripped at her clothes.

Spittle dripped on her cheek. The harsh words drifted into her mind, a far-off echo. She blinked in confusion.

Pain tore through her. Senses sharpened by the agony; she renewed her fight. One of the other attackers kicked her ribs, and the man on top of her punched her in the head.

A SHOCK OF RIVER WATER rushing over her body brought Emerald back to semi-consciousness. Liquid filled her mouth and nose. The current twisted her, and she sank.

Emotionally numb, she looked up at a white half-circle of light. The sight of the moon distracted her from physical pain. So, this was death.

Warm hands closed around her arm. A man swam above her in the water. He pulled her upward, causing the agony of her injuries to rip her from consciousness.

A jarring motion and heavy breathing shook her alert. The pounding of feet on the snow-covered ground thudded in her ears with the pulse of her own blood. She moved her head and sparks shot through her skull.

At her gasp, the dark-haired man who carried her glanced at her. His breath came in white puffs as he carried her across an open field. Soaked, every part of her hurt and she wondered at his urgency. His black-bearded expression was incomprehensible. Who was he?

He slipped, and they almost landed in the snow. Youthful agility and masculine strength helped him recover without falling. Pain tore through her ribs and middle. He didn't stop at her cry but continued running. When would it end?

"Yoboseyo? Yolojushipshiyo." The man's shout came out husky. He slowed to a stumbling walk and tilted his head back.

Emerald looked up, despite the agony the movement caused. In the moonlight, her vision filled with a welcome sight. The gatehouse towered above them.

Home.

"Who goes there?"

"Rick, open up." Her voice, though weak, projected through the frosty air.

The doors yawned.

"We were on the way to find you, Em." George drew a sword.

He and Gael permitted the stranger to carry her in and then barred the gates. The foreign man did not stop. He carried her across the courtyard and up the narrow staircase into the keep. George and Gael followed.

He knelt and laid her in front of the fire in the main room. His body shook and his teeth chattered. The glossy, black of his wet hair reflected the firelight.

She was struck with how handsome his features were. Others bustled around, but she continued to analyze his face. He had a short, well-groomed beard.

He looked as if he ate often, though he wasn't fat. She decided she liked his wide face and tan skin. They were characteristics of the Mountain Realm, or so she had been told.

He met her gaze for the first time and closed her torn shirt without looking at her chest. He tucked his trembling fingers under his arm and shivered. She wondered why her body remained still.

Nina pulled him aside to hand him a blanket. Her gaze shifted to Emerald who marveled at the level of terror she saw there. The struggle to regain control made breathing difficult, and the world drifted away.

FEAR GRIPPED EMERALD as she stretched toward the stone that in other dreams had been the object that saved her. This time, she failed in her efforts to reach it. Stronger than she, the nightmare man bashed the side of her head over and over. It wasn't supposed to be this way. Her head pounded with pain as if the blows fell for real.

"No..."

"It will be all right." A cool hand cupped her cheek. "Please, hold still or you will re-injure yourself." The girl's voice was familiar.

Emerald stopped moving. She wanted to ask where she was. However, no sound came out when she tried to speak.

Something covered her eyes and forehead, preventing her from opening her eyes. She removed it with her uninjured arm. Daylight blinded her until the wet cloth covered her once more.

"Rest, Em. You need to rest."

It was Nina.

The rim of a cup touched Emerald's lips. She drank the soothing herbal broth. She was at home.

"Sing to me, Nina." Her voice sounded raspy and weak as if she had been screaming.

Gentle alto strains sang a soothing lullaby.

Emerald relaxed and allowed the tune to carry her thoughts from the pain. No longer haunted by fear or influenced by terror, she forgot what she had dreamed moments ago. It hadn't been real. There was no danger here.

Time passed in fitful snatches until voices echoed in the sleeping chamber.

"Her fever broke in the night. Sarialla's healing worked. I think she'll be fine."

"She doesn't look fine. What else can be done?"

"She needs rest."

"Who are you talking about?" Emerald glanced around.

"Are you well, Em?" Stephan leaned over and grasped her hand.

It took a moment to recognize him. "I'm fine." She tried to lift her head. "Ah!" She shut her eyes and lay still.

"Don't move. Oh, please don't move, Em." Nina squeezed her other hand.

"I thought I dreamt it." Emerald peeked at them.

Stephan shook his head. A tear glistened in the lamplight as it fell onto the honeybee quilt her mother had made. She lay in bed, relatively comfortable unless she moved.

Try as she might, however, she could not remember what had happened or how she had been injured. More than likely, she was better off not knowing. She willed her muscles to relax.

"I should rest."

Chapter Nine

S houts roused Emerald from slumber. The pounding of boots on the planks of the floor shook the bed in which she lay. Unwilling to face the chore of waking, she did her best to ignore the noise.

"Go outside to play, children," she said.

Deep voices laughed, and rest fled. Men in beige and white military uniforms stood around her with their swords drawn.

"Emerald Stone, come with us. Chief Judge Mason wants to see you." The soldier handed her a piece of parchment.

She clasped the roll of paper. "What does he want?"

"You're under arrest for murder." A cruel smile twisted the man's lips. "Come."

Two soldiers dragged her by the arms from the bed. Pain bit into multiple places along her body as they hauled her from the keep in her nightgown. Several children ran to her aid, but the soldiers held them back. An officer tied her hands and then the two who held her lifted her into the saddle of a nearby horse.

"Ugh..." Unprepared for the shock of agony, her head lolled.

The brutish officer steadied her. "Stay mounted or I will tie you across the saddle." His expression conveyed derision.

Emerald knew her ribs could not withstand being lashed across the beast. So, she exerted her strength to maintain her seat. Oh, how it hurt. Gripping the saddle-horn, she willed her trembling legs to hold her in place.

Was this military detachment from the Capital? She recognized none of the men. Where was Captain Hammond?

The children were gathered in the courtyard and under guard. She counted them. Everyone was here except Stephan and Sarialla. She hoped they had hidden in the library.

The officer mounted a roan mare. "Move out." He waved an arm.

Eight soldiers on horseback followed him. They led the bay gelding she rode across the courtyard, through the gate, and over the drawbridge. The other men detained the children.

The village wasn't far. However, the short ride stretched for an eternity. When they reached the square, the same two soldiers dragged her off the horse and held her arms.

Judge Porter strode forward, grabbed her jaw, and forced her to meet his gaze.

"You will face justice today, Young Lady." He motioned to the soldiers who held her between them. "Bring her."

A noose hung from the gallows. They hauled her up the steps and onto the platform. Her dignity resurfaced, and she stood without support.

None of the local Militiamen were present. Irrational hope forced her to survey the crowd of villagers for help. Unfortunately, however, their expressions of hatred had deepened since she had seen them last.

Funny she should die like this. What had her struggle to survive accomplished? The surrounding faces illustrated the futility of her life. No defense could persuade these people to show mercy.

Who had she killed?

The sound of Judge Porter's gavel silenced the ill-humored crowd.

"Meadowgren court is in session. Chief Judge Helam Mason from Andoshi is presiding." He pointed at the man sitting next to the lectern. "I, Judge Gavan Porter, will conduct these proceedings. We are here to try Emerald Stone of Danalan for the murder of Annie Miller. How do you plead?" His hostile gaze focused on Emerald.

"Who, Your Honor?" She knew no one by that name.

The Judge waved a hand. A wagon rolled forward. It contained a body with a copper sword protruding from the corpse's chest.

Emerald recognized the woman from the Border Road. However, she did not understand how Dana's sword had ended up like that. She had not killed the mother of those children.

Her memory returned in an instant.

Three men had murdered the woman. Images of that night overwhelmed her, and she collapsed. Rough hands righted her. Through the rushing of blood in her ears, she heard the Judge repeat the question.

"I did not kill her, sir." Emerald resisted the urge to shake her head, knowing how much that would hurt.

Clear of the confusion that had enshrouded her over the past, however long, she began to assess the situation. The snow had melted. Warmer weather had caused the body to begin to rot. So, it must have been days since the attack. That realization caused her to comprehend the extent of her own injuries.

"Your plea is noted as not guilty. The witnesses to the murder will come forward." The Judge faced the side of the gallows.

Three men strode through the crowd.

Emerald tensed. They were the ones who had attacked her on the road. The older man had murdered the dead woman with his sword, not hers.

They had baited a trap for her with the children. For whatever reason, they had tried to kill her. Obviously, they intended to finish the job.

"What say you?" Judge Porter gestured for the men to come closer.

The older man appeared to be the picture of honesty. "We were walking along the river and happened upon the woman there." He pointed at Emerald. "She was arguing with the mother here." He swung a finger at Annie Miller's corpse.

"What did you hear?" the Judge asked.

"They were shouting about the children, sir. She wanted to take them to Stone Castle. But the mother said it was against the law and 'the Stones could not have her children, as long as she lived'. So, she killed her."

Boos and jeers erupted from the crowd. Boys near the edge of the platform threw rocks. Emerald avoided them as best she could, but one caught her above the right eye. Sparks exploded in her head, causing her to teeter until she forced herself upright.

Blood oozed from the cut. It was the only mark on her face and neck. To them, she must appear otherwise unhurt.

It made her unpitiable. Emerald ground her teeth. Let them think what they wanted.

The gavel fell four times before the villagers quieted.

"What say you, Emerald Stone?" Judge Porter's expression dared her to defy the man's testimony.

Emerald squared her shoulders. She winced at the pain but raised her chin to face his animosity.

He glanced away.

"Judge Porter, where are the children?" She hadn't seen the Miller's at the castle.

The Judge waved a hand and several soldiers escorted a passel of children from a nearby shop. Emerald recognized the oldest boy.

"Lieutenant Lister, where did you find these children?" The Judge pressed his lips together in a thin line.

"We found them in Stone Castle, sir." The officer's voice carried above the muffled comments of the mob of onlookers.

Upon closer inspection, Emerald observed they each wore cloaks and clothes she recognized. They looked warm and fed, though alert and fearful. How had they gotten to the castle?

Had they escaped while—

The gavel fell again, and the crowd hushed. "Young Man, what happened on the Border Road the night your mother died?" Judge Porter's brows came together as he leaned forward on the podium and focused on the boy.

The young man blanched. "I cannot say, sir." He shifted his gaze to the three men.

"What?" Judge Porter's tone demanded an answer.

The boy cringed. "Sir, please—"

The Judge raised a hand and looked toward the soldiers.

"Your Honor, leave the children alone. They don't know what happened and hold no blame for the actions of others." Emerald wouldn't have anyone hang with her.

"You know what you've done." The Judge took a menacing step. "Admit your guilt. Tell us of the night Annie Miller died."

Emerald stood firm. "It's common knowledge I walk the Border Road in search of orphans." She maintained her appraisal of the Judge. "Stone Castle has been an orphanage and school for generations. When I encountered these children huddled on the road, I knew they were starving. I intended to take them home and feed them. But the girl there," she pointed, "well, her gaze tracked toward the scrub brush at the side of the road as if someone hid there.

"I drew my sword and rushed into the bushes and stumbled across their mother. She asked me to take the children to safety. So, I put my sword away and explained to her that I couldn't because the law forbade me.

"I offered her enough money to buy food. However, as I reached in my purse to retrieve the coins, a flash of steel ran her through from behind. I realized then that her hands were bound.

"Three men lept from cover to attack me. Those are the men, sir." Emerald pointed at the witnesses. "One raised a knife to my throat, but I evaded him and landed a blow to his midsection. Someone clubbed me, and I fell to the ground.

"Desperate to warn the children, I crawled through the brush to the road. I slashed the calf of one attacker, but another pinned me and twisted my arm until it popped. I broke free and as I drew my sword, the man who has witnessed against me tackled me to the ground.

"My weapon was lost and someone kicked my ribs. As I struggled to regain my breath, I heard the older man say, 'Hold her arms, son.' Do you know what they did?" Emerald glared at the Judge.

Unwilling to describe the pain or relive the anguish she had endured, her lower lip trembled. Due to the final blow to the head, she didn't remember everything. But she had felt them rape her. The horror of it chilled her because now everyone would know.

"You are a liar, Young Lady." Judge Porter's eyes narrowed. "The Carpenters are beyond reproach. They've sworn you slew Annie Miller to take her children. They saw you do it and I must find you g—" The wooden gavel began to lower.

"Hold." The Chief Judge's voice resonated with authority. "Judge Porter, don't be hasty." He arose from his seat and strode to stand beside the smaller man. "If she lies, then she will die for her crimes. However, it's simple to tell if she speaks the truth." His well-groomed eyebrows raised in a questioning expression that exposed intelligent green eyes.

"Yes, sir. It's plain to see there are no marks." Judge Porter jerked Emerald's nightgown upward.

As she struggled, the guards raised her arms above her head. Pain drove her to her knees. Naked, she could conceal none of the wounds she had received.

The crowd gasped. Grotesque bruises blotched her thighs and abdomen. Wrapped tight, her ribs remained stabilized. But her arm dislocated from the socket again, and she choked on a scream.

Feebly, she reached for her clothing. The reality of being exposed in front of these people mortified her. She would never be able to face them again, not when they knew she was a whore.

Defeated, she hung her head in shame.

"What are you doing, Gavan?" The Chief Judge ripped the nightgown from his grasp.

It fell, and she pulled it over her body.

"I didn't believe her. The Carpenters are irreproachable." Judge Porter stumbled backward. "I don't understand."

"Fetch a doctor." The Chief Judge lowered to a knee and swung his cape around her shoulders.

The day wasn't cold, but she trembled in shock.

A soldier broke out of the stupefied-immobility that had befallen the crowd and ran for the physician.

She struggled to stay conscious as a strange numbness crept over her. She felt disconnected her from her body. Her gaze drifted to meet the Chief Judge's eyes, and his intense expression held her fast.

"Who killed the mother of those children?" he asked.

"The man who has testified against me," she said.

"Deceiver. My husband and sons are innocent. Judge Porter, you know us. There isn't anyone to take their place. Don't let her get away with it." The woman elbowed her way through the crowd toward the gallows with three young girls in tow.

Emerald recognized Mrs. Carpenter as the woman who had reviled her, 'Stone maiden' she had called her. The words had been a painful epithet then, though they cut deeper now.

The Chief Judge met Mrs. Carpenter's gaze. She halted, causing the little girls to bump into her backside.

"Your husband and sons committed unspeakable crimes." The Chief Judge raised from his knee. "I'm ready to pass judgment. Though, I will listen if they have more to say in their defense." He glowered at the men.

"We're not to blame for this. She is an oath-breaker and shouldn't be taking children to that castle. Who knows what she does to them?" The elder Mr. Carpenter hurled the accusations.

"She feeds them and cares for them," the oldest Miller boy said. "Ask any of them how well they're treated. I did. We ran away while she fought you, but I should have stayed to help." He broke eye contact to stare at the toe of his boot.

"Young Man, did these men use you to capture Emerald Stone?" Chief Judge Mason cut a stalwart figure.

"Yes, sir." Annie Miller's son squared his shoulders.

The Chief Judge faced the Carpenters with a flint-like expression. "What did you do after you raped her?"

The father stood in defiance but eventually wilted under the Chief Judge's gaze.

"We tossed her in the river. It was dark, but I saw her sink. Someone from the other side dove in and rescued her. We threw knives but the current had already swept her away. I should've slit the whore's throat." Mr. Carpenter senior spit onto the gallows in Emerald's direction.

The spittle landed on the Chief Judge's polished leather shoe.

"Guards, seize those men." Chief Judge Mason balled his fists.

The Carpenters fled. When that failed, they fought. The villagers wasted no time, however, and subdued the offenders. They dragged them to face the Chief Judge before the soldiers could even act.

Unrepentant, the father jostled the butcher and cobbler who held him. His chin lifted and his chest puffed out. Blood dripped from the side of his head as he ground bloody teeth and glared.

Emerald met his gaze. The numbness inside her intensified. She wanted him dead. Disgusted, she looked away.

The Chief Judge consulted with Judge Porter and then walked to the edge of the gallows. "Hubert, Roger, and Christopher Carpenter kidnapped, raped, and attempted to murder Emerald Stone. Hubert Carpenter murdered Annie Miller. I sentence them to d—"

Emerald grasped the leg of the Chief Judge, causing him to pause. He looked at her. Emerald stared at Mrs. Carpenter and her three daughters huddled together weeping.

Without a male heir, the family's holdings would be auctioned. They would receive the proceeds but have no legitimate means of earning a living. Mrs. Carpenter could not remarry unless to her husband's stand-in, a single man related to him by blood. It appeared there was none. Therefore, they would be forced to beg, steal, or resort to prostitution in order to survive.

"Sir, please spare the sons, their mother and sisters need them." Emerald had trouble believing she had said the words.

The crowd grew hushed.

The men deserved no leniency, and she struggled with her decision. She hated their cruelty and feared they would commit more crimes. However, the fear and anguish on their sisters' faces moved her.

Mrs. Carpenter stared at Emerald. A spark of hope ignited in the stormy depths of her eyes. It was then that the woman's gaze shifted toward the Chief Judge.

He placed a hand atop Emerald's head. "Justice demands blood for blood. A petition has been made that I show mercy to the sons of Hubert Carpenter. I leave it in the hands of the Creator who is both just and merciful.

"The penalty under the law for rape is emasculation. The penalty for kidnapping is twenty stripes. The penalty for conspiracy to commit murder is five years in prison. The penalty for murder is death.

"Each man will suffer a eunuch's fate. Each man will receive twenty lashes. Hubert carpenter will then hang by the neck until dead. Roger and Christopher Carpenter will serve one day in seven in hard labor in the service of the children of Annie Miller for the rest of their days. These two men will also serve one day in seven in the service of Emerald Stone until death.

"If they infringe on the law in the slightest way, hang them. Furthermore, the Carpenter family has no claim to any child born to Emerald Stone. I terminate any familial bond that could exist in such a case.

"Penalties will be exacted at once. Roger and Christopher Carpenter will report to work in two weeks or face the noose of this gallows." The Chief Judge stepped away from Emerald and struck the gavel.

Chapter Ten

Atop the gallows' platform, Emerald noticed the crowd part for a white-haired man with a neat beard.

"Did someone call for a physician?" Doctor Platt carried a medical bag as always.

"Yes, this woman needs attention." The Chief Judge extended a hand to her. "Can you stand, Lady Stone?"

Concern etched the Doctor's face. He, too, held out a hand to steady her as she gained her feet. Under her own power, however, she descended the gallows' steps and passed Hubert Carpenter. His expression remained hateful. His sons avoided her gaze.

As she walked away, the soldiers marched the prisoners up the stairs to face fate. Without delay, Hubert screamed in agony. It seared her mind.

She kept walking. Roger's cry hung in the air, and then Christopher's. A whip cracked, but she walked onward.

The Doctor opened the door to his office. He ushered her inside the room. When the door shut, the sounds died.

"Sit, Emerald." The Doctor led her to a chair.

She shut her eyes and braced for the pain, but the Chief Judge caught her good arm.

"I think you'd better lie over here." He guided her to a narrow bed along the wall.

Looking into the Chief Judge's eyes she could detect nothing to fear, though fear haunted her. Regardless of what her mind told her, her body trembled and her heart raced. He backed away to speak to the Doctor in gentle tones. Doctor Platt glanced at her and she perceived his pity.

Anguish choked her. Hot tears threatened to fall, but she held them at bay by sheer force of will. Her shame was public knowledge. She had dreaded this day for six years.

The day her grandparents died came to mind. It was the day she had held a stone that made her powerful where once she had been utterly defenseless. Thinking of it now caused her right fist to curl and her jaw to clench. She stared into the past until a touch snapped her back to reality. Startled, she collided with the wall as she shrunk from the Doctor's outstretched hand.

"I won't hurt you, Emerald. Well, at least I won't try to hurt you, but I need to examine your injuries. Do you want the Chief Judge to go?" His kind manner was disarming.

Distrust saturated her thoughts. "If Chief Judge Mason will please turn away, then I prefer he stays."

The Chief Judge nodded and walked over to look out the window. Without further hesitation, the Doctor set to work.

"Please, remove this shift so I can see your injuries." The Doctor helped her take off the nightgown.

His brows knit as he surveyed the damage. He walked to the basin on a cabinet to wash his hands and then examined her further. She cried out when he reset her shoulder and re-wrapped her ribs. Relieved that was over, she gulped air and swiped at tears while the pain subsided.

"Please, I won't hurt you." The Doctor rested a hand on each of her knees.

"There's no need." She kept her legs clamped together.

"Infection wields a mightier sword than even you, Emerald. I cannot allow you to die for modesty's sake."

His eyes entreated her to allow the examination. Trembling, she concentrated on the ceiling and eased her knees apart. When he finished, he helped her dress in her nightgown and covered her to the shoulders with a blanket.

"You are brave to have survived so much." Deep lines etched his face.

He had seen her scars and seemed to understand the story they told, both the new wounds and the old.

"It makes no sense." She referred to the markings etched in the flesh of her left inner thigh.

They had been placed there by the man who had attacked her. He was the same man who had killed her grandparents. She couldn't read the language but hoped the Doctor could.

"No..." The Doctor pursed his lips, a thoughtful expression as he considered the implied question. "I can't understand it either. I'm sorry." Shaking his head, he stood.

He laid the back of a hand on her forehead, then held two fingers to her wrist and nodded. "You should recover within a few weeks if you eat and drink often and rest as much as possible. The tenderness and scarring will subside over time. Someone took good care of you, but that stitch needs to be removed in a day or two." He washed his hands once more.

"It's too soon to tell if you carry a child, but that will become clear in the following weeks. Should you need my services again, please send word. I'll come to Stone Castle if needed." He smiled.

"I delivered you and it would bring me joy to deliver your child." He reached for a towel. "You should rest before traveling home. We'll leave while you sleep." He unfolded another blanket from the cabinet and laid it over her.

She grabbed his arm. "Doctor Platt, how is Sergeant Hume?"

The Doctor sighed. "It isn't my place to relate everything. However, I think he will live, though he will not be the man he once was. I must make my rounds to the sick, but I will visit Liameo for you just to be sure he's comfortable." The Doctor patted her hand, packed a bag, and departed.

The Chief Judge moved to follow him.

Emerald had too many questions. "Judge Mason, where are Captain Hammond and the Militiamen?"

He stopped. "The Governor has called them in for questioning."

"Why?"

"He was under the impression they allowed you to break the law because they were disloyal to Andolin."

"But that isn't true." How could anyone believe such a thing?

"Rest, Lady Stone." The Chief Judge grabbed the doorknob. "I'll find clothing for you and wake you before long."

Emerald frowned. "Why do you, of all people, call me Lady?" The trembling had stopped and her eyelids drooped, but she needed to know.

"If Andolin acknowledged Royalty, then you would be the Queen. I decided today that you would make a good one." He stepped out the door, and it swung shut behind him.

Her displeasure deepened. Was the Chief Judge crazy? If so, there was nothing she could do about it. She had no idea how to assuage the fears of those loyal to the Andolin government. Nor did she have any means to invalidate the expectations of the people who called themselves Royalists.

The factions moved against each other with her caught helpless in the middle. She had chosen to stay out of the political situation. But by doing so, her isolation had allowed little opportunity to speak on her own behalf.

It appeared that others needed no prompting from her in order to form strong opinions. Thus, the division lines were deepening. She sighed. Even if she tried to interfere, who would listen?

Chapter Eleven

A dog whined and nuzzled Liameo's palm. He lay on the floor of the shed at pauper's field with only the comfort of a straw-filled mattress to ease his suffering. Eugenia wouldn't have awakened him without cause, so he listened for the approach of footsteps.

"Thanks, Gene." He stroked the ears of the enormous wolfhound.

The sound of gravel crunching on the road outside the shed let him know that Eugenia had been right. Laying on his stomach, he pushed up from the ground and gained his feet. His back split a little at the healing scabs from the whipping. He pulled on a shirt and buttoned it, hoping to conceal the shameful wounds.

The door to the shed swung open without ceremony.

Eugenia growled, showing off a healthy set of teeth.

The first man in the door took a step back.

Liameo set his hand on the dog's head to still her.

"Your woman's being hung this morning, so get out there and dig a grave," the Private First Class said.

Two other enlisted men from the Governor's Army stood there with shovels. The PFC handed Liameo his. He took it and followed the men to the poor person's cemetery the shed was built beside.

Emerald should not be buried here. She belonged in her ancestor's mausoleum in Danalan. He dug the hole anyway, orders were orders.

The barracks had been overrun with these soldiers from the capital city for days. He had been cast from their midst to the shed. If not for his condition, then he would have been taken south with Captain Hammond and the other local Militiamen to meet the Governor on charges of treason.

"She faces trial today?" He already knew the facts.

The PFC nodded and went back to talking with the two other men.

Emerald's guilt was sure. All the evidence said that she had killed Annie Miller. But he still couldn't believe it. He didn't want to believe it.

Weakened by the serious infection that had ravaged the central laceration on his back, he paused for a breath. Hip deep in the earth, he wiped his brow with a handkerchief from his pocket. In the corner of the cloth was a blue ship with three masts embroidered by a girl he had once known and loved.

She was gone long ago; he just hadn't realized it. All his plans to win her back had died when the news of her guilt had come. He half-wished to die as well.

Inside the cloth was a braided lock of hair. He ran it through his fingers. Emerald had cut it when she had promised to be his wife. It had been a highly inappropriate gesture, of course.

He blushed to think of her love-struck expression on that evening in the corner of her grandparents' cottage. She had stolen a kiss. The two of them had been playing Empire, a strategy game, while the adults discussed the matter of marriage.

"Dig." The PFC kicked a clod into the hole.

Liameo put the cloth in his pocket and continued with the task. It took all of his strength. As he worked, he tried not to think about her. But he dreaded seeing her lifeless body.

The Carpenters swore she was a killer. Roger was an honest man, a friend, so it had to be true. It just didn't feel like it was possible.

The girl Liameo had fallen in love with would never hurt anyone, but...something terrible had happened to her. His mind shied away from what he had learned when he confronted her behind the Judge's barn. She hadn't said it out loud, but he knew she had been raped. It was the only thing that made sense.

Eventually, the hole got deep enough. A wagon pulled up beside the grave in which he stood. He looked up to see the hilt of Emerald's sword sticking straight over the top of the wagon bed.

His lower lip trembled with emotions he had not yet faced. He wished he could lay down beside her. Death would be welcome if she were no longer in the world.

The cemetery caretaker climbed down from his seat. "Need another hole."

A passel of children just now caught up with the wagon. Their faces were traced with tears, but these weren't any of the children Emerald looked after. They were the widow Annie Miller's brood. Liameo laid the shovel across the grave and used it to climb out.

"Grab that sword out of her, Islander. Let's be done with this business," said the PFC.

Liameo walked to the side of the wagon and reached for the sword amidst a cackling chorus. The three soldiers slapped their knees and whooped in merriment. He paid them no mind. Relief washed over him to find that neither of the bodies in the wagon belonged to Emerald. His emotions overwhelmed him.

"You won't weep for that animal when you know what he's done," said the curator.

"I'm just relieved it's not her, Jeffery. Why was Hubert Carpenter hanged?"

"He's the one killed Annie Miller." Jeffery pulled his hat from his head and held it over his heart.

Unable to speak, Liameo took ahold of the sword to pull it from Annie's chest. As he did so, a jolt of heat surged through his arm and into his body. Sword in hand, he staggered backward.

The haze of illness departed from him.

"Where is Emerald?" He needed to see her.

"She's with the Doctor." Annie Miller's son stood holding his youngest sister in his arms.

"Is she well?" Liameo could guess the answer.

The boy shook his head.

"Your woman was ravaged by this cur and his two sons. They're the ones who killed Widow Miller." Lieutenant Lister spoke as he rode up on his steed. "We had it all wrong, and for that, I'm sorry, Sergeant."

The fresh healthy blood that had just risen with the sword's rejuvenating power, drained from Liameo's face. "How can that be?" Anger surged through him as he rallied his strength. "Why are those sons not here to be laid low today?"

"She...had pity on them for their mother and young sisters' sake." The Lieutenant took off his tricorn and rubbed his face from forehead to chin with his free hand. "The Chief Judge would have hanged them if not for that."

The horror of it was almost too much to bear. "I'm not sure I can let them live."

"Chances are they'll die anyway. They've been emasculated and received twenty lashes. They will live out whatever life they have left serving a day each week for Lady Stone and a day for the Miller children." He sighed.

"Perhaps, they can make amends to some degree, though I personally hope they step out of line so they hang for what they did to the Lady." The Lieutenant shook his head, a somber expression pulling at his features.

Jeffery's fists clenched and his jaw set. "I seen what they done and I couldn't have offered 'em mercy."

Liameo couldn't believe what he was hearing. "What did you see?"

"Judge Porter got hot about her denying the charges and lifted her nightgown over her head to show she was lying. But it only proved the Carpenters took everything she had." Jeffery scowled at the dirt.

"I'm sorry you had to find out this way." The Lieutenant put on his hat.

The shock made Liameo numb. "Everyone saw?"

One of the Miller girls started to sob and then several others joined her.

"They did that to her because she wanted to help us." The girl blew her nose on a cloth embroidered with Emerald's initials.

"They said they did it because she broke her oath to you, Islander." Jefferey shook his head. "That was a lie. I think they had their own evil reasons, else why go so far?"

"That was their excuse for murder and rape?" Liameo focused his wrath on the sword, wishing he could run it through Roger and Christopher.

Jeffery backed away and thumped his backside into the wagon wheel. "There's no excuse makes any sense. I figure they's just bad men to do such things to a pretty girl like her."

Liameo clenched a handful of his own hair in his free hand and paced in anguish. It was too horrible to be borne. How had Emerald shown mercy?

He shook his head and took a deep breath. That level of kindness proved she was still the girl he had known. It was what had attracted him to her from the moment they met. Nothing but her loving nature could have allowed her to do such a thing.

"I will not dig a hole for a Carpenter." He tossed the shovel to the PFC who had forced it upon him earlier in the day.

The Lieutenant nodded. The men walked away to dig a grave on the back side of the cemetery. Jeffery led them.

Liameo walked to the shed and took the sheet from his mat on the floor. He returned to the wagon and tossed Hubert onto the ground. With the sheet, he wrapped the body of Annie Miller, giving the woman some long overdue dignity. When finished, he beckoned to the children to gather around the wagon and bowed his head.

"Would you like to say something over your mother?" He hoped they wouldn't leave it to him.

"She loved us," said the oldest girl.

None of the others could manage a word through their grief.

Liameo gathered Widow Miller in his arms and carried her to the graveside. He climbed down into the hole and carefully laid her in the earth. As deep as it was, his head still showed above the top. He wedged his foot across the opening and leveraged himself upward.

The two oldest Miller boys helped him out.

Using his might, he shoved the pile of dirt into the grave with his arms and chest. He wished he hadn't given away the shovel. He needed to get to Emerald.

When the task was complete, he found that the children had gathered rocks to place around the mound as markers. He watched as they decorated their mother's resting place. The gesture moved him.

He vowed to order a stone be carved with her name. That would allow them to mourn her properly. Poverty was cruel to children.

"Where will you go?" He brushed at the dirt that coated him.

"Home." The oldest girl smiled through her tears. "To Stone Castle."

It was the first time he'd seen any of them the least bit happy in the three moons since their father had passed away.

"You are happy there?" He could guess the answer, but craved details.

"Em gives us lots to eat." A boy of around eight piped up.

"I learned my letters from Stephan." A little girl of probably five said, but she was soon shushed by the others.

"Who is Stephan?" Liameo was unaware of anyone by that name. "That's a strange name."

"He's just a kid. We'd better be getting back." The oldest boy herded the others away. "Thank you." He called over his shoulder.

Liameo whistled for Eugenia who had been pointing to birds and rabbits, waiting for his command to give chase.

"Let's take Em her sword."

He walked over to the hut where he had laid the ancient copper sword when he retrieved the sheet. It was covered in caked on gore. He spent the time required to clean it.

A sensation of intelligence emanated from the weapon, and he wondered how it had the power to heal. At their last encounter, Emerald had acted as if the blade had shocked her. The soldiers today had expected it to do the same to him. Two of them had scorch marks on their hands and one of them had an arm that hung useless at his side.

The weapon was peculiar.

Knowing better than to brandish any weapon in town, he slid it through his belt. He wanted to do something to help Emerald. The mortification she must feel caused his soul to shrivel with remorse. The Carpenters had done this horrible thing in his name.

Perhaps, this was his fault.

He had panicked when she told him to return to the sea. He had been so patient for six long years before that. Why couldn't he have just waited a little longer?

He found himself in the hustle of town before he realized he'd even headed that way. When he looked around, he spotted a regally attired gentleman with a diamond-studded dagger on a bejeweled belt. The man could only be the Chief Judge.

Liameo strode toward the man who was engaged in a conversation with a traveling clothes merchant. Liameo had long suspected the salesman to be a grave robber who would sell the garments off a corpse's back. Distaste further clouded his mood.

"I'll take that dress." The Chief Judge offered a pittance from his purse.

"It isn't enough." The merchant complained though he hadn't refused the sale.

"Sir." Liameo tapped the Chief Judge's shoulder. "May I speak to you?"

The Chief Judge turned and his brows crashed together in a disdainful look. "You dare to interrupt my business?"

"Forgive me, sir. I am in town to inquire after Emerald Stone. I am her betrothed." A swirl of emotions played through Liameo's chest, but he still loved Emerald and he would do whatever it took to make right what had happened.

"Sergeant Hume, I presume. You have my sympathies. She's at the Doctor's office resting. I came out to buy her something to wear home. Since she was not permitted the courtesy of modesty when she was taken from her bed this morning. Sentiments were so biased against her as to cause the men to forget their manners." The Chief Judge returned his attention to the merchant.

"Sir, I would pay for a dress and a scabbard for her sword. She is my responsibility." Defending Emerald's honor and claiming her now was more important than ever in the eyes of the people.

"As you like." The Chief Judge squared his shoulders. "I assume you have heard the news."

Liameo nodded, tight-lipped and determined.

"I'll leave you to it then. Again, I'm sorry for what happened." The Chief Judge walked away from the clothes merchant, heading toward a meat pie vendor nearby.

Liameo sensed the man cared less than he seemed to. It didn't matter. Soon he and all the soldiers from the capital city would return there, and Captain Hammond and the Militia would come home.

The important thing now was that Emerald suffer no more injuries, not of word or deed. The one way he could ensure that was to become what he had always hoped to be, her husband. In that capacity, he could protect her...even if she could never love him as he had desired.

Passing an eatery, he realized Emerald needed fortification. He ordered venison, mushroom, and onion stew with rolls and honey-butter be delivered to her at the Doctor's office. Perhaps, she would be strengthened and encouraged by her favorite foods. Shaking his head, he knew it wouldn't be enough to improve her situation.

He formulated further plans as he spoke to the dressmaker and arranged for the delivery of a readymade gown. He noised his intentions to go through with the marriage as he traveled through the village. He stopped in at the girdler who also specialized as a scabbard-maker for a belt and scabbard for the sword. He spoke with each vendor as he perused the marketplace for a silver comb fine enough to make Emerald feel beautiful again.

And when all of his purchases were made, he found himself outside Doctor Platt's office unable to go inside. Staring at the doorknob, he could not force his hand to touch it. She had been wounded in the most intimate of ways, betrayed by the villagers, and shamed in the public eye. If she had not wished to see him before, then she most certainly would not permit him into her presence now.

A carriage rode up and the Chief Judge stepped out. "Have you been to see her?"

"I dare not." Liameo swallowed the lump of emotions in his throat, ashamed to be so cowardly.

"Never fear, I will convey her home where she will be safe."

The Chief Judge took the things from Liameo's arms. The sword shocked him through the leather scabbard enough to make him yelp in pain. He dropped the load of items on the stoop.

"What is that?" The Chief Judge pointed at the sword.

"It belongs to the Woman of the Stone." Liameo didn't want to say too much.

"Then set it in the carriage." He gathered the nice things Liameo had bought and stepped inside the office, shutting the door behind him.

Liameo stared at the door until the carriage horses stomped their feet at a gust of wind. Blinking to clear his mind of apprehension, he went to a window and peered through a slight gap in the curtains. The Chief Judge stood inside the room with his back to Emerald as she pulled the dress on over her nightgown. The Doctor's middle-aged daughter then brushed her hair and placed the comb in at the last.

Emerald was beautiful, though, clearly in pain.

"Are you going to leave that or not?" The footman opened the carriage door.

Liameo scowled at the man and laid the sword on the bench inside the carriage. Emerald would need it to fulfill her divine purpose of restoring the Ancient Empire. He ran a finger over the amber jewel held in the serpents' jaws and realized the importance of his role in breaking the curse. She required a husband.

Chapter Twelve

Dressed in a gown the color of goldenrods with matching slippers and a darker-hued cape, Emerald resembled the Royalty of old, though the dress was modern and fashionable. The Chief Judge rode with her in his carriage as he escorted her to Stone Castle. He had returned her sword with an ornate belt and scabbard.

"Will you come inside the keep?" Unfamiliar with protocol, she didn't know what else to say.

"Not today." He focused on her with intensity. "I must return to Andoshi to report to the Council of Judges and the Governor." He smiled, though it didn't look genuine. "I'm pleased to have met you, Lady Stone. I wish the circumstances had been different." He reclined on the bench. "We will meet again."

Emerald bowed her head and let the driver help her from the carriage. She waited as the man climbed to his seat and whipped the horses into motion. Through the carriage window, the Judge waved goodbye, and she returned the gesture.

With him gone, the children rushed to her side. Enthusiastic chatter freed her from the strange mood that held her captive. Relieved to be home and seeking normalcy, she faced the little ones only to see the awe in their expressions.

For years, she had taken steps to avoid attention. Early on, she had discovered that beauty often caused good men to act the fool, and evil men to behave like animals. With regret, she realized the effort hadn't saved her from the Carpenter's animosity.

Now, because of this dress, the children would never accept her as they had before. Why would they admire her so much? More than ever, she felt like a bloody stone had replaced the heart in her chest.

"Emerald." Stephan rushed from inside the keep and hugged her in a warm embrace. "We thought they planned to execute you. I'm glad you are well." He stepped back. "You're radiant. What did they do, feed you and comb your hair? It's about time someone did." He touched the silver comb the Chief Judge had given her.

Emerald pushed the memory of the trial and the gallows away. Taking a quick breath, she strode from the courtyard and into the keep. Sarialla stood near the doorway and quirked an eyebrow.

"Em." Nina ran to Emerald but stopped short, wide-eyed.

A kind of metal had entered Emerald's backbone, and Nina's reaction proved it. In the fine apparel, she knew she exuded a force equal to nature itself, at once stunning and cruel. She smiled, a ghastly gesture to be sure because it remained untouched by the friendly emotions that usually flowed from her. Injured in both body and spirit, she was not herself.

"Easy now, Nina," Emerald said.

Her left arm hung in a sling, but she opened her arms to receive the girl. Subdued, Nina slid into the embrace. The girl shuddered.

A stranger stood from the padded chair by the fire. Light from the open door shone on him, allowing Emerald to discern his features. Their gazes locked, and a shiver ran through her.

Nina pulled away.

"I am Darrin of Wolfe Mountain." He bowed low. "It is nice to meet you, Emerald Stone." He had a thick accent and spoke with deliberation as if the introduction had been memorized.

The accent and eye color were identical to the man in her memory. Instinctively, she drew her sword and advanced. Confused, she pinned him against the masonry of the wall to give herself a moment to think.

This man couldn't be the one who had killed her grandparents, but the eye color couldn't be ignored. She hadn't known the Wolf Clan to be mountain men. How could they be? But this man was, and the other had been the same except shaven of hair.

"Emerald, stop," Sarialla said.

Emerald hesitated. However, Dana's sword craved this man's blood with an alacrity that compelled her to run the weapon across his throat. His eyes flew wide. He must know she wanted to kill him, though she could see he didn't understand why.

While she deliberated, he parried her blade with a dagger and fled toward the open door. Armed, the boys blocked the way. Nina gathered the little children up the stairs like a hen with her chicks.

Darrin Wolfe's surprise showed on his face. When the expression of alarm faded, he set the weapon on the table. A wounded posture overwhelmed his athletic frame.

"Nan norur salyojuotnundae. Wey narur chookiborigesoe?" he asked.

Emerald understood. Yes, he was the one who had saved her, so why did she want to kill him? This couldn't be the man who haunted her dreams. That man had spoken well in her native tongue, though the things he had said were horrifying.

If this man had saved her from drowning, then he could be the protector Stephan believed in. A shadowy figure...something about that idea sent a chill down her spine. Surely, she should be grateful for the reprieve from death, but she was not. Weariness overwhelmed her and she could not shake the feeling that death would have been a welcome release.

"Panmal hajimayajo?" She resented his use of familiar speech when addressing her.

It was yet one more clue to indicate that he was indeed the shadow man, a person she knew nothing about who knew everything about her.

Darrin Wolfe blinked at the reproof and bowed. This time he didn't take his eyes off of her. She had lost his trust.

Satisfied, she sheathed Dana's sword, turned her back on the mountain man, and went to bed.

IN THE BLACKNESS OF the night, a chilling cry tore Darrin Wolfe from the sanctity of slumber. He sat up in bed. In the sleeping chamber of the castle keep, Emerald's scream echoed off the granite walls once more.

She had cried out like this the night the men from Andolin had attacked her.

The agony of it made him tremble.

Stephan turned up the wick of the lamp. The light increased to illuminate numerous startled children. There was only one person who didn't open her eyes or see her surroundings. Terror twisted Emerald's features.

Stephan and Nina's eyes met across the aisle between the two rows of beds. With a nod, she hurried to Emerald's bedside. None of the children had crawled in with her tonight. Nina had kept them away so she could recover from her injuries.

Nina sang a lullaby. The soothing alto strains filled the chamber. She stroked her mentor's hair.

Emerald's restlessness calmed and she relaxed on the pillow. Darrin watched her clenched fist open and her expression become placid. When at last, she slept in peace, he breathed a sigh of relief.

Most of the children rolled over and fell asleep as if accustomed to the disturbance. The sound of their breathing and an occasional snore should have reassured him. But he remained upright in the large bed, perplexed by the children's reaction. Did she scream in her sleep often? Did that mean Emerald had been sexually assaulted in the past?

He cowered from such a possibility.

Stephan and George had compelled him to sleep between them tonight. They didn't trust him after Emerald's reaction when she had returned from the trial in the village. They were very protective of her, and perhaps they thought he had done something to upset her. What did they suspect him of?

Stephan left the lamp glowing. Nina returned to her bed and stared at the soft light. The worry lines did not ease from her tender brow.

Concerned, Darrin's mind swirled with confusion. In search of answers, he nudged Stephan's shoulder with an elbow. The Prince spoke the language of the mountains and could explain what had happened.

Stephan shook his head. "Go to sleep." He laid on the pillow and closed his eyes.

Darrin lay down but could not rest. When dawn's light entered through the high windows, Stephan and George awoke. They dressed and allowed him to do likewise.

As he approached Emerald's bed, he detected no trace of the terror she must have experienced to utter such cries in the night. Her emerald eyes opened, full of innocent wonder. She had looked at him the same way when he had rescued her. After a moment, hot iron entered her gaze. Eager to escape the searing intensity of her hostility, he hurried downstairs to the breakfast table.

THE DORMITORY CLEARED of males and Emerald dressed in her favorite brown trousers and white shirt. One handed, she buttoned every button even though she normally left the top one open. It felt safer, or maybe it was punishment, or perhaps just a manifestation that life was different now, uncomfortable.

With difficulty, she pulled on a pair of wool stockings and a sturdy pair of shoes. She made a great effort not to think about the Wolfe in the castle. She should make him leave...but curiosity held her in its sway.

The familiar exercise of brushing her hair soothed her anxiety. However, when she tried to use her left hand, sharp pains reminded her of her condition. She hadn't needed a reminder. With a sigh, she left the hair loose. Perhaps Nina would braid it for her later.

Hunger made her stomach growl. Regaining some of her accustomed eagerness, she made haste to the table. She gritted her teeth against her aches as she sat down and gathered the remnants of a sparse breakfast. Most of the children had finished eating and gone to do chores.

Stubborn, she ignored Darrin Wolfe, who finished the meal and took his dishes to the kitchen. The teenager from the Border Road sat at the end of the table, chewing on a biscuit. He hadn't made eye contact though he had glanced her direction.

The biscuits resembled round bricks and she almost broke a tooth when she bit into one. "I'd better soak that." She reached for a bowl and ladled the last of the watery stew over the bread.

"I should have helped you. I'm sorry, Mistress Stone." The boy's voice broke on the word mistress and he blushed crimson.

She perceived his guilty conscience and despite the hard knot of emotion constricting her chest, she wished to relieve his discomfort. The boy had done nothing wrong.

"Tell me your name."

"Ryan Miller, ma'am."

"I'm not married. Just call me Em."

"Forgive me, Em." His blush deepened.

She took a deep breath and let it out. "Do you even know how to fight?"

"Not the way you do." His head stayed down, though the color in his cheeks faded.

She dipped a wooden spoon in the stew. Dubious, she took a bite. Bland and kind of pasty, she ate it anyway.

"My skills didn't save me. You really could not have helped. The Carpenters would have killed you."

He scowled, though he directed his animosity at the table top.

"You did the right thing by bringing your siblings here. Your mother asked me to keep you safe. I'll do my best, but part of that will depend on you. Do you want to learn to defend your family?"

Ryan met her gaze.

Before he wilted, she muted the severity of it.

"Yes, I'd like that," he said.

Satisfied, she nodded and continued eating breakfast.

He got up and took a biscuit outdoors.

"The cold out there couldn't be worse than the chill in here." Darrin Wolfe spoke his language and came to sit opposite her at the table.

"Speak of what you know." She spoke a warning in his tongue. It meant roughly, mind your own business.

He seemed to ponder her words. "I thought you liked me. When I pulled you from the river, you trusted me. The Sage, Sarialla, explained that you've been badly wounded." His eyes and index finger flitted in a gesture toward her lap which the table blocked from view.

Anger swelled in her chest and her face flushed with heat. Her soul fairly crackled with electric currents of resentment. Who was this man to talk to her this way? How dare he?

"If I'd been there, then it wouldn't have happened." His expression held profound sadness. "These things rarely occur in my land, and I don't understand them." He reached out to hold her hand.

Outraged, she jerked from his grasp. "You have no right to speak of personal matters. Who are you?" Heart and breathing rate increasing, she tensed in readiness to launch an attack.

"I can tell you about myself." His shoulders relaxed. "But it's not my place to explain certain things about my people. An ambassador can be dispatched if you request one."

Emerald narrowed her eyes and clenched her jaw. She wanted no more strangers in her home.

"As for me, I am nobly born. We share a common ancestor, you and I, King Krelor of the Mountain Realm." He looked at her expectantly.

She did not soften at the words.

"Anyway," he said, "I trained as an artist, a painter, until my services as a warrior were required. I've long desired to meet you face to face." He smiled at her for a moment before the happy expression collapsed.

She glared.

He folded his hands on the table and stared at them. "I'm sorry I wasn't there in time to save you from those men. Your meeting with the Frenlander distracted me, and I followed her. I wanted to observe her interactions with Prince Stephan. Thus, I was far off when I heard you scream. I reached you in time to save you from the river, but not from what they did." His face flushed with color.

She ground her teeth unable to speak.

"Last night I heard you cry out in your sleep. You cannot know how much it wounded me to hear you suffer." He looked her in the eyes. "However, the others seemed accustomed to your torment. So, I surmised this was nothing new. Hence, there must be more to it. I need to know, has the same thing happened before?"

She launched across the table and tackled him to the floor. Unable to stop, she pummeled his ribs with her right fist until he grabbed her hand with both of his. Butting him with her head, she brought her knee forward to impact his groin. With a grunt, he pushed her off and rolled over to vomit the pasty breakfast.

"You have no right to ask." Her skull felt as though it had split in two, but she climbed off the wooden planks and fled the keep.

Chapter Thirteen

The fresh air braced Emerald and steadied her pace. Without regard for the children in the courtyard, she departed the castle. What she sought was counsel from the dead and she crossed the fields to an expanse of hillocks that housed the ancestors' resting places.

With her good shoulder, she leaned on the stone door of the mausoleum. It opened. A beam of sunlight shone through a slab of quartz in the roof to illuminate the skeletons of her paternal grandparents.

From the doorway, she gazed at the bones but ended up feeling unsure why she'd come. They watched over her and comprehended her feelings, of this she felt certain. However, unlike in times past, today silence filled the tomb. She received no whispered words of comfort.

Disappointed, she pulled the door closed. It echoed goodbye. A feeling of hollowness broadened inside of her.

Turning to go, she came up short.

Darrin Wolfe shuffled a foot on the wide granite step. "I must apologize for my insensitive words. I had not taken the trouble to imagine the pain you endured the other night. You were right to educate me."

Bruises blackened his face. Strange that he should respect her more after being beaten. No matter, she didn't trust him, especially with a hand behind his back.

"What are you hiding?" Reaching for the dagger on her belt, she faced him.

"Please, accept this gift as a token of friendship." His crystal blue eyes sparkled as he presented a bouquet.

Stunned, she stared at the yellow flowers. "Where did you find these?" It was a question she already knew the answer to. Thoughts of that place brought unwelcome memories.

"Your grandmother's garden. Jonquils are your favorite, and hers always come up before any others."

Repulsed, she backed against the stone door of the mausoleum. He had trespassed, stolen, and reminded her of things better left forgotten.

She spun, crouched, and sweep kicked his feet out from under him. Before he could hit the ground, she snatched the bouquet out of his hands. He lay there gasping for the wind the fall had knocked out of him.

"Never go there again," she said.

He nodded, in obvious pain.

Her breath caught as she recognized the ribbon that bound the flowers. "Where did you get this?"

Without waiting for the answer, she pinned him with the dagger at his throat. It prevented a response but she didn't care. The sight of blood trickling from his neck triggered a terrible vision of the past.

Lost. She didn't break free until Darrin's body went limp. Fearing the worst, she withdrew the blade. When he sucked in a breath of air, relief washed over her.

"I apologize." She crawled off of him.

"I'm yours to do with as you please." Sullen lipped, he avoided eye contact. "Under the law, a Shadow's life belongs to his ruler."

Emerald scrambled away in the dirt, holding out the dagger as a defense. Heart pounding as if it might explode, she remembered what Grandfather had taught her about Dana's Shadow. That, in turn, reminded her of what the first rapist, the one who resembled Darrin, had said. It was something she had never repeated to anyone.

Sparks floated in her vision and her head lolled with dizziness. She labored to breathe. Darrin had the ribbon, the one she'd been crying about losing the day the rapist came.

A vision of Grandmother's face unfocused the sight of her natural eyes as the fragrance of flowers filled her senses. The blossoms that day had brought her joy. But dread had loomed in the woods, ready to crush her peace and change her life forever.

The first sign of trouble had been Grandfather's shout of warning and the sound of Stephan tumbling into the well. The four of them had been reciting lessons in the yard after the morning meal. Upset because she couldn't find the emerald ribbon, she hadn't been paying attention to her surroundings.

The Wolf Clansman had tossed Stephan into the well and run Grandfather through with a sword. When Grandmother stood between the attacker and Emerald, he had killed her too. Blood had sprayed in the air before he knocked her to the ground.

The rape was brutal.

However, the man wasn't satisfied with physical brutality. Cruel in both word and deed, the things he'd said echoed in her mind. 'Don't act like this was your first time. I don't care how much you bleed. You are a whore like your ancestress of old. I know your Shadow has been here before me.' His fingers bit into her arms as he held her down in the dirt of the yard.

'Well, filthy whore, how do we compare? A real man is better than a boy, right?' He sneered. 'I'm going to leave something for Darrin to find.' He sat on her right leg and carved symbols on the inside of her left thigh with his dagger.

She screamed until he clamped a hand over her mouth and nose. Desperate, she fought for air. 'Don't make a sound and I'll let you live for a while.' With a sadistic glint in his eyes, he rubbed a handful of grit that burned like fire into the wounds.

As he raped her again, she discovered the stone that saved her life. His skull cracked with a sickening pop, but men don't die easily. It was difficult to know when it was done. The only thing she remembered was the blood, brains, and skull fragments she later washed off at the river.

Through her cloudy vision, Emerald saw Darrin crawl closer. She momentarily returned to the present. Extending the dagger as long as possible, memory swept over her again and with such force that she struggled to breathe. The rushing of blood in her ears sounded like the river that had washed her clean. It pulled her under.

She regained consciousness to discover Darrin Wolfe holding her. Rocking back and forth, he cradled her like a child. All the while, he soothed her with kisses on the forehead and whispered words of comfort.

Panicked, she broke away. He didn't follow. Unsure of her surroundings, she glanced around to find herself near her grandparents' mausoleum. Reality dispelled the last of the vision. She sucked in a breath through clenched teeth.

"I was a virgin." Glaring, she met Darrin's gaze. "He was wrong. You hadn't been there before him, no one had."

"What did you say?" Darrin shook his head as if unable to trust his ears.

"Years ago, he asked me how 'a real man compared to a boy' and left a message for you in my flesh." She spat the words.

"The man who hurt you could not have meant me, Emerald." He swallowed and his throat bobbed. "I've seen every bit of your flesh and read nothing in the scars." Flushed with color, he averted his gaze.

She clutched a rock in the palm of her right hand. "He said your name, Darrin."

The agony of his confused expression deepened and his skin paled.

"What message?" he asked.

She understood that look, grief so deep only the answer to the question could relieve or confirm his fears. She figured he knew the rapist but didn't want to believe it. Unguarded, his expressions were easy to read. Inexplicably, she felt a connection with him.

She couldn't show him what the attacker had carved. No one was welcome to view the intimate location of those marks. Doctor Platt had seen the scars but hadn't been able to interpret the words. That had dashed her hopes because the physician was well educated. So, instead of showing Darrin the true marks, she unbuttoned the top buttons of her shirt and bared the inside of her left breast.

Darrin's eyes narrowed against the sun. He stared at the faded scars until recognition brought horror to his face. Wracked with dry heaves, he turned away. When he finally faced her again, she saw his relief. What had he feared?

"The Renegades defile women and leave bite marks on the corpses." With his forearm, he wiped his mouth. "But I never dreamed it had happened to you." Seated in the dirt, he hugged his knees. "I had never heard of rape until my men explained it." He clenched his fists. "I'm so stupid."

Watching his every move, she re-buttoned the shirt.

"I don't even know what to say, Emerald. Except that I wasn't there the day your grandparents died. My father had been murdered the previous day, and I was taking the body up the mountain to my mother. I returned to find your guards dead and you and Stephan in the castle. From the state of your grandparents' bodies, I understood that the attack had been brutal. But this is far worse than I had feared."

The intensity of his remorse stunned her. Darrin was not the same as the other man. They were as different as the sides of a coin; the form was similar, but the outlook opposite.

"How did you get the ribbon?" She dared to blink her eyes and relax somewhat.

"When news of my father's death came, I ran to your side for comfort. You were asleep in the shade of a tree at the edge of a field of wildflowers. I laid beside you. When you rolled toward me, the ribbon came loose." He smiled.

"Tiny white flowers littered your hair. You were so lovely. I took the ribbon and paid you with a kiss. I had never kissed a girl before, nor have I since.

"When your eyelids fluttered, I feared you might awaken to find me there. I ran back to my men." He looked deep into her eyes.

"I had no right to kiss you, but you can't imagine what it meant. I've treasured that moment all these years. The loss of the ribbon became tied to the worst day of your life, but it ties us together as well. That was my darkest hour." He stared at the dirt. "I know my loss cannot compare with yours."

The innocence of him was a marvel. Had she ever been this trusting and open? The man who had attacked her had done it, at least in part, to torment Darrin. Whatever message lay inscribed on her thigh held the power to crush him.

Her dormant compassion stirred to life.

She didn't have the heart to allow Darrin to be harmed. Whoever had carved the marks must have been close to him. She vowed never to tell him.

Part of her didn't want him to know for a second reason. She had killed that attacker. It would hurt him to know the man was dead.

She gasped. "When have you seen me naked?"

"You swim in the nude, remember?" He blushed and ducked his head.

"Only when no one will see." She stood and brushed the dust off as heat warmed her cheeks.

"How do you suppose a twelve-year-old boy is chosen to be the Royal Shadow and Captain of the Guard?" He tossed a pebble. "I was the only one who could come near you without you knowing."

A few paces distant, she placed her hands on her hips and clamped her teeth against the pain in her shoulder and ribs. "And how was this discovery made?"

"Curiosity." He flashed an impish grin, though he kept his eyes averted. "I ran away from home, drawn by a mystery in the form of a ten-year-old girl of reputed beauty and incredible destiny. I couldn't resist seeing you before my mother gave me away in marriage.

"When I saw you, I knew I belonged with you. Everything about you drew me in. I spent the day watching you work and play and that evening made camp nearby. Before long, the entire Royal Guard was sitting around the fire. They explained what was required to keep you safe." He shook his head.

"I never dreamed of killing. I'm a painter. I wanted to paint you and I showed them my sketches from the day. They said I could paint as I defended you." He looked into her eyes.

"They promised me plenty of time to do both. Thus, it has been, but I have killed in your defense. I would not have chosen that had I understood what it truly meant to take a life. But how does one know until the act is done?"

She comprehended the question all too well.

As their eyes met, she felt a strange kinship. He was the shadowy savior of so many moonlit nights. He had sacrificed much in her defense. Even though she could not comprehend why he would choose to do any of that, she was moved by the fact that he had.

"I never thanked you for saving my life." She bowed her head. "I should appreciate what I've been given, though I didn't ask for it." Striding forward, she reached down to help him from the ground.

He took her hand, stood, and bowed low. "You're welcome."

Mischief caused her to smile. "What does your wife think of you watching strange women bathe?"

"What?" He snapped upright and stumbled. "I don't watch you bathe. I guard you." He looked away. "I'm not married."

Confused, she frowned. "That's right, you've kissed no one but me." She couldn't help blushing, despite vehemently wishing otherwise. "Then why do you wear a beard? It's confusing."

She glanced at his blue eyes, delighted to see him laugh.

"Because I thought you'd like it," he said.

She reached out to touch his well-groomed face. When she realized what she was doing, she pulled back. Hastily, she handed him a cloth from her pocket.

"Your neck is bleeding." She walked to where she had dropped the dagger and flowers as a means to conceal her deepening blush. "I do like it."

Chapter Fourteen

Emerald swept into the kitchen of the keep like a spring zephyr. Bearing the yellow flowers Darrin had picked in Grandmother's garden, she hummed a song Estelle Stone had often sung. She found a bowl and filled it with water.

Jonquils in one hand, she undid the vivid ribbon. Running her thumb over the delicate stitching of her name, she remembered how many times she had been compelled to rip out the thread and start over. Embroidery was an art that required perfection.

Though stern, Grandmother had spoiled her. A smile teased at the corners of her mouth. Despite everything, her life with her grandparents had been wonderful.

She cut each jonquil's stem at an angle and placed them in the bowl of water.

"Look who's happy this morning." Nina trudged into the kitchen carrying a load of wood from the entryway.

"I was thinking of my grandmother." Emerald held out the ribbon. "She gave me this, and I'd like to wear it today. But I can't tie it because of my shoulder. Will you help me?"

Nina's mouth fell open. She dropped the wood and came right over. "It's beautiful. Why haven't I seen it before?" Nimble fingers braided the long, curly hair and tied the ribbon.

Emerald glanced at the girl. "It was lost."

She had rescued Nina during a Wolf Clan border attack on a traveling caravan. Her older sister had borne the brunt of the brutality. Regrettably, the young woman had not survived.

Darrin wasn't the only one who had seen a woman's breast marked with a ring of teeth marks. Nina would have shared that end if Emerald had not come so quickly to their aid. Even so, Nina never left the safety of the keep.

"Oh, I guess that explains it." Nina didn't press for information but walked over to build up the fire. "The blossoms are lovely, Em. It seems like we should have a vase around here somewhere, but I haven't seen one."

Emerald nodded. "Yes, I thought of that. I have one tucked away in my hope chest upstairs." Focused on the flowers, she knew just what to do. "The trick with jonquils is to let them seep after you cut them and then transfer them to fresh water. They ooze a toxin that makes them wilt. But if you change the water, then they live longer."

"How did you know that?" Nina's smile broadened.

"I once cared about such things. Grandmother loved flowers and knew everything about them." Emerald ascended the kitchen stairs. "I'll find the vase."

Darrin knelt before the fire in the main room and fed wood onto it. Striding past him, she pretended not to notice his smile as she climbed the stairs to the next floor. Did he intend to stay? She almost hoped so. Why?

In the chest, she found a vase wrapped in a white, lace tablecloth. Both had been Grandmother's. Expensive porcelain, artisans had crafted the vase across the sea. Careful not to drop it, she made her way to the kitchen.

Darrin wasn't to be found. Was she looking? Of course, not because that would be strange.

As the day wore on, she ran into him several times. He always smiled, and she always tried not to. A hard worker, he learned fast. Stephan and Sarialla helped him find his way around the castle since both spoke the mountain language.

At dinner time, Emerald stood on the steps of the keep. "Come and eat."

As everyone came in, she tallied the children. Sarialla had already gone inside, but Darrin hadn't and didn't come now. Where could he be? With a sigh, she chewed her bottom lip.

Perhaps, he had left the castle after all, unless he was exploring. Without consciously choosing to, she walked away from the keep. She searched the vacant buildings that had once been functioning business and homes for the many occupants of the castle.

The narrow streets provided hiding places for the children when they played games. With a cluck, a stray chicken startled her as she passed an open door. Laughing at herself, she decided that she'd have to organize a chicken chase in the morning.

They needed to find the chicken so they wouldn't lose the eggs. The children would have fun with that. She knew just the perfect prize to offer.

In the bottom of the hope chest, she had found a book of poetry. It had belonged to Mother. Pressed within the pages lay a coral button that had fallen out when she'd picked up the volume. Where it had come from, she couldn't guess, except that coral came from the sea. The children would think it a treasure.

Imagining the fun, she rounded a corner grinning. The sight ahead awed her because the smooth surface of the castle wall featured a charcoal drawing of Andre brushing Dusty. Each detail evoked the joy the boy felt in his work.

To the left was a sketch of Nina in the kitchen, scolding an urchin who'd stolen dough from the bread pan. Emerald giggled. Excited to see more, she hurried behind the building and almost bumped into Darrin.

He leaned against the wall as if hiding. Something in his expression told her he hadn't wanted to be found. Watchful and reverent, it seemed he held the artwork sacred.

The self-possessed, dignity in his carriage lent him an air of power she had not suspected him capable of. It was like when she wielded Dana's sword, or Stephan sang. This was the strongest, most cherished part of him. He obviously hadn't intended her to witness it.

Not wanting to intrude, she turned to go. "Forgive me."

He caught her hand. "Please, I'm sorry. It's fine. I'm just not accustomed to people seeing my work. Well, at least, I'm not accustomed to seeing them see it. Will you stay?" His eyes twinkled with a secret.

Intrigued, she arched an eyebrow. He led her along the curve of the wall to a half-finished drawing of Marta. The little girl grinned as she petted a goat.

"Amazing, she grows every day." Emerald swiped at tears as an excuse to pull her hand from his. "Do you remember the day of Marta's birth?"

Darrin nodded as sadness entered his gaze. That caused Emerald to realize he must remember another day pertaining to the child. Had he been there when the Wolf Clan wiped out the large group of squatters? Only Andre and Marta had survived. Emerald traced the lines of the toddler's face with a fingertip, careful not to smudge the drawing.

"The entire group of squatters celebrated her citizenship because the Andolin authorities could never force her to leave Danalan. I celebrated too." Emerald clenched a fist. Only six moons later had been yet another moonlit night when innocent people perished. "Dinner is ready. We should go."

He touched her arm. "I'll be in soon."

A flash of lightning webbed the sky and a clap of thunder shook the air.

"You'd better hurry." She hurried toward the keep.

Fatigue plagued her despite the fact that her wounds were healing. With a scowl at the mountains, she climbed the steps as the deluge hit. She made it inside before she got too wet. Darrin wouldn't be so lucky and the art would wash away.

Paused in the entryway, she thought of the fascinating pictures. The drawings changed her opinion of him. What would it be like to have such a skill? Just then, the sound of children at the dinner table accosted her with a cacophony of dissident noise. She abandoned the line of thought.

"No, no, Leland." Nina scolded the littlest of the three boys Emerald had saved from the squatters' cottage.

Leland stood beside the table reaching for his brother's bowl of beans. With a howl, he dropped to a sitting position and then threw his head back. When it hit the floor, he screamed even louder and kicked.

Dread for the night ahead caused Emerald to quirk a grim smile. Leland wasn't always this way but was teething and throwing fits. Worried, she strode forward, swept him up, shushed him, and patted his back.

"It isn't easy being little is it, Lee."

He was having a hard time adjusting to life without parents. It hadn't helped that he had still been nursing when his mother died. Nina was doing a remarkable job with him, considering the circumstances that had prevent-ed Emerald from helping much.

Sarialla had done plenty of rocking too. Emerald had noticed. But it wasn't their responsibility to care for Leland, and she determined to be more attentive. Until the tooth came in, he wouldn't sleep well.

"Do you feel better, Lee?"

Lower lip shuddering, he inhaled and stopped crying. With a cloth from a pocket, she wiped his sweaty face and runny nose.

"Let's get dinner, you must be hungry and it smells yummy." She sat at the table with him on her lap. "Do you want bread?"

He nodded and reached out a little hand. At times like this, she felt like kissing all over his face. But she resisted the impulse because of how tired and cross he remained. He let her hold him close as he ate the soft middle out of the slice of bread. Drowsy eyed, he leaned against her chest and con-tinued to calm.

She snuggled him. "Good boy, Lee."

Hungry, she reached for a bowl and ate two bites before Leland perked up and showed interest in the beans. She fed him as much as he would eat and gave him a drink of water. He fell asleep.

With the baby cradled in her arms, she went upstairs. A nap now would help him sleep better tonight. Children seemed to need a great deal of rest.

With a yawn, she laid him in bed and headed downstairs. In the dim-ness, she collided with a sopping wet someone. She recognized Darrin at once. He smelled of rain and the outdoors.

"Forgive me." His hands steadied her on the staircase. "I didn't see you."

Emerald caught her balance. "Please, be quiet, the baby—" Before she could finish, Leland cried.

With a sigh, she walked over and gathered up the little boy. Patting his back, she walked deep into the dim room. On her way past the nightstand by Stephan's bed, she turned up the wick on the lamp. A thoughtful some-one had already lit it.

Offhand, the thought came to her that unless the rain spent itself by morning, she would need to postpone the chicken chase. At the end of the room, she turned around. Darrin was half out of his clothes. Wide-eyed and gasping, she faced away.

"I'm sorry, I didn't realize you were changing." Heat radiated from her face.

His body was more muscular than expected. Her breathing rate increased. The meager hair on his chest and belly was as dark as his beard and head. To her relief, he still wore trousers.

She squeezed her eyes shut. Why hadn't she realized he had come upstairs to change out of wet clothes? Embarrassment blazed across her whole body because he would think she'd looked at him on purpose.

"I should have warned you." His voice was soft and right behind her ear.

Surprised, she almost jumped out of her skin. She hadn't heard him coming or felt his presence. That too was unusual about him.

Her blush deepened as she swung around to face him. With the lamp behind him, she couldn't detect much of his expression. However, his proximity caused her skin to tingle in an unexpected way.

"I should go to dinner." He bowed and returned downstairs.

She took a breath and let it out, his deep voice stirred strange feelings in her middle. Leland fussed on her shoulder, and she realized she'd stopped soothing him. With a jump, she resumed walking the floor.

EMERALD TOOK LELAND to bed with her that night, but he slept little. Every so often, he started crying, and she got up and walked with him. Sometime in the night, she took him downstairs to rock in the rocking chair near the coals of the fireplace. They both fell asleep.

Before dawn, she awoke with a start due to the absence of his weight in her arms. The fire blazed in the hearth. Darrin held Leland in his hands, looking ill at ease. The baby fussed in protest. Emerald jerked to a standing position, wobbling as she gained her balance. Darrin pulled the baby to his chest in some strange hold as he reached out his free hand to steady her.

"He was going to bite you," he said.

She looked Darrin in the eyes and held back a laugh. "The baby seeks his mother's milk." She shook her head at his confused expression and rubbed feeling into her forearms and hands. They had fallen asleep due to the pressure on her elbows as she'd held the baby in the rocking chair. "Leland was trying to nurse."

Color flooded Darin's expression.

She offered a smile and adjusted the crying baby up onto his shoulder, guiding his hand to pat the boy's back.

"Gently," she said.

Darrin nodded. He took to the task of soothing Leland awkwardly at first. Though he soon mimicked her example from earlier.

She pulled her shawl around her shoulders. Her backside had numbed with cold. The fire had only just begun to warm her.

"Did you light the fire?" she asked.

Darrin walked the baby toward her with a little bounce in his step that matched the rhythm of each pat on Leland's back. A smile tugged at the corners of her mouth. Her eyes must have shown her amusement because he paused and blushed.

"Yes."

She inclined her head in a bow. "Thank you."

Leland had fallen back to sleep. It couldn't be more than two hours until morning and she figured Darrin would be fine with the baby until then. With a yawn, she headed up to bed without another thought.

OVER THE COURSE OF several days, Emerald felt her connection with Darrin deepen. They talked as they worked around the castle. Everyone seemed to have noticed the change. However, she was grateful the children held their tongue and didn't tease, especially Stephan.

She kept busy.

Though no one had said anything, she could feel their gaze follow her. She carried a load of firewood through the main room of the keep. Night had fallen and she hefted the last load of wood up the stairs to the library for the evening.

Sarialla sat reading by lamplight before the coals of the fireplace. Emerald knelt to build up the fire with kindling and split logs. The older woman smiled.

"You seem to be enjoying Darrin's company a great deal, Emerald. I notice he often finds work near you. Do you like him as much as you seem to?" Sarialla closed an ancient scroll from the family collection and tied the protective leather covering around it.

"He is a hard worker and his help is much appreciated, as is yours, Wise Sage." Emerald blew on the coals to light the kindling.

"You're welcome to my help." She had a twinkle in her eye. "Have you discussed how long he'll be staying?"

Emerald jabbed the fire with a poker and flames erupted. "No." She flashed a warning with her eyes at the older woman.

"Well, be sure you do before you fall in love with him. He may have other obligations that will take him away."

Emerald's jaw fell open. "I have no intention of falling in love with anyone. I just like talking to him." She stood and dusted off her knees. "I don't care when he leaves." She stalked out of the library, pained by the misinterpretation of her motives.

Chapter Fifteen

Emerald avoided Sarialla for several days. There was an awkwardness between them now that had never been there before. One night, the older woman caught her arm as she crossed the main room of the keep after dinner.

"May I speak with you, Emerald?"

She had dodged this conversation with dogged determination. Sarialla could only have come to Danalan for one purpose, to take Stephan to Frenland, and she couldn't face losing him. Of all the children in the castle, Stephan was the most like family.

She had helped raise him from the age of four. Somehow, he had replaced her younger brothers who had died. For another thing, no one else had known her grandparents and that made him indispensable. How could she live without him?

Looking at the children as they played on the rug in front of the fire, she knew she'd done well to keep them safe and fed. There never was enough to eat in spring. Fortunately, they would plant soon. With more hands to do the work, they could reclaim enough land to grow plenty and to spare.

"Emerald, you can't ignore me forever." Sarialla's voice held kindness and her expression a bemused indulgence.

"I'm aware, Counselor, that you must be leaving soon. I understand what that entails. Perhaps you could allow me to enjoy one more evening of peace before we discuss the matter?"

"I understand your moments of peace are rare." A rueful expression crossed Sarialla's face. "I am indeed sorry to bring up the inevitable exodus. Perhaps, we can delay that conversation, however, if you will speak to me in private?" Her body remained relaxed enough to make it clear she only made a request.

Emerald raised an eyebrow. "The library will be cold at this hour of the evening."

"A stick of wood could remedy that."

Emerald nodded in acquiescence. "Yes, it could. I'll get it and meet you there."

She walked outside to fetch an armload of wood from a lean-to. The heavens had cleared of clouds and it was not as cold as it had been in recent days. She hadn't bothered to put on a cloak and tucked her fingers under her arms to keep them warm.

With a deep breath, she marveled at the familiar taste of wood smoke and animal smells. Swirls fogged the air when she exhaled. The gray flag of her clan with its white tree lay still against the deep blue of the night sky.

"You look well tonight, Emerald." Stephan appeared from the shadows to her right.

She flashed a smile, glad to see him. "I came to fetch wood for the library fire. Sarialla wishes to speak with me."

The two of them bent down to gather split logs.

"I'm not going with her," he said.

Emerald laughed. "Dear brother, I love you for your loyalty." She put her hand on his arm. "Don't you know how proud Grandfather was of your future?"

He shook his head, tight-lipped.

"He was, and I know more than you do about the sacrifices he made to educate you. He spared no expense. I benefited from it as well, though I didn't take to it the way you did." She shook her head at the memories of the hours of study the two of them had been subjected to.

"You don't know what Sarialla expects of me, Em."

"Don't I?"

"I don't feel like a prince." His voice trembled.

"Oh, Stephan, you've been raised by Royalty." Emerald stooped down for more wood. "I was reminded of that by Chief Judge Mason. Indeed, we're poor here in Danalan. But I see what this place has taught you, even if you don't.

"I would have done more for you if I could. I've given you everything these two hands can provide. Be a king for me." Arms stacked high with wood, she paused to receive his response.

"I will never forget what you have done for me." Emotion choked his voice and tears coursed his face.

The depth of his emotion spoke of things she would never discuss. She hadn't realized he knew her secret. How much did he remember about that day, long ago when she had been forced to do such horrible things? Was he trying to thank her for saving his life? She gritted her teeth for a moment.

"Never shirk from your duty to your people, Stephan. No sacrifice is too great when protecting the innocent." She headed toward the keep.

"I will, Em. I'll make you proud."

His words saddened her and she looked back at him. "I will always be proud of you, Brother. If ever you feel you've failed, then think of me at this moment and know it's not possible for me to change how I feel. You're always in my heart."

He sobbed at her words. "I don't think I can do it without you. I'm only sixteen years old." He shifted the load of wood and waved a hand to put her off. "I know you were younger when you had to take on responsibilities beyond your years. But this time, we have a choice. I want you to come with me as Woman of the Stone. I need you, at least for the summer."

She furrowed her brows in thought.

He lifted his chin. "Sarialla says I am to fight a war to regain the better part of my kingdom from Salicor. I could use your advice. Will you counsel me?"

"I..." Emerald looked around the courtyard.

She knew George could take care of things. At least, he could if she wasn't here to draw the ire of the Wolf Clan. A chill ran down her spine as she gazed up at the Impenetrable Mountains and visualized Frenland beyond them.

"My destiny lies along this path, but I fear—"

He laughed, sounding both joyful and relieved. "You've never let fear stop you before. Thank you for coming with me. Everything will be fine. I'm almost excited to get going." He walked past her, climbed the steps of the keep, and pushed the door open with his back.

In the light from the hall, she could see him grin. She followed him in and closed the door behind them.

"You need more help than I thought," she said.

He laughed.

They dropped their loads of wood in the entryway crate with a hearty clamor.

"I'll be in the library with Sarialla for a while." She picked up two pieces of split wood. "Will you put the little ones to bed?"

He nodded and hugged her from the side, tucking his face into her neck like a child. He then departed into the light and ruckus of the main room. A tear traced her cheek and she wiped it away with the back of one dirty hand before she marched to the library.

WITH A RATTLE OF THE knob as a warning to the occupant, Emerald entered the room full of books. She bolted the door behind her to ensure a private conversation. Sarialla sat in a chair before the fireplace, gazing at the glowing coals.

She looked older without her usual animated posture. Emerald laid the wood on the fire and stoked it with a poker. Flames erupted to illuminate and warm the room.

Emerald sat in a chair beside the Sage. She held out her hands to the fire as she settled her thoughts. Would Sarialla object to her coming with them as Stephan's advisor? She sighed. If Stephan wanted her to come, then he would have to ask permission.

"I thought I would tell you a story." The older woman unfolded her hands from her lap.

Emerald's stomach clenched. "As you wish."

"I have traveled to this land many times. In fact, I first came forty-three years ago. I was younger then than you are now.

"Things were different. Danalan teemed with your extended relations. Peace and happiness ruled at the foot of the mountains.

"The elders of your clan were wise and longsighted. The people prospered and everyone had plenty. You know the generosity of your forefathers." Sarialla's smile faded as she adopted a pained expression.

"Some things, however, have not changed. My first encounter with a member of the Stone Clan was the day I met your grandmother, Estelle. I rode along the Border Road and discovered two villagers drowning her by degrees in the river. They had already done their worst. The cowards fled from me as if I were an army."

Emerald sickened at the thought.

Sarialla's expression hardened. "Estelle was such a tiny woman, so frail. They had come close to killing her, but she proved to be made of sterner stuff than I imagined."

Emerald stabbed at the coals with the poker unable to think of a response.

"The Andolin tradition of casting off an unfaithful wife had never taken root in your grandfather's heart. However, he struggled with the knowledge the child might not be his. Your Uncle Edwin came into the world unsuspecting his questionable parentage. No one ever reproached him. He is the one who rescued you from the wolf the day your family died, is he not?" Sarialla tilted her head.

"Yes. He was a brave man and always kind to me as if he had something to make up for. I mourned for him when he died a year later.

"His example guides me still. He was never content with his service to the Clan. He always found more to do."

She shook her head in sadness. "Now I understand his reason why." Respect mingled with pity in her chest.

"And you, Emerald, how do you view such children? For sure, all such products of cruelty do not turn out so well. The attitude of the mother is critical.

"You see, Estelle loved Edwin. I don't know how she did it, but she loved that boy as much as she did any of her other sons. He gave her hope and helped her to heal.

"You understand that her life was never the same after she was attacked. You both have a great reason to be bitter. That grieves me deeply." Sarialla shook her head in a sorrowful gesture.

Emerald clamped her teeth and looked away.

"Though your grandfather eased her concerns with his unfailing love, Estelle lived in fear for many years. She never visited the village again, not even to see her sister, Elaine. Are you to become so afraid?" The old woman leaned forward to capture Emerald's gaze.

Emerald pondered the question. She turned her attention to stare into the fire. Her grandmother had been pale and weak. It was hard to imagine she had ever been robust or healthy.

Somehow, she had borne eight sons and endured their deaths at the hands of the Wolf Clan. She'd loved each of them with everything in her. She gave much of herself to others.

Sarialla was right, however. Grandmother had harbored a cankering fear that felt as if it blotted out the very sun at times. Emerald understood what her grandmother had suffered and what she had feared.

"Grandmother told me what to do if I were raped." She concentrated on the flames in the fireplace. "Somehow, she knew it would happen. I think I inherited my visions from her.

"Anyway, she told me to fight until fighting proved useless. She instructed me to bide my time until the man lost his focus and then strike in any way I could. I looked into her wide, lifeless eyes the day she died and remembered the advice. It saved my life, but the cost was so high."

Sarialla clamped her hand over her mouth.

"This time, I was relieved to die. I welcomed death, but it was snatched from me by one who sought to save me. He didn't realize he was six years too late." Emerald's attempt at a smile did nothing to uplift the melancholy.

Sarialla absorbed the revelation with an expression of compassion. "I can't claim to understand your suffering. I've never been raped. I do know that Estelle worked through it. She was happy again."

Emerald pressed her lips together and knit her brow in concentration. "I don't think I would recognize happiness even if I felt it. I remember snatches of the joys of childhood before my family died. In my mind, I see myself wading through a field of flowers chasing my brothers in the sunshine. I remember swimming in the river on hot days and lying naked on the scalding boulders. I loved the smell of water on those waterworn stones." She shook her head. "I know of no way to become a child again."

Sarialla smiled a broad, generous expression, though a hint of sadness still showed in her eyes. "I do. You'll know it when you become a mother. As you show your child the world, you will experience all of its joys again."

Emerald winced. "What makes you so certain I carry the seed of one of those depraved men inside of me." A tremor shook her spine.

Sarialla's expression dimmed. "I don't know if you are with child. But I know that motherhood will bring you joy. Do you think I don't see you around this castle? I see your influence everywhere.

"These children are in awe of you. Most importantly, they love you. You have a special way with them. Many have suffered so much that it's nothing short of amazing they trust anyone. They trust you."

"I never asked for any of this." The tradition was a well-worn path, but it wasn't a choice exactly.

Sarialla breathed deep. "I realize it's different running an orphanage than having children of your own. To be sure, I can't imagine how difficult it would be to raise a child without a husband. However, I don't think you will face that challenge and I'm glad for you."

Emerald stared at her in confusion. "What are you talking about?"

"Why, Darrin Wolfe, of course." Sarialla chuckled, though her laugh soon ended in nervous fidgeting and furtive glances.

Emerald's jaw dropped in astonishment. "I can't marry Darrin."

"Why not? He's in love with you."

She held her breath as the significance of the revelation pierced her soul. At that moment, everything that had passed between her and Darrin altered.

"But he can't expect that of me. I can't give that to him." She took to her feet and paced as her agitation increased. "There's no way he wants to wed me. He knows I'm unworthy of marriage." Emerald stopped and pointed a finger. "You've made a mistake, Sarialla."

The older woman's hands fluttered until she clasped them together. "I have spoken out of turn. I see my error. Forgive me." With those words, she departed the library in a swirl of skirt and cloak.

The rustle of fabric echoed in Emerald's ears long after the library door closed. The impact of Sarialla's words had done irreparable damage, and she found she could not turn back. Darrin had deceived her.

He wanted to do what others had done, to bruise her flesh with his cruel hands, to force himself inside her with his brutish strength, and shed her blood. She shuddered. How much more of her blood would be required by heartless men?

She vowed he would never have the chance. She would kill him if he tried. Her fear of him surpassed that of any other man. Why had he betrayed her like this?

Fear ate away at her to realize that carrying a child would rob her of strength. The child would make her helpless, so helpless to any man's attack. She trembled in the solitude of her misery. The man who had become a friend was now an enemy.

Chapter Sixteen

The fire had burned out and the library turned cold. Silence rang from the stone walls like the bell in the gatehouse. Emerald thought she might go mad being so alone, but her emptiness faded to numbness.

At last, she unfolded her stiff legs. The chill in her bones amplified the aches of her recent injuries. In the darkness, she made her way by feel to a bed, any bed with space for her.

The soft sounds of sleeping children eased the hardness of her heart but little. Stripping her boots and trousers, she entered a bed. Well-worn bedding already radiated with the heat of a body. She inhaled the soapy, clean smell of the person's skin and snuggled in. With a sigh, her eyelids fell downward.

Tittering and shushing sounds roused Emerald prematurely from her slumber. The dim light of dawn seeped through the high windows. She fluttered her eyelids to behold it and then fell back to sleep as the sound of small feet descended the stairs.

Deep breathing beside her tempted her to drift again into peaceful dreams. That is until she realized the sound was too great and low to be created by a child. Blushing, she realized she must have gotten into bed on the wrong side of the room and slept with one of the boys. No wonder the children had giggled.

When she focused her eyes, the blood drained from her face. She had not cuddled next to Andre, or Gael, or even Stephan, but Darrin Wolfe. A strange thrill shot up her spine.

She pulled back in surprise, grateful he had not awakened. In an odd way, she felt drawn to his sleeping face. She paused, aware of the risk, but unable to break the enchantment with which his halcyon features held her fast.

His eyebrows and lashes were dark against his tan skin. The hair of his mustache and beard was trimmed short and shaved around his cheeks and under his chin. He lay on his back with his lips slightly parted and took breaths of air in and out with the rhythm of his heart. She watched his pulse throb in his neck.

Her ears burned when she imagined what he would think if found her here. She hurried out of bed and pulled on her trousers and boots. With her back to him, she escaped the gravitation like attraction to be close to him one last time.

She had vowed to be rid of him. But her emotions and her mind were at odds. It was hard to remember the reasoning behind the decision.

"I know you've been here all night." His voice reverberated low with sleep, easy, like a caress.

Her eyelids drifted shut for an instant before she stepped away into the center of the room. Knowing he loved her was changing how she thought of him and how she responded to him. These feelings had grown over the past few days. However, she had believed Darrin could never return them.

He was innocent. Good. She was not.

"Do I still frighten you?" he asked.

She paused. Did fear drive her away from him? Likewise, had love drawn her to his warmth? She faced him.

"I didn't know it was you. I made a mistake."

He put his trousers on and came to her in his stocking feet. His features eased into a smile as he looked into her eyes. He grasped her upper arms.

"You have no right to touch me." She pulled away.

He stepped forward. The heat of him warmed her. Did she want him to touch her? Terror made her heart race.

"I want the right. I've fallen in love with you."

She shut her eyes and set her jaw. So, it was true. Her heart tore within her. The urge to weep nearly overcame her anger. How could he do this?

She met his gaze. Projecting fury to mask the hurt, she squared her shoulders. With her head held high, she spoke her native language. She knew his understanding would be limited.

"Wolves are not welcome here."

He winced, causing the corners of his eyes to crease with pain. "I meant no disrespect, Princess." He bowed and descended the stairs.

Her eyes widened and then narrowed. She balled her fist as fury blurred her vision. He had called her 'Princess' in her own language, the same as her rapist had done. Intense animosity overwhelmed her and she swelled with spite for her former friend.

Abhorring her frailty for needing him, she hated him for what he would doubtless do if he knew her weakness. He had shown his true nature. She felt vindicated for her decision to force him out of the castle. However, vindication did not satisfy, it consumed. She burned in a crucible of hatred.

In order to expel the threat, she descended the staircase to the main room of the keep. Darrin's face was ashen and his eyes bright with tears. He stood by Stephan who warmed his hands by the fire. Darrin placed a hand on Stephan's shoulder and leaned forward with his head down. He spoke the mountain tongue.

"She has cast me out. I must leave this place at once." A sob escaped him, but he clamped his jaw and clenched his free hand into a fist.

Stephan's eyes went wide. "What have you done? If you've seduced her, then you're a fool. How else would you expect her to react?" Color flushed his neck.

Darrin took a step back. "No."

The children in the room watched him.

He had his back to the room. "I swear to you that I have done nothing wrong. Last night, someone entered my bed. I knew it was her. I would know her anywhere, but I didn't touch her. You don't know how I felt when she drew herself next to me. I was afraid she was the one seducing me. She wasn't, however, and simply fell asleep.

"This morning, she said she had made a mistake. She didn't know it was me. She is angry, but I swear I've done nothing to deserve it."

Sarialla drew closer to the two men. "Until I told her last night, Emerald didn't know you were in love with her. I had no right to say anything and I'm sorry.

"She wasn't ready to hear it. She may never be ready. She may not even be capable of that kind of love. There's more, something you don't know—"

"He already knows, Sarialla. Apparently, everyone does." Emerald stood behind the three of them.

Darrin spun around to meet her gaze. He absorbed the brunt of her animosity. The others avoided eye contact.

"I would never have hurt you like those other men, Emerald. You slept safely in my bed. If you loved me, that safety would not change. I will protect you until I'm dead. I made an oath."

Agony gripped her. "I don't need you. You've failed me twice. I would not buy your protection with my blood. I'm not a whore! I did not come to your bed on purpose."

His hands trembled. "I need you, Emerald. I admire you. I love you." He stepped toward her. "Marry me, please? I offer you all of me."

Her eyes widened in shock and then narrowed in derision. "I loathe men's 'admiration'. I am full," she slammed her fist into her abdomen, "of men's 'love' for me. You will not own what's left of my body, nor command what's left of my soul. If you want me, take up your sword and claim me."

She backed to the door, grabbed her belt from a peg, and drew her sword to stand at the ready.

Sobs wracked his body and he collapsed to his knees, shameless before the few people remaining in the room. "I never meant for this to happen. You mean so much to me. I only wanted to fill your life with joy.

"You never knew it, but I have fought and bled for you." He pulled his tunic over his head and cast it aside to reveal the scars that riddled his flesh. "I have failed you. Please, kill me, because I can't live with what I've let you become." Tears dripped from his beard and his eyes glossed over.

In her mind, she stepped forward and ran her blade along his neck, reveling in the spray of scalding blood. In reality, her hand trembled and she almost dropped Dana's sword. Her nostrils flared as she struggled for self-mastery.

"This is madness." She fled from his presence.

As she ran across the courtyard, she sheathed the copper sword and buckled it around her middle. She lifted and tossed the crossbar from the main gate, dragged it open, and sprinted away. She didn't care what path she took.

STUNNED SILENCE FILLED the main room of the keep. Darrin realized he had stopped breathing and gasped for air. He would not be executed for his boldness.

Emerald had allowed him to live. The bitterness of the clemency twisted in his gut. This must be the reason she hadn't thanked him for saving her life.

His heart hardened within his chest. Wiping the tears from his face, he glanced at those still in the room. Their presence humiliated him.

"Excuse me." He put on his tunic, stood, and crossed the room to the staircase.

Stephan stepped forward. "She will return. Wait for her."

He stopped with his back to the room. "She would rather die than be with me." The blood drained from his face as realizations struck. He looked toward the west as if he could see through stone walls. "She knows where to find what she seeks. I've killed her."

"What?" Stephan's face contorted in confusion.

Darrin's mind reeled. Would Emerald do what he feared? He brushed off the shock that beset him and ran upstairs.

Stephan followed. "What are you saying?"

"I must go." He pulled on his boots, tucked in his shirt, and ran downstairs to fetch his dagger.

"Explain yourself." Stephan caught up and grabbed a fist full of his tunic.

Darrin met Stephan's gaze as he fastened his belt. "She seeks her enemy at the war front to the west. She doesn't know we're outnumbered. We've held them off this long because she has sheltered in this castle and trained up her own defenders. They will overwhelm us if they see her. I have to stop her." He broke free of Stephan's grasp and ran after Emerald.

STEPHAN MADE A DECISION as he watched Darrin run after the woman he loved.

"George. Rick. Gael."

All the children came running.

"Emerald is in trouble. I'm going after her. If I fail, then you must defend the children." With that, he ran to the armory.

He pulled on chainmail as he gathered weapons of all sorts.

"We're coming with you." George followed him. "Andre, saddle up the horses."

The boy ran to do as ordered while George, Rick, and Gael armed themselves.

"Who will defend the castle?" Stephan hooked a crossbow and quiver of bolts to his belt.

"I will." Ryan Miller's stance held determination.

Stephan clapped him on the shoulder. "Pray you don't have to. But if you do, then listen to Andre." With that, he ran to the stables.

The others followed as they finished their preparations.

Andre cinched the second saddle as Stephan came in. "The horses are ready." Sweat poured off him and he breathed hard.

Stephan nodded to the boy who acted so big. "Keep your eye out for us. We may be pursued on our return. Don't ring the bell. We don't want the enemy to know anything is amiss, and I don't want the little ones frightened."

Stephan accepted a leg up from George who tossed Rick up as well. He then mounted the brown mare and pulled Gael up behind him. They only had two horses and would be pressing them hard to catch Emerald. She ran fast and the terrain was rough.

Andre slid the stable doors open. They took off across the courtyard. The sound of horses' hooves clattered on the cobblestones and echoed off the walls.

DARRIN SPRINTED, FOLLOWING Emerald's tracks. He crossed the fields that separated them until he caught a glimpse of her. How did she get so far?

He needed to stop her from being seen by the enemies who seek to destroy her. Why did she always have to make things difficult for him? The thudding of his feet on the ground and the pounding of blood in his ears set the rhythm of his thoughts.

He hadn't told her the whole truth. In fact, he had deceived her. It was obvious that she hated him for it.

Deeply wounded by her rejection, however, he found her hatred more welcome than her pity would have been. The Stones had named their enemy the Wolf Clan, and she had grouped him in with them. She didn't realize her mistake because she didn't know how the society of the West Wind worked.

He could have explained it to her. She should know the truth about her own people. But he hadn't told her.

He could not bring himself to regret having withheld the information. He loved her and wanted her to love him in return. What love could she have if she lacked respect for him?

Perhaps, if she hadn't feared him, then she would have made him her pet and toyed with him for a time. He contemplated the infinite wrongness of that as he waded across a stream. He rejected it as disgusting. He would never treat her that way and would not accept that kind of treatment in return.

Her unreachable superiority stood between them like a gulf. She was his Future Queen, perhaps even destined to become an empress, and he was the humble Shadow. If she survived this day, then she would one day glory over him. Someday, he would look into her face and see himself as he was, powerless.

A withered branch slapped his face and he sucked in his breath. Why wasn't she slowing? What possessed her to set this pace?

He scowled and pushed himself harder, so he might catch her. Hopeful, he anticipated tackling her to the ground and imagined the electricity of her fury. The thought excited him.

She would not know the truth. She would not look on him as lesser. Today, he would stop her from discovering his secret and the glory of saving her life would yet again be his.

Chapter Seventeen

E merald ran until the sun raised above her head. She headed west, with gray granite hunks of mountain crumbling on her right and the bulk of Danalan descending on her left. Unaware of branches that scraped her skin or underbrush that threatened to ensnare her in these desolate places, she pressed forward.

She passed the crumbling cottages of her kindred dead. Galvanized by their sacrifices, she crossed what once had been fields but had overgrown with brush and young trees. She knew these lands and the revered the names of each clan member who had worked these fields.

Her senses tingled with an awareness of them. She called them to her to witness the end of their Clan. Each man, woman, and child fell in behind her as she hastened toward the west.

The cold did not touch her. Hunger did not touch her. She was not alone, and her company shared her resolve to confront fate.

A grim smile set in her expression and she focused on the horizon. With lungs full of air and feet as swift as the wind, she advanced upon a line of trees. The answer she sought waited somewhere in those woods.

Drawing her sword, she entered the forest. The wind carried a rank smell of decay. Glancing left and right, she saw them.

Dozens of dark-haired men at even intervals crouched at the edge of a clearing. Carrion birds circled above unmoving shapes laying in that clearing. Unafraid, she walked up behind the nearest man and placed her blade at his throat.

He stiffened.

She whispered in his ear. "Why do you trespass here among the dead? Know you not that we have risen against you?"

Without regard for her blade, he sprang forward and stumbled into the clearing.

She forbore slitting his throat but strode out after him with the sword in hand. A volley of arrows whistled across the field. A shaft sank into her left shoulder, causing her to stagger backward as pain erupted in her arm. Other arrows spiked the earth around her.

Two men hauled her from the field. The frightened soldier scrambled after them under the cover of trees. Someone pulled her sword from her hand. She fought with a fist, feet, and knees. The three men laid her down in a drift of leaf litter.

"Princess, why have you come?" The man wrestled her good arm to stillness. "Why do you resist us?" He spoke the mountain language.

Another man pinned her legs to the ground and sat on them. "We are your humble servants."

A third man held her injured arm immobile. "We defend you against your enemies. Lay still and we will remove the arrow."

The man whose throat she had almost cut proffered her a stick. She bit it, preparing for the worst. Her breath came in ragged pants.

"You must not cry out, because it will rally the traitors who seek your life. Do you understand?" The oldest among them spoke. His gaze remained steady in his lined face, though, he did not meet her gaze.

The confusion cleared. She realized it was not as she had feared. These men were what Darrin claimed to be, her defenders.

She ceased to struggle and bit harder on the stick between her teeth. Laying her head in the dry leaves, she focused on the blue sky visible between the budded tree branches. Her nostrils filled with the pungent smell of crumbling leaves and dusty bark.

The men didn't wait. They wrenched the arrow from her flesh, let it bleed for a moment, and then pressed gauze to the wound. Blood scalded her skin but the firm pressure the man applied held her shoulder immobile.

She wanted to writhe with the pain that threatened to overwhelm her. Instead, she held still. The recently dislocated shoulder had caught the arrow.

What a fool she had been. This was no release from her afflictions, only a broadening of them. At least the physical agony came close to matching the intensity of the emotional torment.

She spat the stick out and gasped for breath. The pain made her senses sharpen. The older man spread his cloak over her lower body. She had left home in a shirt and trousers. She was lucky to be wearing boots since she would not have stopped to retrieve them.

She cast her gaze past the dark-haired men who aided her to the spirits who had marched with her. Their faces were grim and set in an attitude of solemn readiness. They waited for her command. She focused her will and their forces shifted, surging westward to meet the enemy.

"Did you see them?" She looked into the faces of the mountain men.

They glanced around, but their gaze returned to her.

"Princess, who do you see?" The older man's dark brows knit in confusion.

"The Stones have risen." It was a proclamation of war.

TIME SPED PAST AND still, Darrin only imagined catching up with Emerald. She had traveled far ahead of him. He glanced back across a clearing. Several of his men from the Royal Guard ran close behind him.

Emerald seemed heedless of anyone else and never slowed. He couldn't catch her. Perhaps, he should have taken one of her horses but she had never outpaced him in the past. Besides, he didn't know how to ride. He snorted out his nose.

"What are you doing Emerald Stone?" He spoke under his ragged breath.

He ran through brambles and leaped a fallen tree. He was already panting. He had to stop her. He hissed an expletive through clenched teeth.

He caught a glimpse of her in the distance. "Emerald. Stop." He squared his shoulders. "Stop!" She should have heard him but she gave no indication of it and entered the tree line.

His heart quailed as he spotted the carrion birds circling above the branches. Terror gripped him. Perhaps, they would both die today.

Focusing on the place where she had entered the woods, he sprinted. With burning lungs, he drew his dagger. The trees were thick.

He spotted her. An arrow bristled from her like some nightmarish thing. Commander Pine and his men feverishly tended the wound.

Darrin ripped his attention away, hand signaling the Guardsmen to fan out around her. His trusted Sub-Captain handed him the sheathed sword he had left at the river the night he'd rescued Emerald. It was the sword of his ancestor and of similar make to the one Emerald carried.

Drawing the copper blade steadied and rejuvenated him with its enchanting power. He breathed deep and prepared to combat the enemy he could both see and hear as they crossed the open battlefield. How were there so many of them? He hefted the ancient sword with grim determination.

"Don't go beyond the edge of the trees. Beware of the archers. May the glory of the moon be with you." He spoke to his men, perhaps for the last time.

The army of outcast dissenters rushed forward. These men had wiped out Emerald's family and attacked her when this line of defense failed. His sword had been named for Dana's husband, Prince Krelor, and never faltered in Emerald's defense. Sleek and powerful, the weapon was deadly.

The art of Darrin's abilities to end life required space to maneuver. He found the right spot and stood his ground. A wave of wolves and men broke around him. Slashing metal met gnashing teeth.

He didn't hesitate. To the same degree he rendered beauty when he held a paintbrush, he dealt death in defense of his ruler. The enemy pressed him until Emerald lay right behind him.

Commander Pine and his men fell bravely to their deaths. Emerald did not see any of it. What did she see? What had she said? She spoke, but Darrin could not make out the words.

War cries ripped his attention back to the battle raging around him. Several renegades charged at him from various angles. He decapitated the first man.

Pain slashed across his ribs from behind. He redirected his blade to skewer the man. An attacker clubbed him over the head.

He tumbled to the ground. The last thing he saw was Emerald. She lay in the leaves, pale, eyes-wide-open to the sky.

STEPHAN AND THE BOYS witnessed Darrin fall. With an aim that surprised him at its steadiness, Stephan fired his crossbow at the enemy who had done it. The man's face contorted, grotesque in its agony.

The brown mare shied, whinnying in terror at the smell of blood. George slung Rick down and jumped from the frightened horse. She pivoted and ran toward home, kicking up dirt and leaves behind her.

The grey gelding did not falter. Stephan had trained on this horse and knew what the beast could do. The question in his mind remained whether he could match the skill of the animal. Dusty was a seasoned veteran of combat, but it was Stephan's first engagement hand to hand.

Gael jumped down to run to the defense of a pile of leaves. Stephan frowned. What was the boy doing? Then he saw who lay beneath those leaves, Emerald. He faltered. They were too late.

A rush of sound came at him. He broke away from the sight of her ashen face. Cold with determination, he drew his sword and didn't think again until no man stood against him.

Blood dripped from his weapons. Gore soaked Dusty's hide. The horse snorted and shook his head as if defying any of the men or wolves to stand back up and challenge him.

Stephan slowed his breathing. He couldn't see any bit of his body that had stayed clean enough to remove the blood from his sword so he could sheath it. He thought of Emerald as he drew a cloth from his pocket and cared for the blade. His hands commenced shaking, and he glanced over his shoulder toward the place where Emerald lay. George lifted her in his arms and carried her toward him.

"Does she live?" Stephan's heart quivered in his chest.

"Yes, it's not a bad wound."

Stephan dismounted. "Take her home, George." He took Emerald from his friend for a moment.

She weighed less than he expected. Did she ever eat? Emotion threatened to overwhelm him. He fought against it because this was not the time.

George mounted and reached down for Emerald.

Stephan hefted her up in front of him. "I'll go check on Darrin."

George nodded. He maneuvered Dusty through the trees toward home. It was tricky because the horse wouldn't willingly step on flesh.

Stephan scanned the scene around him. Blood splattered the trees. Leaf litter captured pools of red as it flowed from gaping holes in men and wolves.

His gorge surged and he doubled over retching. The taste was horrible, though the smell of death was worse. Guilt-ridden, he knew he had done his part to create this backdrop of human demise.

Spitting one last time, he glanced around. It was difficult to tell one man apart from the others. No, there Darrin lay.

His eyes were closed and he did not stare without seeing as so many did. Hope surged, and Stephan ran to Darrin, kneeling beside him. Gael and Rick followed suit.

Stephan touched Darrin's arm. "Can you hear me?"

When he did not respond, Stephan turned him on his belly. The bloody wound across his ribs became visible. Gael whimpered like a child.

Stephan glanced at the boy. "Hand me your handkerchief." He took the cloth and pressed it to the gash. "Rick, can you find me a medical kit of some kind? I didn't think to bring one." Stephan shook his head. "I don't know why I didn't think any of us would get hurt."

Gael handed him the cloth and wrung his hands. "We almost missed it all."

Stephan concentrated on Darrin. "No, we got here in time. I think he'll live."

Rick ran back carrying a bag and knelt beside Darrin. "I found it over where Em had been. I think they used whatever is in it on her. She didn't recognize me."

Stephan nodded. "It's better she doesn't know about this. She's seen more than enough blood already. This would be too much for her. I know she didn't mean for Darrin to be hurt."

Stephan rummaged through the sack identifying its contents as he worked. Cleaning a wound was a grizzly task. Dirt and blood clotted the gash. Cleaning it with the supplies available proved difficult. He didn't spare the supplies, however, because if the wound wasn't cleaned, then it would fester and the man would die.

Darrin couldn't die. Em needed him. She was mad for him and the madness of this fiasco proved it.

Stephan tugged small even stitches with a needle and thread in the flesh between his fingers. Why didn't Darrin wake up? Was anyone else alive?

Stephan finished bandaging the wound and noticed two dark-haired men leaning against nearby trees. He bowed his head to the strangers as they approached him in need of help. He treated their injuries with the remainder of the supplies.

"You must see a doctor as soon as possible. Infection is your enemy now."

They nodded. The war had ended. What happened afterward didn't seem to be of equal importance.

Chapter Eighteen

S tephan came to Emerald's bedside in the keep.

"Are you awake? I have to go." He shook her uninjured shoulder.

She stirred but did not open her eyes.

"You can't abandon her like this, Stephan. How can you leave?" The anger in George's voice put down his stammering manner of speech.

"I must go. The Wolf Clan is destroyed and Darrin's people are finished in Danalan. When they depart into the mountains, they will seal them forever. Sarialla begged them to allow us safe passage to Frenland, and I must go with her. Emerald wished it. Tell her goodbye for me."

Their boot heels resounded on the floorboards as they stomped down the stairs. Angry with Emerald wasn't the way Stephan wanted to leave her, but that's how things stood. She slept under the influence of a pain tonic, and that infuriated him because she had almost gotten herself killed. She had no right to do that, not ever, but especially not over a tiff with Darrin.

Why couldn't she love the man? No. Why couldn't she admit she loved him? She did love him, of that he remained certain.

Darrin was a good man and would cherish her for the rest of her life. Not many men would overlook the abuse she had endured and the torment she still suffered in order to try to make her happy. Why couldn't she see that?

"Nina, are you in here?" He ducked into the kitchen.

"Right here. I'm packing your saddle bag. I wish I had better things to give you." Tears rolled down her cheeks. "I hope you have a safe journey."

Stephan smiled through his sadness. "Thank you, Nina. Don't put too much in there. The whole trip to Frenland takes less than a week. I don't need to scale the mountain you know, just go under it in some tunnels." He patted her shoulder.

"It won't be the same without you." She hugged him and sobbed. "Em, didn't even have the chance to say goodbye. What do you think she'll do? She tried to harm herself. What if she does it again?"

"Now, Nina, don't worry." Stephan held the girl and rubbed her back. "Em will be all right. She knows what I need to do and she supports me. I asked her to come with me, but she didn't really want to leave you and the little ones. She'll be fine."

Nina released him, wiped her tears, and finished packing the saddlebags. Cinching them closed, she strained to hand them to him. He received them with ease.

"Thank you, for everything." He patted her shoulder.

She looked at him and her tears started all over. When Sarialla entered the kitchen, Nina walked away. Her shoulders shook with sobs as she prepared the morning meal.

"There you are, My Prince. We must go. The soldiers escorting us to the entrance of the mountain passages are waiting at the gate." Sarialla had bundled up, despite the warm weather.

"We must go then." Stephan slung the saddlebags over his shoulder. "Nina was my last farewell." He frowned as a thought occurred to him. "Did the Ambassador mention what is to become of her prisoner?"

"She said that Darrin is being taken to the Steward for interrogation and sentencing." Sarialla frowned, a severe expression on her wrinkled face. "I don't understand it. I saw nothing inappropriate in what he did. Loving someone isn't a crime."

Ruefully, Stephan had to disagree. "Em sure thought it was. I hope Darrin will make it through this. Apparently, we have much to learn about our mountain friends, their laws, and their customs."

A white eyebrow edged up Sarialla's face and her lips pursed outward. She shook her head. "It doesn't appear we will have the chance. The Ambassador ordered the mountains sealed. We'll be escorted to the other side and never allowed to enter again under penalty of death.

"I suppose the Steward could overrule the decision, but that's how it stands right now. I have no idea what is required to change the situation either. I fear this is all my fault. Until I said too much, things were going well between Emerald and Darrin."

Stephan laid a hand on the old woman's shoulder. "Of course, it's not your fault, Wise Sage. A solution will present itself, be assured of that. Em will do whatever is required of her, she always does. We'll be back on a visit before you know it." He forced a smile.

"Oh, to be young and full of hope." Sarialla nodded. "You're right, My Prince. Let's hurry on our way so we might travel there and back again."

DARRIN TRUDGED UP THE mountain in bonds. His head swam and his side pained him beyond words, but he pressed onward. Two members of the Steward's Personal Guard escorted him.

The ground leveled for a moment and he glanced down the slope. In the distance below him, he saw the Ambassador's party heading to Stone Castle. What would the woman discover about his actions toward the Princess?

He slipped on a loose stone and landed hard on his knees. He broke his fall with his hands, fortunate they were bound in front of him. Even so, fresh pain blurred his vision with tears and intensified the throbbing in his side.

It wasn't wise to move soon after an injury of this kind. However, that consideration had seemed secondary to the Ambassador. It didn't appear to trouble the black haired, blue eyed women who guarded him either.

Had Emerald survived?

"Get up." The guard behind him gave the order.

Her expression darkened and her hand twitched, then clenched into a fist. Wincing at the woman's inner struggle, he pushed himself to a standing position. His unsteady legs caused him to teeter.

Summoning all the dignity he could muster, he walked onward. Special treatment because of his mother's position of power irked him. If this woman couldn't respect him for the sacrifices he had made as the Royal Shadow, then he would accept his fate.

His curiosity got the better of him, however. "Excuse me, please. Will you tell me why I've been arrested?" How much did they know?

The lead guard ignored him, but the impatient one behind him answered. "You revealed yourself to the Princess. Even a fool can see you are to blame for her arrival at the war front. If she dies, then you will be executed.

"Though, I imagine you'll be required to produce an heir first." The woman frowned for a minute and looked him over. "Perhaps I should put in a request for you." She grabbed his buttocks and slid her hands over his hips toward his front.

Darrin jumped forward, causing her to release him. "Thank you for the offer. Should you choose to do so, I'm sure my mother will consider it."

Heat flooded his face. However, he needed to conceal his outrage lest these women consider him impertinent. Their punishment would be swift.

Dismayed by the information, he came to the conclusion that if Emerald died, he would be a prize to be obtained from his mother. Had men become so scarce that a condemned man could hold such value? He gritted his teeth and struggled to stay out of the Guard's reach.

"Hmmm, I doubt it." The Guard's smile drooped. "Not now anyway. Those of much higher status will line up for you. Perhaps, you don't realize how few men survived the war. A man of any age or situation has tremendous value as a husband these days."

The Guard in the lead came to a halt and looked at Darrin. "Sit."

He obeyed at once, resting on a ledge. Wide-eyed he shook his head to try to stop the dizzy feeling. What of all his boyhood friends? Had the battlefront turned that bloody? He'd been sheltered behind the front lines protecting Emerald. No one had bothered to tell him any of this.

The Guard in the lead stood above the younger woman on the incline with her thumbs hooked on her sword belt. "Stop debasing yourself, Kalia. The implication soils you as much as anyone else. This man will likely be executed and his line will end with him. You know this must be."

Kalia's eyes widened. "But if the Princess does not survive—"

"Your years are not sufficient to obtain the wisdom to understand that the Princess cannot die." The leader scowled. "Everyone else dies, but not her. She will restore that which she takes tenfold. When his body burns on a pyre, then people like you will understand that everything relies on the Future Queen. She will make us mightier than we have ever been."

Kalia bowed her head. "I apologize, Mieda. You're right, of course, but I was thinking of my tiny sons at home with no sister to lead them. I've lost two husbands in this war. My house is ending."

Mieda's expression softened. "He has never been the answer. May fortune smile upon your house. Perhaps the Princess will have a solution to this problem, too. Remember, many others face this dilemma as well." She looked at him. "Are you rested?"

He averted his gaze. "Yes, Mistress."

Mieda pinched his cheek. "It isn't far now. Let's not keep the Steward waiting. Even a mother won't forgive that."

Darrin bowed and followed Mieda's lead. Aside from the fact that he was marching to his death, the utter dismissal of his significance as a human being burned in the pit of his stomach. How could he endure this after being treated with such respect among Emerald's household? He hadn't been patronized like this since, well, since the last time he had visited home.

He quit looking at the scenery as they passed an increasing number of trees of high elevation. Emerald thought he didn't understand her but she was wrong. He understood far too well how she felt, though he had no idea what it was like to be raped.

The mindset it would require to commit such a violation seemed the same that required men to marry against their will in the mountains. No, that wasn't quite true. The callous exertion of power over another human being was one thing but the willful destruction of another's soul felt different.

Emerald must survive. The alternative stared him in the face, though his mind shied from it. Why had she become afraid of him again? Was his loving her the wrong thing to do?

Perhaps, he should apologize.

The thought made his spine quiver with derision. He gritted his teeth as anger swelled in his chest. He would not apologize.

He had saved her life without thanks for the last time. In fact, he was the one who needed saving now. But what help could she be?

His shoulders slumped. Disheartened, he focused on the terrain. No one could help him when his mother found out what he had done.

THE DURATION OF STEPHAN'S journey lengthened due to the fact the mountain men had no horses. They could keep up with a horse at a walk, but tired quicker since they carried their own packs. Stephan worried that a few days was a conservative estimate of the time it would take to reach the other side of the mountain under these circumstances. The problem was that he hadn't brought enough supplies.

"May I have a word with you, Counselor?" They had started the second day of travel and hadn't yet reached the entrance to the passageway.

Sarialla rained in her stallion, Lightning. "What did you say, My Prince?"

He rode Dusty up alongside her and they commenced the long trek once more. He felt bad taking Emerald's horse. The gelding had belonged to Grandfather. However, he had to ride, and the brown mare was younger and more valuable to the farm. Besides, Lightning had covered the mare and she might foal.

Stephan frowned as a thought twisted in his gut. What if Emerald had a baby? How must she have felt to have been treated no better than an animal?

Why wouldn't she talk to him? He missed her already and regretted his anger toward her. How did a woman like Emerald deal with her fears except with force? It was what she knew, and cruelty too much a part of her everyday experience.

"What's troubling you, Sire?" Sarialla asked.

He stuffed his concerns into a familiar corner of his soul. "I wish to discuss the time it might take to travel with these men in tow. I didn't pack the mule with enough hay and grain if it is to exceed a few days before we can replenish our supplies. Also, I wonder if these men carry enough food to make it back if that's their plan."

He glanced at the soldiers in their smoke-blue uniforms as they ran alongside the horses. Their faces showed no indication they understood the

Andolinish language he and Sarialla had been speaking. But then, he had a hard time reading their expressions.

Not one of them would look him in the eye or Sarialla either for that matter. It seemed to be forbidden to speak unless spoken to. Apparently, their society ranked them far below a Prince and his Royal Counselor, and they maintained the distinction.

"I'll inform the Commander." Sarialla nodded in agreement. "There is indeed a reason to urge haste. I delayed speaking to Emerald, because of the unfortunate events that transpired on the day of my arrival. I couldn't ask you to leave her at a time like that, and I would have delayed even further if I'd had the option.

"The fact of the matter remains, however, that we are expected in Frenland. Your Captains will be anxious. It's a reunion that has been long anticipated."

They rode onward until they came to a creek. Sarialla called a halt to water the men and animals. After they drank and filled their waterskins, she approached the Commander of the dark-haired mountain men.

"Commander, do you have a moment to discuss the timeframe of our travels?"

Tight-lipped, the Commander bowed low.

"Normally, the trip takes three days to the Frenland side. We've packed provisions for man and beast to last that long and not much more. I wonder too if your men are prepared for how long it will take to travel there and return. What say you?"

The Commander bowed again and walked out of earshot to speak to his men. After an exchange of supplies, there was bowing and apparent farewells among them. Several men departed amidst the rocks and trees, leaving only the two fastest who squatted down to rest, alert for whatever came next.

Sarialla frowned.

Stephan shrugged. It seemed that no discussion of the situation would take place with these men. "I suppose they won't slow us down much."

Sarialla's expression lightened. "I have something spectacular to show you, My Prince. We're near the entrance to the tunnels. So, I think we'll camp out of doors tonight since the weather is fine." She smiled at him.

He smiled in return at the prospect. "Lead onward, Wise Sage." They continued climbing the ancient track.

Chapter Nineteen

Emerald stared at the Impenetrable Mountains from where she sat, unmoving on the wall of Stone Castle. The wind blew, the clouds rolled by, and days passed. She held the emerald ribbon in her hand, though she had no tear to shed.

The mountains were closed.

No further efforts would be made by Darrin's people to aid or interact with her. She felt fully responsible. It was her careless act at the battlefront that had caused the deaths of so many men. The weight of guilt crushed her soul.

The desolate cliffs and crags above taunted her as the memory of her foolish actions played across their theater, plaguing her with remorse. She had failed to fulfill the Legend of the Stone. She hadn't ushered in a new era of peace and prosperity.

Furthermore, she hadn't opened the mountains to travel. The Modutan Empire was not reunited in trade and commerce. None of that mattered so much as the fact that she had failed her family.

Life had beaten her, and she had allowed it.

Nina brought food, but Emerald didn't eat. The hot tears of others scalded her skin, but she didn't heed them. Even the embrace of little arms did not rouse her from her self-loathing.

It wouldn't be much longer. It couldn't be. Another day passed.

Too weak to move, she stared at the sky from flat on her back. She welcomed death, longing for the release it promised. A hawk rode the air currents above. She watched it soar through the heavens, wishing to join the creature on the west wind.

In her mind, she heard a voice calling her name. For a moment she didn't respond, but the voice repeated. Aware that it was more than a stray thought, she ached with the need to let go. She longed to meet her Creator. Was this what it felt like to die?

She beheld a brilliant figure standing in the midst of the sun. The bright being spoke to her mind, telling her that hope remained. In his marvelous voice, he told her that she had work to do.

The messenger spoke of reuniting the peoples of all the lands in peace. He said she must have the courage to find the way. He said to be patient and she would know the right course.

It was not what she expected, but she didn't argue. She allowed her misery to melt away like frost before the morning sun. The light above her faded to its normal brilliance and she blinked against its harshness.

Emerald sighed and her body trembled, but she found she could go on. She had a purpose. She had not failed the Creator. Indeed, a chance still existed to make all the sacrifices worthwhile.

Gathering strength, she rolled onto her right side. With shaking hands, she reached for a bowl of broth that had long since gone cold. She sipped the restorative liquid, though the effort tired her. Resting her head on her arm for a while, she then consumed the remainder of the life-sustaining food.

Sustenance felt strange in her stomach. But energy built within her frame. She gained her feet and staggered across the chemise wall walkway and into the keep. She would return to the ones who wept, at least for now.

THE MEMORY OF THE GLORIOUS canyon they had camped in before entering the unending night of the mountain tunnels kept Stephan from going mad. This kind of darkness and the maze of caverns was something he had never imagined. In his mind, he had thought of a smooth, obvious road through a manmade tunnel. But though parts of the way seemed carved by human hands, most of the passageways proved rough and sometimes treacherous.

Sarialla never faltered in her lead. They made good progress, not slowed by the two mountain men because the trek itself was slow going. How did Sarialla know which way to turn?

In the light of a candle lantern, he attempted to discern how she guided them. It had been twelve years since she'd visited the South. However, she always knew which passageway to enter at a crossroads. It occupied his mind to consider the question and he welcomed any distraction here in this strange place.

"I thought we might practice speaking your native language, My Prince." She cast her words over her shoulder in his direction.

Even a whisper seemed loud in these caves. "Very well." He spoke the Frenland tongue the best he could. "From now on, we'll speak the language of my people. I admit I need the practice." He'd been shy to use it around her before now.

Her eyebrows shot up. "You speak with excellence. Forgive my surprise, but I didn't realize you maintained this level of proficiency."

He made a face and shook his head. "Flattery will get you nowhere, Counselor. I'm certain my accent is horrific and my grammar will become muddled if you give me long enough. To be frank, I'm embarrassed by my lack of ability. Emerald speaks far better than I do. One would expect me to be fluent. Especially since I spent my first four years in the North."

She laughed. "Not at all, My Prince. You were far too young to have learned much. I'm impressed you remember so well.

"We'll practice pronunciation and grammar. However, I'm not the best teacher for you. Though, I'll have to do for now." She faced forward as they neared a fork in the path.

Stephan observed her. "Why are you not the best teacher for me? Who could be better?"

At that moment, he realized how she guided them. She followed a set of ruts worn in the rock floor. That's how she chose a cavern to enter at a parting of ways.

"Because I am a woman. It would be inappropriate for you to speak as I do." She glanced over her shoulder. "You look confused. Think about it, My Prince. Women speak much faster than men do. We often use a different set of vocabulary. Also, women speak to one another less formally than men do. Thus, you see that you should not speak as I do or you will be considered strange."

Stephan smiled, nodding his head. "I understand." He urged Dusty up alongside Lightning as the passageway widened. "I understand more than you think. I've figured out how you're guiding us."

"Indeed?" She reined in Lightning.

Stephan pointed at the ruts in the floor. "You're following these marks. My guess is they were made by wagons, thousands of wagons."

She gripped the saddle horn and leaned forward with a smile. "You are correct, My Prince. Long ago, my mentor taught me two simple rules about passage under the mountains. Pack appropriately and follow the ghosts of wagons.

"The first time through, I ran out of candles a day short of the end. I had to lead the first Lightning by feel as I followed the ancient ruts of the wagon wheels. You can't imagine my relief when I arrived at that beautiful waterfall at the southern entrance. I kissed the ground. You can be sure, I never journeyed without enough candles again."

He chuckled. "I believe that, Wise Sage."

"I've come several times to visit Danalan. When I brought you to stay with the Stones, I took every last one of Jacob's meager supply upon my return. I suppose you were too young to remember." Her smile faded. "I miss him. We were friends. I've never met anyone quite like Jacob Stone."

ONCE INSIDE THE KEEP, Emerald's eyes took a while to adjust. She leaned on the wall as she slogged into the sleeping chamber. This great room was on the same level as the curtainwall on which she had lain for so long.

She had entered through the upper doorway via the walkway atop the chemise wall that protected the keep and town behind it. She didn't want to climb any stairs or face any of the children until she regained some strength. With her stomach filled, she craved a warm bed and rest.

Voices echoed from the stone walls of the dormitory. She stilled. Those voices were not the voices of any of the boys that lived here. They were voices from her nightmares, the new ones.

Her mind raced faster than her heart until she remembered that Roger and Christopher Carpenter were supposed to be here. The Chief Judge had ordered them to work for her and the children whose mother their father had killed. She breathed deep and straightened her posture.

The two men carried bundles of clean laundry toward the chests in the sleeping chamber.

"I can't believe we're expected to do women's work." Christopher's lower lip protruded.

His older brother stooped to open a chest and tossed in an ironed and folded armload of shirts, leggings, tunics, trousers, and socks. Christopher did the same and then slammed the lid.

"Don't be stupid. They're mocking us because we have no..." Roger's voice trailed.

Christopher patted his brother's shoulder. "I'm sorry Ginny left you. Fred ought to be horsewhipped for giving her the option." He shook his head.

"I'd do it, too, but I'm not in any condition to fight him right now." Roger sat on the edge of the nearest bed, clenching his jaw and his fist as he did so.

Christopher sat beside him, moving slowly as lines of pain etched his face. "Whatever you do, you can't get caught or you're dead. It won't change her mind anyway. If she were pregnant, it might be different."

"Worthless woman." Roger inhaled and let out the breath. "We've been married two years and she hasn't born me a son or any other child for that matter. Now I have one chance to carry on the family name and that cursed Chief Judge denies my rights.

"Well, I don't care what he said. I'll have my son if that whore of a Stone manages to pucker up some gumption and live." His eyes glossed over and his expression slackened into lax lines.

His skin had an altogether unhealthy pallor.

Christopher stared across the room until a frown creased his brow. "I miss father. I don't understand what drove him to do that to her in the first place. Looking around here, I know he was wrong. She wasn't harming these orphans. This isn't the carnal house he believed it was."

Roger slapped his brother's head. "Don't speak ill of the dead."

"I just mean she's not a whore and we really hurt her. She might die and then we'll be executed and Ma will lose the woodshop." Christopher's voice quavered.

"Emerald Stone isn't fit for anything but whoring now. No man will have her except me." Roger met Christopher's gaze. "I will marry her if she bears me a son. I figure the consummating part is already done and as soon as a judge frees me of that cheating wench, Ginny, then it will be legal enough. I'd like to be lord of all of this." Roger flashed a grin, sweeping his arms to indicate the castle and beyond.

Emerald stood still enough that the two men didn't notice her in the shadows of the large chamber. Even in her weakened state, she understood these lazy men plotted against her. As difficult as it was to hear their unsparing discussion, she forced herself to listen to their plans.

"I don't think she'll have you, Roger." Christopher shook his head. "You raped her."

Roger's eyebrows shot up and then crashed down as his fists clenched. "You took her like the rest of us. Just because you weren't man enough to listen to her whimper and withdrew early didn't buy you any leniency with the Judge. I won't let you accuse me of something you did right along with me. Since Pa's dead, I have rights to the child and I plan to claim them. Don't get in my way." He stood and shuffled downstairs.

Christopher stared at his brother's back. He didn't move as two tears fell from his eyes. He wiped them away.

"I should've finished. Then I could fight him for her." He whispered with a pointed vehemence that carried.

"And what would you do with me, boy?" Emerald emerged from the shadows to face him in the light of the high windows.

"What?" Christopher's head snapped around before he froze, wide-eyed.

Emerald offered a wry smile, but her eyes remained focused. "Most importantly, what would I do with you?"

The boy blushed and looked away. "You don't remember me, do you?"

She narrowed her gaze. "There's not much about you I will ever forget, rapist." She spat the last word.

Walking the last of the way to her bed, she collapsed on top of the honeybee quilt. Self-soothing the twisting upset inside her, she caressed the pattern her mother had sewn. Fatigue pulled at her eyelids, but she was not so tired that she couldn't defend herself. As she had collapsed onto her bed, she'd slid a knife out of her boot and concealed it under the pillow.

Christopher stood to face her with his hands clasped in front of him. "I asked you to marry me last year at the Spring Fair. You laughed and said 'I have no use for another boy in my castle, I have enough to please me as it is.' Well, my father heard you say it and that's part of what brought this all about.

"I know now that he mistook the matter. But that doesn't undo what he did, what each of us did to you. I had no idea he meant to kill you. I never would've believed he could murder Annie Miller." His voice grew high. "I guess what I'm trying to say is, I'm sorry." He hung his head.

His apology reverberated off the stone walls like the humming of bees in her ears. After a long while, she let it pass away like the shadow of truth it was.

"You know now why I couldn't wed you, even if I felt inclined to marry a child," she said.

He didn't puff up his chest as she expected. She knew he was grown in stature if not quite mature in other ways. He seemed to consider how to answer. In the end, he nodded.

She closed her eyes against the unexpected tears. The force of her eyelids splashed her face with them. She concealed her sorrow with the pillow. Rolling on her right side, she fought to control her emotions. How could she allow this man to see her this way?

"Who else hurt you, Emerald?"

"A Wolf."

Christopher gasped. "You mean you were captured by a man of the Wolf Clan and lived?" His voice raised high and his eyebrows higher.

Emerald stared at him. All the pain within her welled up like a deep fountain of misery. Could he see her suffering?

"Did I really live after that?" she asked.

He blinked and looked away. "We're both forever changed and unable to wed, but you did nothing to deserve it. I'm worse than a fool. I have blood on my hands." He looked at his palms and his face twisted.

Her bitterness broke forth as quiet laughter. She clenched her jaw and rolled on her stomach. Staring across the open air of the room, she lay her head on the pillow.

"Blood, yes, but not much. You've never taken a life. Even as you spilled my blood, you didn't enjoy it." She gritted her teeth. "You thought you would, didn't you?"

"I wanted you so much." He closed his eyes. "But rape is sickening. I never meant to hurt you." He trembled. "I saved myself for you."

"Your only opportunity." She kept her voice bereft of emotion. "I'm sure you do regret not finishing."

"I can't think of it without remembering you scream. I hope you will one day forget what happened, but I will remember it as penance. You have my word. My life is yours." He descended the staircase.

Chapter Twenty

After several days of incarceration under the guise of time to recuperate, Darrin was called to stand before his mother, the Steward. The High Council of Matriarchs lined the length of the great hall in near darkness. He couldn't distinguish their features until he reached the far end where his mother waited, illuminated by candle-light.

The Steward's chair sat positioned one step down from the empty Royal Throne on the majestic dais. This area was lit with lamps, in the greater light, he could discern his mother's expression. It didn't soften at the sight of him. He knelt, bowed forward, and rested his forehead on the floor.

"Be comfortable." The Steward spoke with formality.

He sat upright on his heels, not daring to ease to the right or left in a more comfortable position despite her having asked him to. The atmosphere in the room was not one of ease. Why make a pretense of welcome when he knew full well that he was a prisoner?

The First Matriarch stood. "Darrin of Wolfe, Captain of the Royal Guard, and Royal Shadow, you will give an account of your actions in regard to the Future Queen. The period in question begins with your revealing yourself to Her Majesty, Princess Emerald Stone, and ends with her injury at the battlefront. You will explain to us every detail of what transpired." The Matriarch's gaze bored into him before she sat once more.

Darrin bowed his forehead to the floor again, mind racing. What should he say? Would anything he told them have the power to make a difference? A stillness fell over him. He resigned himself to tell a brief version of the truth and then wait for their questions.

"On the night the Princess was attacked by three men from Andolin, I had been Shadowing her along the Border Road. When she met the Frenlander, Sarialla, Royal Counselor, my curiosity became piqued. Considering the situation on the road safe, I followed the Counselor to observe her meeting with Prince Stephan at Stone Castle. When the Princess did not arrive within a short time, I hurried to check on her." Darrin's bravado faltered.

"I arrived in time to rescue her from the river where the barbarous attackers had thrown her. She was near death. The only safe shelter was in the castle." He ducked his head.

"I broke the law by taking her home. But I thought it was the only course of action open to me if I wanted to save her life. I apologize for the lapse in judgment that allowed her to come to harm in the first place." He folded his hands in his lap.

"Yes." The Second Matriarch stood. "Our entire civilization is in danger because of your lapse in judgment. You broke the protocol by leaving the Princess unprotected and again by revealing yourself. This does not explain, however, why you tarried in Stone Castle after you had delivered her to safety. What did you tell the Princess that caused her to come to the war front?"

Many voices joined in boisterous accusation.

The Steward raised a hand for silence. "Let us not forget the service this man has rendered to the Princess. We shall ask one question at a time so that all may be revealed in an orderly manner. Indeed, Royal Shadow, I wish to know what would cause you to continue to disregard the protocol and remain in the presence of the Princess."

Darrin noticed the glimmer of hope in his mother's eyes. What did she expect him to say? He knew his life was in jeopardy. This was no casual meeting. His incarceration had been no coincidence.

Every other testimony had been given ahead of his. Though he'd been provided with plenty of time to think of an excuse, nothing would satisfy this court. He had to tell the truth and accept the consequences of his folly.

"Come now, young man. How were you rewarded for your years of service? Did she cast you into a dungeon?" A hunched, old woman sitting midway down the hall raised her voice.

"No, Matriarch." He shook his head. "The Princess lay gravely ill for several days. Prince Stephan asked me to stay until she recovered. I did not wish to offend the rightful King of Frenland. So, I obeyed." He bowed his head.

"And when she did know you, what did the Princess do?" The same Matriarch held out her hands, askance.

"I introduced myself as Darrin of Wolfe. The Princess mistook me for an enemy. She would have taken my life except that she heeded the counsel of the Frenland Sage, Sarialla." Darrin stopped himself from shrugging.

"Once I explained myself, the Princess made requests and inquiries of me. I told her that some things were better explained by an Ambassador, and she accepted my silence on certain topics. She did not request further information or express an interest in speaking with the Ambassador." He did shrug this time and winced at using the foreign gesture in front of these traditional figures because they would view it as suspicious.

"What happened after that?" The First Matriarch leaned back in her chair.

"All progressed well for a while. I served the Princess around the castle in every way she requested. I thought things were going fine until she changed her mind about me." He couldn't bring himself to speak about that terrible day or the tender feelings he had expressed.

Murmuring erupted from the women in the hall. The Steward arose. She stood slim and elegant in her traditional gown of gold.

"How did you offend the Princess?"

Darrin broke protocol to meet his mother's gaze. He pleaded without words for her not to ask this of him. She did not relent. Instead, the questioning look in her eyes intensified.

"I'm inexperienced with women. I've lived in the wilderness for much of my life. Observing the Princess from afar provided little help in understanding what she expected of me." His heart raced.

The Second Matriarch stood. "What happened? We must know every detail."

Darrin ducked his head. "She came to my bed in the middle of the night. It was a mistake. In the morning, she cast me out. That's when she went to the front. I never told her about the war. Somehow, she simply knew." He squeezed his eyes shut.

A pregnant silence filled the room. It seemed as if no one breathed. A dry old woman so wrinkled she looked like she would crack started laughing.

"Withdraw your requests for this man. The Future Queen pines on her wall for him. He's taken." She cackled again.

His skin flushed with heat as he looked at the women around him. "No, you don't understand. She refused to marry me. She—" He'd intended to say she hated him.

"Silence. How dare you slander the Future Queen in this way?" The First Matriarch shook her fist at him.

Darrin closed his mouth and pressed his forehead to the floor. He would die now. He hadn't meant to place Emerald's honor in question. They mistook an innocent encounter for something base. Would he be permitted to explain?

"Precedence applies." The Steward took a step forward. "The law is clear concerning the Future Queen and the Royal Shadow. When Royalty accepts a Shadow, it is a binding relationship and a marriage of sorts. The rights of the Princess supersede all other petitioners.

"With respect, I deny all requests for my son. I defer to the prior claim of my ruler, Princess Emerald Stone. Let it be known from this moment forward that Darrin of Wolfe is the Royal Consort." She clapped her hands once.

The Guard opened the large doors at the end of the hall.

"Return to the Princess and serve her well, my son. Do not offend her again." His mother met his gaze.

Slack-jawed, it took a moment for him to recover. He arose from the floor and bowed all the way out. As the doors shut behind him, he heard a Matriarch ask.

"Is that the second test? Is the Princess rewriting the past?"

He couldn't hear the reply.

DARRIN FLED THROUGH the alleyways and side streets of Steward City. Once he reached the guardhouse where he'd been detained, he reclaimed his sword. He would return to Emerald as commanded. But only because he had no choice.

His pulse throbbed in his skin at the thought of recent events. He hadn't intended to deceive the Council. His mother should have questioned him further. Instead, she had spared his life and put off the husband hunters by accepting the misleading circumstances of his relationship with the Future Queen.

He was relieved not to be farmed out for breeding. But it shamed him that those women believed him to be Emerald's lover. He could hardly see straight for the bitter emotions nipping at his insides. She had rejected him, yet now he was commanded to submit to her every whim.

No.

He would be the Shadow, but nothing more. He would not become vulnerable to further exploitation. His life belonged to the Future Queen, but she would never know it. She didn't appreciate his service, and he doubted she would reconsider her position on the matter even if she understood the details of his plight.

From the day of her birth, the Royal Guard had protected her from the Renegades seeking to prevent the fulfillment of the Ancient King's foretelling. When still a boy, the intensity of his curiosity had led him to abandon brushes and paints in search of the Princess. He'd followed the pathway down the mountain to see the child who would one day restore glory to the people of the West Wind.

He remembered her, dressed in lace and ribbons, picking berries in the patch near her grandparents' cottage. Her hair had caught the rays of the sun, and he had marveled at her cream-colored skin. She was the reason he was in this mess.

The Royal Guard had petitioned the Matriarchs to train him to be a Shadow. It was an honored position many had attempted to fill. A Shadow stood between the Princess and danger.

The difficulty lay in the edict of the Matriarchal Council, who had declared that the people of the West Wind remain undetected by the Princess. That meant that no one else could do the job, except Darrin. Reason being, Emerald sensed the presence of everyone except him.

He had accepted the calling out of a foolish sense of duty and the romance of serving a beautiful girl. Too late, he had realized he had no stomach for war. His gentle childhood had ended with the first kill. Still feeling the guilt of it, he balled his tainted hands into fists.

Displeased, his mother had opposed his calling as the Shadow. She had wished to protect him. In the end, however, she had conceded to the will of the Matriarchal Counsel. In her wisdom, she had guessed how difficult his life would be. He was always in danger and lived out of doors in the elements.

Naïve thoughts of Emerald had filled his days and infiltrated his dreams. Over the years, he'd become obsessed. His chin dropped to his chest.

He'd fulfilled the edict to go undetected until the end. Emerald had never realized he was there, even when he was so close. However, he had failed to save her soul from the destructive forces of evil men and their terrible lusts.

He stuffed a pack with supplies and hurried out of the deserted guardhouse. There was nothing he cared about in this city anymore, aside from his mother and his paintings on display in the Royal Residence.

Urgency hastened his footsteps. He'd been held for five days in darkness, but he'd counted the changing of the Guard to keep track of time. He should be dead right now.

His mother had spared his life. However, being the son of the Steward guaranteed he would one day pay for his crimes. The truth couldn't be overlooked forever.

He had spoken to the Future Queen, touched her, and laid beside her in bed longing for her love. It was more than enough to condemn him when Emerald's true feelings were known. The conundrum was that she had a penchant for trouble and still needed his protection.

Exhaling, he shut his eyes and stopped in the shade of a building on the outskirts of the city. She despised him and yet he continued to serve her. Was anything he did going to be enough to save her?

Those men had such terrible power to break her. Why didn't he have the power to mend her? The fact that she hated him came to mind.

He pushed away from the masonry and trudged up the south side of the valley. Once over the ridge, he started down the steep slope of the mountain. It took a day to hike to Stone Castle. That would provide him with plenty of time to hate himself for still being in love with her.

Chapter Twenty-One

The children discovered Emerald at bedtime and piled in with her. She made room for each of them. Marta toddled over to cuddle. Nina's expression remained brooding, but she snuggled in too. Andrew broke the rules and came on the girls' side of the sleeping chamber. He climbed into the bed next to Emerald's and gazed at her in the lamplight.

By their response, she understood she had done something terrible. Languishing on the wall for those three days had been worse than any other risk she'd taken. Remorse melted the hardness from her heart with tender feelings of love. The burden of their need and the self-reproach she felt for hurting them weighed heavy.

That guilt doubled when she considered how soon she needed to leave.

"I'm sorry I frightened you." She spoke in soothing tones.

They fell asleep but rest evaded her. In the darkness, she pondered the future. After the vision in the sun, her fear and trepidation had disappeared. Purpose and direction had given her confidence.

Shifting her position between the children, she stroked Marta's silky curls. This simple act made her heart swell, causing tears to well up and spill over with the realization that she may never return. It couldn't be helped.

She decided to undertake the journey that would lead to the fulfillment of the Legend of the Stone as soon as may be. It was impossible to know where the quest would end, but she understood where it must begin. As soon as her strength returned, she would scale the Impenetrable Mountains. She needed to meet with the Steward and pass the tests of the Ancient Southern King.

The children wedged her in place, and she focused on enjoying the closeness of loved ones. The self-imposed isolation endured on the wall had been weakness haunting her. It hadn't been a reality, because these orphans needed her and she needed them too.

A lump of sadness formed in her throat. Enlightenment made the pain of leaving poignant but did not change her mind. Regrettably, these children were linked to her suffering.

"Oh, Stephan, where are you?" The stars winked outside the high windows in the velvet dark.

STEPHAN LED DUSTY FROM the caves and strode into the twilight world of the northern side of the mountain. He strained his eyes to gather the details of the foothills and plains of Frenland. Feeling the weight of his responsibility to rule, he sought a connection. He hoped for something familiar, a reminder of his heritage.

Nothing.

His shoulders slumped. Then the wind shifted and the smell of the grasslands filled his nostrils. It caused a slow smile to spread across his face.

Sarialla chuckled. "You do remember. I thought you might. You were only a little boy, but you loved to play in the tall grass."

The horses whinnied and danced at the prospect of fresh grazing. Stephan almost allowed Dusty his freedom before Sarialla grabbed the bridle. She gave a curt shake of the head.

"I must caution you, My Prince. We must not leave the safety of the mountains just yet. My daughter and a legion of female soldiers conduct patrols between the mountains and the planes. She would discover us in an instant, with deadly consequences. We cannot enter the grasslands."

Stephan patted Dusty's neck to soothe the animal. Starlight reflected on the sea of grass as it rippled in the wind. It was so exquisite that he hadn't imagined the danger there.

At that moment, he knew he would never go home again. A sharp pang of homesickness reminded him of Nina and her simple meals. He laid down on a blanket in the lush grass, wishing for a hug.

WORK FILLED EMERALD'S days. Mounting the curtain wall, she surveyed the plowed and planted fields outside the castle from beneath the brim of a straw hat. With a satisfied sigh, she rubbed her sore shoulder. Her other muscles ached in pleasant ways, but she was sure the crops would yield well this year.

Nina climbed the steps to the top of the wall in a rare outing from the keep. She'd been increasingly bold lately. That made Emerald so pleased for the girl.

Nina and the Miller girls had taken the domestic chores in hand. The keep was in good order. It hadn't required much to train them in the way the household ran.

Several girls had shown interest in joining the morning archery practice. That gave Emerald joy. She flashed a smile at Nina, enjoying the freedom from worry the end of the war had brought.

"It's good to see you out," she said.

"It's good to see you happy." Nina avoided Emerald's gaze.

"At this moment, all is well. I'm going to hold it as a treasure for later when hard times come again."

Nina nodded. "The midday meal is ready."

Emerald had traded most of the armory for supplies in town. So, there was plenty to eat. The villagers had been fair and, in some cases, friendly. The most welcome news had been of Liameo's recovery. It had eased her mind more than expected.

"I wanted to ask you about something. Did your group of squatters have Royalist ties?" Emerald asked.

Nina frowned in thought. "It wasn't like that, exactly. But my father said we should go with them because Danalan was fertile. He wasn't afraid of wolves. My mother had died, and I think he had designs on you." She blushed.

"Oh, well, hmm, I suppose you know how that proposal would have fared." Emerald hugged Nina. "I love you."

The girl wrapped her arms around Emerald's middle and held on as tight as she could. "I love you, too."

Emerald rubbed Nina's back. "The villagers say that the Militia, including Captain Hammond, has been reprimanded by the Governor. The inquiry found them partial to Stone Clan philosophy. That irritates me because it isn't true." The butcher's wife had told her all these things.

"I wish everyone could be like we are." Nina still hadn't let go.

The thought was pleasing. "Me too, but they aren't."

George strode across the courtyard below them. He had taken over many responsibilities of late. To her surprise and delight, he was a natural leader.

He hadn't forgotten to check the road once. To everyone's joy, he had discovered a waif named Tarah. Seventeen and reserved, she had captured his shy heart.

"Do you think he'll ask her to marry him?" Nina released her hold around Emerald's middle and held her hand as they walked together along the wall.

"The Spring Celebration begins tomorrow. I plan to give them my blessing." What she'd seen of Tarah's character had pleased her and she wished them joy.

"Good." Nina lifted Emerald's hand and looked at it. "You need a bath."

Emerald laughed. "Indeed."

Rich, dark earth dusted her clothes. It satisfied her to see it beneath her fingernails. The soil's gritty reassurance comforted her because this land gave life.

Though arduous, she and the boys had cleared new growth out of two overgrown fields. They had planted dry beans. Barring disaster, the crops would yield enough to feed any number of additional children this winter.

The unrest in the South had opened a new type of refugee influx. Unfortunately, it appeared that the trend would only worsen. She could not turn away the needy, especially now that it was safe to live in Danalan.

"The food is getting cold," Nina said.

"I'm still full from breakfast." Thoughts of politics always drove away Emerald's appetite.

"Well, I'm not. See you inside." The girl smiled as she ran down the steps and into the keep.

Things had changed since the Wolf Clan had been eradicated in the final battle. Emerald moved to sit atop the battlement. It was nice to be able to make plans for the future.

She intended to parcel out land to the orphans as they matured. George and Tarah would be the first to inherit acreage. She wanted to form a community.

She planned to recommend that the men travel from their homes to the fields each day. In that way, a cluster of homes could be built so that no one would ever be isolated or alone. Each family could support the others through sickness and childbirth as the years passed.

The future excited her, but she had to put those aspirations aside because she would soon complete the preparations for the journey she must take. She felt compelled to leave and had only hesitated this long in hopes of good weather.

Andre slammed the door of the keep on his way out with a plate of food. He spotted her atop the wall and ran over to the stairs of the curtain wall. She wondered how he didn't send food flying in every direction.

Panting, he came to her side and set the plate in her lap. "I saved you some."

She put her arm around him. "Thank you."

"I helped make it." He didn't pull away.

She tasted a forkful of ham and beans. "Mm, it's good." She let go of him so she could hold the plate steady and keep eating.

He watched her until she winked at him.

He went to sit on the crenellation next to hers on the battlement. "I like to cook."

"You like to eat."

He laughed and nodded. "What's the difference? If I'd known the cook got to sample the fare, then I'd have been helping in the kitchen long before now."

"Well, I'm glad to see it." She set down her empty plate and considered telling him about her plans to leave.

Where should she enter the mountains? Would she need to climb to the top? She didn't want to get caught in a spring snowstorm.

The gray forbidding peaks loomed overhead, and she held her tongue. She fought back her emotions and stared up at them. The enormity of the task she must perform was overwhelming, but her courage rallied. She squared her shoulders and attempted to penetrate the mysteries of the mountain as she scanned the craggy surface.

"Do you think Darrin's all right?" Andre had adopted her gaze at the mountains.

The question startled her because she had shoved her misgivings about that man deep. "I don't know."

"Do you think he'll ever come back?"

"No." After what she had done, he would never return. She leaned forward and took Andre's hand. "I hope you know how much I love you."

The boy smiled. "I know." Just then the brown mare whinnied in the horse stables below. "I'd better go see what she needs."

She released his hand and he was gone. For the first time, her resolve to journey into the mountains wavered. How could she leave that boy?

Just as it seemed hopeless, a possible solution came to mind. The boulder inscribed with the curse of the Ancient Southern King was believed to be near the entrance. Stephan and Sarialla had recently used those tunnels to go north.

Grandfather had taken her there once. If she could find the doorway to the mountain, then the quest would be half complete. If not, then she needed another way.

The soaring peaks looked forbidding. However, it was the capable men that defended them that struck fear in her as never before. One of those men, in particular, made her sick with anxiety and self-reproach.

Her cheeks burned with shame, but she wasn't sure why. Embarrassed by Darrin's declarations and her own behavior with regards to him, a profound sense of confusion overwhelmed her. Try as she might, she could not solve the puzzle or resolve her feelings.

The primary concern she had was that she must certainly have created an enemy. Darrin had said he loved her. But she knew love was an emotion closely related to hatred.

Love was a strong emotion that only lacked pride and fear to become corrupted into something dark. What would she do if Darrin hated her? Did he have the power to stop her?

Chapter Twenty-Two

Stephan enjoyed the sunrise from his grassy spot high above the plains. After three days of near darkness, the land delighted him with vivid greens and a bright sky of blue. Compared with the caves, even the air felt different. The inner-mountain had been cool and close, but outside, the wind never stopped. It whistled through rocks and whipped the horses' manes and tails.

Restless, Dusty danced as if he wished to run wild. Lightning, however, stared across the foothills toward the sea of green. Unmoving, he breathed in and out in a steady rhythm.

Sarialla's expression mirrored the white horse. This place was part of them. He wondered if it was part of him too, but everything felt unfamiliar.

Deep snow remained banked in the shady places around them. He calculated the sun shone directly on this side of the mountain only when high in the sky. That meant they needed to ride fast to use the daylight. The chilly wind sent a shiver along his spine. He slipped on a pair of gloves and mounted Dusty.

"Shall we go, Counselor?"

Sarialla and Lightning blinked in unison. He marveled at their similar expressions. Were people unusually connected to horses here?

The vast pastureland was ideal for grazing. However, the incessant wind and shorter growing season might be less conducive to farming than he was accustomed to in the South. The ground here appeared free of obstacles and easy to plow. As a ruler, he must consider every possibility to improve the lives of the people.

"It's good to be home." Sarialla mounted with greater ease than had been her custom of late.

They traveled eastward between lichen covered pillars of a fallen archway to enter an ancient causeway. Massive earthworks and preexisting rock formations concealed them from any possible notice of the people on the plains. It felt strange not to have the two soldiers of the West Wind following them. However, sometime in the night, the men had disappeared.

"How long do we follow this road, Counselor?"

"More than a day, My Prince."

Even after hundreds of years of neglect, no grass grew between the stones. The respect he had already acquired for the architects and stonemasons of the past deepened. The wonders of this land heightened his curiosity about the people.

Once in a while, the road forked toward the plains or reached upward to a recess in the mountainside. He imagined ancient cities at the end of those roads or rock quarries and mines. Why did no one live here?

Another thing bothered him. Why hadn't the mountain men known about the tunnels? They had been visibly shocked when shown the southern entrance.

"Wise Sage, why are there no people here? There should be many inhabitants, but I've detected no one. How are the mountains defended against invasion from Frenland?"

"This is the Sacred Mountain, My Prince. No one lives here by decree of the ancient rulers. No one needs to defend it, except the Creator. It is the highest and most inhospitable of the Impenetrable Mountains. It divides the east from the west." Her eyes sparkled as she pointed upward at the jutting sides of the mountain that impaled the clouds like the chipped blade of a stone ax.

"Are the people of the mountains divided?" he asked.

"Yes. Darrin's people are called the West Wind. Tomorrow we will leave this road before we enter the territory of the East Ice. The eastern mountains curve northward and are covered with treacherous glaciers, everchanging. Ancient writings say the nature of the people is equally unpredictable."

Stephan focused on the aged woman. "Have you met anyone from the eastern mountains?" He broke eye contact to rub a scratch on Dusty's saddle. "Are they as conflicted about Em as the Westerners?"

Sarialla shrugged. "I wish I had encouraging news, but no one has ever returned from the East Ice. A year ago, a battalion of rebels was forced to flee onto a glacier by my daughter's forces. Their bodies slid back like so much frozen fish. The Valkyrie fled in disarray. Valerie was indignant, or so I was told."

Stephan considered the implications.

"We've been pressed near the glaciers for years, My Prince." Sarialla's shoulders slumped. "I left epistles for the East Icers, seeking a diplomatic relationship. I elicited aid in the fight against my brother but the messages were ignored. Well, I should say, they disappeared mysteriously and no reply ever came.

"The Easterners won't help, Sire. Moreover, I fear they are watching for a sign of Emerald's rise to power. I don't know if they will be as divided as the Westerners or not, but they are aware of the Legend of the Stone. I informed them."

Stephan eased the furrows of his brow and laughed at Sarialla's guilty expression. "It seems that Em can go nowhere to escape the expectations of others. I reassure you, Counselor, that Emerald expects more of herself than anyone. She doesn't aspire to riches or power and never has.

"In fact, it is my belief that if the Wolf Clan had not come, then she would live a quiet life. If she were whole again, that is." He glanced at the precipitous angle of the mountainside.

Sarialla's lips pressed together.

His mind wandered to forbidden topics. "Em used to play with dolls. She pretended they were babies and dreamed of a future husband, a farmer or a beekeeper like her father.

"She changed after Grandma and Grandpa Stone died. She wouldn't wear a dress or hair ribbons and burned the dolls. Months passed before she spoke a single word to me.

"We have never discussed that day. Now it has happened all over again. Do you think she'll give birth? The people of Andolin aren't kind to unwed pregnant women." These things were hard for him to say.

Sarialla sighed. "I could not tell if Emerald carries a child. George is worried too. She will be protected. Of that, you may be sure.

"Besides, Ryan said the villagers were appalled by her wounds. They were shocked that the Carpenters had done something so base. Emerald's show of mercy on behalf of Mrs. Carpenter and her daughters moved them. Things will improve." Hope blossomed in Sarialla's expression.

Stephan scowled, incensed by how Emerald had been treated. He fidgeted with the saddle horn as heat radiated from his cheeks. Ryan had related the entire series of events after Emerald had returned to the castle.

Stephan gritted his teeth, he hated that everyone knew Emerald had been raped and had seen her broken body naked in the town square. Why had they been allowed to do that? How had she endured the mortification and still shown mercy?

"I don't think I'll make a good king. I could never be merciful to men like the Carpenters. I would have killed them with my bare hands. You saw what they did to her." Tormented, he glanced at the older woman for comfort.

She reached across to rein Dusty in and pulled Lightning to a halt as well. "I saw it." Pain creased the corners of her eyes. "Justice is needed in Frenland, My Prince."

She stabbed a finger toward the plains. "When you become the King, make just laws and enforce them. Emerald would not have had to thwart justice if the laws of Andolin protected the innocent wife and daughters of Hubert Carpenter. Be thoughtful and wise, because we are not like Andolin. Frenland is much worse."

STEPHAN OPENED HIS eyes before the sun lightened the sky. Had a noise awakened him? Crickets chirped. He heard nothing out of the ordinary.

Sarialla's story of the East Icers returned to mind. What if they had noticed the fire? Sitting up, he pushed the fear away with hopes that the horses would warn them if anyone approached.

Instead of worrying, he planned ways to win a war with few trained soldiers and scant resources. The simple answer was that he couldn't. He needed to acquire men and supplies and a place to train them.

With a sigh, he realized that a bigger problem remained. How could a wicked populace be converted to the proper rule of law? Sarialla had described King Salicor, Prince Byron, and Princess Valerie to him while in the caves. They ruled with a cruel grip on power and tight control over the armies and the people of the land.

Byron and Valerie were Salicor's generals and rotated duties around the kingdom. This year Byron recruited for his army and oversaw the training of his soldiers. Valerie had fought at the front last year and now guarded the border with the mountains, raising cattle. That beef fed the armies.

Salicor sent orders from the Capital City, Soniashi, to his personal army at the eastern front. He relied on trusted Commanders, most of whom had been part of the original forces from the far North that he had used to win the kingdom.

Over the years, the rebels had been slaughtered to near extinction. So, unless bored, Salicor seldom inspected the forces or harassed the enemy in person. He had little to fear.

Stephan wondered how to repel such a well-supplied and motivated fighting force. Without cutting the legs out from under the body, he couldn't. Salicor's generals, Valerie and Byron provided stability. If the two of them defected, then the armies could fail.

Stephan's frown deepened. How did Salicor keep Byron and Valerie in line? Sarialla was their mother and was owed their first allegiance. If Salicor had lied to the twins, then Sarialla could persuade them of the truth.

Stephan grabbed the hair above his forehead in a fist. If he captured the twin generals, then Sarialla could convince them of Salicor's deception. He would need to divert Salicor's army long enough to do it, though. Where could he hide the rebel forces from the enemy's wrath in the meantime?

He tossed the blanket aside and slipped on his boots. In the gray of the morning, he climbed the embankment and stared at the grasslands below. He breathed deep breaths and pondered the problem.

Smiling, he knew the answer, he would pound Valerie's army and steal the cattle. He would strike from the foothills of this mountain until he could sweep northward to confront Byron. But where would he obtain the forces he needed?

He walked further from camp and an idea teased. Salicor's men were terrified of the East Icers. Terror was a double-edged blade but effective when used with skill. He could use their fears against them by employing deception.

He would inform Sarialla and the Rebel Captains of his intentions when he met with them in a few days. But it would be imperative that they keep the strategies secret. The people of Frenland would not understand what he was about to do.

In the west, he could use most of the rebels to impersonate the people of the West Wind. By attacking in this way, they could raid supplies and cause confusion among the Valkyrie. If they stored the stolen supplies in the Sacred Hills and moved along this hidden road, then that part of the plan might work.

He could not use terror on the plains. He needed tactics. The reason being, that he wanted to win the hearts of the people.

What could he do to wear General Valerie down and yet keep his forces from annihilation? He exhaled and dropped onto the grassy slope. He plucked at the grass and stared at the blades in his palm.

The wind swept them away.

That's it. He could burn the plains and let the wind fight his war. The details of his plan came together. Sunrise flooded the landscape as if the fires already burned.

DARRIN WATCHED FROM beneath the cover of a clutch of under-growth rich trees. Emerald had several children out in a meadow practicing archery during the last hour before sunset. She appeared thin and weak.

Indeed, her left shoulder seemed to cause her lingering pain. She could no longer hold a bow steady enough to hit the mark. It was a shame because she had been a skilled marksman.

She taught the orphans how to aim and track a target. They laughed and teased as the inexperienced children made their mistakes. He hadn't seen her smile this much in a long time.

She was fine. She didn't need him. His heart stormed with pain.

What was he going to do? He was on his own and no longer received support from his people. His mother believed he had obeyed her edict to return to the Future Queen's presence as Consort. But he would rather die.

The chatty group of orphans meandered toward the castle. Emerald wasn't with them. When had she disappeared?

Determined to see her one last time before he returned to face the Council of Matriarchs, he went after her. He wouldn't burden her with his death. In his own way, he simply wanted to say goodbye.

He followed her tracks to the river. She often came here after a dirty day's work. This was her favorite spot. It was near the ruins of the cottage where she'd been born.

He gave her plenty of time to wash her clothes and bathe, thus allowing her the privacy she craved. After a while, however, he expected her to emerge from the foliage at the river's edge. She didn't.

Worried, he snuck closer to check on her.

He had no wish to catch her bathing. The sight of her that way was more than he could bear. Once he had watched her and longed for her until the weight of his desires had crushed him. After that, he had learned self-control for the sake of self-preservation.

With a deep breath, he braced himself and peered through the bright spring leaves. Fully clothed, she crouched on a rocky outcropping with a hand in the water. Her fingertips caressed the surface in an absentminded gesture.

She hadn't bathed or even undone her hair. The expression on her face as she stared across the river was profoundly sad. It shocked him to see her confront her emotions. She seldom did that.

"Goodbye." She stood.

The warm hues of a sunset filtered sideways through the trees. A fish jumped after a swarm of insects. The splash seemed to distract her from her thoughts. She knelt and washed her face. Then, fleet as a deer, she crossed the rocks and ran toward the castle.

What did she mean by 'goodbye'? Was she saying farewell to this place or something else? Perhaps, she had detected him, but that was impossible.

She couldn't have known his intentions. So, what then? He had to find out.

Chapter Twenty-Three

Emerald leaned against the doorframe of the library. When Stephan had wanted an answer to a question, he'd looked for it in a book. She fixed her gaze on the shelves of leather-bound volumes and scrolls. This place didn't hold answers for her, though words from the past built her road forward.

She heaved a sigh and longed for Stephan. With regret, she wished she had the chance to say goodbye to him. He had asked her to come with him. If she hadn't gone off in search of death, leaving everyone who needed her behind, then she could at least have bid him farewell.

She adjusted her feet and stood upright. Perhaps, she should not have feared to go with him. After all, he would only have needed her for the summer.

Realization struck and her shoulders slumped. She alone was responsible for the Ambassador requiring him to go north. Because of her, he had been forbidden to return.

Thoughts of Stephan only brought the pain of regret. She pushed away from the doorframe and fled. In the darkened stairway, she collided with George's substantial chest.

"Ah." She squeaked.

"Emerald." He stammered as he took her by the upper arms.

Steadied, she backed away from him and squared her shoulders. "Sorry, George, I didn't see you."

"I can understand that, but I thought you would have heard me." He stepped forward. His boot thudded on the wood step. "I was looking for you, Em. I have something important to talk about."

"Of course. Let's go to the library." Emerald strode into the room and parted the drapes for more light.

"There is a matter I want to discuss with you. I wish to marry Tarah at the Spring Celebration. I love her. She's the sweetest girl I've ever met." His cheeks blushed crimson. "I can't live without her. If she doesn't say yes, then I don't know what I'll do."

Emerald smiled until his last statement locked her in a knot. "If she says no, then you won't do anything, George." Her voice came out low and icy.

His jaw worked without sound for a moment. "I'd never hurt her, Em. You're right. If she doesn't want me, then I'll accept it. I won't hold it against her."

Emerald held his gaze. "I think she will consent to be your wife. I perceive, she has feelings for you that mirror your own. But I worry you're too big for her. I don't see how you can…" She shied from him. "I mean to say, mating would surely hurt her, and you must not do that. I will kill you if you do." Tears clouded her vision.

From behind, gentle hands closed over her shoulders and turned her to face him. He embraced her. Enveloped in his arms, she wept.

How could it work out well for Tarah? How could she be unafraid to marry George? Emerald trembled and he stroked her hair. At that moment, understanding dawned.

Compassion. George would be kind and patient with Tarah. They would find happiness.

He touched her face and changed the dynamic of the embrace as his fingers caressed her skin. Undeniable, the heady feeling was hard to incorporate into her way of thinking. It both thrilled her body and made her mind recoil at the same time.

She lifted her head to look into his eyes. To her surprise, she discovered an unexpected depth of emotion mingled with a chasm of pain. Stunned, she couldn't move.

"George?"

His thumb stilled her lips. His eyes shut and his arms fell to his sides. Her breathing came fast and shallow. Confused, she realized part of her had responded to him. She had trusted him, thrilled at his touch, and wanted him to touch her more.

"How long have you felt this way?" she asked.

He opened his eyes. "I've loved you since the day we met. Respect and admiration have only deepened my feelings. I'll always care for you, Em."

He swiped a tear from her cheek. "Over time, I realized I could never make you happy. I know you don't care for me the way I care for you and that's fine. I love Tarah. My bond with her is stronger than with you because she returns my feelings." The sadness in his eyes lessened.

"I didn't know." Emerald shook her head. "I never knew."

Something had altered inside her. She needed to ask him what. He had revealed it, so perhaps he had the answer.

"George, did you know I wasn't a virgin? Is that what changed your mind?"

His expression collapsed. "No. That changes nothing." He held her hands. "I mean, I know it does for you, but not for me. I'm sorry you've been hurt, both before and this time. I want to kill Roger and Christopher every time I see them."

He rubbed her fingers. "I hope you don't think of yourself as impure." He flushed. "You are virtuous. Believe me, because I know what a whore is. My mother was one."

She gasped but felt terrible for it as his blush deepened. He turned away with his shoulders hunched. She touched his arm.

"What's the matter?" she asked.

"I'm not worthy of you. Even if you cared for me, I would never act on my feelings. I'm glad they faded, and I found Tarah.

"I've told her what I am, and she doesn't mind. She said we can't help who our parents are, that it's our actions that matter. Now, I've shamed her by admitting my feelings for you. I guess I am like my mother." He started to leave the room.

Emerald jumped in the way. "George, you are not in love with me. You may admire me but you don't love me like you love Tarah. Not because you're unworthy, but because you found more than infatuation.

"Tarah deserves you because she returns your feelings. I'm not capable of that kind of emotion. I cannot love." The pain of this conviction made her bold.

Unflinching, he absorbed her declaration. In answer, he brushed her cheek with his fingertips. Her eyelids fluttered and her breath caught.

"Why do you think your body is ready?" His question penetrated. "It's because your heart has been given away, not to me, but to another."

She furrowed her brow and held his gaze. Confused, she would have asked him what he meant. Before she could speak, he shook his head and left the room.

Alone, she bolted the library door. Heart pounding, her breath came in gasps. What had just happened?

Heat ascended her neck as she remembered the seductive way his touch had sent fingers of sensation through her middle. Her gorge surged to remember it and she had to swallow hard to keep from vomiting. On shaky legs, she collapsed on a chair by the fireplace.

Her troubled head sank into her trembling hands. She had done something reprehensible. What if other boys felt the same way as George?

Gael smiled when she came into a room. Did that mean he loved her? He was only a boy, but she had thought the same way about George.

His touch had stirred her body. The remembered sensation deepened and her skin throbbed with desire. Who wouldn't like this feeling? She ached for it even as she hated herself for the weakness.

Her body was ready, but to do what? Marry? He had said she'd given her heart to someone, but to whom? She couldn't fix her mind on anyone.

Images of the men she knew raced through her mind, each one a poor fit. Even Liameo, whom she had once loved, wasn't right. How could she have committed her heart to someone when she didn't even know she'd done it?

Chills washed over her like water from the well. George was wrong. She could not love. It was her body that betrayed her. Her heart remained as she had always believed, a lump of marred stone.

Faced with a problem she never thought to have, she wanted to run. She couldn't trust her body. What would become of her when men learned of the power that they possessed over her?

Hating her weakness did little to strengthen her resolve. Her stomach was still unreliable. Her eyes flew wide.

Perhaps, her stomach held the key. Was she with child? Did that do things to a woman's body?

Shame made her cheeks burn. She ground her teeth and clenched her fists. Fearing the worst, she had no way of knowing for sure. Her womanly cycle didn't come often when she hadn't been eating enough. But before her body had a chance to prevent her, she made the determination to go in search of destiny.

Did mountain men stone unwed pregnant women like Andoliners sometimes do? She pushed the thought aside. Why had she wasted time? Tonight, she would tell the children she must go.

Resolved, she strode from the library and assembled the orphans in the main room of the keep. Hardened, she barely looked at them. Her voice was heavy and unyielding.

"I will leave Danalan in the morning."

An outcry of disbelief rippled through the group. George's spine snapped straight and he avoided her gaze. She didn't look at him either. This wasn't his fault.

"To tell you the truth, I've been planning this journey for weeks. During my time on the wall, I felt as though I had failed. I wanted to die. However, a vision from the Creator gave me hope. I must fulfill the purpose of my birth and open the mountains."

Protests arose, but she held up a hand. A strained silence fell over everyone. Nina chewed a fingernail. Roger scowled and threw a scrub brush into a bucket. He and Christopher had been cleaning the floors.

"My life was spared for this purpose. Perhaps, it is impossible, but I am willing to try."

Nina and the little ones rushed toward her. She sank to a knee and embraced them. Marta couldn't possibly understand, so she hugged her and kissed her curls.

The young boys from the cottage clung to her and wailed in distress. When had they become so attached to her? Overwhelmed, she wept with them.

THE MORNING AFTER THE announcement to the children, Emerald set out alone. She had kissed them and tried to reassure them that everything would be fine, but she had a hard time believing the words. How could it be fine if she wasn't with them?

Her pack weighed her down, but before long the food that made it heavy would dwindle and disappear. Time was of the essence. She hurried along the track and across the bridge.

Perhaps for the last time, she caressed the granite workmanship of her ancestors. With a sigh, she set off on an easterly trek along the Border Road. She planned to reach the great stone carved with the words of the Ancient Southern King by nightfall the next day. After that, she would search for the tunnel under the mountains.

She hadn't traveled far when she sensed Roger ahead. It would be difficult to avoid him. He was sitting in an open area on a boulder with a good view of the road. There was no easy way around.

She kept walking, determined to power through.

He held a bouquet of wildflowers. When his eyes fixed on her the look in them softened. She didn't bother to hide her distaste, or what could only be a sour expression on her face.

"What are you doing, Roger?" she asked.

He stood to face her. "I need you to stay, Emerald. I thought I had more time to tell you how I feel about you. But your leaving has changed my plans. You don't know what you mean to me. By that, I mean to say, I love you." He went down on one knee and held out the flowers. "Will you marry me?" His brows raised expectantly.

Emerald knew Roger's true nature. From his own lips, she had heard his reasons for desiring her hand. He wanted a son. Christopher did too, but the child was not his.

She didn't want the baby. Didn't want to keep it. Didn't want to carry it. But how could she give it to this man? Unthinkable.

The child wasn't even born yet. Perhaps, she wasn't even with child. Roger was taking a terrible risk. Then she remembered what he wanted more than a son. He wanted Danalan.

Due to the close quarters, she drew a dagger rather than a sword.

"I'd rather you not do that my dear." Roger swept past the blade to hold her close.

He forced a kiss on her lips. Repulsed, she recoiled in revulsion and shoved him. Pain tore through her left shoulder and she cried out in anguish.

The cry encouraged him. He pressed her, causing the weight of the pack to topple them both over. Landing on her back, the impact knocked the breath out of her.

Her weapon skidded off in a cloud of dust. Fixated on the blade, she reached, flexing her fingers. She could not reach any blade.

Roger pressed her down like a turtle on her back. His hands bruised her breasts. His mouth sucked her neck.

The weight of him drove away reason. How could this happen? On the verge of hysterics, she gasped and sobbed, pushing him away.

"No." The sound of her scream brought her focus. "Roger, stop."

"What, my dear?" He raised his head to look her in the face.

His hand slid down her side to lift her shirt. She slammed his jaw with the heal of her hand. Unphased, he grabbed both of her wrists with one hand. His gaze lowered to ogle her breasts and abdomen.

"You are." Awe filled his voice.

"Let me go." She rolled onto her side and slammed him to the ground.

With a jerk, she covered herself and freed her arms from the shoulder straps of her pack. Flinging dirt in his face, she regained her feet. Putting some distance between them, she drew her sword.

He wiped the dust from his eyes and crawled forward. "Marry me, Emerald."

Surprised at his tenacity, she let him get too close.

He grabbed her hand. "I need you. Please, be my wife." His eyes revealed his desire, not sexual, but something else.

Out of sorts, but no-longer panicked, she tried to wrench her hand free without dislocating her shoulder again.

"You are insane." She kicked him in the gut and tucked in her shirt. "I could never allow you to have power over Danalan."

He grunted in pain. "Then give me my son, that's all I ask."

She wished she could run him through, but the current situation hardly warranted his death. How could it? He possessed no weapon with which to injure her.

"What if it's a girl?" She couldn't think of anything else to say.

"Well, I've thought about that and decided I still want her." He sat on his heels. "I've always wanted children. You seem to have had your fill. So, you should give me this one. I will take good care of the baby."

He pulled something from his shirt pocket. "You would need to nurse it until it could be weaned, but I'd care for it after that. I have my mother and sisters to help.

"It would be a burden off your shoulders. Clearly, you don't welcome motherhood. But I want to be a father." He held a pair of tiny shoes. "Just give me my child, Emerald."

Frustrated, she clenched her jaw. "I'm probably not even with child."

He smiled. "Your breasts are bigger. The areoles have darkened since I saw them at your trial." His grin turned lecherous. "Pregnancy looks good on you, Emerald."

"Stop looking at me like that and stop saying my name. You have no right." She paced away searching for something reasonable to say, but her head wouldn't cooperate. "The child probably isn't even yours, anyway."

Roger stood and walked toward her. His manner had relaxed. "My father is dead and Christopher didn't finish what he started." Shoulders squared. "Think well. This child isn't an orphan. I am the father.

"I want the baby more than anything and you don't. What happened to you has killed your motherly instincts. I share blame for it, but I hope you won't punish the infant for the mistakes of others." His eyebrows crashed together as he took her by the forearms. "Have a little compassion, please."

Shaken, she considered his words. Was it true? If he was right, then he deserved the child.

What kind of woman would give up her baby? Not a woman at all. She was something else, a twisted, horrible thing she hated.

"You may have the child. If I live, then I will return it to you."

A genuine smile blossomed on his face. "You won't regret this." He chuckled as he touched her belly. "I'll be a good father and teach him to carve wood. I won't make the mistakes my father did, I promise you that." He kissed her forehead.

She shoved him away. "Stop touching me."

He nodded. "Anything, you say, My Beauty. As long as you keep your word, I'll do anything."

"Then let me pass." She scowled. "Get back to work and don't cause trouble. If I return to discover you've been up to no good, then you will have proven beyond a doubt the scoundrel you are. I wouldn't give any child to such a man."

Queasy, she repressed her misgivings. It had to be this way. She didn't want the baby. The thought of it made her sick.

"You look pale. Let me help you with your pack."

He lifted it for her to slip into. The weight settled on her shoulders. He scrambled to retrieve her dagger. With his shirttail, he wiped the dust from it before sliding it into the sheath at her waist.

"Good journey to you. Hurry back." He grinned.

She wanted to knock all his teeth out. Instead, she strode away without returning his cocky wave. Shaking her head and muttering under her breath, she plodded onward.

The sun shone. The birds sang. She hardly noticed.

She had done what she must.

She vowed that she would not regret the decision. The child would be better off with someone who wanted it, even if he was the most despicable of men. Certainly, Roger's mother would treat the baby as part of the family.

Sick about her choice, Emerald chewed her fingernails. She would probably die on this trek, anyway. Oddly, that dark thought comforted her. She quit biting her nails and marched ahead.

DARRIN EXERCISED ALL of his self-control to remain concealed during the exchange between Roger and Emerald. Blood pounded in his ears at the audacity of the blaggard, touching her that way. He had understood little of what was said, but the satisfaction on Roger's face as he parted ways with Emerald caused Darrin to follow him westward along the Border Road.

He could kill the man. There were many places to hide a body where it would not be found. Even as he fantasized, however, he knew he wouldn't go through with the plan.

He had never murdered anyone. In the defense of his Future Queen, he had killed, but that wasn't the same. After all, Roger wasn't even armed.

Darrin paused to scrutinize the man's limp. Had he put on a show of strength in front of Emerald? Now that he presumed himself to be alone, the pretense had vanished.

He was pale and becoming winded. A grim thought occurred to Darrin. There was no need to kill him, whatever ailed Roger Carpenter would claim his life soon enough.

Chapter Twenty-Four

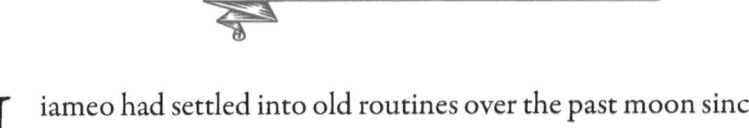

Liameo had settled into old routines over the past moon since Emerald's trial. Tonight, he patrolled the streets of Meadowgren, riding his chestnut mare, Allura, with Eugenia the wolfhound beside them. If Captain Hammond had been wiser, he would have continued to assign duties far from the center of the village.

As it was, Liameo patrolled the streets around the Carpenter's wood-shop. The family residence was above the shop. All was quiet. Even the fire had been banked for the night, judging by the lack of light from the windows and smoke from the chimney.

Liameo hoped to catch his former friend, Roger, breaking the law. Then he would have grounds to fight him and perhaps, whittle off more of him than had already been lost. Liameo laid his hand on the ax at his belt. A curl of the lip betrayed the pleasure he would take in laying Roger out.

He shook his head. No. It was better to move past this den of the wicked. Reluctantly, he urged Allura along a darkened street.

Before long, he encountered a cloaked man with a limp.

"Halt. What business do you have this late at night?" It was strange because Eugenia hadn't barked any warning of the man's approach.

"Just headed home, Sergeant." The man attempted to disguise his voice, but it was Roger.

"The law has you under curfew for your crimes, Roger Carpenter. I'm taking you to see the Captain." Luck was on Liameo's side because the Captain was eager to hang Roger and needed no real excuse to do it either.

"Please, don't be this way. I was on a noble quest." He laughed under his breath.

"I don't want to hear it. Move." Liameo watched Roger eye Eugenia and then turn to obey.

At the Militia Fort, the guard on duty ushered them inside the picketed walls. Liameo dismounted and tied Allura to the hitching post. He knocked on the Captain's cabin door.

A disheveled and sleep-deprived Captain opened the door to reveal the five sleeping children inside. He grabbed his boots and stepped outside. When he looked closer at Roger, he smiled a wickedly satisfied grin.

"I knew you'd be here before long." He laughed.

"Captain, Roger was out after curfew." Liameo wished he had more to accuse him of.

"That'll suffice for a few lashes." The Captain opened the door again and pulled a whip off the peg just inside it, shutting the door once more.

"No, please, not more lashes. I won't be late again, Captain. You have my word." Roger whined.

"Your word?" Liameo wanted to rip the man apart.

"Not good enough." Captain Hammond jutted his chin in the direction of the whipping post. "Bind him, Sergeant."

"I have a reason for being out." Roger backed away, avoiding Liameo's reach.

"This should be good." The Captain followed the two of them toward the post.

"I needed an education." He chuckled even as he bumped into the post in the center of the yard. "The Widow Blaine was teaching me how to please a woman again after what was taken from me. So, you see, this wasn't even for me."

"Whoremongering is a serious accusation." The Captain stepped forward.

Roger wiped his mouth with his sleeve. "We were only talking, mostly."

"Ginny took you back?" Liameo couldn't believe that.

"What need do I have of that cheating wench when I have won the heart of a queen?" Roger stood tall.

Liameo punched him square in the jaw. It felt good. He would have done it again, except the Captain grabbed ahold of his arm.

Roger picked himself up off his back and spit blood on the ground. "It's true. Emerald Stone is carrying my child and has promised the baby to me. Now, what do you say to that?"

Captain Hammond was a large man, but nothing compared to Liameo. There was no holding at bay the rage those words incited. He pounded Roger with his fists.

The fiend was fast and pulled a knife. At the sight of the blade, Eugenia took over the fight. It was soon ended.

"Gene, stop." Liameo had caught his breath.

Whimpering on the ground, Roger held his shredded arms close to his body.

"Damnation, Sergeant, go fetch Doctor Platt." Captain Hammond shoved Liameo in the direction of the gate.

Liameo kicked the knife to a safer distance away as he moved to obey the order. He ran, rather than take the time to saddle Allura. As luck would have it, the Doctor was home. The two of them returned with a medical kit without delay.

In the meantime, the Captain had dragged Roger into the company barracks for triage. Compassionate, even in this instance, Doctor Platt stitched the wounds on Roger's arms. He then inspected his broken teeth.

"This is assault, Captain. It's a crime. I want to see the Judge." Roger spoke through split and swollen lips.

The Captain laughed. "You'll have your chance in the morning. Now, be silent."

"What's this?" The Doctor touched a darkening stain on Roger's calf.

"It's nothing." Roger pulled his leg away. "An old wound."

"Captain, I need to see that." The Doctor's expression was serious.

"Strip his trousers." The Captain barked the order and two men obeyed.

Liameo almost vomited at the sight of the gangrene gash and spreading infection on Roger's leg. However, it was the absence of what belonged between his legs that drew away most of the men's attention.

"I need to take the whole leg." The Doctor met Roger's gaze.

"No, you can't. I won't let you." Roger pulled a blanket over his lower half.

"You should have shown this to me much sooner. I could have helped you then. You didn't tell me, because I might have suspected your guilt. Am I right?" The Doctor's voice was grave.

"Guilt? I'm the father of the heir to Danalan. It was worth it." Roger grinned, though blood dribbled down his chin when he did.

"What is this?" The Doctor looked to the Captain.

"He's a liar. Whatever he says doesn't make any difference. He has no claim, even if it were true. The Chief Judge already ruled on the matter." The Captain clenched his jaw and glared at Roger. "Let him die, Doctor, the man is scum."

The Doctor frowned. "Perhaps, it is the Lady I should speak to."

"You can't. She's gone east to fulfill her destiny or some such. But she vowed to give me the baby. You'll see. When she gets back, you can all see." Roger passed out.

"Captain, I have to take that leg, or he will die." The Doctor opened his bag and removed a knife and a bone saw.

"Do it."

SECRETED AWAY IN A dense forest near the glacier, lay a camp of rebel soldiers. Enshrouded by the dark of night, Stephan strode through the midst of the subdued people. He ran his hand through his lengthening hair and straightened the clasp of his cloak.

If Nina were here, he'd ask her to cut his hair, but that would be a mistake. The men in Frenland wore long hair. He sighed. Would he ever fit in?

He stopped in front of the command tent. The Command Counsel, comprised of Sarialla and the rebel leaders gathered inside. He planned to present his ideas to them tonight.

Worry made him hesitate because they might disagree with the tactics and abandon him. The need to try overcame his concerns, however, and he stepped into the tent. Eight faces greeted him with varying levels of confidence. Each head bowed.

"My Prince, we're at your service." Commander Helen Scion was an unprepossessing woman of sturdy build.

Sarialla had spoken of her warmly. Though not tall and quite young, she was seasoned in battle. A capable officer, she had earned her position as Commander by leading rebels from the far western provinces.

The name of the village she hailed from escaped him. Oh, right, these people were named for their place of birth. Scion.

"Thank you, Commander Helen, of Scion." He gestured to include everyone. "Thank each of you for coming. We have much to discuss and the longer we're together the greater the danger. So please, settle in and be comfortable. I'll be consulting the map often."

Without needless chatter, the group sat around a table, leaving the head open. Wind rattled the tent, and the flames danced in the lamps. Stephan took the open place and looked at each man and woman for a time.

"The plans I offer are secret and must remain so if we are to succeed. We have little in our favor. My return has not caused masses of citizens to rally to our cause. In fact, most don't know or care."

Silence prevailed in the room.

The expressions Stephan observed ranged from anger to tight concern. "There's no use being disappointed that people are too frightened or apathetic to fight. Even if they pledged loyalty in the past, I've been a long time coming.

"To be honest, sixteen is full young to rule. But I am ready and I will restore justice to this land. Your sacrifices will not have been in vain."

One corner of his mouth tipped upward. "There is an advantage to obscurity. If our enemies underestimate us, then we can use misdirection as our ally. Fear of the unknown will be our friend."

He stood to lean over the map and plunged a finger downward. "The people of the western mountains have long been silent. But their wind sweeps the plains and has great power."

He slid his finger to the center of the map. "The Sacred Mountain is not populated and can be used as a safe haven for our forces. There is a road we can travel from near the edge of the glacier where we are now to the Sacred mountain. It will allow us to remain undetected by the enemy patrols on the plains. Also, there is an abandoned city that we can use as a shelter for women, children, and the elderly. The city will serve as a perfect place for the healing of our wounded."

"The women will fight, Prince Stephan." Commander Helen's face held a stern expression with her lips pressed thin.

He relaxed into a smile as his mood lifted. "I understand the merits of women warriors, Commander. I also know that children need mothers and that a woman's health can be delicate when she's pregnant."

He crashed his brows together and addressed the group. "I will not squander one of our greatest strengths before the hellish brutality of Salicor the baby slayer. We must have a future."

"Yes. Yes." Several Commanders pounded fists on the table in agreement.

Stephan held up a hand as his determination solidified. "If we use the wind as our ally, then we can deploy our forces to win the hearts of the people by raiding enemy soldiers."

He moved a hand on the map. "It works like this. We'll start a small fire. Fed by the wind, it will threaten an encampment. The soldiers will be forced to fight fire by day, thus exhausting their strength."

He closed a fist and met each Commanders' gaze, one at a time. "Then at night, we will send in raiding parties to harass and plunder. Our forces will be fresh and will easily overrun them. Without supplies, the soldiers will resort to taking from the people and lose popularity."

Commander Grist leaned forward with a scowl on his face. "You wish to burn the plains, My Prince? Won't we be left with a wasteland? Wouldn't that cause the citizenry to hate us?"

Stephan met his gaze. "That's why we must be careful to set fires the soldiers can put out before a serious loss occurs." He stood up straight. "I've been told it's impossible to sneak past General Valerie's Valkyrie Army. The patrols are tight and the women skilled. Until we wear them down, we must use the best spies and the most skilled infiltrators to accomplish our ends. So, I'll need a list of names."

The Commanders nodded.

"What of the raiding parties, Sire? It doesn't seem like you need the most experienced forces to steal supplies. What do you plan to use us for?" Commander Brighton, a middle-aged man with unclouded eyes gestured at the group with his hands.

"You are correct, Commander Brighton. I'll answer you in due time. I think new recruits sprinkled with capable leaders could do the job in the west.

"I'd like to train them at an ancient fortress along the hidden road. Sarialla and I passed the location on our way here. It will suit our purposes." Stephan hoped they would see the wisdom in the next arm of the plan.

"Perhaps you're asking yourself how I will entice recruits to our cause. I can't, not at first." He gathered their full attention. "I intend to buy them."

The eyebrows of several Commanders shot upward to a chorus of inhalations and mutterings. Sarialla remained silent.

"What?" Commander Helen's face flushed beet-red.

Stephan met her gaze. "I plan to purchase slaves from the villages."

Helen Scion writhed in her chair but held her tongue.

Commander Gentry sat up, though he was unable to straighten his hunched spine. "I thought, My Prince, that you opposed slavery. Also, I'm curious about where you'll get the funds to purchase this slave army? Did you find hidden treasures in the mountains as well as roads and crumbling cities?"

Gentry had been silent throughout the meeting, until now. In fact, he had seemed to doze. Though grizzled, Stephan knew the other Commanders took their lead from him.

"I will entrust you with the second phase of my plan, but only if you are with me." He planted his hands on the tabletop.

One by one they bowed their heads, including Helen.

"There is no treasure in the mountains. We will get the funds another way and I'll explain that in a moment." He stood straight. "You know me better than I thought and I suppose it's because you knew my parents, at least by reputation. I do not believe in slavery. But we must do what is necessary to win the war."

Several Commanders nodded in agreement.

"My Prince?" For the first time, Sarialla sounded concerned.

"Do not fear, Counselor. I have no desire to compel anyone to fight. Innovative thinking is what I propose.

"A well-bred horse can purchase twenty children. A fine warhorse buys a dozen women or eight strong men. I plan to empty the countryside of innocents before any major battles."

A slow, fierce smile spread over Helen's features. "I know where to find the animals you need, My Prince. With the skilled forces you have in this camp alone, we could steal a thousand horses from Salicor's army."

Stephan met her gaze. "Our plans must proceed in secret because the Rebels will not be stealing the horses."

Sarialla laughed. He looked at her, but she shook her head. Perhaps, she had guessed what he planned, though he doubted she would approve of the details.

Commander Gentry lifted a hand. "Then who will acquire them for us, Sire?"

Stephan held their gaze in grim determination. "The people of the East Ice. At least that's what everyone, including our own citizens, must forever believe."

"Why all the secrecy, Sire?" Helen looked confused.

"Because we're going to have to slaughter some of the more recognizable animals. The carcasses will enrage Salicor's army to the point they disobey orders and attack the glaciers in retaliation. In this way, the East Icers will aid us in liberating this land, even if they are unwilling allies at first."

He knew Emerald needed Frenland freed in order to fulfill the Legend of the Stone. He hoped by drawing the people of the eastern mountains into a war, it would help her chances of reuniting the Modutan Empire in peace. It was a gamble.

Chapter Twenty-Five

E merald placed her palms on the rock of her troubles, a great red sandstone boulder. History stated that it had been cut from the heart of the mountain that towered above her. The memory of Grandfather Jacob's voice reciting the inscription overwhelmed her with longing for that day so long ago.

She remembered how she had hugged his side and hid her face from the curse written here. Not so today. Now, she had embraced her call to fulfill the Legend of the Stone, though she did not know how she would accomplish the task.

With a sigh, she walked away from the stone and broke camp. She had slept at the foot of the proclamation last night. Since dawn had broken, she needed to move onward in search of the entrance to the tunnel beneath the Impenetrable Mountains.

The one bright spot was the weather.

Breezes from the south created a balmy morning. She followed a track marked by the long-ago passing of wagons through the rocks and rills of the mountain. Stephan must've come this way. Just thinking this made her long to see him.

What was he doing in Frenland? Perhaps he led an army into battle. More than likely, he was only starting his preparations for war.

Her shoulders slumped. She'd failed him. He had asked for her help, and she'd gone off in search of death.

Death still appealed.

What joy did life hold when comprised only of duty, sacrifice, and suffering? Surely, the Creator had something better waiting on the other side of the veil. Rest and healing would be enough to satisfy her.

With a deep breath, she determined not to fail in her quest. The dusty terrain climbed at a sharp incline. Ignoring her thirst, she increased her pace. Always alert, she searched for any sign of a cave that could be the entrance to the passageways under the mountain.

The road faded, though worn rocks and markers remained as guides. At higher elevations, the trees thinned. Rocks and scrub brush provided shelter for the creatures of the mountain. She trudged over a rise and discovered a stream. Removing her boots, she crossed it and soothed her tortured feet.

Two days of walking had taken a toll. She set her pack on the other side, drank, and filled a waterskin. The surrounding scenery held tranquil beauty.

Tufts of grass covered the stream's edge. Round rocks highlighted by the sun's golden rays interspersed the landscape of the waterway. Sparse foliage added relief to the yellow shale of the mountain slope.

She dangled her toes in the stream and ate a piece of venison jerky. As she chewed, she made plans to catch a fish for dinner. She sighed and abandoned the idea as she looked up the track ahead. Wherever this road lead, she must go.

She dried her blistered feet and put on socks and boots. With a grunt, she lifted the pack onto her back. Much to her dismay, it felt heavier than ever. She ignored the ache of muscles and pressed forward.

Not having gone far, an unexpected sight greeted her. The reddish color of sandstone crept into view. A tall waterfall lay at the end of the crimson box canyon. Water had carved the rocks so that lush vegetation had a place to flourish on the floor.

Stories of old told of the creation of the Southern people, speaking of a place like this. The Creator had taken a soft stone and carved the people. His breath had brought them to life, and their red hair and ruddy beards were a testament of his love. The story had always pleased her.

Was this the place where life began?

Birds flocked to the paradise. She ran to explore it for artifacts or signs. The ancient road remained aloof on a wall of the canyon. Below her on the right were rabbits and waterfowl, though no large game.

The waterfall increased in magnitude as she drew closer. A spectacular pool of crystal blue waters lay at its base. What would it be like to swim in those depths?

The ledge ended. The canyon curved and the path stopped on a blank slab of sandstone. There was no way around or through. She pressed and pried and searched for an entrance but in the end, was forced to surrender.

Kicking a rock in frustration, she descended to the canyon floor. The day had passed far too quickly and soon the sun would set. So, she determined to search for the passageways on the morrow. Biting a lip, she worried she wouldn't find the way inside. But that seemed unlikely since she had a mandate from on high.

The rumble of her stomach reminded her of practical concerns. Perhaps, she would have fish for dinner after all. The pool held plenty.

She discovered a ring of rocks where a recent fire had burned. It looked like the best place to camp. So, she gathered wood and started a fire.

Stephan must have been here only weeks ago. The thought comforted her in a sad kind of way. She stared at the fire while the logs burned to coals. She didn't want to dwell on the past, but she couldn't help feeling regret that he had gone north without her.

Shaking off those thoughts, she found a suitable sapling, cut it, and whittled the end to a point. Once tempered over the fire, she was satisfied with the spear. Tossing another log on the fire, she tiptoed barefoot across the grass to the beach at the water's edge.

In the evening light, the crystal depths sparkled. She spotted what she sought. Her first and second attempts failed, but persistence soon had a nice sized fish wiggling on the end of her makeshift spear. The herbs she had picked on the trail would flavor it deliciously as it baked in the embers of the fire.

WATCHING A MAN DIE should be hard, but Liameo only felt hardened. Doctor Platt stayed with Roger in the Militia's barracks, since he was too ill to be moved. It took three days.

Upon the last breath of a man who had been a friend for many years, Liameo breathed a sigh of relief. All the men were in their bunks when it happened late one night. The rasping for air just stopped. The Doctor sat by lamplight beside the cot where Roger lay, haggard from his vigil. He checked for a pulse and then pulled the sheet over the body.

"I'll inform Captain Hammond." The Doctor stood from the creaky, straight-backed chair.

"Thank you, Doctor." Liameo got out of bed, dressed, and beckoned to another man who was still awake.

The two of them went to remove the body. Liameo grasped under the arms, and the other man held the solitary foot Roger had left. They hefted him outside and tossed him in the empty wagon in the yard. Crickets chirped in the warm, night air. A wrong had been set right.

"Sergeant, come with me." Captain Hammond stood in the doorway of his cabin and pulled on his boots. "Walk this way." He headed toward the stockade. "In the event of Roger's death, Judge Porter has ordered you to be placed under arrest on charges of wrongful death. It's a formality."

"Sir?" Liam asked.

"I know, it's not true and I'll testify of that. The Doctor will also show evidence and give his opinion that Roger died of the wound Emerald dealt him when he attacked her. You will not be punished, though, you will be discharged from the Militia." The Captain opened the door of the stockade with a key from a ring he held.

"I don't understand, sir. I did nothing wrong." The discharge mentioned could only be dishonorable. It hurt because he had maintained distinction for six years in the Militia.

"It isn't about you." The Captain ushered Liameo inside. "It's about Emerald. You need to be free from your obligation to the Militia in order to marry her. I should have found a way to let you out years ago."

He held up a hand. "You must visit her grandfather in Humetown and obtain his blessing. I know you have gone a dozen times before, but this time you will succeed. You have to."

"And if I don't?" Liameo sat on the cot inside the cell, remembering the many occasions he had bargained with the old man for Emerald's hand to no avail.

The Captain locked the door.

"I have sent for the Judge. It'll all be set within the hour. Pack up and head south as soon as you are free. You don't want to be here when we go in to remove the children from Stone Castle." The Captain rubbed his face with both hands.

"I don't understand why they can't stay until Emerald returns." It wasn't right.

"Apparently, the law requires it." The Captain shook his head. "The Governor ordered them out."

"I thought she had adopted those children." Liameo stood up and held the bars of the cell.

"No. She wasn't permitted to do that since she isn't married." The Captain paced the dirt floor. "A single man can adopt, but not a woman. Though, why she is subject to our laws is beyond me. It isn't right."

"I'll adopt them, well, some of them. How many does she have?" Liameo ran a hand through the waves of his hair.

"Too many. Don't worry about the children. Judge Porter and his wife will take them in until good homes can be found for them. He has already been making arrangements." The Captain cocked his head as if he had heard something in the yard.

"How much money will that take? I feel obligated to pay for their up-keep." The expense would likely take most of his hard-earned savings, but Emerald would want the children cared for.

"Good evening, Sergeant." Judge Porter strode into the small stockade with Doctor Platt on his heals. "I hereby rule that you are not guilty of any wrongdoing. This letter is proof of your exoneration. Hello, Captain." The Judge nodded at Captain Hammond.

The Captain pulled a sealed letter from his shirt pocket. "These are your discharge papers, Mr. Hume."

Both men handed over the documents.

Accepting this was not easy for Liameo. "May I ride ahead to the castle? I need to assess the situation and see if I can find any clues regarding Emerald's whereabouts. Moreover, I can't let the children panic or put up a fight when you come for them."

The Judge nodded. "Try not to upset them. All will be well. I give you my word."

Liameo clasped the Judge's hand in a firm grip. "Thank you, sir. Please, wait for me before you finalize any placements. I know Emerald is partial to several of the children. Therefore, I want to do what I can for them so that when she gets home, she...won't kill me."

The Captain chuckled.

"As you wish, Mr. Hume." The Judge led the way out of the stockade. "I have a letter of recommendation for you to present to Albert Hume. That is the name of her mother's father, is it not."

"Yes." Liameo and Emerald shared a single great grandparent.

"I have a letter for you, too."

"So do I."

The Judge, Captain, and Doctor handed him letters.

Overwhelmed, Liameo took the letters and stared at them. Emerald wouldn't be happy to know of these plans. Why had she left the children? More importantly, when would she return?

"It feels like we're conspiring against her." Liameo couldn't help feeling like this smacked of betrayal.

"Not so. We're acting on her behalf in order to right a terrible wrong." The Captain put his hand on Liameo's shoulder.

"She needs our protection. I only regret I didn't offer it sooner. I should have believed in her innocence." The Judge's posture slumped.

"It is her delicate condition that concerns me the most. Find her if you can and bring her home safely." The Doctor met Liameo's gaze. "Roger was a horrible man, but he told me of the signs that convinced him she is with child. I think he was not lying about that part at least. Though, I know she would never promise away her child."

"She can't be pregnant." The icy fingers of fear wrung the life's blood of courage from Liameo's heart. "It has to be lies. She would never surrender her own child. Particularly not to Roger, especially after what he did."

The Judge took ahold of Liameo's forearm. "Why did she reject your proposal?"

Liameo looked up at the dawn-stars with a great sigh. Should he tell them what he suspected? He had no proof.

"She could not accept him." Doctor Platt drew the men's attention.

"Why?" demanded the Judge.

"I examined her after the trial and discovered that the Carpenters are not the only men to have brutalized our Emerald. The Wolf Clan took more from her than we ever suspected." The Doctor shook his head.

"And you saw evidence of this?" The Judge sounded shocked.

"Faded scars. The kind of marks I've seen on corpses," the Doctor said.

"Yet, she survived." Awe pervaded the Captain's expression.

"Did you know?" The Judge faced Liameo.

"No. Though, when I confronted her behind your barn, she almost told me. I think I guessed it then. You asked me why she didn't marry me. I think it's because she can't...tolerate the thought of being touched." He remembered the panic she had exhibited when he prevented her from escaping the conversation.

"That's why she would promise to give the child to Roger. If he convinced her it was his, she'd be relieved to be rid of it. I don't think she views it like a baby at all, but something that has been forced upon her." The Captain, a father of five children, seemed to understand.

The Doctor turned away from the men, showing a hint of the trauma he had witnessed in his troubled expression as he did so.

"That child is the heir of Danalan." The Judge met Liameo's gaze. "If Emerald can't accept the little one, then whoever claims the baby will have power over the entire land. You cannot fail to obtain permission to marry her. This is more than a matter of the heart. It is a matter of state. There are things we can do..."

"What things?" Liameo felt helpless.

"Would you be willing to forsake your citizenship, take the name of Stone, and adopt enough of the children to begin to populate Danalan?" The Judge's gaze intensified.

Liameo considered far-reaching implications.

"Yes."

Chapter Twenty-Six

In the early morning sunlight, Liameo rode across Stone Bridge. The clop of Allura's shoes echoed throughout the calm. Eugenia remained alert and stayed close.

A hunch had been strengthening in his gut since Emerald's near death at the trial in Meadowgren. Digging her grave had started him thinking about burial, specifically the resting place of her grandparents. The thought wouldn't leave him.

He had to know if the bodies of Jacob and Estelle Stone offered any clues. If he found something, then he might be able to persuade Albert Hume to agree to let him marry Emerald. When the older man knew what she had gone through, then he would understand the wisdom of consenting to the union. After all, Emerald had wanted the marriage at one point. Perhaps, that would be enough.

Deep inside the granite slope of the Impenetrable Mountains lay the tombs of the Stones. An ornately carved mausoleum stood at the crown of the catacombs. This is where Emerald would one day rest...with him alongside her.

Liameo dismounted and tied Allura to a stone hitching post.

"Sit, Gene."

The dog obeyed.

He approached the white marble door with more than a little apprehension. Pushing it open, he found the remains of Jacob and Estelle Stone laid on the slab. They were little more than dried bones, though their clothes were still preserved.

The smaller of the two figures had a detached and badly broken skull. The other wore men's clothing with a bloody stain around a stab wound to the ribcage. Upon closer inspection of the breast pocket, Liameo spotted a piece of folded parchment.

It was a sealed letter from Jacob. Blood had soaked the outside of it but faded over time. Liameo popped the seal and read the epistle, though it was addressed to his father.

Jacob's humble plea that Liameo Senior return with his son so the courtship could resume moved Liameo to tears. He swiped away the moisture from his face. The mention of Emerald's wishes to sail the seas with her husband made him chuckle. Oh, how he missed that girl.

"I knew it. Thank you, sir. You too, ma'am. I will honor your wishes." Liameo bowed to the bones.

He exited the tomb and pulled the door firmly closed. He mounted his horse and headed toward the castle. Eugenia barked a friendly greeting to George as they crossed the drawbridge and went through the open gates. Andre stepped out of the stables to stand in the morning sun in the courtyard, watching.

"She isn't here, Sergeant." George's expression was troubled.

"This isn't my normal visit. The Governor of Andolin has ordered all of you removed. If I can't find her, then Judge Porter and Captain Hammond will have no choice in the matter. Where is she?" Liameo leaned forward in the saddle.

"Gone." He stammered. "Headed east with all the food she could carry. She isn't coming back anytime soon."

Liameo dismounted and handed the reins to Andre. Eugenia licked the boy's face.

"Where would we go?" Andre's lip protruded in a pout.

"That's what I'd like to discuss. George, may I have a word with all the children?" Liameo grappled with the decision to follow the Judge's recommendations, but it was the only option if he wanted to help Emerald.

"Andre, tend to the animals and then come inside." George led the way into the keep, leaving the gates open.

Once inside, Liameo removed his hat and stood by the entryway. George gathered the children around to listen.

"Is there anyone here who could help me find Emerald?" Liameo still held out hope that he might be able to track her down and bring her home.

Silence filled the room.

"She left us." Nina stood in the doorway at the top of the kitchen steps.

"She'll be back." Andre had just come in from outside.

"I think so, too." Liameo patted the boy's back. "However, there is a problem. The Governor has ordered you all to leave Danalan."

An uproar of adverse reaction took a moment to subside.

"Marta can't be ordered to leave. She was born here." Andre brushed off Liameo's hand.

He went down on one knee to look the boy in the eyes. "And who will care for her?"

Andre's lip trembled and tears threatened to fall.

Liameo stood and addressed the group. "Six years ago, Emerald agreed to marry me. If I can obtain her maternal grandfather's permission for the marriage, then I can adopt some of you."

"No." George stepped forward. "Get out."

"George, she loved me, and still would if not for what happened." He couldn't even say it, though he thought they would understand what he meant.

"She doesn't love you now." Nina wiped her wet hands on her apron and strode two steps toward him.

"Yeah, she loves Darrin." Andre scowled defiantly.

"Who is Darrin? One of you?" Liameo scowled a bit in response.

"No, he's from—" Andre was cut off by George's large hand covering his mouth.

"Emerald's business is not yours to know. Now go." George spoke softly, but the threat was clear.

Liameo surveyed the faces of the children, noting their consensus. His hand shook as he took Jacob Stone's letter from the knapsack slung across his chest that hung at his side. He read the letter out loud.

No one spoke until Nina strode forward to take the note from his hand. She read it in silence. Shaking her head, she handed it to George and walked back to the steps and down to the kitchen.

George read the letter and nodded. "It's true."

"But..." Andre cried openly now.

WOMAN OF THE STONE

It wrenched the heart to see him like that. Liameo went down on one knee again and drew him into an embrace. "It's going to be all right. She's coming back, maybe not soon, but she will return."

Andre sobered up a bit. "How do you know?"

Liameo smiled. "Because I know her, better than you think I do. She loves you and when she loves it's all the way."

Andre took a deep breath and let it out. "What do I need to do?"

Liameo put his hands on the boy's shoulders. "Be patient for a few more days. Don't resist the Militia when they come for you and wait patiently at Judge Porter's home. I will take this letter to Emerald's grandfather and obtain his consent for the marriage. Judge Porter will then be able to declare Emerald and me married. I'll take the name of Stone and renounce my Andolin citizenship. Then I can adopt you. Would you be all right with that?"

He nodded.

"Then it's settled. I can adopt all of you if you like, or other arrangements can be made. There are several tradesmen who would take on an apprentice for the right price. That would be good for some of you boys to think about. The blacksmith is a friend of mine. He would be good to work with. It's a valuable skill." Liameo hoped to drum up some enthusiasm.

"Rick is good with metal." Timothy smiled.

"I'm good at carving." Gael chimed in.

Liameo stood. "See? Things are going to work out."

George shook his head and frowned. "Not for me. I turned eighteen yesterday."

A young woman on the other side of the room gasped.

Liameo walked over to her and took her hand. "Tell me your name."

"Tarah." A deep sadness entered her gaze. "George and I were going to be married."

"And why can't that happen now?" Liameo saw the dilemma, but he had a solution.

"We'll have nothing. I have no skills, no money, nowhere to take us." George hung his head, hands limp at his sides.

"Tarah, if I adopt you and you become a Stone, then you can marry George." Liameo let his offer sink in.

She ducked her chin and nodded without meeting anyone's gaze.

"Everyone, think these things over. I'll be back within a week." Liameo departed the keep, retrieved his animals, and headed south toward Hume-town.

Chapter Twenty-Seven

Days passed as Emerald searched within the canyon for the entrance to the mountain passage. In the heat of the day, she sweated while climbing the wall near the falls. She hoped a different point of view would yield results.

Mist coated everything and made rainbows in the sunlight. She twisted to look at them, relied too much on her weakened left arm, and lost her grip. Cartwheeling, she hit the water.

The impact stunned her. Caught in the turbulence of the waterfall, she tumbled in the torrent of bubbles until she hit the bottom. Clasping a handful of sand, she gained her bearings and launched away from the falls to emerge gasping for air.

"Looking at rainbows." Disgusted with herself, she stomped out of the water and cast off her sodden boots and socks on the hot sand.

Out of habit, she reached for the weapons on her belt and discovered the dagger missing. A streak of panic chilled her spine. She must have lost it in the pool.

With teeth bared, she undid the buckle and laid the belt on a rock along with her boots, and knives so they would not be ruined. Fortunately, she'd left her sword safely at camp. Even though there had been no indications of a single living soul in these mountains, she didn't feel comfortable stripping her clothes to let them dry.

The need to find the weapon caused her to wade into the pool. She dove in search of the dagger. It wasn't just any weapon. It was the one she always carried into battle; the same one her attacker had used on that terrible day so many years ago.

She surfaced for breath and submerged again. Repeatedly, she searched for the blade to no avail. An unwelcome stillness crept over her as she tread water in the pool.

Apprehension deepened as she swam ashore, and it was more than regret over losing a fine weapon. The etching on the blade was unique. A clue.

Who had the previous owner been? She had believed the dagger would one-day lead to the answer. Now, she would never know because she couldn't understand the marks carved in her flesh.

She shivered in the sunlight, shed her wet clothes, and sat in the soft grass by the water's edge. With hands trembling, she wrung her hair and undid the braid. She lay down but could not afford to fall asleep, because her skin was too fair to remain exposed for long without burning. Inconsolable, she rested until she had mastered her fears.

NESTLED IN A THICKET of bushy young trees, Darrin watched Emerald climb by the falls. He had never seen her this curious. What was she doing?

If she was looking for the entrance to the passageways, then she was going about it all wrong. Near the mouth of the box canyon, he had spotted a trail marker left by the soldiers escorting Prince Stephan. He had followed it to the mouth of a tunnel under the mountain.

The entrance was concealed by an optical illusion and the natural distraction of this paradise. He should have told her the instant he had found it. In fact, he should tell her now. He shook his head as he folded his arms across his chest and kept watching her climb.

As quick as anything, Emerald fell. She hit the water with a clap that caused him to wince. Leaping to his feet, he hesitated long enough to realize she wasn't coming up for air.

Stripping his belt and boots, he ran and dove into the pool. Where was she? He could see nothing but bubbles until a flash of silver captured his attention.

He swam to the bottom. From his new vantage point, he saw Emerald push off in the other direction. She swam clear of the turbulence without noticing him.

What had caught his eye? Lungs burning, he spotted metal and grabbed it. He needed to avoid detection yet wanted a better look. A gap behind the falls provided the solution, and he swam there. Concealed by the waterfall, he climbed on a narrow ledge and tucked his legs out of the water.

Emerald dove in again. Why was this weapon important to her? It was the same one she always wore.

He looked, squinting until dread clawed at his stomach. The blade had belonged to his brother Allan. How had Emerald gotten his brother's most prized dagger?

She'd killed him.

Darrin's heart quailed. Why hadn't he ever found Allan's body? His hands trembled as he tossed the weapon along the ledge. With arms wrapped around his knees, he stared at the scene etched on the blade. A wolf devoured a hare as a crow watched with its beak open wide.

As a boy, he had admired his brother's work. Now he saw it in a different light. The art depicted violence in nature, seeming to excuse it as the natural order.

The strong destroyed the weak. That was why Allan had joined the traitors who opposed the Matriarchs. It was the reason he had killed their father.

Allan had devoured Emerald's soul.

Darrin shut his eyes. His brother must have murdered their father as a diversion, knowing that Darrin would escort the body home. It left Emerald vulnerable. The betrayal was overwhelming. Darrin rubbed his face with his hands.

Emerald had lied.

He grabbed the cursed blade and dove toward shore. No one else was in the pool, and he didn't spot her right away. She would want her trophy returned.

She had defeated his brother and saved Stephan's life. Perhaps the price had been high, but she had her memento. He wouldn't keep it from her.

Sunlight glared on the surface of the pool as he stalked through the shallows. He wiped his face and wrung out his shirt before he noticed her. Despite the cold water, his body responded to her nudity. She lay on the grass, hair free and fiery in contrast to the creamy whiteness of her skin.

Perhaps she slept because she didn't see him. Fixated on the way the fine hairs of her body captured the rays of the sun, he crossed the sand. The curve of her breasts drew him in and the curve of her hips with the dark red hair between drove him mad.

Filled with desire, he moved closer. The dagger's blade flashed in the sun, blinding him for an instant. What was he doing?

He fled.

The thoughts he'd entertained shamed him and his breath came in shallow gasps. Until now, he had never looked at her as an object to satisfy his desires. It sickened him to have fallen so easily into that trap.

What had he been thinking? He hid his face in his hands. The impulses he'd indulged were callous and offensive. He rejected them, but for an instant, he had felt that way about her.

He loved Emerald. Yes, he wanted her, but he needed her to want him back. He didn't love her title, even if she would one day be a queen.

He admired the woman who gave so much of herself to bless others. Her thoughts and feelings mattered. So, what could have caused him to look at her the way he had a moment ago?

Blame for what Allan had done to their father, misplaced as it was, explained everything. Impotent fury tortured his soul, and he punched the tree in front of him. Blood ran from the split knuckles. However, the pain could not distract from the depth of his anguish.

It wasn't her fault.

She had survived what must have been a brutal attack. How she had accomplished that was beyond his comprehension because he knew she had been brutalized. Defeated.

Every night he had slept in Stone Castle, he had witnessed her relive the terror of Allan's assault. There was no deception. Was there?

Lust left him. He studied her in search of understanding. Instead of power, he schooled his desires to that of empathy. Even from this distance, he could see tears streaming from her eyes. Despite the warmth of the day and the brightness of the sun, she had now curled in a ball, shivering.

The blade in his hand was no trophy. It was hope. The last dignified opportunity she had to find out why she had been hurt and who had done it.

She had kept the truth from him. Blood drained from his face. He had seen a string of bodies left in the wake of the Renegades and what they had done to the women.

What if Emerald couldn't show him the true markings his brother had left in her flesh? Modesty would have prevented her from revealing them because of where Allan had placed them. The intimacy of the location was why Darrin would never have noticed the scars.

He collapsed in the shade of the thicket. He hadn't meant to rob her of hope. Regret made him tremble as he stared at the blade, though he could not bring himself to tell her the truth.

STEPHAN LED THE MAIN body of rebel subjects in a stealthy exodus toward the Sacred Mountain. Five Commanders stayed behind with the most skilled riders divided between them. Their secret orders, when carried out, would doubtless incense the enemy.

He glanced behind, in search of Commander Helen of Scion. She hadn't approved of the slaughter of horses as a terror tactic. Regretfully, the most celebrated animals were far too recognizable to sell without someone guessing their origins. That marked them for death. Weeping, she had told him straight out that she could not obey this order.

For some reason, he had admired her for the emotions. He'd asked if she would keep the secret, and she'd vowed she would die before divulging the plan. He'd accepted her word and let the matter drop.

Helen caught him looking at her. "My Prince?" She guided her battle-worn horse alongside him and bowed her head.

He hadn't intended to speak to her yet.

The rocky trail they followed led along the edge of the glaciers and was often treacherous. They traveled single file to disguise their numbers. Overcast, he hoped the rain would obliterate the tracks.

"I appreciated your honesty in the meeting." He needed her to understand his reasoning.

She glanced ahead and behind them but no one was close. "You don't know how relieved I am, Sire." She bowed her head.

Her obeisance darkened his mood. It put a wedge between them. That was counterproductive since he desired to make a friend of her.

"I suppose my position as an absolute monarch will always intimidate people. It is admirable that you haven't allowed it to compromise your principles. Thank you for that." He nodded at her.

She nodded in return, though she kept her eyes on the trail ahead of them.

"I plan to institute a body of elected officials to help govern the people," he said. "It will check the power of the monarchy. I hope you run for election as soon as the kingdom is stable enough. Half the seats will be reserved for women."

Agape, she bowed her head. "As you wish, My Prince."

"We must teach the citizens of this land, that we're not only fighting against a cruel dictator but we are fighting for freedom. Salicor is evil. He needs to be stopped, but we can't end up like him or we have failed. My plans seem harsh to you, but they save human lives."

Helen's brows knit. "Many of our forces fight for vengeance, Sire, including me. But I'll do my best to see the wisdom of standing up for a cause that is right and not simply opposing all that is wrong. I can help others do the same."

"I appreciate your support, Commander." He thought of Emerald. "This idealistic part of the plan could heal the hearts of the people. Please, do not keep it a secret."

Helen's expression softened. "I'll do my best."

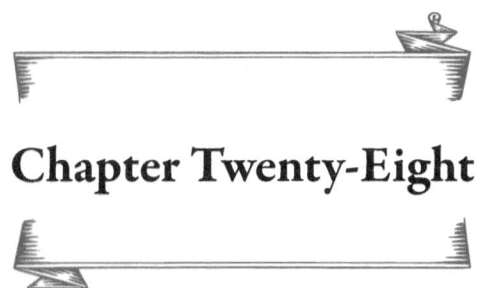

Chapter Twenty-Eight

Liameo arrived in Humetown during the mid-morning bustle. The weather was particularly fine in the southern provinces. Flowers and trees were in bloom.

Several passersby tipped their hats or curtsied in greeting. Over the course of a lifetime, he had made many friends here. After all, this was Humetown and he was a Hume.

His family lived in Ando Bay. They were often out to sea on one or the other of a fleet of merchant ships his father owned. But at least once a year, they came to Humetown. It was usually for the plum festival at the end of summer.

Albert Hume's grand house sat on the south of town amidst a vast orchard of plum trees. He worked just as hard as any hired hand. Liameo had always admired that about his great uncle. He was rich but he never allowed it to make him lazy.

Plum blossoms swirled in the air as Liameo rode along the lane to the house. Allura snorted and shook her head. Eugenia bounded into the orchard grass after some creature, though she soon returned with nothing.

That was a relief. What would he have done with it? Perhaps, he could have presented the kill to the cook at Albert's house. Liameo sighed.

Worry caused his brow to crease. Other than Jacob Stone's letter, he had precious little to offer Albert Hume. Especially when it came to a bride-price.

Normally, a dowry was required of the bride's family. But in this instance, with Emerald's wealth of lands, it was expected that the prospective bridegroom pays the family of the bride for her hand in marriage. So, instead of marriage being a boon, it was a burden on him.

Opportunistic families in Andolin had long exacted such bride-prices of the Stone Clan. Of course, none had ever totaled the amount that Albert had the right to ask for Emerald's hand. Reportedly, incredible fortunes had been offered. Albert had refused them all, thus far. It was truly incomprehensible.

Liameo rode into the courtyard of the house. The stable boy ran forth to take Allura and Eugenia into the cool structure for fresh water. The animals knew the boy.

"Thank you, Gib," Liameo said.

Gib bowed and continued about the business.

Liameo straightened his jacket and strode to the front door. He used the brass knocker to summon the house worker. A little old woman opened the door in a gray dress and white apron.

"Hello, Mrs. Cook, may I see my great uncle today?" Liameo removed his tricorn hat.

Mrs. Cook frowned. "That depends on how long you're willing to wait. I just sent the midday meal to the far end of the orchard. We don't expect him home until he's tuckered himself out." She pulled the door wider and stepped aside. "Wait in the library, please."

"Thank you, Mrs. Cook." Liameo knew the way and the routine.

He pulled a book from a shelf and found a comfortable spot on a window seat. It was an epic sailing tale. He had begun reading it last autumn and not had the opportunity to finish.

As the evening drew near, the door opened. It was only Mrs. Cook. Out of respect, Liameo stood.

"Mr. Cook has prepared a meal, young man. Come to the kitchen and sit with us to supper." She held open the door expectantly.

Liameo placed the book in its proper place on the shelf and followed her to the kitchen. It was an honor to sup with this couple who had served the household since they were children. The lamp in the kitchen combined with the light and warmth of the fireplace made the room hot, though welcoming.

"Good day, sir. Thank you for inviting me to dinner. It smells delicious." Liameo shook the old fellow's hand.

"It's good to have you come, Liameo. I had hoped you would still make the journey, despite the news we received of late regarding young Emerald." The man's voice quavered with emotion. "I knew you would be the one who came for the right reasons. I knew you wouldn't allow the hurtful things they did to her scare you away." Tears spilled over his wrinkled cheeks and into his long beard.

"Hush now, husband, we don't know why he's come." Mrs. Cook served fried fish and overboiled greens onto the plates. Neither one of them had many teeth left with which to chew.

Liameo's stomach turned to realize how widespread the news of Emerald's rape had traveled. His shame over it had not lessened. Though, he knew she held no blame, he had a hard time letting the issue drop. Probably because he felt partly responsible.

"I still want to marry her." He sat at the short table all knees and elbows since he was so much larger than these little old people.

Mrs. Cook offered thanks to the Creator for the meal, and the trio ate in silence.

Mr. Cook cleared away the dishes. He brought over a basket of rolls and a crock of honey butter. "She likes this type of food, I hear. Honey. Her father was a beekeeper."

Mrs. Cook eyed Liameo. "Ethan Stone camped in the orchard for months before Mr. Albert consented to allow Ellora to marry him."

"If that's what it takes, then I'll do the same." Liameo didn't like the look of skepticism in the woman's eyes. She seemed angry.

"It won't do you any good." Mr. Cook buttered a roll. His hands shook with old age as he lifted it to take a bite.

"Why is that, sir?" Liameo swallowed his disappointment.

"Mr. Albert will never agree to the marriage until he sees his granddaughter and she says what she wants." Mrs. Cook scowled at Liameo.

"She did love me...once." He didn't have the words to explain what had happened.

"Then she'll love you again." Mr. Cook offered a grin with very few teeth in it. "She isn't fickle, I think. It's just that life's been hard. She needs to find her way."

Liameo nodded in agreement. "I'm sure you're right. Though, it may be more pressing than that." He stopped short of expressing his deepest concern.

"A child?" Mrs. Cook whispered.

"What did you say, wife?" Mr. Cook cupped his ear.

"Doctor Platt said it's too early to be sure. However, one of Emerald's attackers swore she had promised him a child. I know the man was a liar." The muscles of Liameo's back stretched the still sensitive scars tight as he balled his fists in anger.

"I hope you made him pay for those words." Mrs. Cook trembled with rage as she took to her feet.

"I did."

"He's dead then?" Mr. Cook looked hopeful.

"Yes. Though I didn't kill him. I just ruffed him up a bit. He had concealed a wound Emerald had dealt him when he attacked her. The leg had festered with infection. He died hard." Sharing the grim news darkened Liameo's mood.

"Serves him right." Mrs. Cook paced the floor with shuffling steps. "Ellora's girl deserves better than any of this."

"Ellora's girl deserves a good man like this boy, wife." Mr. Cook patted Liameo's hand. "Though none will ever be good enough to please Mrs. Cook." He chuckled.

She harrumphed.

"What would it take to convince you, Mrs. Cook?" It was wise to feel out the situation. These people may have an influence over Albert.

"If you don't know, then I'm not going to tell you." She walked out of the kitchen.

"Don't mind her. She just wants things to be how they should have been. They're never going to be that way." Mr. Cooks eyes dimmed of luster.

The old man looked away. "Take a roll or two, in case you get hungry while you wait. I'll have Mrs. Cook bring you a blanket. We'll make sure our grandson light's the fire."

Liameo thanked the man for the meal and returned to the library. Someone had already lit the fire and the lamp. Outside the window, it was pitch black.

The entire conversation with the Cooks had been humiliating. He had held back the letter written by Jacob Stone. It was clear that it wouldn't have made a bit of difference.

Angry, he paced the floor.

The door swung open and there was Albert Hume. Just as tall as Liameo, he filled the doorway with his wizened, older man, toughness. He held Liameo's gaze for a moment as if sizing him up.

"What was your part in it?" Albert wasted no time in getting to the heart of the issue.

What was the answer to that? "I think I caused it when I confronted her about the oath of marriage that she made to me six years ago."

"She actually did promise to marry you?" Albert's hostile posture eased into one akin to despair.

"She couldn't keep the oath, sir." Sadness to have to be the bearer of bad news weighed on Liameo.

"Couldn't? Why?" Albert narrowed his searching gaze.

"She wasn't pure, or, well, I don't know if that's the right way to say it. Anyway, she had been hurt before." Liameo couldn't look the man in the eyes.

"Hurt how? Raped? When?"

Liameo rubbed his face and walked to the window. "I think it happened on the day Jacob and Estelle Stone were murdered. Doctor Platt examined her after the trial in Meadowgren. He said there was evidence of a brutal..."

"Say the word." Albert's voice was low, dangerous.

Liameo faced him, ready for an attack. "She was ravaged. Not just raped, but brutalized mind, body, and spirit. She can't abide the touch of a man."

"So, she refused to keep her oath? Can anyone corroborate this accusation?" Albert was the one to pace the room now.

"Yes." Liameo unbuttoned the pocket of his jacket and removed the stack of letters.

"Breaking an oath is a serious legal breach, not to mention a betrayal of trust. I had thought better of her. I knew her to be an honorable woman."

Albert accepted the letters and sat down at the table to read them by the light of the lamp.

Liameo watched the expression on the man's face change as he read each one. Albert's hands trembled at the blood-soaked missive from Jacob Stone. Shaking his head, he reached into a pocket for a handkerchief and covered his face weeping.

"She was so innocent." Albert wiped his nose. "And now the Cooks tell me she has promised her unborn child to the very man who hurt her. How could she do such a thing? She knows her child will rule Danalan one day."

"It can't be true." Liameo walked toward the fireplace. "It makes no sense."

Albert groaned. "Yes...yes it does."

Liameo bristled with hostility as he faced the man. "She wouldn't do it. The girl I knew would never be so foolish. She's smart, sir. This kind of blunder is so incredibly reckless as to be insane."

Albert nodded as if appraising the new information. "This kind of hurt is a kind of madness. She believes the lies these wicked men have told her. They've convinced her that she is unworthy, unfit, unlovable to be sure, and perhaps even inhuman. You say she's smart, but you don't understand how words can worm into an impressionable mind and rot a soul from within."

Liameo wasn't a violent man, but he wanted to kill Roger all over again. More than that, he wanted to murder the man Emerald had killed six years ago. He wanted to crush these men before they could take away the girl he had loved.

Death was too good for them. A dark desire to hurt them for what they had done twisted his lip. He gripped his fists so hard the knuckles popped.

"Would you be the child's father?" Albert stood beside the table; the letters spread out before him.

"There is no child." A vicious pain ripped the words from Liameo's throat.

Albert's head tilted forward in a defeated posture. He braced himself on the edge of the table. His eyes were closed.

"Then who will inherit the kingdom? The next man who takes what she cannot give? Or shall we leave it to you to force the issue and put her with child?" Albert met Liameo's gaze.

The words crushed him. "It will not be like that. She has a passel of orphans that she cares for. One of them was even born on Danalan soil. Her name's Marta and she's only a year or two old, but she looks like she could be Emerald's natural daughter.

"I know you read Judge Porter's letter. So, you understand that the law is on my side. I plan to adopt some of the children. But I need your consent for the marriage before I do that."

Albert shook his head. "Emerald isn't even there. How can that be legal?" He held out a hand. "I know it is legal, but it isn't right. It's not justice." The older man's eyes beseeched Liameo. "How can I do this thing when I know how much it will hurt her?"

"I won't hurt her." Liameo closed the distance between them to stand opposite the older man across the table. "I'll protect her."

Albert held his gaze, taking in a deep breath.

"Why?"

Surprised by the question, Liameo didn't have an answer.

"You want her land?" Albert's tone held accusation.

"I will work it with her. But that's not what I was thinking of. She needs me, and I gave her my word a long time ago that I would be her husband. My word is unbreakable."

Determination filled Liameo with a sense of strength. It was the same feeling that had carried him patiently through the past six years. He relied on it to sustain him come what may.

"Horse manure." The old man poked a finger dead center in Liameo's chest. "I think you're probably like your father, and the first thing you'll do is take over.

"I read Jacob Stone's letter. Emerald was smitten. Lovestruck. It seems clear to me that you'll bend that little girl to your will just like you did all those years ago.

"She would have agreed to anything in order to be your wife and you would have made a selfish king. You would have destroyed her. You did destroy her.

"She was willing to abdicate her place as a ruler. Why? Because she wanted to sail the seas with you.

"She didn't want that because she loves the sea. She's never seen it. She did it because that's what you wanted. So, what makes you think you've changed so much?"

Liameo held his breath, stunned by the words Albert had spoken. Was it true? Certainly, he had never intended for it to happen that way.

It was possible that his father had desired to sidetrack Emerald's divine purpose as Woman of the Stone. He had political aspirations in that direction. Liam sighed.

The plan had almost worked, too. If she had become Mrs. Liameo Hume the third, then she would have given up everything. That realization staggered him with its implications.

"So, you think the Creator punished her because of me?" Anger overwhelmed the remorse he had felt a moment ago. "What kind of God could be so cruel?"

Albert shook his head and braced his hands on the table again. "The Creator doesn't punish people. People punish people. Life isn't fair, but it has a purpose."

"What might that be?" Liameo's anger caused him to be cynical.

"Choice and accountability. Without either one, there's no purpose. That's why it's so wrong to force Emerald to marry you against her will." Albert leveled his gaze on Liameo.

"Then you are the one responsible for destroying her. I at least would try to restore her dignity, her family, her...life. She is the Woman of the Stone. But she can't be that to anyone without the things I have the power to return to her. Believe me when I say that I love her because I always have." Liameo's heart swelled with the need to make this right, both for Emerald and for himself.

"Then you admit you were wrong?" Albert grabbed up Jacob's letter. "Do you give me your word that you will marry her for the proper reasons and never allow anyone to abuse her again?"

Liameo nodded. "You have my word."

"Then so be it."

Albert walked to the corner of the room and sat at a writing table. He wetted a quill in a bottle of ink and penned a letter. Sanding the parchment to dry the ink, he then folded it.

He carried the letter to the table. From the heat rising from the lamp, he melted a wax stick. He dolloped the red wax on the edge of the paper to seal it and pressed his signet ring into it.

"Take this letter to Judge Porter." He laid it on the table without looking at Liameo. "I'm going to bed and I suggest you not be anywhere near here when I awake."

Liameo picked up the letter and departed.

Chapter Twenty-Nine

E merald abandoned the paradise of the sandstone box canyon and climbed the mountainside. The difficult terrain invigorated her limbs. She admired the rocky spires and reveled in the aches of her straining muscles, pushing the limits of her endurance.

Scrapped and bloodied from the climb, she pressed forward and upward. The throbbing of cuts and bruises increased her determination to fight her way above the world that stretched below. Inspired by the evidence of the Creator's hand in each crevice of the rock and every breathtaking vista, she desired to touch and see it all.

As a reward for the pain and weariness, her heart filled with the joys of the mountain. It had become sacred to her. With the occasional rock that dislodged and tumbled away, so did her cares.

Light and sound became crisp and clear. What would it be like to sleep on this mountain? How bright would the stars be tonight?

The sun lowered on her left in a glorious sunset. Without warning, the cry of a hawk rang out above her head. With an iron grip on the rocks, she snapped her gaze to see the creature. Gliding on the air, it soared higher.

Peace filled her with a sense of belonging. This mountain felt like home. She hastened her ascent.

LIAMEO RODE ALL NIGHT and only stopped along the journey to Meadowgren when the animals needed rest. Driven to see Judge Porter and square away the business at hand, he pressed Allura and Eugene to their limits. He'd already lost so much time these past years, and he could not wait to achieve his...obsession.

It was an obsession. He hadn't ever thought about it that way. But without a doubt, the desire to marry Emerald had consumed him. Now that it was about to take place, he knew he needed to adapt. Grow.

After all, he would soon be a father. He smiled as he rode into the yard of Judge Porter's house. It was mid-afternoon and Andre came out from the Judge's stables for Allura and Eugenia.

"Thank you, young man." Liameo ruffled Andre's hair. "Let me help you with the animals so you don't miss any part of what I have to say."

Andre grinned. "Then you got permission?"

Liameo winked. "Yes."

Andre whooped. However, his enthusiasm quickly drained away. A look of concern clouded his expression.

"I wasn't lying when I told you she loves Darrin." The boy hurried to water the animals.

Liameo unbuckled Allura's saddle and hefted it from her back. "You need to tell me about this man."

Andre handed him a curry comb. "Will it make you mad?"

"No." Liameo accepted the comb and set to work brushing Allura.

"Why?" Andre put a scoop of oats for the horse in a feed bucket on the wall.

Allura responded with enthusiasm.

"I suppose it's because I don't believe she would ever marry anyone of her own free will." Liameo kept brushing.

Andre chuckled. "Well, you have that right. The instant she realized he loved her, she almost killed him." The boy related the whole of the events.

The story broke Liameo's heart. Emerald had fallen in love, real love, with a man from the Mountain Realm. She'd responded to the feeling just as expected. That made it all the more tragic.

"Walk with me inside." Liameo led the boy into the house.

EACH DAY, EMERALD EXPLORED more territory. Certain the mountain people lived here, it seemed impossible that she could not find them. However, there was no trace of a populace.

Soon, she would reach the summit and that worried her. Perhaps, there would be a dromedary path to traverse the spine of the mountains. Any sign of civilization would be welcome.

The supplies in her pack had dwindled quickly. There wasn't much she recognized as food in the vast reaches of this stark and wild environment. Without her bow, she could only hunt using snares and there was little time for that.

What did these people eat? She began to wonder if they existed at all. She'd broken most of her nails while climbing and chewed the rest with worrying. What did the Creator expect her to do?

Strange evergreen trees with dusty blue fruit sprang up sporadically. They nestled in the crags of granite, sinking roots into the crevices with firm fingers. This place was full of newness, yet older than any history she had ever learned. The thought comforted her as she pressed onward.

Eventually, she found a level area to rest and make camp. Though difficult to find wood, a fire felt nice during the chill of the evening. She drank from her water skin as she surveyed the rocks and trees in wonder.

This place brought her hope for the future. It was as if the Creator had put together a mountain for no other purpose than for her to enjoy. If so, then he had taken more care when forming her than she had previously suspected.

Warmth swelled in her chest.

What did he want her to become? A better version of herself, of course. He had plans for her.

Surely, he would be pleased when she had accomplished the task set before her. Could she be happy then? In this sacred place, she trusted the Creator's wisdom. He was as close as the rocks. The fading sun was his smile and the wind his sigh.

STEPHAN STOOD ON THE crumbling battlement of the mountain fortress as a chilling gale assaulted him with sleet. The stronghold was being repaired in preparation for defense. However unlikely an attack might seem; it was just good tactics to be ready.

The facilities housed and trained both warriors and war horses. At present, he had few of either but he hoped that would change soon. Everything depended on his plans working.

He pulled his gray cloak closer around him. Having already dispatched spies into the grasslands, an occasional fire had been reported on the plains. He would lead his first raiding party tonight and he prayed to the Creator for success.

His forces struggled with hunger in order to send their meager supplies with Sarialla and Helen. The two women oversaw the settling in of the mothers, children, and elderly. Concealed in a hidden city higher up the valley, they would be safe on the side of the Sacred Mountain.

Not a single horse had emerged from the east, despite the passing of several days. He found it increasingly difficult to resist his doubts. He feared failure.

Perhaps, Helen had been right. The Frenland people loved their horses. What if other Commanders felt the same way as she did, but had chosen not to say anything?

What if they had abandoned the cause? Time would tell. His empty belly provided no comfort.

EMERALD'S CAMPFIRE burned to embers. She lay looking at the stars shine in the ebony sky. The crisp air did nothing to distort the beauty of the heavens, and not a single cloud reached these heights tonight.

A streak of light caught her eye. A star fell southward. She wondered where it might have landed, thinking of Liameo somewhere down there. She hoped he was safe? Would he one day go home to the sea?

More stars slid across the heavens.

"It's raining fire."

Chapter Thirty

Liameo had no idea what he was stepping into when he entered negotiations with the orphans of Stone Castle. He had presented the letter from Albert Hume to Judge Porter who immediately dispatched a written record of the marriage by courier to the Governor as well as to the Hall of Records in Andoshi. That's when the work began.

"Nina, please, you can't stay angry with Emerald forever. She loves you." Liameo had followed the upset twelve-year-old girl into the woods near the Judge's house.

Nina shook her head. "If she did, then she would not have abandoned me to die."

Liameo couldn't help but chuckle. "I won't let you die."

Nina faced him. "How can you still want to help her after everything she's done?"

Liameo's mood sobered. "What has she done?"

"She tried to kill herself after Darrin proposed marriage and now, she has left us. I don't think she's coming back. She's going to die and then what will everything you are trying to do matter?" Nina's body couldn't hold still for waving her arms and pacing through the trees.

"Tell me everything." He was beginning to realize that Emerald had kept many secrets.

Nina talked for hours, telling tale after woeful tale of hardship and heartbreak. When she had done speaking, the two of them had walked the entire perimeter of the property of the Judge. In the yard of the Porters' home, they stopped to enjoy the last rays of the sun.

"I'm sorry for everything you've been through, Nina. It is possible that Emerald will not return. The dangers of her quest are formidable, but that does not affect you and me. Will you be my daughter?" Liameo did not extend the offer lightly. Nina was special and he would be proud to be her father.

The girl's expression turned to one of deep thought. "Rick will apprentice with the blacksmith in Meadowgren. The traveling peddler who buys all of Emerald's furs has agreed to adopt Gael because of his carving skills. The Miller children are to foster with the Carpenters and Ryan is to apprentice there. What will be my future?"

Liameo hadn't really considered that. "What would you like to do?"

She glanced his way. "Mrs. Porter says there is a couple with a dairy farm near here who have agreed to foster two or three girls. They have cows that need milking and sons who will grow up to need wives. But I don't want to do that. I want..." She shook her head and faced away from him.

"What would you like to do, if you could?" The hesitancy to answer intrigued him.

Nina faced him with color in her cheeks and determination in her eyes. "I want to plan cities in Danalan. I've read about it in the library at Stone Castle. I've even drawn some plans.

"Stephan took them with him when he went north. He thought my ideas were good. I know I could do it with a little more schooling. But...that all depends on Emerald coming back home. Doesn't it?"

Liameo frowned. "Judge Porter petitioned for us to return to Danalan without Emerald. Though the request is not likely to be granted by the Governor. So, yes. If Emerald never returns, then you will not be able to have that wish. What else might suit you?" The girl was fascinating.

"If I were a boy, then I could study just about anything. A horse breeder has requested a couple of boys. Timothy is excited to go but Andre refuses." Nina's shoulders slumped and she shook her head slowly. "There's really nothing else I'd like to do. Em has ruined my life."

Liameo's heart ached to explain to the girl that he felt exactly the same and was equally wrong. "I wanted to be a ship's captain and sail across the sea. Emerald was willing to be my wife and see the world with me. I wanted to show her the Splendor Islands, where my grandmother was born. It's so beautiful there..."

Nina looked up at him. "What will you do?"

"Well, I'm not part of the Militia anymore. My father disowned me after I joined. So, the life I had planned is not an option.

"I had hoped to farm Danalan at Emerald's side. Since I have no lands of my own, farming won't work." Liameo sighed. "I guess I'll have to talk to Judge Porter. I need an income so I can support any children who will allow me to adopt them. It sounds like everyone has other plans, though."

Nina shrugged. "Everyone has a place to go except Tarah and George, Andre, me, and Marta, and of course the three little boys, Benny, Sam, and Leland. I know Tarah is eager to accept your offer so she can marry George."

Liameo nodded. "Then let's speak to George and Tarah."

Nina's expression was obscured by the darkness. "I...want to be the first one you adopt."

Moved, Liameo hugged the girl. "I'd be honored."

STEPHAN SWEATED THROUGH sword practice in the yard of the ancient fortress. He circled his opponent but as he did so, detected a strange vibration through the soles of his boots. Everyone stopped in mid-action.

"Horses." The lookout shouted down from the newly constructed wooden tower.

Stephan sheathed his sword and ran up the battlement to see a mob of horses thundering his way. Strange riders stayed back as the horses charged through the open gates. The leather-clad riders were bald with their skin painted white and black. They looked inhuman. The trainees clutched their weapons.

"Corral the horses," Stephan shouted the orders to the recruits, his enthusiasm unrestrained.

After a moment's hesitation, they obeyed.

With a bow, he waved his thanks to the men impersonating East Icers. Only he, the two Commanders with him, and Sarialla knew the men were not what they seemed. The painted men picked up the raided supplies Stephan had placed outside the fortress in a covered wagon. Their life was not one of ease. They did not take the wagon itself, only the food.

His spies had reported that Salicor's Captains were engaging with the inhabitants of the glacier with increasing frequency. Isolated groups of Salicor's men were falling into disarray. They were scattered by the certainty of death if their Captains persisted in the folly of war with the East Ice.

Stephan's ruse was working.

The sale of these horses would fill the fortress with freed slaves. He hoped some of them would be eager to fight for their continued freedom. Trading all the horses they could spare; the hidden city had already half-filled with children.

Stephan visited them often. It humbled him to see their uncertainty in the face of liberty. They didn't know what freedom meant or how to act. He hoped they would soon figure out how to play as children should, without fear of the whims of a selfish or cruel master.

He planned to visit the hidden city again soon. Playing with the children relaxed him. It helped keep him focused on the important things. Every time he looked at one of the little children of this land, he thought of the orphans of Stone Castle. He longed to see his brothers and sisters but it comforted him they lived in a free land.

Glancing at the horses now filling the courtyard, he counted fifty and three. He wasn't much of a judge of horseflesh, but he could tell these were fine beasts. He smiled as he patted one of the beautiful creatures on the flank.

"It seems the East Icers have brought another gift. What do you say, Commander Brighton, will these horses fetch a good price?" he asked.

Commander Brighton smiled. "They will bring a high price. The East Icers are indeed generous, Sire." He busied himself checking hooves. "These are the finest horses I've seen in a long while."

Everyone standing within hearing distance of the conversation seemed in awe. They marveled at the latest tribute the East Icers had paid to the Prince. In truth, these were fine horses.

Some of the young men of the group commented they had seen this kind of horse in Salicor's personal army. Rumors circulated as to where the Icers had obtained them and why they brought them to Prince Stephan. Commander Brighton winked at his Prince. Stephan grinned.

EMERALD DISCOVERED a lake high up on the Sacred Mountain. Smooth as glass, the water rested on the backbone of the earth. Humidifying the air, it stretched before her like a woman at rest.

A crack of thunder demanded her attention and she looked to the east. Dark clouds climbed the mountain with astounding speed. The brilliance of another arc of lightning struck a current of power in the air that created a strange smell.

Sensing the need to take cover, she hurried toward a rocky outcrop. The storm's path tracked across the lake and rain swept over her in a wave. It hit her skin like a myriad of tiny feet. She had never experienced anything so wonderful.

Emotion burst from her like the rain from the clouds as it filled her senses. Great sobs of joy shook her body in the same way the thunder shook the air. Leaning outward from her shelter, she let it wash the tears from her face.

"I wish I could stay."

When the rain ended, the snow fell. Emerald hated leaving the lakeside. It was so lovely here. She had gotten soaked, but her pack remained dry underneath the outcrop of rock.

She would need better shelter for the night, however. Perhaps, she could find a small cave or the bowl of a pine tree. She scanned the terrain in vain. There were no large trees within sight.

To the northwest, there appeared to be a craggy area that might conceal a suitable place to shelter. Her joints had stiffened as she'd waited out the rain. She abandoned the slim shelter of the outcrop of rock and headed toward the summit. The snow swirled around her and bit her skin with stinging sharpness.

"Thank you." She whispered to the Creator at the sight of a large opening in the rock.

The cave was large enough to stand in, dry and untroubled by the wind. It extended deep into the mountain. She stayed close to the entrance, unsure of what pitfalls might be concealed by the darkness.

She could see nothing except the outline of the twilight sky against the mouth of the cave. It didn't matter. Fumbling with numb fingers, she undid the strings of her pack.

She stripped her clothes and hung them on crags in the cave wall. Slipping into a dry shirt, she grabbed a fur-lined cloak and wool blanket from her pack to make a bed. Shivering until the fur warmed her, a calm feeling brought sleep despite the thunder of the storm.

Chapter Thirty-One

Darrin was caught in the open during the downpour. He was still unwilling to allow Emerald to know he Shadowed her. Following her to the cave, he hesitated before going inside. However, there simply was no other shelter to be had.

He waited until he could no longer feel his hands and feet. When the convulsive shivering of his body stopped, he recognized the signs of hypothermia. He was dying, though he almost preferred that fate than the one he faced now.

He peered into the cave. In the flashes of lightning, he saw her sleeping and crept past. Stripping off his wet things, he searched his pack for dry clothes. Everything had gotten soaked. The agonizing cold drained his strength.

How could he ask her to let him lay beside her? What would she think of him? Would she allow it or let him perish?

In the next burst of light, he found her looking at him. Covering what he could of his body with his hands, he backed away. However, she didn't respond the way he feared. Seeing and not seeing at the same time, she came toward him.

Stumbling, she skinned her knee and yet held his gaze. He stood frozen by indecision until she embraced him. She felt so warm. When she began to tremble, he picked her up and carried her to bed.

She clung to him, looking into his eyes. Strangely, there was no sign of recognition. Furthermore, she made no move to indicate she wanted him to do anything. After a moment she stared off into the depths of the cavern.

Her breathing rate increased as her heart pounded against his chest. She was having a vision. He had seen her have them before. The vision stayed with her for quite some time. When it ended, she relaxed against him and closed her eyes.

What had her vision revealed? She hadn't uttered a word and seemed not to know him. She had saved his life. He laid a bittersweet kiss on her forehead, simultaneously enduring and enjoying the feel of her in his arms.

THE HOWL OF A WOLF haunted Emerald. A shock of cold jolted her body, but she couldn't awake from the vision. The lobo led her through the mountains.

Naked in the rain with her hair loose and matted to her body, she scrambled to follow him. She skinned her knee. Red-hot blood mingled with the rain on her skin.

She breathed in the smell of wet fur. When she looked up, he stood before her. His strange blue eyes met her gaze. He panted a white cloud and his tongue hung from the side of his toothy jaw. For an eternity, she searched those eyes.

She felt no fear as she gazed into the soul of the creature. He had something to show her. He ran.

His muscles bunched and elongated as he covered the uphill terrain with ease. She did her best to follow. Climbing the rocks, she found him in the mouth of a great cave.

She pursued him into the belly of the earth and a light appeared. Down they went until they neared a curve in the cavern. In that moment of anticipation, she stopped. Her reluctance to take the next step caused the vision to end.

DARRIN SHIVERED AS her warmth seeped into him. The feel of Emerald's body next to him felt so pleasant that it caused him physical pain. Why couldn't he control himself?

His desire for her threatened to overwhelm his good sense. It would be easy to take her here and now. He slid his hand along her shirt covered hip. She sighed.

Their faces were so close he could feel her breath on his cheek. She trusted him. He couldn't betray her, but if she wanted him, then he could be with her. They were practically married after all.

He pulled her closer and kissed her. She tensed and stopped breathing. It seemed clear she didn't want him. The pain of rejection sliced deep.

Bitter about what had caused Emerald to fear him, he took this one chance to find out for sure what had happened. Running his hand up from her knee to mid-thigh, he searched for the scars he feared to find there. Yes, it was Allan's name etched in her flesh.

Emerald pushed his hand away. He let her have some space between them. After what Allan had done, he couldn't blame her for not wanting a Wolfe in her bed.

Darrin squeezed his eyes shut. He clenched his fists and rolled onto his back. With everything in him, he wished his brother hadn't done this unthinkable thing that had caused so much misery.

Their mother would mourn.

IN THE LIGHT OF DAWN, Darrin found himself cuddled next to Emerald in warmth and comfort. She had her hand on his chest and her forehead tucked under his chin. The intimacy of it aroused him. He pulled away, desperate to escape.

He left her, though he hated to go. She moaned and leaned into the place where he had been. The frigid air hit his skin with a chilling, though not undesired effect.

She stirred.

He grabbed up all of his things and hid in the back of the cave where darkness concealed him. His clothes had frozen. He worked the fabric with his hands until it became pliable enough to wear.

Shivering, he reached inside his pack to find his wool socks and tunic. Even wet wool offered some warmth. He made sure no ice had formed inside his boots and slipped them on.

Just then, he noticed that Emerald had arisen. She looked stunning in the morning sunlight. He broke away from the sight of her to continue packing.

He glanced back to find her dressing. He swallowed with difficulty. This kind of desire couldn't be healthy.

Perhaps, he would have been happier if his mother had given him in marriage to someone else. He could have fathered children and brought his mother grandchildren. Granddaughters.

He scowled. Even his own daughter would have more status than he did. What made women more important than men anyway?

Danalan seemed like utopia. Emerald ruled with such a gentle hand. Everyone in her care loved her. He loved her.

He shook his head, realizing he needed to be honest with himself. No one ever really had a claim on Emerald. She had left her home behind to wander the Sacred Mountain and for what purpose he had no clue.

The only thing he knew for sure was that she seemed more at peace here than he had ever seen her. Didn't she love the orphans in Stone Castle? She had seemed to love them and to love him as well, at least for a while.

Casting a glance her way, it startled him to discover her missing. Her things remained, but she had disappeared. Just then the cave behind him brightened.

To his amazement, the cavern reached deep into the earth. He gathered up his pack and descended the rock steps. What was this place?

Another crystal in the roof of the cave illuminated and he traveled all the way to the bottom. Around a corner, he found a large granite door. He ran his fingers over an inscription that instructed him to push a block of stone in the side of the cavern. He did so and the door sank into the floor.

A marvel opened before his eyes.

The sound of Emerald descending the steps behind him alerted him in time to find a place to hide. How had she known about the Imperial City? It had been lost for four-hundred years.

The vision must have guided her, and that made him question his assumptions. What kind of woman was she? Perhaps, she really was a god. Despite her destiny as the Future Queen, she had always seemed so human before this moment.

THE LIGHT OF MORNING penetrated the darkness at the mouth of the cave. Emerald awoke, expecting to see the wolf of the vision. Disappointed, she realized there was no sign that a wolf had ever been here.

Alone.

Snow covered the landscape like the cloak wrapped around her body. It dazzled her eyes as the sun reflected off the icy mountaintop. It reminded her of the diamonds she had seen on the hilt of Chief Judge Mason's dagger.

The air had grown frigid. She stood but didn't look at the snow for long because her bare feet started to freeze. Shivering, she found something to wear and dressed in a hurry.

Her clothes from the day before had frozen stiff on the cave wall. She folded them to fit into her pack. Hungry, she sat down to eat a hard biscuit.

Memories of her vision returned. She gazed into the black unending depths of the cave. This had to be the place. How had there been light here? She scrutinized the walls around her to discover writing chiseled in them.

She could make no meaning from the inscriptions, but a diagram depicted a clue. Where could such a device be hidden? She strode out into the landscape beyond the shelter of this special place.

Surely, the cave was a doorway into the body of the mountain. She took a deep breath of the clear, cold air. Within the secret places revealed to her, she hoped to find the people she sought.

The panoramic vista from the top of the mountains stunned her. It seemed to reveal the entire world. She could see the entirety of Danalan and also much of Andolin all the way to the hazy sea.

She had never beheld such a vast body of water. As she gazed at it, the earth curved away. How strange.

"Stephan always said the Earth was round." She shrugged and chuckled.

Facing north, she beheld the legendary land of Stephan's people. Where was he down there? Was he well? A good feeling came over her. He would be happy for her if he could see her now.

Oh, how she longed to share this place with someone. It wasn't Stephan that came to mind, however. To her astonishment, she wished Darrin were here.

He could appreciate this place. He could tell her so many things about this land. Where was he?

An ache in her chest intensified and tears piqued in her eyes. Was he the one George had talked about? A lump formed in her throat. Would she ever see Darrin again?

She took a deep breath, trying to shrug off the oppression of her regrets. Moving forward would bring her joy. Looking back only made her weak.

Perhaps when her mission was complete, she would be given a second chance with Darrin. Part of her wished it. However, she did not dare to hope.

Right now, she needed to find the device depicted on the cave wall. Where could such a thing be? From her dream, she knew it made the passageway bright as the noonday sun.

Perhaps it caught the sun and focused the rays downward. What could do such a thing? Could a mirror do that? Yes, the device could be a mirror, round and adjustable.

It wasn't long before she spotted what she looked for, a large metal mirror. She took a cloth from her pocket and wiped it clean of water spots. Adjusting it until she saw a woman. The image startled her. She had never seen a reflection in a mirror.

She knew about mirrors because a peddler had sold them at the marketplace last year. The sun shining off of them had caught her attention along with many other passersby. She hadn't gone close enough to draw the man's attention, because she had no money. But she had observed the reactions of others as they looked into the wondrous things.

Of course, she knew what she looked like. She had seen her reflection in water but this was different. The image she saw now was a surprise.

The beauty of the woman in the mirror impacted Emerald's self-image. Until now she had not comprehended what others saw in her. Looking past the attractive features, she discovered softness around the lips and eyes, grace in the gentle curve of the neck, and dignity in the upright posture. She almost didn't believe what she beheld.

In her mind's eye, she had always viewed herself as hard and unyielding not lovely and innocent. She frowned at the reflection and the change made her smile. She tried out a few more expressions and giggled at the results.

Well, how did this amusing thing function? Mounted on a framework it could be rotated in various ways. She rotated it and found the sun. Blinded for a moment, she stepped aside.

When the spots cleared from her vision, she realized the light could be focused into an enormous crystal lodged in the granite. More mirrors dotted the spine of the mountain.

It didn't take long to focus a handful of them in the right places.

She hurried back to the mouth of the cave. Gratified to see that light filled the cavern, she gathered water and jerky for her expedition. Leaving her pack behind, she went down into the marvelous cave.

The rough floor became smooth steps. Brackets for torches had been carved into the walls. Of course, this passageway would have to be lit at night, except perhaps on a full moon.

The muscles in her legs ached. She didn't want to think about the climb back. So far there had been no side passages. Where was the bottom? The tunnel leveled out and curved.

She stopped to catch her breath.

Overcoming her apprehension, she took the last few steps to behold a marvel. A vast cavern full of light filled her view. She couldn't believe her eyes, however, because gigantic crystals hung from the ceiling as if she were inside a geode of enormous proportions.

"Woah." At her feet lay a city of glass nestled within a crystalline shell.

She stumbled over loose stones as she searched the glorious dwelling places in hopes of finding the inhabitants. However, a layer of dust covered everything. No people lived here.

Her heart sank. She hadn't found what she sought. The mountain people did not live in this ancient marvel.

Why then had she been shown how to get here? What was she meant to learn? Curiosity caused her to investigate a building that could only be referred to as a palace. It stood at the focal point of the city and all the streets led to it.

She mounted the perfect marble staircase to be greeted at its top by full-sized statues of a man and a woman. They had been chiseled from enormous quartz crystals. The couple gazed into one another's eyes.

Their right palms touched but were twisted opposite one another so their lips kissed the back of the other's hand. Intimate. She could only guess at the cultural significance of the gesture.

The couple wore gold crowns on their heads. Was this Prince Krelor? Emerald took a sharp breath. Could that be her ancestor, Dana the Stone-hearted? The resemblance of the statue to the image in the mirror she had seen moments ago stunned her.

The softness, the dignity, the grace was all there, but the statue deviated in one important way. In Dana's expression, Emerald perceived ambition. In those eyes, she detected a hunger for power.

Relief washed over her. She had no such personal desires. That meant she would never become like Dana.

She walked away from the magnificent city. There was much to occupy her mind as she climbed to the surface. At least she knew it was real. Her life had a purpose. Even though she hadn't found the mountain men, she had found a treasure of reassurance.

Perhaps the people lived on the northern side of the mountain. It seemed possible that some valley sheltered them. She resolved to head down the northern slope. If she didn't find them, then she would seek Stephan. Surely, Sarialla would help her find the mountain people.

DARRIN OBSERVED EMERALD'S reaction to the Imperial City. Whatever she had expected to find here, the city seemed to disappoint her. Though she sometimes gaped in wonder, she did not smile. For whatever reason, the city upset her.

She never guarded her expressions when she thought herself to be alone. She seemed so childlike in her openness at these times that he had felt like he had known her all of these years. He shook his head. He had been a fool.

The statue surprised them both. It looked so much like her. She belonged here.

It stunned him that she didn't investigate further. Instead, she headed up the cavern to the crest of the mountain. Why had she climbed the Sacred Mountain if not to find this great city and rule in majesty? What did she want?

He watched her ascend, but he couldn't bring himself to leave this treasure of ancient workmanship and wonder. While the light lasted, he investigated every nook of the palace and much of the city. Many caverns joined with this vast gem bubble, but only one seemed to be the main thoroughfare down to the passageway under the mountain.

He descended by candlelight until he found what he sought. Yes, this had to be the crossroads where wagons had come up to the Imperial City or continued traveling to Frenland or Andolin. Perhaps his mother would have these tunnels guarded.

He found his ink frozen solid, though the caves felt moderate. Everything that had thawed was wet, even his charcoal for drawing. He needed to leave his mother a note. So, he dried a bit of parchment over his candle lantern and used his own blood to write the message.

He addressed the epistle to Lady Celeniurisa, Steward of the West Wind, and told her how Emerald had found the Imperial City. He inscribed directions to the city, both from here as well as from the upper entrance. He weighted down the parchment with his brother's dagger. His mother would understand Allan was dead.

Chapter Thirty-Two

Liameo swung his ax. At the final stroke, the tree fell with a cracking swoosh. Nina and Andre cleared the branches from the trunk with hatchets. George wrapped a chain around the log and led the chestnut mare, Allura, as she dragged it to the sawmill.

It was a new life for a new family.

Liameo had adopted Tarah, Nina, Andre, and Marta. Tarah had married George, and the couple had adopted Benny, Sam, and Leland. All of them had renounced their citizenship in Andolin and taken the name of Stone. Now all they needed was for Emerald to return.

Liameo wiped the sweat from his brow. "Children, come over and eat." He sat on a stump and inspected the basket lunch Tarah had prepared for them this morning.

Nina and Andre were both red-cheeked and thirsty.

"Should we wait for George." Andre took a long drink from the waterskin and passed it to Nina.

"No." Liameo chuckled at the way Nina rolled her eyes. "He'll probably stop at the shack to eat the mid-day meal with Tarah."

"Oh." Andre reached for bread and ham.

"Oh, is right." Nina shook her head.

Liameo laughed outright at the exchange. "Yes, they're newlyweds. I suppose that means they need plenty of space to figure out how all of that works." Anyway, he wasn't sure how that could work with Benny, Sam, Leland, and Marta running circles in the one-room shack.

Nina frowned and then scowled, fanning her flushed cheeks with her hand.

"What's wrong now?" Andre spoke around a mouth full of food.

"Nothing is wrong. We should be happy for them." Liameo spoke before Nina could react. He began to eat his meal even though the food stuck in his throat a bit.

"Emerald will never..." More color flooded Nina's cheeks, though it looked more like anger than embarrassment.

"I understand, Nina, and it's all right. She doesn't have to...do whatever it is they're doing in order to be my wife." Liameo knew what the law said about it, but he didn't care.

"What are you talking about?" Andre brushed the crumbs from his lap and stood as if ready to go back to work.

"We're talking about being kind to Emerald when she returns because she's going to be surprised to find out she's married to me." Liameo had no desire to traumatize Andre with details he wasn't old enough to understand.

He nodded solemnly. "She's going to be mad, but then she'll be happy again. She never stays upset too long." He trotted away to use his hatchet to cut the larger branches into firewood.

"If she doesn't let you do it, then you'll have to force her." Nina's angry voice cut deeper than the hatchet chopping wood.

Agape, Liameo simply stared at the girl in shock. "You can't mean that."

Nina looked away at the clearing they had cut this past week. "Once will be enough."

"I won't do it, so quit burdening yourself with such repulsive thoughts." He stood and hefted his ax.

"You'll have to." Nina shot him a cold look. "The law requires it or the marriage won't stand. We'll lose her."

Liameo stood in indignation. "We won't lose anything because we are not subject to the laws of Andolin anymore. I'm sure the laws of Danalan do not require it." He stomped toward the nearest tree and swung the ax.

Chapter Thirty-Three

E merald never found a living soul on the mountain. She exhausted her supplies and found she had no choice except to abandon her search for a populace. She would seek Stephan's camp.

Using her best judgment, she walked out of the mountains into a vast grassland. From a higher vantage point, she thought she had spotted a village. Now that she had entered the sea of green, she could see nothing but waving blades of grass taller than her head.

Hoping she was headed in the right direction, she pressed forward. Thirst drove her forward even when hunger had robbed her of strength. She paused to dig into the soil beneath the grass, hunting for a pebble to suck on. It would slake her thirst.

If night fell and she still had not found water, then she would suffer for it. She licked her dry lips, but that made them sting. There were no pebbles.

To pass the time as she walked, she imagined ways to disguise her Southern looks. Winter was long past, so a hooded cloak was out of the question. Perhaps some kind of shawl could conceal her red hair except that she didn't have one.

The cloth in her pocket might be big enough. She could tuck her braid down the back of her shirt. Yes, that just might work.

Even as she reached for the cloth, a ring of horses encircled her. They moved like the wind in the grasses. There was no escape. She had detected them too late. How had their riders known she was here?

The helmed figures stared at her from atop tall horses. One woman smiled. It was not a pleasant expression.

Emerald scrutinized them. She thought they were all women. Their chainmail obscured some of their curves, but it was still apparent in their hairless, sun-bronzed faces.

All married men in the South wore beards. Andolinish women were not permitted to be soldiers. Was this land different? Yes, Sarialla had said something to that effect.

"We have ourselves an invader, girls." The smiling woman spoke the Frenland tongue.

Emerald understood what she said and corrected her.

"I'm a visitor, not an invader. I hope I find myself welcome." She looked at the face of each woman surrounding her.

"You speak our language well. Are you not of the South then?" The leader no longer smiled.

"I am Emerald Stone of Danalan. I come in peace."

"Peaceful travelers do not carry weapons nor wield sharp tongues. Who are you? I doubt indeed you are the Woman of the Stone." Even under her helm, the leader's frown could be detected.

"You have no reason to doubt my word." Emerald drew up to her full height. "I do not lie."

The woman smiled with more mirth this time. "Then why have you come to Frenland, Emerald Stone? To be sure, your mission lies in those peaks at your back."

Emerald met the leader's gaze. "I couldn't find a living soul in those mountains, though I saw many wondrous things. Without further guidance, I fear I have failed in my purpose. I cannot live with that, so I seek a wise woman from your land to aid me in my search."

"Oh? What, pray tell, is the name of this Sage?" The leader arched an eyebrow.

"Sarialla, Royal Counselor." As soon as the words left her mouth, she knew she had made a mistake.

With a hand signal from the leader, the others drew their swords. The rasp of metal reverberated in the air. Emerald stayed her hand. She had no strength nor did she have any desire to fight these women.

The leader prodded her horse forward and slipped Emerald's sword from its sheath. Stunned that the sword allowed the woman to handle it,

Emerald stood agape. Who were these warriors? Surely, they were not Salicor's soldiers.

The leader kicked Emerald in the jaw. Her head reeled, but the blow hadn't been hard enough to break anything. The pain was significant and the bruise would be a choice one, but she wasn't badly hurt.

"Bind her and lash her to my horse. We shall see how fast a Southerner can run." The wicked grin flashed again.

Emerald already knew how sharp the blades of grass could be. She imagined being dragged through it and mentally shuddered. Outwardly, she showed no sign of weakness. These women would not be merciful. The leader, in particular, seemed jaded and perhaps cruel.

"May I have the honor of your name, leader of many?" Emerald looked up at the smiling woman as another soldier bound her hands.

The leader frowned. "No, you may not." She tied the other end of the rope to her saddle horn. "Ha!" Her horse took off like a shot.

Emerald was jerked from her feet and dragged all the way to the village. The individual blades of grass left her covered in bloody cuts. However, the sea of supple greenery shielded her from injury.

There seemed to be no rocks in these grasslands and she was thankful for that. She did have one painful problem, however. Her shoulder had dislocated again, and agonizing waves of pain washed over her.

Covered with dust and blood she managed to gain her feet. This preserved her dignity but took all of her strength. She received a kick to the head, though this time from a different soldier. It sent her sprawling on the ground for the second time.

"You'll do well to learn to stay where you're put, Woman of the Stone." The new aggressor sneered.

The leader drew her sword and rode her horse alongside the woman, placing her blade at the other's throat.

"Do you presume to act of your own authority?"

"No, General. I would never disrespect you. I apologize for offending you. Please, forgive me." The woman paled.

To Emerald's surprise, the leader's blade did not pull away from the woman's neck. It drew along the vulnerable skin between helm and chain mail. A rivulet of blood flowed from the woman's neck. At the last instant, before severing an artery, the General withdrew her weapon.

"You'll do well to remember to stay where you're put, Danielle of Trent."

"Yes, General, I will remember." Danielle didn't move.

"Clean up the prisoner and bring her to me in the town hall. I'd better not see another mark on her or you'll bleed for it." The leader untied the rope from her saddle.

"Yes, General, as you wish." Danielle clasped her fist and brought it to her chest.

Two other women cut the bonds at Emerald's wrists. They were raw and bleeding, but whole. What happened next startled her. They ripped off her clothing and tossed her into a horse trough.

"Get cleaned up for the General." One woman dunked Emerald's head under water for a moment.

Several others laughed at the joke but Danielle frowned.

"What happened to her shoulder? It doesn't look right."

Rough hands pulled Emerald out of the trough and poked at her shoulder.

"Looks dislocated, Commander."

"I'd better not get the knife for this." Danielle waved for them to follow her.

Pain and humiliation seemed to be the order of the day. Emerald was shoved down the main street of the village in the nude. The villagers expressed mixed feelings about what they saw, though most mocked her. A few men tried to get a handful as she walked by but were beaten back by the soldiers escorting her.

Once inside the town hall, Emerald's gaze fell on the General. She sat at a table writing on a piece of parchment. Emerald thought it must be a letter to inform someone of her appearance in Frenland. It boded no good.

The General sat unencumbered by helm or chainmail. She was dressed in trousers and a linen shirt with a dagger on a simple leather belt. Her long blond hair was braided and hung the length of her back.

She was not a large woman by any stretch of the definition. By Emerald's standards, she was short, slight, and quite flat bosomed. But her features were delicate and fine.

As her fingers moved the quill to write her epistle, a similarity struck Emerald that she hadn't noticed until now. Her sharp intake of breath caused the General to pause her writing and look up. She didn't seem to notice Emerald's nudity but looked her straight in the eyes.

"Do I look like her then?" the General asked.

"Not so very much. But when you were writing just now, your mannerisms resembled her greatly. Are you Valerie then?" She hoped her words would not offend the woman further. One could not afford to have an enemy of this caliber.

"You may call me, General." Valerie's gaze drifted to appraise Emerald's body.

The slow deliberation caused Emerald to flush from head to toe. She'd never been scrutinized like this before. She held still, hoping it would be over soon.

Valerie's gaze stopped on Emerald's abdomen. "Are you pregnant?"

Emerald flushed anew. "Yes, General, I suppose I am." She had a hard time getting the words out.

Valerie's right eyebrow lifted. "Are you wed?"

"No, General. I'm not." Emerald hadn't believed she could blush any deeper, but she did.

Now both of Valerie's eyebrows lifted. With a circular motion of one finger, she indicated that Emerald should turn around. Emerald complied, enduring an equally thorough appraisal of her backside until she came full circle.

"Send her to a physician for that shoulder." The general picked up her quill and continued writing. "Oh, take her to the smithy as well." Valerie dismissed them with a flick of the wrist.

Emerald marched out without looking back. She hoped this doctor would be close by and that the guards would keep the men off of her as they had before. Valerie's attitude had begun to annoy her.

EXHAUSTED, STEPHAN herded stolen cattle up the grassy foothills of the Sacred Mountain. He led the survivors of his raiding party. Above him, an ominous sky of roiling gray clouds threatened a deluge.

A lump solidified in his throat at the sight of Helen of Scion. His raid had been a catastrophe. Twenty-seven Rebels lay dead, tied to the saddles of their horses. Eleven others had been wounded. Most could still ride, but the worst off lay in the captured supply wagons.

There had been eight wagons instead of the usual two or three and a hundred head of cattle. The escort of guards had been tripled to twenty-four seasoned soldiers with eight slaves driving the wagons. Valerie supplied Salicor's army with beef and grain. His men must be getting hungry.

Stephan had laid in ambush for the supply wagons with five groups of ten raiders. He had been sure he was over prepared for whatever came along the road. However, Valerie had outsmarted him by sending so many.

If not for the defection of several of the escort soldiers, then all might have been lost. Valerie's edict that anyone who lost supplies or cattle to the raiders would be executed had put fear into her own forces. It caused most of the escort to fight to the death, two to desert, and three to surrender.

Stephan swallowed against nausea. There had been too much bloodshed. That wasn't what he wanted.

"Commander Helen, I think it best to postpone the raid you planned for tonight. Send your five groups of ten soldiers on patrol instead. I'd like your help interrogating the three defectors who surrendered themselves to me today." He sighed. "The raid didn't go well. We took heavy losses. This can't happen again if we are to be successful."

Helen surveyed the riders herding the noisy cattle and the wagons carrying the wounded.

"Yes, Sire." She bowed her head and rode off to dispatch her fresh raiders on patrol duty.

They rode away along the road. Each group of ten peeled off at equal intervals to descend to the edge of the grasslands. Stephan hoped they would at least be able to provide some warning if Valerie chose to invade the mountain tonight. She would want her cattle back.

Helen returned to ride alongside him as the wagons continued eastward along the hidden road.

He rubbed his hand down his dirty face. "It appears the General has ordered her escorts to fight to the death. They face execution if they lose the supplies they protect. We were almost defeated." He kept his voice low so no one else would overhear.

Helen's eyes were as dark as the sky. "General Valerie doesn't value life. She'll use any tactic available to repel you, Sire." Her frown deepened.

"What are you not telling me?" Stephan had become accustomed to Helen and could sense her moods.

She unclenched her jaw and met his gaze. "My Prince, will you permit me to tell you the story of my village?"

"Tell me the tale." His heart grew heavy with a sense of foreboding.

From what he had learned of Helen, she held darkness within her. He had recognized that right away. He felt drawn to her because of that kinship of loss.

He thought he understood her because of it. Though he remained cautious as well. That much anger held danger and unpredictability.

"I was younger than you are now by a year when Salicor sent his niece to inspect the villages of the region." She spoke as the last light made its way through the heavy cloud cover. "Valerie started in the most remote territories of the west. Thus, she came to Sion.

"My village was poor and not of much consequence to King Salicor. However, Valerie came to ensure our loyalty. A secondary purpose was to collect taxes."

Stephan cleared his throat. "I hear his taxes are quite high and there is little he does for the people. For example, the roads are not good and his way of caring for the poor is slavery or a quick death. Were you ever a slave Helen?"

She looked away and for a moment, he thought he saw her blush.

"No, Sire. I am yet a virtuous woman."

"Is that what slavery means then?" This time he blushed and looked down, fidgeting with Dusty's reins. "I did not realize." He glanced at her.

She held his gaze. "When you informed us you were taking slaves, women, and children as well as men, I thought you intended to—" She shrugged, shaking her head. "—well, it doesn't matter what I thought. Your intentions were to free them, not to use them for any other purpose." She looked away. "My sister is a slave, that is if she yet lives."

He tried to catch her eye but couldn't. "I hope she is alive and that we free her soon. Does anyone else in your family still live?" He guessed at the answer.

"No."

Her voice was not as brave as he had expected it to be. It sounded vulnerable. She differed from Emerald and he knew why. Helen had never been raped. His understanding caused hope to rise within him and he struggled to figure out why.

"Valerie burned my village to the ground." Helen bowed her head. "We had nothing when winter arrived and few of us survived to see the spring. My parents and grandparents starved to death. My older sister sold herself into slavery to buy food to keep me alive long enough to walk to the nearest rebel camp. I have been fighting for you ever since, My Prince."

"How many years ago was this?" His real question was less tactful. He doubted a slave would live the number of years he guessed she would answer. It was likely her sister had died.

"Six."

He looked at her in surprise. She was only five years older than him, maybe closer to four. An odd, warm feeling filled his chest. He looked away for a moment.

"Do slaves survive so long? Please, forgive my ignorance."

Her face conveyed puzzlement. "It all depends on the master. A weaver bought her. It's hard work, but skilled and therefore valuable. She may yet live."

They rode on in silence. He hunched his shoulders and stared at his hands. A thought occurred to him and he sat up straight.

"How old was General Valerie at the time?" He'd always thought she was about the same age as Emerald.

"Fifteen years of age, My Prince." Bitterness infused her tone. "How could a girl my age be so cruel? The tales of her would turn your blood to ice, Sire."

Stephan clenched his jaw. He had listened to many such tales in recent days. His initial hope of converting the General now seemed foolish.

"When I am king, she will be brought to justice. You have my word, Helen." He reached out and she met him halfway for a quick clasp and release of fingers. He hadn't anticipated the thrill that shot through him as he touched her.

"Why aren't you married, Commander?"

She ducked her head. "Because I'm unattractive, Sire." Her voice gave evidence of her pain.

He laughed and shook his head. "I'm sorry, but you are not unattractive, Helen." He met her gaze to witness the depths of her anguish.

"I'm as ugly as you are handsome. Don't dally with me, My Prince. Excuse me." With a bow of the head, she rode off to survey the line of wagons.

His jaw dropped open. He snapped around to look straight ahead. Had he been dallying with her? Never in his life had he been accused of being insincere. Not one person had ever said he was handsome either.

Chapter Thirty-Four

E merald's shoulder felt better since it had been reset. However, the physician had taken liberties during his examination that she would have liked to reward with a well-placed knee. Apparently, when compared with Frenland women, her breasts were large and her body shapelier. It had the effect of driving men to distraction. Since she hadn't a bit of clothing to conceal her charms, she was forced to endure it.

On a positive note, the men were short and slight as well as the women. If she were armed and fed, she should be able to defend herself quite well against them. At the moment, however, she indulged in a few cruel fantasies concerning the men who pressed the guards with such urgency.

Clenching her jaw, she did her best to ignore their base words. It was good she didn't know the meaning of most of their foul language. As it was, their hand gestures communicated more than enough.

She had long since tired of blushing. In fact, she was just plain tired. However, the torture wasn't over yet.

The General had mentioned the smithy. As they approached the open structure, Emerald could feel the heat of the fires on her skin. Why would the General order her here?

Sweat dripped from the greasy haired assistant. The older blacksmith worked with hammer and anvil, pounding out something or other. Emerald could not see what. The blacksmith never even glanced her way.

The assistant hurried to the fire and grabbed a metal rod. Emerald's guards shoved her to her knees and held her arm immobile on a block of wood. The man pressed the brand against her wrist.

Screaming in pain, Emerald fought with all her strength, but it was too late. The guards cuffed her upside the head and drug her down the street. They cast her into a filthy one-room shack with bars on the door.

"You behave in there and we won't lock you in the stocks at the town square."

Laughter greeted the comment.

"If she wasn't already pregnant, then she would be after that."

More laughter followed until the group of guards settled in to watch the shack. They were hard-pressed to keep the townsfolk away. It seemed the men were not easily put off.

Despite her outrage at having been branded, Emerald gave the guards no trouble. What did the mark mean? She tried to think about something else in an effort to distract herself from the excruciating burn.

She took a cleansing breath and focused her mind. She was grateful she hadn't stumbled into this particular difficulty without the guards' protection. She imagined what might have happened if she'd come into town unaware.

The men of this village seemed to have no qualms about their actions. Even with a sword in hand, she would have been unable to fight all of them. Especially since she had not eaten or drunk today.

No, she was better off a prisoner. Prisoners had rights. She hoped they would bring her something to drink soon.

Her mouth felt like it was full of sand. She took a raspy breath. Her wrist felt like it was on fire. Why would Valerie do this to her?

UNUSUAL NOISES AWOKE Emerald from slumber. She had lain in her small prison for two days. To her astonishment, a shirt and loaf of bread sat inside the door of her cell.

She hurried to eat the bread. It was not plain fare, but airy and made with honey and fruit. She did her best to save some, at least until she put on the white shirt.

It was a man's shirt. Even so, it was barely big enough for her to wear comfortably. Gingerly, she rolled the right cuff up so it wouldn't rub on her still healing brand.

It felt wonderful to be clothed again. She hadn't expected such a fine garment. When nothing but water and moldy bread had come for her over the past two days, she had worried the General had forgotten about her. The rattle of a key in the door to her cell warned her before it opened.

"Out of there and come with us." A guard stood in the doorway.

The full sun shone in Emerald's eyes. Its warmth felt welcome on her face and legs. The white shirt looked stark against her dust coated skin. She must look terrible. The thought caused her to smile.

A guard slapped her head. "What makes you so happy this morning?"

"I was just thinking that the men of this village wouldn't find me so appealing today." She ducked her chin but couldn't quite suppress a grin.

"You don't need to worry about that." The woman shook her head. "The General has satisfied their needs. Even with you around, she still managed to turn their heads. I think it challenged her though."

The other guard snorted with laughter. "She seems to like a challenge."

Emerald stared at the women. What did they mean by that? It couldn't mean what she thought it did. Certainly, Valerie was not what they implied.

"I don't believe it," she said.

The two women laughed.

"You are innocent, aren't you?"

"Not too innocent, I think. Pregnant women don't get that way by accident."

Emerald ducked her head even deeper. The walk across town had changed from her first experience. Many looked, but none showed much interest. She ignored the fact this might be evidence of the veracity of the guard's words. Oh, how Sarialla would weep if it proved true.

The sound of a door opening to slam against a wall brought Emerald back from her thoughts. A well-dressed man strode out of the town hall. In one fluid movement, he mounted a heavily scarred warhorse.

As ugly as the horse was the man was that handsome. His wheat-colored hair shone in the sun. It fell straight to his shoulders.

Emerald realized the other women were staring. They had idiotic expressions on their faces. She realized she must look about the same and dropped her chin to her chest.

When he saw her, the frown on his face disappeared. A smile took its place. Such a transformation enhanced her opinion of his looks and her body had much to say about it.

Surprised by the physical reaction, she felt heat flush her skin. She looked away from him altogether. Barely able to see straight, she walked into the town hall. The guards were a step behind.

Emerald still felt exposed. After all, a shirt only covered so much and this one less than most. It barely covered her buttocks. Regardless, she should be grateful. At least the man had not seen her without it.

Despite the door being off its hinge, the room remained in good order. Valerie did not sit at the table, however. She paced the floor with a severe frown on her face.

Oddly, the color in her cheeks heightened her allure. Emerald had thought her pretty before. Now she was forced to elevate her estimation, with much displeasure. Beauty was not a virtue.

Just as Emerald thought this, Valerie looked at her. Tumbling into those brown depths would be an easy thing to do. They seemed to absorb information against a person's will.

Not that Emerald had anything to hide. She squared her shoulders. Ignoring the pain, she met the General's gaze.

"I see my brother has been to see the prisoner." Valerie's lips curved upward at one corner.

"He left her a little something to remember him by."

The guards snickered.

Emerald frowned at the women.

A wry smile contorted Valerie's face. It did nothing to enhance her looks. In fact, there was no mirth behind it.

"She is a woman after all." Valerie shook her head.

Emerald stopped herself from denying it. That would be ridiculous. She was a woman, but she was not whatever they were hinting at. Had that been Valerie's brother who had left this hall in anger? Was he the one who had given her the shirt and bread?

"Don't look so surprised. It makes you look like a child. Maybe that's what drew him to you. I like the young ones too. Byron and I were cut from the same cloth, so to speak." She held up a finger to stop Emerald from answering the accusation. "Don't speak. Remember your place, or you will have your lessons repeated."

Emerald held her tongue. Perhaps it was the fact that she no longer felt accustomed to wearing clothes, but all of a sudden, this shirt made her squirm.

Did Byron have some kind of payment in mind as a reward for giving it to her? The idea made her skin crawl and the bread turn in her stomach. Her gorge rose.

The two guards stepped away with distasteful looks on their faces. Vomit was not something anyone appreciated. In this musty hall, it smelled doubly bad.

"You two, clean that up." Valerie took Emerald by the arm and dragged her out of the building. She kept a rapid pace, though her stride was not as long as her captive's.

Emerald had no trouble keeping up. Her lack of shoes made it uncomfortable, though. Thankfully the General had grabbed ahold of her good arm.

They didn't stop walking until they reached the edge of town. Valerie unlocked a cottage door and pushed her inside. She stumbled and landed on the planks of the floor. A severe look, including a single arched eyebrow, was her reward.

"You've got to take better care of yourself or you'll never carry that child to term. Who is the father anyway?" Valerie came in and closed the door of the single room residence.

Emerald gathered herself up by the light from a small window. "I'm not sure."

Valerie burst into laughter.

Emerald had her hands around her throat in an instant, squeezing with all her might. Valerie's eyes flew wide with surprise, but not panic. She exploited Emerald's injured left shoulder to free her neck with ease.

Once put off, Emerald regained self-mastery. She quit attacking. Valerie, however, took much longer to find some level of self-control. She rained blows upon Emerald until her fists bled.

Covered in bruises and bleeding from a split lip, Emerald didn't move from her spot on the floor. Her entire body hurt, with one conspicuous exception. Valerie had refrained from injuring her belly.

Breathing heavily, Valerie sat in a high-backed chair. "I take it, you did not consent to bear this child. How many men did it take to best you?"

Emerald curled into a ball and covered her ears. How could a woman be so cruel to another? Emerald wept for what Sarialla would suffer when she discovered what her daughter had become.

"You will answer my questions, slave." Valerie came down on one knee and grasped her jaw in a cruel grip.

"I hope I never find your mother." Emerald met her gaze with compassion. "It would kill her to know you acted this way."

Valerie's eyes went wide. "You weep for my mother's sake?" She indulged in another burst of mirthless laughter. "If I had known that's what it would take to kill the witch, then I'd have written her a well-crafted epistle years ago." She released Emerald's jaw and returned to the chair.

"She told me such wonderful stories of you and Bryon when you were children." Emerald sat up. "She was so sad to have lost you to Salicor. Even I, who have lost everything, pitied her. I pity her even more now. My family is merely dead, but you've been ruined. What happened to you is far worse."

Emerald spoke with boldness, but not from anger. The tragedy before her tore at her heart. Even as she suffered at Valerie's hand, she knew it was Salicor's influence that had twisted a gentle child into a monster.

Once again, the depths of Valerie's gaze pulled her in. The general seemed to draw out every thought and feeling in Emerald's heart. In the end, Valerie was the one who looked away.

"I suppose you know what you're talking about," the General said.

Emerald wiped the tears from her cheeks with the sleeve of Byron's shirt. "I did nothing to earn this shirt, Valerie. You must believe me. I can't repay him the way you think I should. I'd rather be naked."

A slight but genuine smile lifted the corners of Valerie's lips. "He offered to buy you from me."

Emerald gasped.

"Don't worry. I refused him, though the amount he offered was more than I had expected. I've never heard of a slave worth even one piece of gold, but he offered much more." Valerie snorted. "It gave me pleasure to deny him his plaything. He doubled the price and when I refused him still, he got angry and left. I don't think he'll be back, so you need not concern yourself."

"You wrote the letter to him?" She didn't know what to think.

Valerie leveled her gaze on Emerald. "Yes, but it contained instructions that the message should be forwarded to the King."

Emerald sprang to her feet. She couldn't suppress a smile. She did manage not to hug Valerie, however.

"Then my brother will know I'm here. Thank you, Valerie. I don't know what resources he has, but I'm sure he'll pay any ransom you could ask. Though, I don't know how I'll ever pay him back."

Valerie's brows crashed together. "Your brother?" She stood.

Emerald was taken aback. "Stephan."

"Prince Stephan is not your brother." Valerie paced. "Are you telling me Sarialla hid that brat in the South all this time?" Her neck grew red.

"In Danalan, yes. I was eight when your mother brought him to live with us. He and I were raised by my grandparents until they died." Emerald's voice caught. "I raised him on my own after that. We are orphans, but family all the same."

"How did they die?" A glint in Valerie's eye and the set of her jaw betrayed suspicion.

"A lone man took their lives." Emerald didn't want to answer, but she had learned her lesson.

"What did that man take from you, Emerald?"

The muscles in Emerald's jaw bunched and tightened until her teeth squeaked. "Everything." Full of venom, the word came out a raspy whisper.

"Not everything. You lived. Did he?"

"No." A muscle in Emerald's cheek twitched.

"How old were you?"

"Fourteen."

"Already a woman. You should count yourself lucky. I was five and I did not have the satisfaction of vengeance."

Emerald gasped. How could anyone do such a thing to a child? The color drained from her face.

"You are not fourteen now." Valerie's expression remained impassive. "From what you said earlier, a lone man did not put you with child. Thus, it must have happened again. Tell me."

Emerald took care not to lock her knees lest she pass out. "I take in orphans. Each night, I walk the Border Road to look for unwanted children. They come from far and wide. The villagers often direct them there. We have an agreement, I accept any child, sick or well, infant or adolescent." Emerald shifted her weight.

"Not all of the villagers think what I do is right. Most of them blame me for the misfortunes that have beset them for the last forty years. A clan of evil men killed my entire family, often raiding the people of Andolin along the borders as well.

"Those men are dead now. In any case, a man from Andolin and his two sons kidnapped a woman and her children to lure me in. They killed the woman and assaulted me." Emerald hadn't moved from her place in the middle of the room. Her voice remained flat throughout the entire telling of the tale.

"I doubt they just let you live to talk about it. Is there no law against murder in the South?"

"There are strict laws and the men received punishment."

Valerie frowned. "But how did you survive?"

"They threw me in the river. A man on the other side rescued me. He took me home where Sarialla saved my life. I didn't thank them for it then, but I am glad now."

"You're glad of it now? Now that you are a slave to be beaten or raped or treated ill in any fashion, how can you be glad now?" Valerie shook her head. "It must be the child. You find joy in your child. Am I right?"

"No." The thought both startled and shamed her in rapid succession.

"No? Then what are your plans for the baby?" Valerie asked.

"I have agreed to give it to the father." A hot flush radiated from Emerald's cheeks.

Valerie's jaw dropped. "Tell me the man is dead. Why was he not executed?"

Emerald focused on a crack in the wall. "I asked the Chief Judge to show mercy."

"Why would you do that?" Valerie shook with anger.

"In Andolin, women cannot hold property. His mother and three younger sisters would've lost everything. I couldn't let that happen. They hadn't done anything wrong." Her voice trembled.

"So, you let him live. You begged for his life. More than that, you promised to bare his child?" Valerie shook her head and paced the floor.

"What else will you give him? Will you spread your legs for him again? Perhaps you delight in the feel of it." She skewered Emerald with a glare.

"Do you like it when they force you?" Valerie balled her fists. "Is that the kind of relationship you have with this man? What is his name?"

Emerald couldn't stop her lip from trembling. Her voice would not obey, either. So, she met Valerie's glare with one of her own. How could anyone think such a thing?

"Speak." Valerie's hand slammed on the table.

"He has no manhood with which to threaten me. He spends two days a week working in my fields or around the castle. One day of service is for the children of the mother who died and the other is for me. He makes his reparations. I found I could not deny him when he expressed a desire to raise the child."

Valerie sat in her chair and drummed her fingers on the table. "How did he convince you to give up your baby to a rapist and a murderer?" Her gaze pulled Emerald in.

"He said my desire to be a mother had died. He admitted responsibility for his part in that. He pleaded for me to think of the child.

"He said this babe would not be an orphan and that I could not treat it as such. He declared his fatherhood and asked me to marry him. I refused.

"He insisted that he should be allowed to raise the child after it was weaned. I promised him, that if I lived, then I would return the child to him one day. I did the right thing, Valerie, the only thing. I don't want this baby." Emerald's knees threatened to buckle beneath her.

Valerie stared into her eyes for an eternity. "Tell me how you feel after the child has suckled at your breast for a year. I wonder if you will still despise your daughter then." With those words, she departed the cottage.

Emerald stood agape until tears spilled from her unblinking eyes. Blinded and shaken, she lay on the cot and wept. Valerie had known the exact thing to say to hurt her most.

Chapter Thirty-Five

E merald snapped awake as the door to the cottage swung open.
"Get out of my bed." Valerie's voice slurred.

She had a man with her. A strong odor accompanied them. Emerald's nose wrinkled in distaste.

The two fondled and rubbed against one another until Valerie lost her balance and toppled onto Emerald. The man laughed and Valerie giggled. Emerald wriggled out from under her and stood between the General and the townsman.

"What's happening here?" she demanded. What was wrong with them?

"I brought home a friend. If you want a turn, I'm sure he will oblige you." Valerie spoke so indistinctly that Emerald had trouble understanding the words.

"You need to leave." Emerald pushed the man back as he teetered forward. "The General is not well."

"Oh, Emerald, don't be such a prude. It's fun. You'll like it." With those words, Valerie leaned over the side of the cot and retched.

Emerald felt the blood drain from the upper half of her body at the smell but managed to shove the man out the door. She slid the bolt home with a clack. In the light of a lantern the general had carried in, she noticed Valerie had fallen asleep.

Trying not to breathe, she cleaned up the mess. With that accomplished, she pulled off Valerie's boots and loosened her clothes so she could rest in comfort. What had caused her to act like that?

It still smelled horrible. Emerald sat in the chair beside the little table. She shouldn't be tired, but she was. Her thoughts made her weary. After a while, she leaned over and fell asleep.

THE POUNDING OF A FIST on the door awoke Emerald with a start.

"Oh." She jerked her head upward and winced at the complaint of a sore muscle in her neck.

The unseen fist pounded again.

"General, you told me to wake you at first light. General?" A woman on the outside of the door spoke.

Valerie didn't move. Her chest rose and fell, but she gave no indication that she heard the soldier. In fact, she snored.

Emerald stood and slid the bolt open. The next time the soldier knocked on the door it swung in on its own. The woman peered into the room.

"She's sleeping." Emerald massaged her aching neck.

The woman glared. "Yes, and I know why, too. It's no excuse. She must get up." The soldier tromped over to the cot and shouted. "General."

Valerie jumped out of bed. She moaned and wavered on unsteady legs before she sat on the cot. Both hands raised to rub her head and cover her eyes.

"There better be a war on."

"Funny, General. You told me to wake you at sunrise. I've done my duty." The soldier left the cottage without bothering to close the door.

"Oh, my head. Shut it." Valerie moaned.

Emerald closed the door. "Are you all right?"

"Mind your own business." Valerie glared at her but soon gave up.

Emerald folded her arms across her chest. Whatever was the matter, it hadn't improved Valerie's disposition. What would it be like to see a genuine smile from her?

Valerie stood and walked over to the washbasin. Her hands shook as she poured water into it. She set down the pitcher, stripped, and washed her body. Scars marred her flesh. Emerald looked away but was soon hit in the head by a pair of trousers.

"One of my friends left these. They might fit." Valerie finished dressing in her black and red uniform.

"Thank you." Emerald sniffed the garment to see if it was clean.

"Well, you're not much use to me half naked. I guess if you're not going to run away, then I'd better put you to work." Valerie crawled around on the floor looking for her boots. She found them under the table Emerald had slept on.

"You mean to tell me you didn't post a guard?" Emerald found that impossible to believe.

"You mean to tell me you didn't check?" The hint of a smile brightened her expression.

Emerald chuckled, but the feeling didn't last. "I had other things on my mind."

Valerie clapped Emerald on the shoulder. "I should not have said those things to you. I should've given you a hot cup of tea and been done with it."

"That would've been nice." She smiled.

"No, not nice, it tastes terrible. However, it would cure what ails you." She pointed at Emerald's belly. "I have to drink it from time to time. But you don't see me dragging around any brats."

Emerald felt the blood drain from her face.

"Have a seat before you faint." Valerie shoved her into the chair. "How can you stand to be so weak? You don't want it. So, why not just kill it? You've killed before, it's no different."

Emerald stood with her hands trembling.

"I have defended myself against my enemy, but I've never taken an innocent life and I don't plan to start."

"Innocent?" Valerie snorted. "That child is going to bring you nothing but misery. Mark my words. If you don't do it soon, you'll regret it for the rest of your life."

Heat suffused Emerald's neck. "How do you know?"

Valerie met her gaze. "I had a daughter when I was thirteen. I thought I was old enough to care for her. I did my best. I defied the whole world to do it, too. In the end, she died anyway."

Valerie looked away. "She got hurt. She was so little, barely a year old. One day she was fine and the next she was dead. What a waste, huh?"

Emerald hugged Valerie in a fierce embrace. Her tears fell freely and after a moment so did Valerie's. The women sobbed as they held each other.

"What was her name?"

"Lily."

Chapter Thirty-Six

Darrin waited in the tall grass as another patrol passed. He hunted the leader of the women soldiers, the one who held Emerald hostage. He didn't know her name, but she defended the border against the raiders who pretended to be from the mountains.

Darrin knew better than to fall for the deception. The men that attacked these women warriors were from Frenland. The real question was who lead them?

Perhaps it was some ploy of Stephan's. Darrin hadn't seen the boy yet. If he had, he would've asked for help to rescue Emerald.

The concealing cover of darkness fell over the land. He held his position. His trap had been set.

He plucked at a blade of grass and inhaled the heady, fertile air of the plains. The light faded fast near the mountains and tonight would have little moonlight. His plan was well laid.

He needed to capture the ruthless, carousing leader. Then he could offer to spare her life in exchange for Emerald's freedom. Thus, he planned to take the Princess far away from this war and this lascivious enemy.

Emerald had walked straight into this woman's ambush. It was as if she hadn't known the soldiers were there. That was strange considering her gift for noticing the presence of others.

Darrin had trailed the Future Queen and been just far enough behind to avoid being captured along with her. He hadn't suspected he would be unable to free her. Nor had he imagined she would be treated with such cruelty by this woman.

He'd been a fool not to let Emerald know he Shadowed her. He should've told her so many things. He looked up from his thoughts.

A patrol approached. He resolved to tell Emerald about his brother, his people, and perhaps even how he still felt about her. When she was safe, he would tell her.

The patrol began to pass without noticing him. As usual, the leader brought up the rear. This woman had piqued his curiosity from the beginning. She was so wily that she had spotted him as he had tried to work his way closer to Emerald.

She had almost captured him each time he had attempted a rescue. His narrow escapes had been sheer luck at times. Yet, he sensed she was feeling him out, testing him to determine what kind of figure he was and where his motivations lay. She was a skilled hunter and took her time, leaving nothing to chance. He matched her tactics.

In regards to the possibility of being captured and the cruel methods this woman would employ to purge him of information, he had no illusions. He'd seen the aftermath of one such interrogation. The man had been dismembered in the most horrific manner.

He watched the woman as she passed him. She was a strange blend of the sensual and the brutal. She took men with a ravenous appetite. If they yielded then it appeared pleasurable. But if they sought to dominate, then it turned sadistic. She was always the aggressor and the conqueror. Yet, Emerald had chosen to stay with her, and he couldn't begin to guess why.

At the last possible moment, he stood. The leader's sharp gaze found him. The others had ridden out of the line of sight and he hoped he was right about what this woman would do.

After a moment's hesitation, she signaled to her soldiers to continue on without her. They obeyed and Darrin found himself alone with this strange woman. After several minutes of stillness, she urged the great beast she rode toward him.

The intelligent horse would be her downfall. The animal loved honey. Darrin had been hard pressed to find it and the herbs he needed to make his plan work. But he had placed a sticky ball of the concoction in the tall grass, level with the horse's mouth. Just as expected, the horse smelled it and ate it before the woman could stop him.

Darrin smiled at the sight of the toppling animal and the sound of what must be cursing from the woman. She was now trapped with one leg pinned under the unconscious beast. It had worked better than he had hoped.

She couldn't reach her sword and she couldn't flee. Capturing her had been too easy. It felt as though he had been guided and he recognized the blessing.

Without moving a muscle, he waited until he was certain his enemy was as helpless as she seemed. She talked more than he had anticipated. But he couldn't understand anything she said. When she ceased to struggle and ended her speeches, she made an exasperated exhalation and lay back in the grass.

He took this opportunity to tramp down the tall grass around them to provide an arena for negotiation. He spoke little of her language. Would she laugh at an attempt to communicate his demands?

"Your life is mine." He had planned out some of what he needed to say in her language.

She responded with so much vehemence that he couldn't catch a word.

"No, I need you..." What were the words? He hadn't studied this tongue since he was a child. "...to give me...woman..."

He didn't know the right title for Emerald. Did they even know who she was or how important? He took a step closer to the Frenlander.

Silence prevailed between them. In an amazing contortion, the woman pulled off her chainmail shirt. She tossed the heavy thing away.

"Have it your way." She unbuckled her belt.

He watched her hands, expecting her to seek a weapon. She did not. Looking at her eyes, he felt drawn into the dark depths.

They pulled in the starlight. Nothing escaped them. Her long-sleeved undershirt clung to her body and she smiled at him seductively, though her gaze held only satisfaction.

He set his jaw and held his ground. Without a doubt, she must have a weapon concealed somewhere. He had to make sure she didn't get the better of him.

"Hands." He moved closer.

She held her hands above her head.

He came down on one knee beside her and captured her wrists. Slender. Almost against his will, he met her gaze.

She intrigued him and never more so than now. He found her expression both hard and soft at the same time. But more than that he saw the recognition of his dark hair and light-colored eyes. She knew he came from the mountains.

She smiled at his hesitation.

"Kiss me." She spoke his tongue with an enthralling accent, her body language so come hither he almost didn't process the words.

His jaw dropped.

She capitalized on the opportunity to draw herself up and kissed him open-mouthed. He pulled back, but she held him, thrusting her tongue into his mouth provoking startling sensations. He pushed her away.

She looked surprised.

With more force than necessary, he slammed her to the ground. He flipped her onto her stomach. Anger swelled in his chest.

His actions wrenched her trapped leg. She screamed and fought with violent though ineffective force. He matched her fierce resistance and pinned her down with her arms behind her back.

"Please, stop. Please, don't." A certain quality in her tone spoke to him, reminding him of something. But he couldn't put a finger on what.

"You should not have done that." He concerned himself less with causing her pain as he did with not letting her have the upper hand. He searched her for weapons, finding several.

"I'm sorry." She sobbed herself breathless and stopped resisting. "I won't do it again. I'll do anything you like, just don't take me like that." Her body shook. "Turn me over, please. I'll do anything you like. I'll make it good for you. Just treat me like a woman." She dissolved into hysterics.

He bound her hands behind her back with a short length of rope. She spoke his language, so he understood what she said, though it made no sense. He suspected her of duplicity since pleading seemed out of character.

She struggled again. He slammed her back down, resting his full weight on her. How could he have let her do that to him?

This vile woman, who rutted with every man she met, had tried to seduce him. But it hadn't worked. Perhaps, that was why she pretended to cry.

He flipped her over to see what her expression betrayed concerning her true emotions. With a face slick with tears, she seemed the visage of anguish. She opened her eyes and relief washed over her features. Her throat worked to get the words out.

"Thank you."

He paused in his efforts to ensure she didn't escape long enough to realize she had ceased to fight him. He heaved great breaths of air. The struggle had been intense.

"What are you afraid of?" he asked.

"I'm yours." She exhaled and inhaled. "I will not resist you, just let me be a woman. Join with me as a man joins a woman, not as men do. Please."

He recoiled from her, shaking his head in revulsion. "I didn't come here to rape you." He ground his teeth. "I'm not that kind of man." His distaste for the thought warped his tone.

He backed far enough away from her to collect himself. Pulling a cloth from his pocket, he held it to a bloody scratch on his chin. The cloth itself reminded him of Emerald and that soothed him.

The woman watched. "You said, you needed me and I agreed to let you have me. But then you flipped me over." She glared at him. "What was I supposed to think? Who are you?" Her brows crashed together.

He could not avoid a sullen tone. "I am the Royal Shadow. I've come to retrieve the Princess. You—" he pointed at her, "—are holding her prisoner. I'll trade her life for yours. If I spare you now, will you release her?" His mood darkened. This had not gone as planned.

She squared her shoulders and adjusted her arms beneath her. "And if I refuse? I suppose you would take advantage of what you've discovered about me to get what you want."

Anger surged within him that she would accuse him of such intentions. Yet, he hesitated to tell her the truth because it might be the only threat capable of intimidating her. No, he couldn't even pretend to be so despicable, not even for the Future Queen. He sighed and broke eye contact.

"I might end up killing you, but I would never rape you," he said.

"Then how did you plan to get me to agree to your terms?" She sat up the best she could with her leg trapped beneath the horse and her hands tied behind her back.

He stared at her. "I bested you and spared your life. You are honor bound to repay me life for a life. I want hers."

"Honor? You think I have honor?" She laughed in what sounded like genuine amusement.

He stood up and came over to her. She quit laughing. Her eyes were wide, like a frightened child. He folded the cloth in his hands to the clean side and took a knee beside her. He brushed strands of hair from her forehead and wiped the tears from her cheeks.

"I know you do." He stood and looked down at her. "Emerald wouldn't have stayed with you if you didn't."

She swallowed. "The King will kill me if I let her go."

Darrin took a deep breath through clenched teeth. "Then come with us."

Her eyes opened wider, but she didn't answer.

"We need supplies. You would be rewarded by the Steward of the West Wind." He hated speaking for his mother.

"How could you guarantee that?"

He clenched his right hand into a fist. "I know what she will do because I am her son." How had he lost control of this situation? "Will you set Emerald free? Will you come with us?"

The woman gazed at him for a long time. Once more, her eyes drew him in. He started to see why she was so popular with men.

"Well?" he asked.

"Kiss me."

His brows shot up and his heart jolted into a breakneck rhythm. He wasn't so much angry as frightened.

"Why?" he asked.

"I need to know what kind of man you are. If I'm going to trust you, then kiss me." She held his gaze.

"No."

"Then you can't have her."

He closed the distance between them. "I will not betray my duty to the Princess."

"Your Princess doesn't even know you're here." She laughed without mirth. "Besides, what obligation could you have to her if you will not trade a single kiss for her freedom?"

Exasperation growled forth from him. He paced away and back. His brain refused to provide an alternative course of action.

"How can a kiss convince you to trust me?"

"Believe me." Triumph gleamed in her eyes. "One kiss from you will tell me all I need to know."

He knit his brows and beseeched her with his eyes not to ask this of him. However, she held his gaze without relenting.

"Fine." He squatted to heave the horse up enough for her to slip her leg out from under the enormous animal.

The horse wasn't dead, only sleeping, and would soon awaken. If he had to kiss this woman, then he would do it standing. He didn't feel comfortable laying over her like some kind of predator.

She attempted, to no avail, to gain her feet. He reached under her arms and lifted her to a standing position. She was petite.

He wasn't tall compared to Southerners, but he was a head taller than this woman. It made him feel masculine. She made him feel masculine. He cleared his throat and dropped his hands to his sides.

"You'll forgive me if I don't untie you." He didn't trust her.

She stood still, observing him. "There are two conditions to the kiss. The first is that I end it. The second is that you don't resist. Do you agree?"

Darrin swallowed. What kind of woman was this? He nodded.

He resented everything she now forced him to do. He hated the situation worse because a small part of him was curious. What would it be like to kiss an experienced woman?

Her expression sobered. "Sit down and lean against the horse."

Darrin scowled. What did she hope to accomplish with this? In the end, he relented and sat as directed. She straddled him front to front. He clenched his jaw against the feel of her.

"Are you ready?" She seemed serious about the kiss. But more than that, she was sweating and stalling.

Perhaps, she wasn't toying with him.

"Put your hands wherever you like." She spoke this instruction in a sensual tone that didn't quite match her body language.

The bravado made her seem vulnerable. He hesitated. Unsure, he put his hands on her knees.

"Kiss me." The edge had gone from her voice.

He met her gaze and she drew him in. Thoughts of duty fled. She was a beautiful woman.

"I just want to say—" He leaned toward her lips.

She closed the distance and stopped him short of whatever it was he had planned to say. Her tongue parted his lips and entered his mouth. She seemed to expect something from him that he couldn't deliver and it left her hesitant.

She eased into more of a teaching role. Patient, she seemed to enjoy demonstrating ways to elicit pleasure. The kiss evoked a primal response in him. When she allowed him to meet her halfway, the feeling intensified.

For a long time, his mind remained aloof as he repeated the things she taught. He wasn't sure when it happened, but she stopped initiating and he took over. She had drawn the kiss out and made it so sensual that he had somehow gotten overwhelmed. Before he knew it, he slid his hands up her hips and pulled her body to him.

The instant he realized what he had done, he broke away gasping and filled with desire. He'd been caught up in the kiss. The intimacy hadn't been simply physical. She'd shared herself with him, given part of herself.

Her gaze remained unguarded for a moment. Sadly, the vulnerable woman he'd witnessed within withdrew behind a veil. It had to be this way.

He pulled back. However, part of him hated to see it end. That part shamed him.

"Forgive me." Whether he spoke to her or to Emerald he didn't know.

The woman got to her feet and walked a few steps away. "Don't tell Emerald I did that. I had no right. You belong to her." With her head down and her body turned away, he couldn't see her expression.

The shame of what he'd just done sunk in to weigh on his chest. His grief was both emotional and physical. He wanted to cry and vomit at the same time. Through great effort, he managed to clamp down on those urges as he climbed off the ground and stood.

"I'm the one who betrayed my oath." He felt like he owed her for what she had given him. It had meant something to her. "Thank you for the kiss." It had meant something to him too.

He'd learned a lot about her and it changed his mind. She was far different on the inside than her actions had led him to believe. She lived a hard life, as he did. It was a lonely life.

The men she kept company with obviously didn't fill her need, at least not for long. It was both like and yet unlike this kiss. It didn't last and yet the consequences could never end. Would he ever forget it or the feel of her body in his arms?

This was a colossal mistake. It would have been worse if he had allowed it to go on. Fortunately, some part of him had stopped at the last moment.

He knew the part of him that loved Emerald had overpowered everything else. His love for her had saved him from disaster. He pulled a knife from his boot and walked up behind the woman.

"I broke my word to you when I ended the kiss." He cut her bonds. "I think you know why." He cast the cut rope to the ground and walked a few paces away through the tall grass.

"Does Emerald know you love her?" The woman rubbed her wrists but didn't face him.

"I told her once, but it meant nothing to her." His voice came out thick with emotion.

"You're wrong." She wiped her eyes. "Is that why you serve Emerald in secret? So, she can never hurt you again?" She faced him.

"I've failed her so many times." His lower lip quivered. "Please don't let it happen again."

"Why didn't you stop them from hurting her? You are her protector, aren't you?"

He stiffened. "I wasn't there." He looked her in the eyes. "Just like I'm not there now."

Her gaze hardened. "How would you get her to safety?"

"I'd find a way." He ground his teeth.

"With no food and the exertion of climbing a mountain making the possibility of miscarriage so much the greater, why would you risk it?"

Blood drained from his face and neck. "Miscarriage?"

Her shoulders slumped. "You didn't even know she was pregnant?"

He looked away. Was that what Roger had been so happy about? Was that why Emerald had been so afraid?

The woman walked toward her horse. "She's better off with me. I'm feeding her and protecting her. It won't happen again. You have my word."

He growled. "Impossible. She cannot stay in Frenland."

"No, Emerald cannot go with you, not until you have a better plan." She folded her arms across her chest.

"I'll take her to Prince Stephan. He'll protect her."

She laughed an unkind, mocking noise. "That whelp will not last another moon. His forces are all but destroyed. If you place your trust in him then you will fail."

Darrin drew himself up to his full height and strode over to confront the woman. "Then I'll take her under the mountains to her home. I just need the supplies to make it through."

"I won't give them to you. It's a foolhardy plan. She's better off with me." She nudged the horse with her knee.

"Just who are you, anyway?" He leaned over her with his face in hers.

She squared her shoulders. "I am General Valerie of Bluebird Vale. I give you my word, Shadow. She will be safe at any cost. Have no fear."

Darrin stood agape but managed to slam his jaw shut and kneel. "Please, forgive me, Your Highness. I didn't know who you were."

Heat flushed his skin. He had kissed Sarialla's daughter. Salicor was King of Frenland and the twins were next in line to the throne. This was a Princess he'd been fooling around with, not some low Commander. Well, that explained the fact that she had mastered his language. The gift must run in the family.

At that moment, the horse awoke. The beast shook his head and took to his feet. To Darrin's surprise, he seemed quite steady. Valerie gathered her weapons, slung her chainmail shirt onto the horse's back, and mounted.

"Return for Emerald when you have a plan and the means to carry it out. Prove to me that you'll do a better job than you have in the past. Also, she has to want to go with you. I won't force her." With that, she rode off in the direction the patrol had gone.

Darrin stood there with his regret and uncertainty. Neither one was easy to stomach. He glared after Princess Valerie. He, foolhardy? They would see who was the foolhardier between them.

Chapter Thirty-Seven

Over the next few weeks, Emerald followed Valerie everywhere, at least when the General was in the village. Valerie's patrols along the border and occasional visits to check on the range cattle detail to the west kept her busy, but Emerald stayed occupied as well. She did a variety of work to earn her keep. She carried messages, cooked, cleaned, and tended an extensive vegetable and herb garden.

At night, she slept on a cot the General had moved into the cottage. They often had time to talk. Much to Emerald's relief, Valerie didn't bring home any more men from the village. She did talk about men, however, but only because it seemed to amuse her to see Emerald blush.

One night in the cottage, Valerie sat at the table writing letters home to the families of soldiers killed by raiders. Her jerky movements and sour expression spoke volumes about her mood. Emerald took her time sewing the second sleeve on her dress. It would be complete tonight and she looked forward to wearing it in the morning. Her trousers had grown snug as her belly swelled.

Valerie finished the letters and put away her ink and quill with a clatter. A grim look descended on her expression, accompanied by an unhealthy need in her eyes. She licked her lips.

"I'm going out."

"Why, Valerie? What can you find out there?"

Emerald's heart rate increased. If Valerie kept squandering her strength with men, she would not live long enough to regret it. Men were not to be trifled with. They were dangerous.

"Comfort."

Emerald shook her head. "Torment is what you will find, nothing more."

Anger flashed across Valerie's features. "You don't understand. I want to kill something, anything. Even you are not safe from me."

"You're not an animal." Emerald set her sewing aside. "You are a woman. You have a choice."

A mirthless smile twisted Valerie's face. "I'm a bad woman, Emerald."

"No, you're not." Emerald stood and crossed the room to her friend. "You do what you do to hurt yourself because you were hurt." She touched the General's shoulder. "But no one can hurt you anymore."

Valerie's expression contorted and a sound approaching a sob escaped her. "You're wrong, Em-Emerald." She pushed away and opened the door. "You'll find that out tomorrow when my uncle arrives." With those words, she fled into the darkness.

EMERALD HAD ARISEN early to pull weeds in the garden before the heat of the sun made the day unbearable. She noticed Byron arrive an hour after sunrise. He met his sister in the town hall, and when the twins came out, their severe expressions gave evidence that they had argued.

As Valerie approached, she said nothing about what had been decided but instead walked Emerald straight to the Smithy's. The soot-covered man extracted a different brand from the fire with his leather gloved hand. Emerald trembled but submitted to the torture.

She knew Valerie wouldn't do this if it wasn't critically important. The second brand seared into her forearm, a little higher than the first. It meant her ownership had changed. She tried not to whimper.

Valerie put her to work in the farthest part of the garden and told her to stay there. By midday, she suffered for lack of water under the hot sun. She also felt ill due to the new brand on her wrist.

A sunhat and gloves along with the newly completed long-sleeved summer dress protected her delicate skin from sunburn. The thin material allowed her skin to breathe, but it didn't help with thirst. Being pregnant helped with nothing, of course.

She focused on the dress in an effort to distract herself. It felt strange to wear a dress again after so many years. Sitting on a stool in the garden to rest, she took off her gloves and wiped the sweat from her brow. When was the last time she had worn a dress? She gritted her teeth as the memory of her trial returned.

Talking with Valerie had helped her work through a few things. However, the first rape still tormented her. It wasn't something she could forget.

Living in a cottage again had been uncomfortable at first. Going to the well for water had made her agitated. It took a while to figure out why.

After her grandparents had been killed, she had taken Stephan to Stone Castle, because she felt safer there. She had believed he didn't know what had happened to her. After all, he was only ten years old and had been tossed into the well. He hadn't seen what happened.

When she had pulled him up with the bucket, he was exhausted from swimming. She had walked toward the castle and he had followed. Had he heard the assault? For certain he had seen the blood on her dress. Perhaps, he had dismissed it as part of the gore that covered her arms and face.

It was too late now, but she realized she should have talked to him. Instead, she'd left him in the empty castle and gone back to take care of her grandparents' bodies. What must he have thought as he sat there all alone?

"Emerald."

She looked up to see Byron standing beside her. She hadn't anticipated seeing him here. The look in his eyes surprised her. It caused her to suspect the sweat on his brow hadn't come from the heat of the day. She concluded he was afraid and guessed why.

"Emerald, do you trust my sister?" His serious tone let her know this was a more important question than it seemed.

"Yes."

"Then you must trust me." He extended his hand and she took it. "Do not get angry in front of my uncle. Come with me now. Valerie told me to tell you that I'm not a rapist."

He guided her out of the garden to the town hall. When she saw Salicor, for there could be no mistaking the aura of authority that radiated from the man, she wanted to run. He was handsome like his nephew. But even his age could not soften the cruel bent of his expression.

Valerie stood beside him, her features pale and drawn. She glanced at Emerald which caused Salicor to notice her approach. He came at her, cast her sunhat aside, undid the laces of her dress and forced it to her feet. His sharp intake of breath and lecherous smile elicited a full body blush from her, but she held her tongue.

Salicor took the three steps between him and Valerie and landed a solid fist to her stomach. "You should have told me about this lovely creature the instant you found her. You'll pay for that."

Valerie had doubled over but now straightened to face her uncle, holding her midsection with her hands. "I sent a message through Byron right away. I'm sure he forwarded it to you. But I'm afraid he claimed her for himself before you could get it."

Byron smiled. "Uncle, how could I not take pleasure in this exquisite creature? I didn't think you would mind since she was already with child. I'm sure you noticed." His hand swept down to caress Emerald's swelling belly.

It took all of her strength to keep from pushing him away. His words made her hot with anger. His touch, however, was torture.

She had been having dreams about him. The dreams frightened her with the intensity of the passion they stirred. How could she imagine such things about a man she had only seen once?

"I noticed." Salicor took a step toward Byron. "Then this is not your handiwork? You wouldn't be lying to me would you, Nephew?" His black eyes bored into Byron's brown ones.

Byron showed all of his perfect teeth in a disarming smile. "I received the letter from Valerie about three weeks ago and came to see for myself. She had the poor woman locked up in a filthy cell. She didn't have a stitch of clothing. I made myself welcome." His fingertips traced a line up her belly to her breast and circled the nipple.

Emerald's breath caught in her throat. She swallowed to keep from uttering a more incriminating noise. She had never been touched like this. Her breast betrayed the reaction, but her heart raced in fear.

"You see? She didn't complain." He let his hand drop to his side.

"Not much fight in her then?" Salicor adjusted his stance.

"No. Not in this one, Uncle. This one knows what she likes." Byron took Emerald in his arms and leaned in to kiss her.

The kiss startled Emerald so much that she held her breath. Dizziness overwhelmed her and she started to black out. He pulled back breathless and pressed her head to his shoulder.

"There, there, my sweet, it won't be long now."

"You had no right to her, Byron." Salicor's attention fixed on the lines of her body.

"I had every right, Uncle. I paid Valerie twenty gold pieces for her. I'm sure, when I tire of her, she'll fetch a similar price. It was a good investment."

"Twenty gold pieces? You could buy forty slaves for that. Byron, you're a fool." Salicor paced.

"If you want her, I'll let you have her for fifteen. It isn't fair, though. She likes me." He reached down to run a hand from Emerald's knee to her inner thigh.

She gasped and clutched his shirt, pleading with her eyes for him to stop. If his hand went any higher, she'd panic. His eyebrows lifted a fraction as his fingertips paused on the scars etched in her flesh.

Color climbed Salicor's neck. "I don't need your leavings. Take her. Go have your fun." He drew a knife from his belt and jabbed it at Byron's crotch. Byron avoided the blade, though he did not let go of Emerald. "If you ever take what is mine again, I will remove your motivation. Do you understand me?"

Byron's face drained of color. "Yes. It will not happen again."

Salicor sheathed the knife and grabbed a fistful of Valerie's hair. "As for you, Niece, I have something more to discuss with you." He grasped her buttocks and shoved her into the town hall.

Emerald shot toward her friend but Byron caught her. He clapped a hand over her mouth. Holding her firmly, he picked up her dress and dragged her away.

"Don't say a word."

His expression frightened her, but all she could think about was Valerie. What must she be going through? How could she endure it?

Salicor must have done this over and over. Was he the one who had raped her at the tender age of five? Tears flowed down Emerald's face. She didn't realize where Byron had taken her until he cast her on her cot in Valerie's cottage.

"You are mine now."

His silhouette filled the doorframe. He shut and bolted the door. In a swift motion, he drew the curtains on the window.

Emerald trembled in terror. What was he saying? He had assured her that he was not a rapist.

She had believed him. That was a foolish thing to do. She realized it too late.

However, he didn't attack. Instead, he sat at the table and rested his head in his hands. The lines of his body spoke of his grief for his sister's plight, and perhaps ab it about his guilt for allowing it.

Tears flowed down her face. It was all too horrible. How could Byron let this happen to his sister? How could he just sit there while his uncle hurt Valerie? What kind of man would do that?

"Why don't you stop him? You could stop him." Anger clawed past the lump in her throat.

"I can't." It was a whisper from a man immobilized by fear.

Emerald pulled the sheet from the cot to cover her nakedness and stood. "What do you mean you can't? You are a man, a warrior. Fight him. kill him."

She wished she had a knife at Salicor's throat right now. She would not hesitate to spill his blood. In fact, she wanted it so much she could almost taste the iron.

"He hurts you more if you fight him." Byron balled his fists in his hair. "He's too strong."

The shock of his words made the blood drain from her head. Could men be raped? It was the last thought she had before oblivion swept over her.

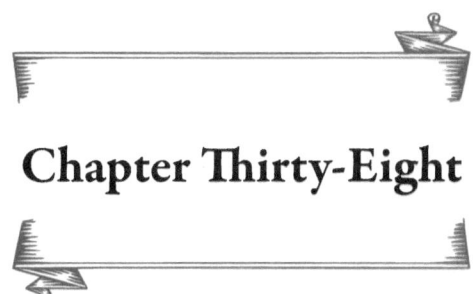

Chapter Thirty-Eight

Emerald awoke on her cot with the sheet tucked in at her shoulders. Byron knelt beside her with worry evident in his expression. Tears coursed his face.

"I'm sorry." She intended so much more than those simple words could express.

He reached out to stroke her cheek with his thumb. She knew he meant it as a comforting gesture, but her body took it the wrong way. Evidently, he had been told she had been raped.

She sensed that he did not intend her any harm. That was what the gesture had been meant to communicate. However, the heat in her cheeks betrayed the sensual nature of her response. She closed her eyes in an effort to force the feeling away.

"You want me to touch you?" His voice filled with surprise.

Emerald opened her eyes, meeting his gaze with force.

"No."

His chin lifted. He nodded his understanding. Standing up, he paced the floor.

"You've never been with a man before, have you?" He looked at her now, standing still, waiting for the answer.

Anger clouded her thinking process. She was naked under the sheet and couldn't move much without exposing herself. Despite this, her hands became restless, eager to rip something to pieces. She clenched her fists and her jaw.

He knelt by her bed. "I don't mean rape, Emerald. It doesn't have to be like that. Making love is different. It doesn't hurt. You're not afraid. It's a wonderful sharing between two people, an intimate dance of give and take."

His breathing came fast and shallow as he reached out to tuck a strand of hair behind her ear.

The look in his eyes was pure desire. Emerald had never seen a man look at her quite like that before. It frightened her. She could never live up to his expectations.

She shook her head. She would never allow him to...make love to her. It was a new concept. She pushed his hand away.

"I don't love you, Byron. I could never do what you say. I don't do that."

He rested his hand on the side of the cot and sat back on his heels. "Valerie was right to protect you. You can't take much more abuse. It'll kill you. Without your innocence, you would be destroyed. I won't take it from you." He stood, looked at her, and then sat in the chair.

"However, I'm afraid you will have to share my bed." He held up a finger to put off a response. "I assure you; it is the safest place for you." He gave her a rueful smile. "You should rest. I'll be back to get you after a while." He left the cottage.

EMERALD COULDN'T REST. As soon as Byron shut the door, she got up and put on her dress. She felt dirty. She washed her face and arms, dressing the tender brand with bandages.

Gritting her teeth, she gripped the edge of the table. A myriad of thoughts ran through her head, but there was nothing she could do except honor her friend's sacrifice. Valerie had given her to Byron in order to save her from Salicor.

Right now, Valerie was paying a terrible price for it. Emerald couldn't just stand here, but she had to, didn't she? Suddenly, she could force herself to be still no longer and turned to go to her friend's aid.

At that moment, Valerie stumbled into the cottage.

The look on her face said everything. Emerald rushed to her side but knew better than to touch her. Instead, she shut the door.

Valerie took the few steps to her cot and collapsed onto her belly. Her eyes closed, and some of the tension in her body slackened. The rasp of her breathing eased.

Emerald knelt beside her, unable to keep from crying out. She had to put her hand over her own mouth to stifle the sobs that shook her shoulders. However, nothing could be done about the tears that streamed her face.

Words proved impossible at a time like this. Her only hope was that her presence would comfort her friend. From experience, however, she knew that nothing would help.

EMERALD STAYED WITH Valerie until Byron returned to the cottage. He didn't wake his sister or say a word. He just helped Emerald from the floor beside Valerie's cot and guided her out the door. Once outside, he pulled the door closed and rested his head on the wood for a moment.

He didn't linger but led Emerald to his horse. He lifted her onto its back and mounted behind her. With his legs, he and urged the rough looking horse into motion.

They departed the town at a gentle pace. He held her around the middle. It felt like a possessive gesture but also helped her stomach not to be jarred by the movement of the horse's hips.

For some reason every time the horse took a step it sent an odd sensation through her belly. It was uncomfortable though not painful. At that moment she felt a strange movement within her. She'd never felt anything like that before and it startled her.

Byron splayed his hand across the place where she'd felt it. He seemed to be waiting to feel it again. When nothing happened, he leaned his head over her shoulder to smile at her. His brown eyes sparkled with delight.

"I'm sorry." Her cheeks blazed with heat. "I didn't mean to do that."

"You didn't." His breath caressed her ear.

Their faces were so close. Despite herself, she glanced at his lips. Her ears throbbed with the flow of blood and the feeling spread.

Byron smiled at her embarrassment. She knew he wasn't oblivious to her other reaction either. To her relief, he didn't comment on it.

"It was the baby, Emerald. He kicked."

"What? Can it do that?" She put her hand next to his.

He moved his hand to cover hers and adjusted it to the right spot. There it was again. It was a tiny bump, difficult to detect on the outside, though she felt more on the inside.

"I felt it." She giggled.

"Haven't you ever felt a baby kick before?"

He still held her hand, but his touch was light and his eyes were focused on the road ahead. She shook her head. It seemed strange that she didn't remember her mother carrying her younger brothers, but she didn't.

"No, I know nothing about babies before they're born. I know how to care for children, but I didn't even understand how the process worked until...I was compelled to understand it." She pushed his hand away.

"I thought you grew up on a farm." He leaned around to look her in the face. "That's what my sister said."

Emerald blushed. Memories of what she'd seen on the farm came back to her. She pushed the thoughts away.

"I didn't know people worked the same way. We are different from animals, you know." She tensed. "At least I thought we were."

"Don't worry, we are." He rubbed her arm in a reassuring fashion. "At least most of us are."

Emerald drew a breath and let it out. Even if it was a lie, she felt better for hearing it. Her experience and recent observations had caused her to think people could be far worse than animals.

She didn't like the ramifications of that. She hoped he was telling the truth and that she had been mistaken somehow. Personally, she could never find out for sure, but she hoped he was right.

Chapter Thirty-Nine

The landscape of Frenland had altered somewhat. There had been several fires during the two weeks Darrin had been gone. He had managed to find the northern entrance tunnel under the mountains and steal enough supplies to get Emerald and himself through.

It had taken a frustrating amount of time. What if Emerald wouldn't come with him? How could she be safe with the whole world burning around her?

As he approached the village, it surprised him to discover that there were no patrols. The entire army had abandoned the town.

A full moon ascended a night sky clear of clouds. Smoke emanated from the ash of a recent blaze, and several homes at the edge of town had been consumed. At first, he thought that Valerie's cottage had burned as well. But it remained intact.

Not a soul stirred as he strode up to the residence. The door stood ajar, the inside black as coal. They must have gone.

He pushed the door further open and inhaled the stench of death. His heart jolted. He dropped his pack to rifle through it for a candle.

"Shadow, is that you?" Valerie spoke the mountain tongue in a weak, dry voice.

Relief washed over him. "Yes." He rushed forward.

"Don't touch me." Panic filled her voice and she reached out to hold him at bay.

"What's wrong?"

Her arm relaxed onto the cot. His eyes adjusted and he could see that she lay on her belly. All was not well.

"You need not worry about Emerald. My brother has taken her into his care. She will not be harmed." Her breath came in labored pants. "It's good you returned while I can still direct you."

She paused again to draw breath. "Byron is training soldiers at the midland camp. If you go east to the next village, then walk due north for two days, you'll find him."

She muffled a whimper. "We concealed my injuries. Please, don't tell her about me. It's good you came in time to be here when I pass. I didn't want to die alone."

Darrin clenched his jaw. "Rest easy, no more harm will come to you, Princess."

In the darkness, he spotted the outline of the oil lamp on the table. He took it out to the smoldering poles of the burned out home next door and lit the lamp. Placing the glass over the wick to protect the flame, he returned inside to see if anything could be done to save Valerie.

She lay with her eyes closed.

He brought the table and chair over to her bedside. Nude beneath a sheet, she reeked of infection and filth. He lifted the covering, but she stopped him.

"Don't...I don't want you to touch me."

He lowered the linen. What he'd seen was bad enough. Someone had cut gashes into her back. They'd been sewn shut but infection had taken hold. Why hadn't anyone tended to her needs?

"Please, Princess, let me make you comfortable. I will prepare a broth that will take away your pain."

Her eyelids closed.

He heated a metal cup of water over the vent of the lamp. When it had warmed, he stirred in some herbs. It would put her to sleep.

"Drink this and all will be well." He held the cup for her.

When her breathing had slowed, he knew she had fallen asleep.

While she couldn't protest, he found several washcloths to clean her with and fetched a bucket of water. She'd been brutalized in a cruel fashion and her wounds treated poorly. He cut the stitches out of her back and cleansed each wound with his special medical kit from his mother. The task proved laborious and gruesome. Her intimate parts were heavily scarred and recently torn front and back.

Who could've done this terrible thing? She was a woman. Her body was sacred.

Until today, this part of a woman had remained unknown to him. How could any man desecrate her in this way? Anger raged within him because she deserved better.

He sewed the last stitch in the most private of areas, observing that women were much more complicated than men. Life grew within them and somehow issued forth from them. Even seeing did not solve the mystery.

Men's bodies seemed straight forward in comparison. A man's involvement in the process of creation was brief. It was no wonder women ruled over men if this was what happened when women were not protected.

He placed a dry cloth between her legs and covered her with a clean sheet. Finding a blanket in a trunk, he laid it over her. Carefully, he turned her onto her least injured side so she could rest easier.

Whoever had taken advantage of her weakened state would find his sword an unwelcome intrusion when he returned for another go around. Darrin left the bolt open on the door and replaced the table. He set the chair in front of the door so it would squeak when the intruder came.

Lowering the wick on the lamp, he lay his blanket beside Valerie's cot. He drew Krelor's sword and laid it with the hilt beneath his palm. The sword agreed with him and the thrum of its power kept him alert.

As he lay there waiting, he tried to put the new injuries out of his mind by pondering the scars he'd seen on Valerie's body. Her back held horizontal scars by the dozen, including the three fresh matching slashes. There was an S-shaped brand on her right buttocks that sent a chill down his spine. However, her legs were the worst. They were covered by faded burns severe enough that he wondered how she had survived them. Perhaps, one day he would ask her to tell the story.

If Emerald were any indication, however, then Valerie would be angry that he had involved himself in her private matters. Even though he was trying to save her life, she wouldn't thank him. He finally understood that pushing away his help was the only means she had of reasserting her self-control.

The women were similar in that way. Their shared suffering had tempered them like swords in a forge. Their inner forms were of the same metal. They could not bend, only break.

IN THE GRAY LIGHT OF dawn, the chair squeaked. Darrin shot up and flung the door wide. He knew the man's guilt by the look in his eyes. He ran him through all the way to the hilt, twisting for good measure.

The grotesquely disfigured man died without a word and Darrin drug the body over to the burned-out cottage next door. He dug a shallow grave, placed the wretch in it, and covered him with ashes. The smell of the fire would mask the scent of his decay.

Darrin spat on the grave.

He washed his hands at the well and returned to the cottage. After bolting the door, he drew the curtain of the little window. Fatigue overwhelmed his spirit and he prepared to sleep on what he suspected had been Emerald's cot.

"You killed for me?"

He sighed and found the lamp. Turning up the wick, he met Valerie's gaze. He couldn't stop thinking about what she had been through at that man's hands.

"He would've raped you again. That is why he came isn't it?"

Her hand trembled. "I told you not to touch me." She looked down at her body and then back at him. "You had no right." She broke off and sobbed into her pillow.

"I did what needed to be done." Anger blurred his vision. "Don't think I took pleasure from it. The sight of your injuries sickened me, and I would kill any man who had done that to a woman. He was lucky I showed mercy, and so are you."

Darrin stalked over to the farthest corner of the room. He clenched his fists, wanting to slam at least one of them into something, but he knew she was frightened. Willfully, he relaxed his fists, because he did not wish to panic her.

"I'm sorry to have disobeyed you, but there was no other way. I would prefer that the mystery still stood between us as much as you do. But you needed my help. There is no way I could let you die, not when I had the power to heal you." He avoided her gaze.

"I'm going to live?" Her words were a whisper. Then the look in her eyes hardened and she let out a harsh laugh. "I will have my revenge on my uncle. I swear it."

Darrin sighed.

"Rest...I need to rest. May I sleep here?" He indicated the other cot with his hand.

He bowed his head. If she cast him out, then she would likely not survive. She needed further care.

All he had come for was to retrieve Emerald, but a sense of duty bound him to help Valerie recover. She needed his protection while she could not protect herself. After all, she had been willing to die for Emerald, and that meant everything.

"Yes." The severity of her illness showed in her watery eyes. "You may stay." She rested her head on the pillow and exhaustion eased from her features.

Darrin turned down the wick on the lamp and slipped off his boots. He had made the cottage as secure as he could make it. So, he really should sleep, but he couldn't. Taking a drink from a water skin in his pack, he stared at Emerald's cot. Would her scent still be there?

As he slept in her bed would she be safe in her new place? Would Byron keep his word? What kind of man let this happen to his sister?

A man like that could not be trusted.

Darrin knelt by the cot as if approaching a shrine. He touched the blanket. Once again, he had come too late. A lump formed in his throat and he took deep breaths to dispel his unshed tears.

Unfastening his belt, he slipped off his leggings. He lay them and his sword below where his hand would rest. The room was stifling hot with the door shut. He pulled off his tunic and lay down beneath the sheet.

Turning his head to the side, he inhaled. "Emerald."

Chapter Forty

After two days ride, Emerald and Byron arrived at a villa outside the army training camp. It was his home, complete with servants and luxuries she had rarely seen. The way Byron lived stood in stark contrast to Valerie's spartan cottage. She wondered if there were more to it than a mere difference of taste.

True to his word, she slept safely in his large bed. His flirtations drove her body wild. Her heart, however, remained inexplicably aloof.

Aside from the flirtations, he allowed her to choose the level of intimacy they shared. He was right, she needed to protect her innocence. Without it, she would feel cheap, tawdry. She would suffer like Valerie, believing she was bad and letting her actions mirror that belief.

Emerald could see that road did not lead to happiness. If she had fallen in love with Byron, then it might be different...perhaps. For now, however, friendship was all she desired.

Working in the household was the one relief she had from the isolation and boredom of life as a slave. She washed the laundry. She scrubbed floors. The other servants spoke to her rarely, however, and she languished in loneliness until Byron returned from his duties at the end of each day.

In the dining room, she served a meal the kitchen staff had prepared.

"Would you like more? What did you say was in this?"

He smiled with a warmth of affection she craved. "Chicken braised in red wine, with crispy bacon bits, mushrooms, and onions." He accepted her offer.

"I'd like to learn to make this, but I don't think we have red wine in the South. How do you acquire it?" She was seated opposite him and continued eating the delectable meal, particularly enjoying the mushrooms in the sauce.

"I'm sure you have noticed the vineyards surrounding the villa." He drank from a glass beside his plate at the table.

"Yes, is wine made from grapes?" She put together the clues.

"Fermented grapes, bottled for preservation." He laid his hand on the bottle next to his glass.

She had tried the drink when she had first come to Frenland. However, she had not cared for the way it made her feel and had partaken only of water thereafter. She scrutinized the bottle. Knowing somewhat about fermentation and the taboo it held among her people, she wondered at the use of it among this nation.

"It lowers your inhibitions." He touched her hand.

"Is that why Valerie acts the way she does sometimes?"

He withdrew his hand. "I wouldn't know." He wiped his mouth with the linen napkin from his lap and laid it on the table. He stood to leave the dining room.

"And you had hoped I would behave the same way?" The possibility stunned her because she had believed his motives to be pure.

He shook his head and smiled. "No. I simply hoped the wine would help you put aside your fears long enough to feel passion."

"Because I don't, right, and this will help?" She lifted his glass and stared at it.

He sighed and walked to her side. "No. Intoxication does not change one's true feelings."

She lowered the glass to the tablecloth. "I...don't know what you want from me." That was not true, he wanted her to lay with him rather than beside him.

He took her in his arms and kissed her gently. "I need you to be happy."

"I...I'm sorry." Heart pounding, the corners of her vision closed in on her.

"I'm the one who is sorry." He gathered her in his arms and carried her to the bedroom. "Fear not. I will not take you against your will. I just wish I could convince you of that." He sat her in a chair by the window and went to dress for bed.

Through the open window, she could see the distant peaks of the mountains, glorious in the moonlight. If only Darrin would rescue her. But he was far away, and even if he were not, he would not come.

Her last words to him echoed in her mind, as painful as ever. Yet somehow less true...less indelibly written upon her soul. Something had changed, though it did not help her current predicament.

Byron came toward her, carrying her nightgown. He took her by the hand, causing her to stand. With nimble fingers, he undid the laces of her dress and let it fall to the floor.

Trembling, she stood helpless in his grasp. He kissed her neck and his hands roved her back until he pressed his body to hers. The terror she felt caused her to cry out, though she dared not resist him.

Panting, he released her. "You see? Passion is..." With space between them, he caught his breath and then frowned. "Forgive me. I forgot how afraid you are."

Tears coursed her cheeks.

He handed her the nightgown.

She clutched it to her, trying to cover as much as she could.

"How can I help you to overcome this?"

She shook her head. There was no way.

"I think you're wrong about that. I know you want me." He went to the bed and laid beneath the sheet. It was a warm evening.

"How can you say that?" It made no sense that he should think so.

"You talk in your sleep."

"I do not." No one had ever told her this before. It mortified her what she might have said.

He chuckled. "Yes, you do. The first time we slept in this bed together, I mistook you for being awake. You let me kiss you."

"I did?" She shuddered to believe it.

"You had awakened me by calling my name." He pulled back the covers on her side of the bed.

Humiliation flushed her skin with heat. "I did?"

"I continued to kiss you, thinking you would reciprocate, but you never did. The instant I moved to mount you, well, let's just say, I realized my mistake." His tone remained light.

Agape, she could not think of a response. He hadn't hurt her, even though she had given him a reason to. What could it mean? Perhaps, he actually wasn't a rapist.

She walked toward the window.

What did her unconscious actions mean? Yes, she was attracted to him. However, she had not considered herself capable of this. She had called his name in her sleep and enjoyed his advances up to a point.

"You didn't force yourself on me?" She had to be sure.

"Of course, not. I will never hurt you, Emerald. I gave my word." He rolled onto his side, facing away from her half of the bed.

She stared at him until, eventually, his breathing leveled and she knew he was asleep. He'd given her much to think about. The needs of her body were betraying her. She wondered how much longer he could keep his promise if she continued sending mixed indications of how she felt.

The moonlit mountains drew her to the windowsill. As if she could see through them to her home, she gazed for hours. Memories of the carefree days of her childhood comforted her as if she were once again wrapped in the arms of her mother. Oh, how she wished she could speak to her about this.

Perhaps, she would have the answers. Mother had loved Father. She had given up a career as a famous singer and the riches of her prestigious family to marry him.

Emerald shook her head. These feelings for Byron were only lust, merely physical attraction. The reason they were so confusing was that he was Sarialla's son. She had loved him ever since she was a child and had heard Sarialla's stories of him.

Love made sense. This kind of platonic love changed things. She breathed a sigh of relief and went to bed. Able to sleep in peace for the first time in days, she dreamed of home.

Chapter Forty-One

Darrin had to give Valerie sleeping tonic each time he cleaned her wounds. But she never said another word about it. Despite his best efforts, however, her recovery progressed slower than he had hoped.

He needed to go to Emerald.

It surprised him that no one bothered them in this cottage on the outskirts of town. He remained cautious, though, and did the household chores at night. He took long walks in the grass alone until Valerie recovered enough to walk with him.

The first time he took her outside the cottage, she stopped cold in her tracks.

"The fire got so close." Wide-eyed, she surveyed a damaged cottage on the left and a pile of ash on the right. "I almost burned alive."

The grass was scorched right up to the edge of the mud brick wall that surrounded her somewhat isolated home. That wall and the ceramic tile roof of her cottage were probably the only things that had saved her. He looked more closely, thinking of the village in general.

"Why did you choose this cottage?" He thought he knew the answer. It wasn't for convenience. This cottage was far from the army encampment north of town, including the horses she loved.

"I don't like fire." She walked out into the grass at the edge of the burned area.

He followed. "You chose this cottage long before Stephan started lighting fires. Is it because of the burns on your legs?"

She swirled around to stick a finger in his face. "Keep your nose out of my business." With that, she promptly passed out.

He caught her and turned to carry her back to the cottage, but as he did so, she awoke.

"I can't go inside, not yet." She clung to him in utter weakness.

"As you wish, but please tell me what happened." He'd learned that a soft answer often turned away her wrath.

"Lay me in the grass." Her strength was spent.

Very carefully, he placed her on her side, because he knew it pained her greatly to sit.

Eyes closed, she made a pillow of her arm and took a few minutes to catch her breath.

In an effort to be patient, he sat cross-legged where she could look at him easily.

"Perhaps, I will tell you my tale, if you have something worthy of exchange."

He frowned, finding it difficult to open up after so many years of secrecy.

She fell asleep, and he watched her for the better part of an hour as the grass waved the moonlight around them.

"My brother is a murderer and...a rapist," he said.

Her eyes opened, causing him to wonder if she had truly been asleep or not.

"You mention this because..."

"He is the one who destroyed Emerald. I only recently discovered this." He avoided her gaze.

"And you kept it from her." It wasn't a question.

"She killed him."

"I know, she told me."

"My brother."

She laughed darkly and rolled partly onto her back to look up at the stars.

"I never even knew he was dead." Anger overwhelmed his good sense.

"She cast his body in the well." Her voice was conversational.

Stunned by the revelation, he couldn't think of a response. So, he took a walk. Apparently, Emerald had finally talked to someone about what had happened. Good.

He shook his head. No, it was horrible. He didn't want to know any-more.

"I needed a purpose if I were to go on living after my daughter died." Valerie's voice carried in the night air.

He stopped. This was his one chance to hear Valerie's the story. He returned to sit beside her.

"Salicor offered me the opportunity to revive an ancient tradition. The Valkyrie. He said I could raise my own army of women and lead them. He wanted me to become a general."

Darrin knew better than to interrupt the story with questions. In fact, he was surprised she was speaking of such personal things at all. It meant she trusted him.

"He gave me twenty-five horses and two dozen of his castoff slaves. The horses were half wild and the girls were broken of body and spirit. I could relate to them." She had a blank stare.

He lay on his side, looking into her eyes so she didn't have to exert herself with speaking loudly.

"Our first assignment was to collect the taxes in the far-flung village of Scion. We arrived late in the evening and set up camp outside of town. Sometime in the night, I was bound, gagged, and kidnapped from my tent. The men tied me to a pole and carried me to the village." She looked off into her memory, speaking almost as if to herself.

He dreaded what she would say next.

"They had a bonfire burning in the center of town. Without ceremony, they hefted me over the flames. I screamed as my bare legs burned and struggled hard enough for one of the men to lose his grip.

"He dropped me into the flames. In the process his shirt sleeve caught fire. He ran.

"In an effort to stop the spread of fire, the other man chased after him. He inadvertently dumped me out of the flames as he did so. I rolled around in the dirt until the sound of sizzling flesh ended.

"Helpless, I watched as the town caught fire. The burning man hadn't stopped running. No one could catch him.

"The thatch of the homes hung low over the alleyways. As he passed by, they lit up. The fire spread until most of the village was consumed.

"My Valkyrie came to my rescue, stole a wagon, and hauled me to the Sages for healing. It took me a year before I could ride again. When that day came, my uncle ordered me to return to Scion and kill every living soul. My women were trained by then, and their ranks had swelled to over a hundred strong. We followed orders, mostly." She shrugged.

"I remained obedient to Salicor's commands until I captured Emerald." She met Darrin's gaze. "She saw something in me that I had never known I possessed. There was no hope for me until she loved me. I couldn't comprehend it at first. I probably still don't understand, but I wanted to be worthy of it. So, I changed." She stared at the swaying grass, deep in thought.

He nodded, though he frowned. "She has a special way about her. I thought she loved me too."

Valerie held him captive in her gaze. "You know better than to accuse her of being insincere. She isn't capable of it. Her feelings for you run deeper than you realize. Yes, she is conflicted, but you are her match. She is well aware of it."

THE CONSTRAINTS OF slavery chafed Emerald. Though the brands on her wrist had fully healed, the curtailment of her ability to choose for herself rubbed her mind raw. She longed to resist. But she forced herself to submit because she needed to keep her unborn child safe.

There was no way to leave.

Subdued, she smoothed the fabric of her dress against her round belly. She sat on the windowsill and gazed at the smoke-blue mountains. She didn't hear Byron enter the room. But she sensed him beside her now and smiled wistfully.

He kissed her cheek.

In order to stop him from touching her further, she took his hand and held it. He seemed satisfied. Standing behind her, he pressed his body against her and kissed the top of her head.

"Why do you watch the mountains?"

"I dream of home." She moved his hand to feel the movement of the baby within her belly, holding it in place. "Sarialla told me that motherhood would change me. I didn't see how that could be true, but it is."

"What do you mean?" He put his other arm around her and placed that hand over hers.

"It's hard to explain. This child is not just an ugly reminder of a nightmarish experience, it's also a part of me."

"The two things are not connected." He moved to meet her gaze. "You have to know that. If a man punched me in the jaw, and the next day I found a treasure buried in my field, I would not hold the man responsible for giving it to me nor owe him any part of it. This child is yours alone."

She shook her head. "I made a promise."

"What promise?"

She couldn't look at him. "It doesn't matter. I don't want to talk about it."

"Fine, but you know how I feel." He stooped to lay a kiss on her belly. "I've ordered us a bath."

"I wish you wouldn't." Why did he always do this type of thing?

"As long as you share my bed, then you and the baby are safe. If I cast you off, then any man in the household has a right to you. Do you want that?" Worry lines etched his face.

She hurried to shake her head and walked toward him. "No. Of course, not."

At that moment, the servants brought in the bath.

When they had gone, he stripped his red and black uniform and stepped into the steaming tub.

The sight of his body had become familiar. It didn't frighten her anymore. As comfortable as she had become to seeing him naked, however, it did not excite her. Nor did it lead to any kind of longing.

She had expected it would, but she felt nothing. In fact, as time went on, she felt less attracted to him than in the beginning. Inexplicably, she loved him more than ever.

He held out a bar of soap expectantly.

With a sigh, she helped him bathe. She lathered his hair and rinsed it with a clean pitcher of water. This wasn't her preferred way of serving him.

But this was a slave's duty. Taking a washcloth, she washed his back and shoulders.

"You're tense." She laid down the cloth and massaged the muscles of his back.

"There are other ways to ease my tension." He had relaxed forward under her ministrations. "Ugh, yes, right there."

She ignored the innuendo and worked the tight muscle with her thumbs. Was she causing him so much strain? She knew the answer and regretted it. He was a kind man and didn't deserve to suffer…deprivation.

"I thought you had no trouble finding willing partners. So, why should my refusal be anything to you?" He was so handsome, almost perfect.

"I'm keeping up appearances." He laughed, but it sounded strained rather than natural.

"Is that better?"

"It will have to do." He stood and waited for her to hand him a towel.

She had never noticed the mark on his right buttocks. "What is that?"

"Come here and find out." He faced her, bursting in fullness.

She scrambled away, repulsed by the object of her terror.

He bent to pick up a towel and dried himself as if she hadn't responded as she had. Uncovered, he stepped onto the mat. Slowly, the threat diminished.

At last, she blinked.

"If you weren't talking about this, then what?" He dried his hair and walked to the bedpost to fetch his robe.

She worked hard to steady her breathing. "The brand."

"Oh." He put the robe on and tied it.

She wrapped her arms around her knees. "Valerie has the same one."

He laughed bitterly. "Yes."

"I thought the scars on your back were war wounds, but they're tally marks, aren't they?" The level of her tension escalated until she couldn't feel her hands.

"Eight times, he took me." Byron met her gaze. "My uncle."

Emerald's breath came ragged and fast. "She has dozens, maybe a hundred."

"One hundred and forty-three." He faced away.

Too stunned to weep, she closed her eyes and prayed for her friend. How could she endure it? How had he endured it?

"Why do you let it happen?" she asked.

He laughed an even darker expression of anger. "We were only five when it started. What could we do then? I guess, we learned to please him, or at least I did. The marks are punishment. It's the times he didn't count that hurt the worst; Valerie has none of those." He shook his head. "It's your turn for the bath."

"Please, don't make me." Trembling afresh, she buried her face in her arms.

The sound of his footfalls on the floor alerted her that he was coming.

He took her by the wrists, lifting her into a standing position. "Everyone is owned by someone. If you are not owned by me, then he will find out and come for you."

"Salicor?" She could see it was not a threat.

"Who else?"

He untied the strings on her dress and pushed it to the floor. Breathing heavy, he seemed to be making up his mind. Reluctantly, he released her wrists and stepped aside.

She hurried to the tub and sat, glad to be somewhat covered by the water.

"It isn't right that he should be permitted to hurt so many people." She washed as quickly as she could. "You offer too much, you and Valerie both. I have nothing to give in return."

"Nothing?" He walked over to kneel beside her, taking a bar of soap and running it all over her body. His fingers glided across her skin. "She was willing to die for you." His eyes focused on her thighs.

"I would die for her too. We are friends." Emerald took the soap from him.

"That's what I thought. Well, then you have only one more secret to share with me tonight." He met her gaze.

She cocked her head in confusion.

"The scars. How did you get them?"

She bowed her head, knowing he didn't mean the ring of teeth marks on her breast. He had already explored those tonight.

"Show me."

Humiliation locked her up tighter than a rusty hinge.

"Why? Do you read the mountain language?" she asked.

"I do."

"Valerie can't."

He smiled, such a handsome man.

"Fine." She turned the flesh of her inner-thigh so he could read the marks.

He went for the lamp and returned, looking at the marks closely.

"It's a name. Allan."

"Allan." She had waited so long.

"He caused all this?"

She nodded, though her mind was elsewhere.

Byron took her hand, and the gesture brought her back to the here and now.

"I can fix everything he did to you."

"How?" No one could fix it.

"Make love to me. Let me make love to you. Love me, Emerald." He clutched her hand to his chest.

She shook her head uncontrollably and tried to pull away.

"No. I can't."

"Your fear is irrational. Well, it's rational, but disproportionate to the threat. Resolve it." He held her gaze until she understood what he meant and then he parted his robe.

This was the last thing she wanted. How could she choose to allow this kind of intimacy outside of marriage? Her fears held her captive. She had to begin to break free. If he were going to hurt her, then he would already have done so.

She faced reality.

Perhaps, his body was a weapon, but it was also a part of a human being. The man was the one to fear, not the hideous part of him she couldn't face.

She reached for a towel.

"That's it?" His body deflated before her eyes.

"I guess so. I...was afraid of nothing."

All these years, she had cowered away from men. She had been unable to face the thought of that thing. But it wasn't what she had feared at all.

His expression of surprise held her attention. "Nothing?" He shook his head and stood with his body on full display. "I am not nothing. I'm magnificent."

She looked down at the bathwater, but couldn't control her reaction to the humor of the moment. She stifled a giggle. Fortunately, he was laughing too. It had been a joke, a brag, and an expression of his infinite confidence in his sexual abilities.

Something about that confidence had always attracted her to him. She could never have it. But she admired him for...believing in himself.

Chapter Forty-Two

Darrin was impressed by Valerie's courage. She was frail, but never gave up trying. Though he had no courage to say it, he wondered if she would be able to make a full recovery.

Weeks passed before she could sit without pain.

"I think it's time to go, Shadow." They ate a stolen loaf of bread at the table in the cottage. "I plan to reclaim my place as general." She looked at him, her spoon poised above a bowl of broth. "I'll use my forces to defeat my uncle or die in the attempt, you have my word."

He wasn't sure what to say. He wanted to go to Emerald but worry for Valerie nagged at him. How could she survive with such reckless plans? He kept eating.

Valerie sighed. "I didn't tell you before. But I resisted my uncle when he came to take Emerald away. The lie had worked. Byron had been granted permission to take her to safety. But I could not let him punish me for doing the right thing.

"I just couldn't let him have his way with me, not even one more time. I hadn't planned to try to kill him. Perhaps if I had, then I would have succeeded. Instead, I was left to his cruel pleasures."

Darrin forced himself to swallow. He couldn't quite meet her gaze. The muscles in her jaw bunched.

"Thank you for saving my life." She laid down the spoon. "I hesitate to ask for more help from you. However, if I defeat Salicor, then Emerald will be free. Stephan is liberating all the slaves.

"I didn't lie to you about Stephan being defeated before his fight begins. But I will join my Valkyrie Army with his and perish with them. Will you help me?" she asked.

Darrin had waited for her to say something like this. He'd noticed a change in her since the first time they met. She didn't attempt to manipulate him anymore. Even now, she asked for his help without trying to seduce or dominate him.

Furthermore, her offer had great value. Without his help, she would have little chance. His testimony on her behalf could convince Stephan to let her live. Emerald would want him to help her brother and save his life if possible.

Darrin gritted his teeth. "How do I know Emerald is safe? What if I continue to leave her with Byron and something terrible happens?" He pushed away from the table and paced the room. "She would want me to help you. But what she wants and what she needs are often opposites. I should go to her."

Valerie's shoulders slumped, though her expression remained impassive. "You'll need this then." She leaned over and put her finger in a knothole of a floorboard and jerked. "I saved her sword for her. It wasn't easy to conceal her identity as the Woman of the Stone from my uncle. I didn't even tell my brother." She held out Emerald's sword to him. "She'll be missing this, I think."

Darrin's jaw dropped. "How are you holding that sword?" Valerie shouldn't have been able to touch it.

"What do you mean?"

"No one can handle it without the sword's permission. So, if you're able to wield it, then you are special indeed."

Valerie shook her head and thrust the hilt into Darrin's palm. The jolt that struck him knocked him to the ground. Hissing in pain, he backed away unable to feel his arm.

"Keep it away from me. I've never been able to touch it. Mine is its mate but the two have opposing mindsets." Darrin stood.

He pulled Krelor's sword from the scabbard where it hung by the door. It bore the ancient ruler's name on the blade and two wolves formed the hilt in a struggle for a sapphire. Their tails formed the hilt guard.

"You act as though these swords are people, as though they have a will of their own. It's preposterous." Valerie looked at the lettering on the blade of Emerald's sword.

"That's what it feels like when you wield one of them. Emerald's sword was named for Queen Dana the Stonehearted. Mine was named after her husband Prince Krelor of the Mountain Realm of old. I feel his remorse and his desire to make amends to her." Darrin stared at Krelor's sword and focused on the connection he felt.

"I feel powerful when I fight for Emerald." He looked at Valerie. "I am powerful when I obey the will of the sword." He shook his head. "It's hard to explain." Darrin extended his sword so she could see the two side by side. He felt warmth and peace flow up his arm.

Valerie, on the other hand, sucked in a breath, backed away two steps, and raised the weapon as if to strike. She shook her head, looking at the sword in her hand. Carefully, she sheathed it.

"I see what you mean. This sword hates the other one. What did he do, this ancient Prince?" Valerie's brows raised.

"I don't know." Darrin frowned. "History recorded that she betrayed him, not the other way around. No wonder Emerald seemed so conflicted when she held that sword." He hadn't realized there was such a difference between the influences of the weapons.

"I feel an overwhelming sense of malice emanating from it." Valerie met his gaze. "I understand malice, but this is deeper."

"What did Emerald do when you took the sword?" he asked.

Valerie flashed a mischievous grin. "Nothing. She looked about as surprised as you did." She squinted at the hilt of the weapon. "I felt something too. It was like a sisterhood, a deep affection. I had no idea what to make of it. So, I put it out of my mind."

Darrin arched an eyebrow. He had observed Valerie's affection. He frowned because he also remembered how willing she had been to suffer and even die for Emerald. Just how much influence did these swords have? He strode over to sheath his, eager to get it out of his hand.

"I'll help you find a horse but then I must go to Emerald. Keep the sword until your quest is complete. Stephan will believe you if you show it to him. If it abandons you, then your mother will know how to return it to Emerald. I hope you are successful."

"And you as well. Keep her safe, Shadow."

Chapter Forty-Three

Stephan led his forces northward from the foot of the Sacred Mountain. Village after village and town after town pledged their loyalty to him as he forced the Valkyrie to retreat. Helen reported that Valerie wasn't leading them.

He delighted in the ease with which he could outsmart the new Commander. But where had his foe disappeared to? Where was the General?

Dismissing his questions, Stephan signaled his troops to advance. They charged forward to see the women warriors retreat from yet another village. This time, however, the Valkyrie set it ablaze as they fled. The tactic gave them enough time to escape. But the consequences for the villagers would prove disastrous.

"Do not pursue them. Help save the village." Stephan's orders were obeyed without delay. Even so, chaos reigned.

People and animals ran in every direction. Smoke and flames confused the narrow streets and made the alleyways treacherous. In the midst of this, he heard a baby cry.

Through soot and falling embers, he found a cottage half alight with fire. Inside he heard the child. He ran to the front of the home to discover a woman ramming the door with her thin shoulder.

"I can't get it open." Her voice was high with desperation.

He picked up his pace and braced himself to hit the door. Whatever had been blocking it moved. It was enough for him and the woman to enter the cottage.

Blinded by smoke, he followed the sound of the baby's cry. The woman with him reached the child first.

"Help the mother. She's right there." The woman grabbed his hand, guiding him in the direction he needed to go.

His eyes burned. He couldn't see anything, but he stooped to grab the mother under the arms and dragged her out. Just as he pulled her free of the house, the eave collapsed on his head.

He hardly had time to register his own cry of pain before someone knocked him to the ground. The woman who had gone with him into the cottage ripped off his burning shirt. The flames burned her hands.

Tears cleared the soot from his eyes so he could see better. He helped the woman pat out the last of the hot spots in what was left of his hair. Involuntarily, he wailed in agony.

The woman disappeared into the smoky street. Where had she gone? She'd saved his life and he didn't even know her name.

Clenching his jaw, he staggered to his feet. Worried for their safety, he pulled the mother further away from the fire as the heat intensified. He placed her crying baby in her arms.

It relieved him to see them unharmed. "Mother, wake up. You must take your child to safety. The fire is spreading."

The mother coughed and opened her eyes. Horror overtook her features. She squeaked in fright, gathered her baby, and fled.

"Come away from the flames and sit here." It was the woman from before.

She had returned with a bucket of water. She had a pack over one shoulder. He fixated on the liquid. His face and chest still felt aflame.

"Come, rest while I tend you." She looked deep into his eyes.

He took one step and collapsed.

STEPHAN RETURNED TO consciousness on a hay-filled mattress on the dirt floor of a hut. He had a strange taste in his mouth. It was probably a tonic of some sort, something for the pain.

The woman who had helped him rescue the mother and baby worked on his injuries. Despite blistered hands of her own, she cleaned and dressed his neck and shoulder with care. The intensity of her focus masked her discomfort. But he could see it around her eyes.

"We're safe here for a while longer." She applied a poultice to his damaged skin.

Each separate word registered until he comprehended their meaning. "You saved my life. Thank you." His voice sounded as dry as his throat felt.

She gave him a sip of water. "You won't be quite so good looking after this."

He laughed. Though when he did, he winced in pain and coughed. For the second time in his life, a woman had said he was handsome.

Was it true? Or rather, had it been true? He knew the left side of his head and face had been burned. It seemed more reasonable to assume this woman recognized him and attempted to flatter him.

"Who—"

She put her finger to his lips. "Save your strength."

His throat moved in protest.

She leaned down to press her cheek against the unburned side of his face. "Don't make my sacrifice vain. Live, boy, and I will one day reward you."

She pulled away to meet his gaze. He saw a deep sadness there. She was lying.

The chill of terror shot through him. How severe were his burns? Emotion clutched him with physical force. He struggled to breathe past the constriction in his chest and the lump in his throat.

"I just want to go home." He sobbed.

The woman leaned down to kiss the corner of his eye. "Hush now, it will be all right." She kissed his cheek. "Please."

Why had he left Stone Castle? His head spun with the images of loved ones he would never see again; Nina, George, Andrew, all the boys, and the little ones. Emerald. He keened in anguish.

A strange softness stopped his cry. He tasted the salt of his tears on the lips of the woman who had saved his life. His eyes flew wide.

Hers remained shut.

He had never been kissed on the lips before. He didn't know what to do. However, if he died, then at least he would die knowing he hadn't missed this.

Her kiss was chaste.

He marveled at her tenderness. She wanted him to live, so much so that she would do anything to calm him. Was there still hope?

She parted their kiss. "I always keep my promises." Her eyes opened and the strength of her words showed in them. "Now you must keep yours. Be still." With that, she worked on a burn on his forearm.

He watched her in fascination. She had transformed in his estimation. She had to be a loving soul in order to care so much for a stranger.

"Are you a nurse?" he asked.

Surprise opened the door for mirth in her stern expression. She had dimples. He liked dimples.

Her eyes brightened. "I've never been accused of any such occupation." Her smile withdrew. "Now rest."

He relaxed to watch her through half-closed eyes. He enjoyed the look of her. The pain tonic must have been a good one because he fell asleep.

STEPHAN AWOKE IN THE night to find the woman lying next to him. Her closeness comforted him, but the pain had returned. His body trembled.

She slept, tucked between his arm and his chest with her head on his good shoulder. He could feel her body along the side of him. She was warm and soft.

He laid a feather kiss on her forehead and pulled her closer. Her head tilted back. In the near darkness, her deep brown eyes opened to look into his.

"I want to kiss you." He hoped she would say yes.

He felt her amused expression as much as saw it since the light coming through the shattered door of the hut had grown dim. The fires must be out.

"Many men have said that to me, but I only kiss a man once."

"Why?" His pain increased moment by moment but he didn't want to distract her from answering his questions.

She sighed and relaxed her head onto his shoulder. "I learn all I need to know about a man with the first kiss. Why should I repeat the exercise?"

He looked at the ceiling as his eyes watered. "Just what did you learn about me that could be so different than what I learned about you?"

Her eyelashes brushed his skin.

"I learned you've never been with a woman. You are virtuous. That's something I can never be and would give my life to preserve. I thought people like you no longer existed. But it turns out I was wrong."

Her answer confused him. "Aren't you pleased to have been mistaken? Doesn't it give you hope to find that goodness still exists in this ravaged land?"

She trembled, gooseflesh rising up on her skin. He held her closer and rubbed her upper arm.

"Hope? What hope is there for one like me?" Her voice held none of the strength or confidence she had shown earlier.

"There is always hope." He relaxed into the figurative weight that settled on his shoulders.

In his capacity as the Prince, he had heard many tales of horror and woe. He prepared to hear another. He gathered his wits in order to judge what could be done to correct the wrongs that had been committed.

She lifted her head and met his gaze. "Don't expect me to confess my sins to you." All softness left her.

She pulled away, stood, and walked to the broken doorway. Her feet were bare. She wore a long-sleeved undershirt that covered her to mid-thigh. Her legs were...melted.

She folded her arms across her chest and stared at the night.

"Your sins or the sins of others committed against you?" A violent tremor overtook him at the loss of warmth beside him.

She sent a sharp sideways glance his direction. "Somewhere along the way, they became the same thing." Her voice filled with heavy remorse but her chin stayed up.

"You doubt I can judge you rightly?"

She looked him straight in the eyes. Her countenance collapsed. Her hands fell to her sides and she dropped to one knee, bowing her head.

"Forgive me, Prince Stephan. I didn't know who you were." She kept her head down.

His heart leaped and quailed at the same time. She had not known him. It was a hopeful sign. Yet, now that she did know who he was, what would her response be?

"Forgive you for saving my life? Never. You are brave and selfless. I owe you much." His voice cracked.

She met his gaze. "Listen to me when I tell you that at first light this town will be overrun by the Valkyrie. I came here searching for you, My Prince. My heart has changed and I wish to fight against my uncle.

"I have vowed to slay him and the woman he promoted in my stead when he left me for dead. I will defeat Danielle of Trent and reclaim my place as general of the Valkyrie. Then I can lead my army against Salicor. They will follow me. You have my word; I will not betray you."

It felt as if a great stone descended to crush him. How could he have invested so much of himself in this woman who had been his enemy? She claimed now to be his friend. He looked deep into her eyes. Despite the testimonies he had heard and all the skirmishes he had fought against her, he knew her to be sincere.

"What has caused this shift in loyalties, Valerie of Bluebird Vale?" He swallowed the painful lump in his throat.

She came to his side knelt. "My Prince, do not trouble yourself with my sorrows. I am nothing to you." She relaxed the concern out of her expression and replaced it with ease he sensed she did not feel. "Take the reward I promised, and then I'll find a Sage to assist you."

He couldn't help but laugh at the horrible twist this night had taken. "The most famous lover in all of Frenland offers a disfigured boy on the verge of death the chance to feel a woman's breasts?" He snorted and looked away. "I should be overcome with lust and grope you freely, except I've gone and done the damnedest thing and fallen in love with you." His voice choked with anger, offense, fear, and the supreme unfairness of it all as he trembled near the point of convulsions.

She remained as if paralyzed by his words. With a shake of her head, she reached for the pack. Quickly, she mixed him another tonic.

"Why didn't you tell me the pain had returned?" Her tone was urgent and filled with accusation. She lifted his head with one burned hand and held the cup to his lips with the other.

He didn't want to stop feeling or go back to sleep. She would be gone when he awoke. He drank the tonic anyway and let her lay his head down, resigned to what must happen.

Regardless, the fact remained that she was incredibly gentle and attentive. The pain in her hands seemed to mean nothing to her if it meant his comfort. Two tears slipped out of the sides of his eyes.

"If you go for help, you'll be recognized. I can't stop what they will do to you." He clenched the muscles in his jaw and almost passed out from the pain.

"I will go anyway. There is still time to warn your Commanders of the attack." She kept her gaze on him.

He met those fathomless eyes and became enveloped in their openness. "Don't stay out of pity, but if you want to," his throat tightened with emotions, "lay beside me once again and let me imagine you are simply a remarkable woman that I happened to meet here in Archtown on a hot summer's night. A woman I'm free to love. A woman I can marry."

She blinked and tears raced down to her chin. Her burned fingers raised as if to wipe them but stopped short. She looked away.

"You don't know what your words do to my heart." She stifled a sob and got up to go to the open door. A breeze blew her blond hair back from her face.

Her response surprised him. They also made him helpless with hope at the same time. Hearing those words from her meant more than he had imagined possible.

Everyone had said she had no heart. They said she was a savage killer with no remorse or any shred of humanity. Lascivious, that was what they said...and worse.

Valerie inhaled the night air. "I will not make love to you, Stephan, though I want to, and I've never made love to any man before."

The emphasis she placed on the words 'made love' gave the phrase a depth of meaning that differentiated it from the acts of physicality he knew her to be infamous for. The news shook his understanding to the core. Her confession forced him to restructure his thinking more than once in order to absorb the impact.

"I would never defile you by making love to you out of wedlock. But I would hold you close to me for a while if you wanted." The pain tonic lessened his grip on consciousness.

"I am a selfish woman and wicked to let you persist in this delusion." Her lower lip trembled. "My Prince, you don't love me. You are hurt and you look upon me with injured senses. Your sensibilities are stirred and your compassion piqued by a rare moment of tenderness.

"It is out of character for me to behave this way. Your first knowledge of me is more genuine. I'm a bad woman who does bad things and I will meet a bad end. Do not mourn for me when that day comes." She dressed and gathered the rest of her things into her pack. "Goodbye."

She left him alone.

Chapter Forty-Four

E merald cleared away yet another dinner Byron had not had time to eat. Weeks had passed and her belly had grown round with the child she carried. She heard him enter the house.

His face lit up when he saw her. "Come with me."

He led her through the hallways to the door of the sheltered courtyard and its lovely gardens. The sun was setting and he helped her up the steps of the short tower. The view was breathtaking.

Thousands of troops had amassed at the training camp. The tents were aligned with precision. She marveled at how the ranks had swelled in the months since she had arrived here. Her heart sank to realize that these men stood in opposition to Stephan.

"I can't stay here, Byron." She faced him.

His enthusiastic expression turned to confusion. "I thought," he took her hands in his, "you liked it here with me."

Was there no other way except to break his heart?

"I would rather die with my brother than to be used as a pawn in his destruction."

"I'm not using you, Emerald. Valerie told me that Stephan is your foster brother. I simply thought you felt something for me." He met her gaze.

"I love you, Byron. But I am the Woman of the Stone. I am not a slave, not really. Hiding in your bed is not something I can continue to do." She wanted him to understand.

"You love me?" His head shook as if he couldn't believe it. "I knew—"

She put a finger to his lips. "I love you. Truly, I would do almost anything for you. But I am not in love with you."

He took a step back, stopped by the railing. "Give me a chance to prove my feelings for you. Lay with me tonight, let me worship you, Woman of the Stone. I am yours to command."

The softness of the plea entreated her on a level so deep and painful she almost consented. If she thought it would make him happy, then she would have lived the lie. For a moment, she thought she actually could permit it. But the old fear clawed its way to the surface and overcame everything else.

"I must go."

His countenance darkened in the twilight spreading across the land.

"No."

She fled from the tower, though there was nowhere for her to go except to his bedchamber.

EMERALD LAMENTED THAT Byron no longer made excuses to spend time with her. Over the course of many days, he kept busy drilling the soldiers. He worked to the point of exhaustion and said little when he came to the villa at night.

She tried to talk to him but he had become moody and distracted. He didn't touch her as he had before. His brown eyes held none of the warmth she cherished, and he never smiled.

She hadn't realized how much she had treasured their closeness. The bond between them had been a comfort. Now, it felt like he was punishing her.

Alone in his bedchamber, she wept more and more frequently. Stoic in his presence, she kept her sorrow secret. If he knew how much his silence hurt, then she would be a greater burden. She regretted the burden she already was and had no desire to add to it by complaining.

Tonight, she had already gone to bed by the time he finally came home. She wasn't asleep, however, and had lain in bed for hours missing him. He kept to his side.

She needed forgiveness, but he offered none.

The sorrow grew too great. She could not hold back the tears. When sobs racked her body and she could no longer muffle them, Byron rolled over and reached out to her. He did not prevent her from burying her face in his chest.

She cried without restraint. He held her close, stroking her hair. When she regained some self-control, she noticed something else. He had responded to her closeness. In that moment of recognition, her body locked with tension.

He pulled away. "I'm sorry."

She let him go, though she was glad he did not turn his back. Moonlight flooded through the open windows. In the semi-darkness, she could make out something of his expression.

"Haven't you ever loved someone without mating with them?"

"No."

She was taken aback. He stared at the ceiling. There was that little line of concern on his forehead that she had come to despise.

"I know you love Valerie. What about her?" she asked.

His eyes squeezed closed, and she feared he had shut her out as well. He rolled away from her. She had almost fallen asleep when he rolled onto his back.

"My uncle has a twisted sense of humor." Byron's voice was raw with anger. "He likes to make people do things they don't want to do." He said nothing more for a long time but now Emerald lay wide awake.

She wouldn't force him to tell her this. With all her heart she hoped it hadn't happened. She believed there was a limit to cruelty. What if she was wrong?

She touched his arm, but he avoided her. He probably didn't want to admit what had happened. Though it must weigh on his mind. She couldn't leave him to suffer alone.

"He brought me a bound and gagged girl with a hood over her head. He said she was my birthday present. I was thirteen.

"I didn't want to, but he made me do it. He laughed when it was done and showed me who the girl was. I hated him for it.

"Angry and ashamed, I did fight him that day. He and his men beat me until I wished to die." His shoulder slumped. "It was a long time ago."

His words horrified her. She couldn't stop her lip from trembling. Tears flooded her eyes.

"Byron, I'm sorry."

He winced. She slid her body next to him and hugged him. He tried to push her away.

"Don't, Emerald." His voice reverberated with shame.

"I don't condemn you. I would never judge you." She held him around the middle. "Allow me to weep for your hurt. Let me mourn for the loss of all that is sacred. Let me love you, Byron."

Upon hearing her words, he rolled on his side and hugged her with a fierceness that spoke of his need for comfort. Like a child, the tears came all at once. His body shook with them as his cries rent the night air.

She pulled his head to her bosom, stroked his hair, and rocked him. It was a terrible thing he had suffered. Her heart went out to Valerie as well. The act had distanced the twins and it showed in their actions toward each other as adults.

It was cruel beyond words that this had happened to two people who must have once been so close. Without their parents, and in the clutches of a madman, they must have relied upon one another for strength. Salicor had taken even that small comfort from them.

Somehow, Emerald found a way to push her anger away. She focused on the man in her arms. He needed her to find some way to make this better. She was all he had.

No, that wasn't true. He had his mother's love. Sarialla had never forgotten her son nor given up on winning him back.

Byron cried himself out. Eventually, his breathing slowed to match hers. Perhaps he was ready to hear her. She wiped the tears from his face.

"May I tell you something?"

He took a deep breath and his body gave one last shudder.

He nodded.

She smiled and, on impulse, kissed the crease in his forehead. "Even though I'm from Danalan, I have been connected with your family all my life."

His eyebrows raised in question.

"Your mother saved my grandmother's life long ago. Don't look so surprised. Sarialla is a great healer and a wise woman.

"She's been visiting the South for over thirty years. She was eighteen when she first came, though my earliest memory of her was when she was already what I considered old. It wasn't so very old I suppose. But I was eight and thought everyone was old."

Byron smiled, though his body remained tense. She kissed his brow again. However, the crease did not go away this time.

"Sarialla told me a story one night. I'd been avoiding sleep because of my nightmares. My entire family, except for my father's parents, had been killed a couple of years earlier. It was hard for me to understand."

Byron hugged her close for a moment and then moved to rest his head on the pillow.

She met his gaze. "Your mother told me about her children. She talked about how precious you both were. You did a lot of cute things when you were little." She brushed his hair away from his eyes.

He gave her a brief smile but looked troubled.

"I didn't understand what twins were. When she explained to me the bond you shared, I was amazed. She actually giggled when she told me how happy your father had been when presented with both a son and a daughter. I knew they loved you. I knew they had been happy." Emerald sighed.

Byron stilled.

"Even at that young age, I knew their happiness hadn't lasted. The sadness in Sarialla's eyes told me something terrible had happened. The depth of her sorrow made me dread what she would say but I listened anyway. I couldn't help myself. She's an excellent storyteller." She played with his hair.

He brought her hand to his lips before releasing it.

She hadn't realized she was nervous and gathered her courage. "As children, your mother had shared a close relationship with her brother. She understood the bond between twins because she was one. It was her greatest sorrow when Salicor betrayed her.

"He killed your father when he stole you and Valerie. Oh, how Sarialla wept when she told me of that day. I felt so sorry for her."

Byron grasped her hand again. "You, who had lost your entire family, felt sorry for her?"

She flushed. What if he didn't believe her? She couldn't get comfortable. She adjusted her position a couple of times and put more space between them.

"I know it sounds disloyal. I really did love my parents and younger brothers." The corners of her mouth jerked upward for an instant, though pain wrenched her heart.

He leaned forward to kiss her eyes and closed the distance between them. He put his arms around her and tucked her head to his shoulder. She couldn't see his face but she could feel his heartbeat. It steadied and comforted her.

She rested her hand on his side. "Somehow, I understood that losing your children was worse than having them die. The two of you were always on her mind and in her heart. She did everything she could to get you back. Your mother still wants you back, Byron."

He hugged her tighter.

"You wouldn't recognize her if you saw her. She looks much older than Salicor. Her worries have worn her out before her time. She has never slackened her efforts to overthrow him and reclaim you and Valerie. She will never rest while he has power over you.

"I didn't know someone could love like that. I learned a lot at your mother's knee. Even as an adult she tried to teach me. I wish she could have saved you and your sister from your uncle. I wish there was something I could do." She clenched her fists. "I could kill him with my bare hands for what he has done." She fought tears with anger.

Byron held her so tight her shoulder ached. "You must never do it, Emerald. Promise me you will never go near him. You must promise." His voice broke and he eased his grip.

She took a deep breath. "If I ever see him again, I won't hesitate to act. His cruelty must be stopped. I am no longer paralyzed by my fears. What he could do to me is terrible. But even if it cost me my life, I would be glad he was dead."

Byron's eyes flew wide. "You must not fight him. It's not just you that I worry about. Think of the baby. He must never get this child." He grasped her shoulders and shook her once. "Promise me he will never get your son."

Fear engulfed her. "I promise to protect the baby, Byron. I'm sorry I frightened you. You're right. There's nothing more important." How could she have forgotten to protect the baby?

Relief flooded over his face. A torrent of tears followed. His body surged over hers and she felt his need for her grow.

Her heart raced out of control. He didn't heed the tension in her body. He kissed her lips, her neck, and crossed a line he hadn't before.

"Byron, stop."

He didn't hear her. His face pressed between her breasts. His breath came in ragged irregular bursts.

His touch frightened her. Suddenly, he pushed her nightdress up over her round belly. It was past her breasts before she could decide what to do.

He kissed and caressed her. She pulled the nightdress down to cover as much as she could. But he went lower with his mouth. She squirmed in his grasp, and he pulled up from her for a moment in the dark.

She screamed. She could feel him there.

"Oh, Emerald." His body trembled.

She screamed and the sound of it drove away reason. Her mind filled with the color red. Her heart beat as if it would explode. Sparks overwhelmed her vision and her ears went deaf.

Chapter Forty-Five

Emerald awoke to the sensation of fingers pushing the hair back from her face. The dark of night concealed the person who touched her. Confused, she called out the only name she thought it could be.

"Byron?"

The hand stilled.

The memory of what Byron had done came back to her all at once. Nausea gripped her until she vomited. Drenched in sweat, she grasped handfuls of grass in order to crawl away. Exhausted emotionally, she collapsed, having no courage to face him.

He had followed her. When her hands fluttered in protest, he stilled them. She writhed free.

"Don't touch me."

He obeyed.

She sobbed out the fullness of her heartache until her strength was spent.

The sound of crickets soothed her until she realized they were out of place. She hadn't expected to hear them here in Byron's villa. One must have gotten into the house.

Her eyes flew open. Where was she? How had she gotten into the grasslands? She lay in the tall grass, alone. Where was Byron?

Her breath caught in her throat as the blood drained from her face. She knew what he had done. She felt her belly.

Relief flooded over her when the child moved. She felt no pain. She was whole. But he had raped her, hadn't he?

How could he do that? After everything they had shared, she had never believed he would force her like that. Had he even known what he was doing?

Surely, he had heard her tell him to stop. Surely, he had felt her push him away. He hadn't paid any attention.

"Oh, Byron, how could you?"

Her shoulders shook with sobs, mourning the loss of trust.

She swept the tears away and sniffed her nose. She had loved him. Even still, he had wanted more. He had taken more by force. Outrage surged within her chest.

She took a breath through clenched teeth. Where was he? She would tell him what he had done was wrong. She would pummel him with her fists. He needed to understand that he could not do this.

She stood and thrashed through the tall grass. There was no one anywhere nearby. She could see nothing but the line of the mountains to the south.

"Where are you? Coward. Come and face me."

She spotted the outline of a man in the grasses and charged at him. Enraged, she impacted him hard. The two of them fell to the ground. She vented her rage against him with her fists. He offered no resistance.

The wind blew the clouds away, allowing moonlight to illuminate his face. She gasped with her fist in midair. It wasn't Byron. It was the man who had occupied her dreams so often of late. Her protector.

"Darrin." She whispered in his mountain language. "You came for me. I knew you would come. I prayed every day."

Relieved, she kissed his face though not his lips. He didn't resist. But he didn't respond either, a cold fish in her arms.

His expression in the light of the rising moon was not cruel. It was firm, resolute. He stood and walked some distance away.

"We'll head home in the morning." He spoke to her in her native tongue with much of his accent gone.

"Home?"

"Your home." He lay in the grass.

Her lower lip trembled. Relief turned her spine to jelly. She would be free. Her emotions overwhelmed her until a burning question seared her tormented soul.

"Did you kill him?"

"Byron lives."

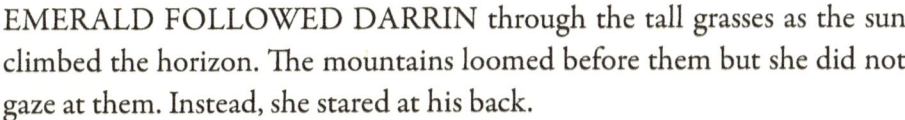

EMERALD FOLLOWED DARRIN through the tall grasses as the sun climbed the horizon. The mountains loomed before them but she did not gaze at them. Instead, she stared at his back.

He wore a gray tunic. It looked good with his black hair and blue eyes. It angered her that he looked so incredibly good because it was a distraction. She was angry at him for rejecting her attempts to talk about last night.

He kept up a grueling pace. She was dressed in nothing but her nightgown. Even her lack of shoes did not slow him down.

Did he blame her for what had happened? She blamed herself, but he had no right to. What choice had he given her?

Why couldn't he have saved her before it happened this time? Why hadn't he been there? She started to cry. Blinded by tears, she ran into the back of him and they knocked heads.

The impact stunned her. When she reached for her forehead, she lost her balance. He caught her as she fell. But disoriented as she was, she was no help. He laid her in the grass.

Through her tears and sobs and runny nose, she couldn't see much. He handed her a handkerchief. That gesture made her weep all the more as she wiped her eyes and nose.

"I'm sorry." The passion in her words and the sincerity in her eyes should tell him she meant more than a simple apology for running into him.

His rigid expression softened. "All is forgiven." He spoke his language.

Her sobs returned, though more from joy than pain.

"I never meant to hurt you." She spoke his native tongue because the words had a deeper connotation and entered the heart more easily.

He helped her up.

"We will not speak of it." He started walking, though slower this time.

BAREFOOT, EMERALD PERMITTED Darrin to carry her over the rocky terrain near the secret entrance to the mountain passageways. Exhausted, she laid her head on his shoulder and closed her eyes. She didn't want to admit how much the journey had taken out of her.

The absence of the sun, caused her to open her eyes. Cool dry air caressed her flushed cheeks. He set her on the smooth, dry stone.

His touch remained brusque. She regretted his attitude. Part of her wondered how to make it up to him. Another part of her fumed because he made it so difficult.

Were men always going to have the last say in her life? Why didn't she have any control? Her frustration continued to build though she dared not act on it. What could she do that didn't seem foolish?

She could see nothing in the tunnel, not even her hand in front of her face. She didn't like the absolute dark. She lost her bearings.

"Darrin?" Her voice echoed.

A sharp noise made her jump. She saw a spark and then a flame blossom on a torch. He placed the torch in a bracket on the wall and rummaged through a pack at his feet, producing a cloak, wool socks, and a rough wool tunic.

He pulled on the second tunic and slid the cloak and socks in her direction. He didn't speak. In fact, a strange stillness pervaded this ancient place. She sensed the history; it strummed her senses in an unsettling way.

"Thank you." She spoke in an effort to dispel the feeling.

His spine straightened.

She sighed and padded over with bare feet to put on the cloak and socks. She left the hood back but held the cloak closed. She hoped he would speak to her now that she was sufficiently covered.

He motioned for her to follow him and started walking. She didn't hurry. If he wanted to upset her, then she would resist letting him. But it hurt.

Her emotions were so near the surface these days. It made it hard to.... What? She barely recognized herself. Emerald Stone was not a crier.

How could she know how to behave when she couldn't trust her own reactions? She guessed it had something to do with the baby. She had become fond of the life growing within her. Though she had discovered that carrying a child complicated everything.

She wasn't angry about the indignities she had yet to face. But she did wonder how something so big was going to come out. Women did it all the time. Surely, she would be fine. She did not feel reassured in the least.

STEPHAN LAY IN BED watching the rain fall outside his window on the mountain slopes. Sarialla had left Helen in charge of the Rebel Army and had brought him to the hidden city in an effort to nurse him back to health. His burns were severe and painful.

However, nothing oppressed him more than the loss of hope. Most days he wished he were dead. Though that would come soon enough.

News from the front discouraged him. There was one exception, however, because Valerie had kept her promise. She had reclaimed her place as general of her army and turned the Valkyrie against her uncle. Even now, she swept her forces northward, taking villages in Stephan's name.

He knew she stood little chance of long-term success against Salicor. In the end, she would be killed. When he thought about her, worry and sorrow oppressed him.

His mood darkened as he stared at the stonework of the fortress wall. Frowning made his healing skin hurt but he couldn't help it. Besides, it hurt regardless of what he did.

A knock sounded on the door. He gritted his teeth. Another knock.

The urge to yell swelled in his chest but he resisted it. He had yelled enough in the delirium of fever to bring him embarrassment enough to last a lifetime. He feared everyone knew of his infatuation with the former enemy general.

"Enter," he said.

Sarialla peeked into the room. "I hope I didn't wake you, Sire." Her eyes were wide with concern.

"I wasn't sleeping."

He looked out the window at the rain as it fell in sheets. A drip commenced in the corner of the room. Both he and Sarialla stared at it.

"Horses continue to come in from the East Icers." Sarialla walked over and sat in a chair at his bedside. "Though troop numbers are dwindling, they still manage to have sporadic success. I wish we could afford to send reinforcements but I advise against it. We are too few in numbers to stand against Byron's fresh troops."

Stephan sighed. It didn't matter either way. Rumor had it that Byron had mobilized his forces and moved to join with Salicor. Soon the final battle would take place.

Stephan feared defeat. Even his best strategies held little hope. He would simply be overwhelmed by superior forces. It had all been in vain.

"The time has come." He met Sarialla's gaze. "I will ride at the head of my army to face our enemy. We will see what happens."

He would face his end on his trusted horse, Dusty, and with a sword in his hand. A strange glimmer of hope flashed within his soul. He couldn't explain it but miracles happened from time to time. He prayed for one now. His people needed to be free.

EMERALD RESTED ON THE floor in an alcove beside the main tunnel under the mountain. Darrin had left her to search for food. Though where he planned to find it, she didn't know.

Water was abundant in these peculiar alcoves. Thus, she wasn't thirsty. But hunger had made her ill and she worried about the baby.

They had traveled through the tunnels without speaking. Darrin had given her all the food he had, but it hadn't been much. What had he gone through to find her? He looked half-starved and exhausted, yet he never relented.

Pity filled her heart.

The stone beneath her drew her body heat away. Her sore muscles had stiffened and she didn't have the strength to stand. Sometime during the past day, she had caught a chill. It wasn't cold here, but it wasn't warm either. Without enough food to fortify her, exhaustion plagued her.

Darrin hadn't seemed to notice her distress. To be fair, she had done her best to conceal it. She had her pride after all. She wouldn't beg him to stop when she knew they must go on or perish.

When, at last, he had stopped to rest, she'd been grateful. However, she hadn't said so. If only he would talk to her about whatever he was feeling, then she could explain.

Her entire body ached. She couldn't help but fall asleep even though it didn't seem wise to do so. Her last thought was to wish Darrin had left a candle.

Chapter Forty-Six

Darrin slammed his fist into the granite wall of the cavern. He had found help in the Imperial City and come back as fast as he could. She should be right here.

"Emerald." His voice had grown hoarse from calling her name. He turned to the men with him. "We must find her."

His desperation echoed back at him. Where could she be? Had she moved?

The men ran with him and the light of their torches danced along the walls of the tunnel. He spotted another alcove ahead. It was further away than he remembered, but there she lay.

"She's here." He jammed the torch into a bracket on the wall and collapsed to his knees at her side. "Emerald, wake up." He touched her arm. The heat of her skin through the thin fabric of her nightgown felt as hot as fire. "Emerald?" He grabbed ahold of her.

She moaned but did not awaken.

"Run ahead and find my mother." The men gathered around him as he lifted her from the floor. "The Princess is sick." He carried her as far as he could, but his strength was spent. "Be careful with her." He handed her off to another man to carry and followed them as best he could.

Why had he left her alone?

The last few weeks had been torture watching her sleep with Valerie's brother. The man had ignored her and she had cried so many tears over him. It was obvious, she wanted Byron, loved him. Yet, the man had attacked her anyway.

Darrin had never seen her so fragile. She was with child and he worried over her. Still, her determination had impressed him.

She clearly understood the importance of pressing onward. Not once had she complained. He rubbed his face with his hand as he ascended to the ancient city.

One of the men clasped his elbow to help him along as they came out of the tunnels. It was day and the Imperial City dazzled his eyes with its freshly polished beauty. He cared about nothing except Emerald.

Unable to look her in the eye, he had kept his distance these past few days. It was guilt over failing her in so many ways. He couldn't bring himself to look at her belly, because the assault that had caused the pregnancy was his fault. Everything was his fault.

The man guiding him stopped at the doorway of a white stone building. Darrin entered but came up short when he saw Emerald lying exposed on a bed. His mother and her nurses wiped Emerald's body with wet cloths.

"Darrin. Here." His mother paused in her flurry of activity to point to where she wanted him. "Strip off your tunic and hold her skin to skin in a sitting position. Your body will help draw down her fever without causing her to go into shock. She's too weak to do this alone. You need to help her deliver the child."

His eyes tracked the action, but his mind wouldn't work.

"Now, son. There isn't much time." His mother took him by the shoulders and shook him. "She's losing the baby."

Without another thought, he stripped to the waist, casting his tunics who knew where. He lifted Emerald into a sitting position and held her upright as he leaned against the wall. Labor was already heavy upon her.

He did everything his mother asked, and still Emerald cried out. She was delirious. She didn't even know he held her. He willed her his strength.

She had to live.

FEVER RAVAGED EMERALD'S body. Delirium kept her from waking but prevented her from resting either. Where she was or how she had come here defied her ability to comprehend.

A myriad of faces swirled around her. She swatted at them like flies. Who were these dark headed strangers?

Her body hurt. She couldn't get warm. Some kind of pain came and went. It kept waking her each time she settled down to rest. The voices of people around her buzzed in her ears, but she couldn't understand them.

The pain intensified until she thought she would go mad. Perhaps, she was already so because nothing made sense. She wanted to weep, but she had no strength. Only the pain kept her from oblivion.

When it ended, she shut her eyes and lay still. Someone shook her shoulder. Why were they so rough?

She opened her eyes to behold the face of a tiny baby boy. His fists trembled, but he didn't cry. Clumsy, she reached for him.

The woman who held him placed him in her arms. He weighed nothing on her chest. She kissed his sticky, wet head and looked into his eyes.

Her mind filled with wonder because it seemed as though he looked at her too. What had happened? Her throat felt dry and at first, her voice wouldn't come.

"Are you my son?" She smiled at him. Even in her weakness, she could do that much for her child.

While she watched him, his fists stopped trembling. He wasn't cold anymore. With one last look at his tiny face, she could no longer resist the abyss of forgetfulness that dragged her away from him.

DARRIN HELD EMERALD and her son. When the nurses carried her away, he was left holding only the infant. He wept for the dark headed boy who never drew breath. He wept for Emerald who had spoken to her child with such love before his death. He wept for himself too.

"This is my fault, Mother. I let this happen."

His mother embraced him. The room had emptied. The nurses had gone with Emerald.

"I'm so sorry, my son." She kissed his hair.

She urged him to lie down and placed a blanket over him. He held the tiny, lifeless boy in his hands, keeping his little body warm against his chest.

Darrin's mother caressed her son's cheek. "I know what it's like to lose a child...and now I know what it's like to lose a grandchild. We will get through this, Darrin. The Future Queen will live. There will be other children." She was so kind in her reassurances.

He wept anew. "The child is not mine, Mother. I've never—" he shook his head, "—you don't understand." He met her gaze. "The men who beat Emerald and threw her in the river last winter did this." His shoulders shook and he clutched the baby to him.

The Steward's reaction was subtle, though Darrin could read his mother's distress. She appeared calm and continued to soothe him, but the news hit her hard. When it was known that her assumptions had been wrong, he would die.

Even Emerald could not forgive him for this.

EMERALD AWOKE TO A general feeling of unwellness. She found it difficult to open her eyes. When she did, she discovered a haggard man in a filthy tunic sitting beside her bed.

He was the only color in a pure white room of polished stone. His face was ashen. He looked as if he were not in good health.

Asleep, he held her hand as he leaned on the side of the vast, down-filled mattress. His face was toward her. She noticed the deep purple splotches under his puffy eyes. Did she know this man?

He seemed familiar, but she couldn't place him. He should be taking better care of himself. Was she responsible for letting him get this way?

He should smell like soap and warm skin, not stale sweat and filth. Why were the knuckles of his hand split and crusted with blood? Had he been in a fight? Why would he do that?

Someone had hurt her. The impact of the realization helped to clear her head, though it oppressed her spirit. Did he fight that man?

Thinking made her head throb. It also made her aware of pains in other places. She didn't want to feel pain.

Her mind shied away from it. She closed her eyes and forced herself to be still. Before long, the oblivion she craved loomed up to engulf her.

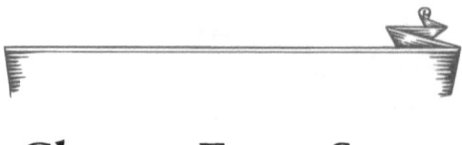

Chapter Forty-Seven

Byron met Valerie under a white flag of truce in the middle of the open plains. She once again led the Valkyrie and looked well. He'd had a change of heart after Emerald had gone. His tolerance for evil doing had ended.

His sister met his gaze. She seemed to detect that something was amiss with him. She had a sense of things like that.

The wind tousled her hair. She tucked it behind an ear. It made her look very much like the child he remembered.

He found it hard to speak past the lump in his throat. "I failed you, Valerie."

Stiff shouldered, she met his gaze. "What happened?" Her voice remained level.

"I fell in love." A tearful smile tugged at his expression. "Emerald didn't." He shook his head. "I should have just accepted it. But instead, I did something terrible. Or I almost did. She thinks I did.

"I was on the threshold. If she hadn't screamed, then I would have done it." He swallowed. "I've never heard a scream like that."

He shook his head to clear the memory that rang in his ears. "Do you know what it's like to want something so much you just take it?" He averted his gaze. "I'm a monster."

"Didn't the Shadow come?" Tears slid down Valerie's face. "He should have arrived weeks ago. Why didn't Darrin come for her?"

"He came in through the window the instant she started screaming. He must have been around for a while. Food kept going missing.

"He never made himself known. If he had, then I would have told her. But he didn't, and I didn't. I was selfish.

"The Shadow spared my life." He laughed his bitterness to the wind. "He believes Emerald loves me, but I know for certain she doesn't.

"She sat on the windowsill of my bedchamber staring at those mountains every day, waiting for him." Byron allowed all of his sadness and regret to show in his expression. "She talks in her sleep."

Valerie wiped her eyes. "I know." She glanced his way. "She talked about you once. I think she liked you from the moment she saw you.

"But Darrin was there first. I've never seen the kind of love he has for her. I was jealous for a long time." A rueful smile flitted across her face. "In the end, brother, we only have each other. Will you fight with me against our uncle?"

Byron met her gaze. "I will fight our uncle but I beg you to go to Emerald." He swept his arm toward the mountains. "Be safe with her. Tell her I'm sorry. Help her get over it.

"You know what this has done to her. I worry she won't ever trust anyone again. Why should she when I betrayed her so completely?" He shook his head.

"I'll go fight our uncle. But I can't bear to watch you die. I love you too much, Valerie." His voice thickened with emotion.

She looked into his eyes for a long while. "If you would take up Emerald's quest, then you must take up her sword. With this weapon, you will stand a fighting chance. It cuts clean through armor." Valerie proffered Byron the ancient copper sword.

Byron drew the sword he already wore.

Her jaw dropped and she pulled back. "How did you obtain Darrin's sword? These are ancient weapons and do not yield their use to many." She put her weapon away.

"When the Shadow drew his blade, it shocked him. He dropped it to the floor with a clatter. Enraged, he continued forward. We fought to a standstill. I didn't realize he was holding back. He said for Emerald's sake, he wouldn't make me suffer for what I had done. It was obvious he would have preferred to punish me unto death.

"Instead, he simply adjusted Emerald's nightgown to cover her and lifted her in his arms. I offered to provision them, but he ignored me and took her away. I let them go and ordered they not be pursued."

New tears washed Valerie's cheeks. "I doubt he understood you, Byron. Darrin speaks next to nothing of our language." She looked away. "I will go to Emerald. Though, I need to tell you something first." She paused and avoided his gaze.

"Tell me anything."

Her cheeks blossomed with color. "I've been with many men. But I've only kept one child. She was yours."

"Lily was mine?"

He couldn't believe it. Each breath he took became labored. His chest felt crushed.

She met his gaze. "She wasn't perfect and only lived a year, but she was—" Valerie choked on her tears, "—she was beautiful to me. I gave her all my love, all the love I had given you."

He reached out but pulled back and looked away. He hadn't touched his sister since that terrible day when they were thirteen. He sobbed and tears coursed his face.

"I'm sorry, Valerie, so sorry."

She rode up next to him, leaned over, and embraced him.

WHEN EMERALD AWOKE the chair beside the bed sat empty and a different person stood over her. A woman with cold hands massaged her abdomen. The woman's fingers caused pain and Emerald cried out.

One cry wasn't enough. She screamed. The woman backed away.

However, the memory of her touch made Emerald scream again. So many people had hurt her. When would it end?

A man in blue burst into the room. He rushed past the woman. Horror on her face, the nurse fled.

"Emerald, it's all right." He took her hand. "You are going to be all right." He pulled the blanket over her.

Had he done something like that before? He seemed familiar, but the man she remembered had a beard. This man seemed more of a boy without one, though his face was lined with fatigue.

"You are safe, Emerald."

His voice sounded familiar. She looked at him more closely. Was it really him? She pulled his hand to her face and inhaled his scent.

"Darrin." She closed her eyes.

He relaxed and sat in the chair. "Yes, it's me. We've been worried about you."

"We?" She smiled as she enjoyed the connectedness of the word.

When he didn't answer she opened her eyes, though it took great effort. He had a grave expression on his face. His lips pressed into a thin line. Her face must have voiced her question because he didn't wait for her to ask what was wrong.

"The child returned."

She frowned in confusion. "Speak your own language. I don't understand you."

"Your child returned to the heavens." His features crumpled.

"I don't have a child, not yet." She reached for her belly only to find loose flesh. Panic clawed at her heart. "No."

The baby wasn't there. Where had he gone? She'd given birth. It was too soon.

"I saw him. I held him. Where is my son?" She focused her gaze on Darrin in wretched disbelief.

"Your son lived only for a brief time, Emerald. The child came too early. Do you understand what I'm saying? He wasn't breathing." Darrin looked as if he would be sick. "I'm so sorry for your loss."

She couldn't breathe. "Darrin, where is my son?"

She wanted to see her baby. She needed to hold him and keep him warm. Where could they have taken him?

"Emerald, we have honored him according to the ways of old. Your son has been burned on a pyre in the mountains. His essential elements are enshrined on display in front of the Imperial Tombs."

"You burned my baby? How could you? He was so little and helpless. Why?" She shook her head back and forth. "Why?"

Darrin leaned forward. "It's been three days. You almost returned to the heavens along with him. If I had been forced to lay your body beside his, then I would have thrown myself upon the pyre with you."

He bowed his head. "I'm sorry I didn't take care of you." His voice broke. "It would be better if I had never been born. My failures are complete. I am to blame for your son's return to the heavens. Punish me, Princess." He bowed his forehead to her hand where it lay on the bed.

"I want my son." She shook her head back and forth on the pillow. "I need to hold him. He needs to nurse or he'll die. Please, bring my baby to me. I want him."

A LOVELY SMELL FILLED the room, like some kind of flower. Something touched Emerald's lips and warm liquid ran down her chin. A cloth caught the drip.

It took a while to focus her eyes. They were dry and her throat sore. When she parted her lips to run her tongue over their chapped surface, the Lady who sat by her bed tipped another spoonful of broth into her mouth.

Emerald tried to swallow but choked instead. It took all her strength to roll on her side and cough it up. She gasped for breath.

Living was too hard. She closed her eyes and would have gone back to sleep. But the Lady sitting beside the bed wouldn't allow it.

"My son tells me you speak our language. That's good because I speak little of yours." The Lady folded her hands in her lap.

"I had a son. They burned him." Emerald stared at the wall. "I'll never see him again. He was so little. So very little."

Chapter Forty-Eight

The tramp of boots on the stone floor rang loud as the wearer ran down the hallway and into Emerald's bedchamber. The person did not stop politely at the door but burst onto her bed in a flurry. Whoever it was smelled of horse, leather, hay, and sweat.

"Ergolute-oon."

Emerald sneezed into the pillow. The rude visitor took her by the shoulders and pulled her up. She had no strength to hold her head, so it rolled backward.

"Emerald, ergolute Valerie." The woman reached out to support her head.

It was hard for Emerald to focus on the face of the annoying woman. Her head was so unsteady, she couldn't keep her eyes from crossing. Did the woman say her name was Valerie?

"Do I know you?" She scratched out a dry whisper.

"Oon isange, ni, Emerald.' The woman smiled.

Emerald recognized that smile and spoke in the Frenland tongue to her friend. "Do you know your brother raped me? I lost the baby. Someone burned him. I think I've gone mad."

Valerie kissed both of Emerald's cheeks. "I think you are through the worst of it now, my friend. Yes, I know my brother raped you. That is why I came.

"When I found out where you had been taken, I came to the foot of this mountain. I raced up and down shouting your name. Finally, your Shadow came.

"It's my fault this happened, but you must forgive me. I never believed Byron would hurt you. I trusted him to keep you safe. The next time I see him I will horsewhip him. You have my word."

The muscle in Emerald's cheek twitched. "I'm not in love with him, you know. I'm in love with the monster who burned my baby. Is that the right word?" The connotation in Frenland for the word monster was extremely derogatory.

Valerie chuckled and eased Emerald down to lay on the bed. "They're all monsters."

Emerald smiled, though she felt so weak.

Valerie shifted her attention to the bedside table. "Is this what passes for sustenance in this place? Well, you'd better take in every drop or they'll be burning you by sundown." She picked up a bowl of broth and a spoon.

"You won't let them burn me, will you?"

"Of course not. You are going to get better. Eat this or I'll beat you senseless." She held out a spoonful of broth.

Emerald did her best to obey. However, most of the broth dribbled down her chin. Valerie didn't criticize. She just draped a cloth around her patient's neck and continued spooning in the broth. The simple effort of swallowing left Emerald exhausted.

"Well done." Valerie set down the bowl. "Now rest for a while. I'll go get some more of this disgusting stuff. It smells like mushrooms. I thought you hated mushrooms." She flashed a mischievous grin.

"You know I adore them."

"My mistake."

EACH TIME EMERALD AWOKE, Valerie was there with a bowl and a spoon handy. One day Emerald had finally had enough.

"You could at least say 'hello' before you stick a spoon in a person's mouth. If I don't get something besides broth soon, then I'm going to be the one breaking heads around here."

Valerie put a hand on her hip. "Oh, you are, are you? Well, in that case, you'll be happy to know I brought gruel." She smiled a wicked grin and shoveled a spoonful into Emerald's mouth. "Enjoy."

"I'll get you for this." Her threat came out muffled by the mouthful of bland food.

"Nothing would make me happier than to see you well enough to best me in combat." Valerie grinned but her expression soon sobered. "I need to ask a favor."

"What can I do for you?" Emerald lifted her arms to indicate how weak and helpless she still was.

Valerie looked her square in the eyes. "Grant me asylum." She bowed her head. "Please, Your Highness."

Emerald's jaw fell open. "What did you call me?"

Valerie avoided her gaze. "It's not a swear word. It's a title of respect reserved for Royalty. I'm serious, Emerald. I can't go back to Frenland. They'll kill me."

Emerald's brows crashed together. "Who will kill you?"

Valerie tossed up her hands. The gruel sloshed all over the place. She set down the bowl and mopped up the mess on her hands and knees.

"Everyone. My uncle wants me dead because I betrayed him. The people want my head because I did my duty to my uncle. You know how zealous I was to do my duty to him." Her head popped over the side of the bed to reveal a raised eyebrow.

"You are my only hope, so I'm glad you finally have some color in your cheeks. What do you say, Princess? Can I stay with you?"

At the sound of the dreaded word, Emerald wrapped her arms around her head and flipped over to bury her face in her pillow. "Why do people keep calling me that? I'm not a Princess. I will never be anyone's ruler."

Valerie didn't answer.

Emerald looked up to find her friend had gone. Anger gave her strength. She tossed the pillow across the room and got out of bed. On shaky legs, she left her bedchamber for the first time since they'd brought her here.

In passing, she noticed there were two male guards posted outside the door. She marveled at the stone hallway. There was natural light coming through the translucent ceiling.

"Stop right now, Valerie." She tripped over her own feet and landed hard on her hands and knees.

The guards swooped in to help her up, but she swatted them away. She was too angry to be embarrassed about falling on her face wearing nothing more than a sheer fabric nightgown. It was probably see-through. Doubtless, she'd feel mortified later.

Valerie stopped, crimson-cheeked. "I was counting on you to help me. I didn't expect you to throw a tantrum."

The guards on either side of Emerald drew their swords. Apparently, they did not need to understand the language of Frenland to consider this a fight. Emerald pressed their hands down to lower the blades.

"It does not become." She reprimanded them in their language.

The men bowed to her and sheathed the weapons.

Valerie did not speak. Belligerence was a talent she excelled at. She employed it now as she crossed her arms in front of her chest.

"You and I throw fits for the same reasons." Emerald softened her expression. "I will help you in any way I can if you will just assist me back to my room."

Valerie swept forward to catch her by the elbow. She helped Emerald walk back to her room, and tucked her in bed.

"Thank you for your protection." Valerie bowed her head.

"Has anyone ever accused you of being stubborn?" A smile jerked at the corners of Emerald's mouth.

"No."

Their laughter echoed through the hallways of the palace.

Valerie sat down in the chair and folded her arms. "I know you're tired. But I've already guessed at too much of the answer to wait, so you'd better tell me now. Why did you throw a fit when I pledged my fealty?"

Perplexed, Emerald couldn't think of an answer.

"Let me rephrase, why can't you stand to be referred to as a Princess?" Valerie looked her in the eyes.

For the longest time, Emerald didn't speak. Her heart was stricken by an old wound. In the end, she decided that if there was anyone in the empire that she could talk to about it, then Valerie was the one.

"I think the first time it happens must be the worst." Emerald looked into her memories. "The details still haunt me. He was a small man, like all of these fellows around here. I didn't realize it for years because he had disguised his appearance, but he was a mountain man."

Valerie nodded. "He must have called you Princess, just like all these people do. Was it a term of endearment?" The mirthless smile made a brief appearance.

"I was fourteen years old and unarmed. He had just tossed my brother in the well and murdered my grandparents. He threw me down in the dirt, forced up my dress and began to rip me in half.

"He chanted as he thrust, 'My Princess, my whore, My Princess, my whore.' When he stopped thrusting and his eyes rolled back in his head, I bashed it in with a stone. I didn't stop pounding until nothing remained of his skull but a bloody stain on the ground." Emerald looked up from her recollections. "Those kinds of things stick with a person."

Valerie nodded, a slow gesture with a severe expression. "I'm glad you killed him. The rock was a nice touch, very resourceful. I wish there had been one handy my first time, or my hundredth. I suppose you figured out who haunts me. He's no memory, not yet. I think my brother might make him one, though."

Valerie's revelation surprised Emerald and troubled her. "If Byron kills Salicor, then I will forgive him. At least, I hope I will...someday."

Valerie sighed. "Byron is sorry for what he did. I don't know if that makes a difference. He told me to tell you he was sorrier than you will ever know. He apologized to me too. I guess he told you. Anyway, I told him about his daughter." Valerie's eyes projected the continuation of her thoughts.

Emerald lay stunned. She hadn't guessed this much. What a terrible, misguided thing to do. Catching herself in judgment, she reached out to her friend.

Valerie took the hand she offered. "He didn't know Lily was his. After it happened, Salicor had sent him away to train with the army. I didn't see him again until we were grown. By then I didn't want to talk about it. I'm still not sure why I told you."

Emerald flashed an approximation of the General's trademark smile. "You and I are cut from the same cloth. We both fell in love with rape babies. We made fools of ourselves trying to make something good out of a bad situation. I'm not sure anyone else would understand."

Valerie seemed to ponder the words, holding tight to her hand. "What was your son like?"

Emerald met her gaze and smiled past her tears. "He was beautiful."

Tears spilled down their faces as they wept together for a while.

Valerie wiped her cheeks. "I knew you'd see it my way."

Chapter Forty-Nine

Stephan received a courier with the news that General Byron had joined forces with Valerie to fight against Salicor. This prompted him to hasten his pace across the plains. As he approached the twins' armies, a Commander from each force broke off and rode toward him.

The two officers bowed their heads. The woman spoke first. It wasn't Valerie.

Stephan tried to suppress his disappointment. However, it must have shown on his disfigured face. A glimmer of recognition showed in the Commander's expression.

"I am Ashlyn of Cairn. I lead the Valkyrie in the absence of General Valerie who has gone to the aid of a beloved friend. I hope you will accept my pledge to serve you with all faithfulness and diligence, My Prince." She inclined her head.

The other Commander's spirited horse refused to remain still. "I'm Commander Harry of Westvale. I'm at your service, Sire. General Byron has not returned from his reconnaissance mission. He placed me in command in his absence." The Commander looked a little nervous, not unlike his horse.

Stephan wondered what it could mean. "When is General Byron expected back?"

Commander Harry lowered his gaze. "He was expected yesterday, Sire."

Stephan frowned. "Where did he go? Has anything been done to assure his safety?"

Harry squared his shoulders. "General Byron ordered us to await your arrival. He said that if he did not return, then I should subject myself to you and fight in your defense, My Prince."

Concern etched the young Commander's face. "The General rode in the direction of Soniashi. His mood was, well, it was dark. He's been like that for a while.

"It was worse as he rode away. He didn't look back. I don't think he believed he would return and he wore that strange old sword." The Commander's throat bobbed as he swallowed. "I wish I had more to report, Sire."

Stephan couldn't be sure if it was good news or bad, but there was no helping it now. "We will march to Soniashi. Commanders, when will your forces be ready?"

Both Commanders sat straighter in their saddles.

"The Valkyrie Army is ready."

"We're ready too, My Prince."

Stephan squared his shoulders and set his jaw. "Very well then, Commander Ashlyn, take the left flank and Commander Harry, take the right. Today we liberate the Capital."

Both Commanders bowed before they rode off to lead their forces. Stephan continued the ride he had led for half the morning. Before noon, they would engage in bloody warfare.

He should have had his mind on the battle ahead, but all he could think about was Valerie. Where had she gone? Was she safe?

It was the one bright spot and the biggest mystery. Who was this friend Commander Ashlyn had referred to? He thought about the rumors he had heard about a red-haired woman from the South. Could Emerald have followed him here?

When the thrice ringed city came into view, it lay shrouded in smoke. "What's happening?"

Sarialla squinted. "I don't know, Sire."

They rode closer.

"Something isn't right. Look at all the fires." Stephan noticed the gates of the city were thrown wide.

As they approached the gate in the outermost wall, several small bands of soldiers fled the city. They scattered before his forces. The streets already flowed with blood.

"Do not pursue them. We enter the city together." Stephan suspected trickery, but the carnage before him was real.

He waved Commander Harry in with his army to clear the third ring of any surviving enemy. He progressed toward the gates of the second ring. When he approached it, he sent Commander Ashlyn and the Valkyrie in to secure it.

No one stood in his way. He continued into the innermost ring of the city. The palace stood before him. All was still.

The rebel forces at Stephan's command secured the innermost part of the city, including the Royal Palace. With this accomplished, Stephan and Sarialla dismounted. They strode toward the Hall of Kings.

Stephan's men pulled open the great doors. En masse, they rushed in to find no one alive to challenge them. Bodies littered the ornate blue marble floor.

Stephan's eyes adjusted to the dim lighting. He spotted a familiar sword protruding from a golden breastplate. The blade had pierced the man's heart.

Stephan strode forward to clasp the hilt. A strange sensation of bonding passed from the weapon to him. He pulled at it, but it didn't move.

He ignored the hideously contorted face of the dead man and put his foot on the golden suit of armor. This time he pulled harder. The blade came free.

It was Darrin's sword. There could be no mistake because it was etched with the name Krelor. How had it gotten here?

Behind him, Sarialla cried out. Stephan whirled, at the ready to defend her. However, she was not in danger. Horror and sorrow mingled with torment in her expression.

"My son." She collapsed to her knees and grasped the hand of a fallen man.

The young man lay face down in a pool of blood. He bristled with half a dozen crossbow bolts. Was this General Byron, Sarialla's lost son?

He must have come here to kill his uncle. With Salicor dead, the remaining leaders must have fought for control of the city. Judging by the body count, they had fought almost to the last man.

Byron had done the impossible and had paid with his life. But what had made him do it? Or who? And how had he obtained Darrin's sword?

Chapter Fifty

Darrin stood square of shoulder and stern of expression. He and another man guarded Emerald's room through the night. He had brought Valerie to the Imperial City and she had saved Emerald's life.

As a reward, he'd been granted a stay of execution. At least until such time as the Princess might pass judgment over his actions and failings. In the meantime, he had been reinstated as Captain of the Royal Guard.

Darrin was Captain. Yet, he had lost the respect of his men. Regrettably, only a handful of them had survived the war.

The entire culture and people of the West Wind had been reduced. There were sixty-two women, one hundred and forty-three children, and thirty-two men. Among the men, twenty were old and only a dozen ranged between the ages of fifteen and fifty, including him.

The Council of Matriarchs and the Steward had interrogated him. He told them everything in explicit detail. They were not pleased.

Something his mother had said led him to believe they were keeping something from him. Emerald was in danger. He sensed fear from the Matriarchs and it left him wondering what they were planning.

The replacement watch rounded the corner at the end of the hall and strode toward him and his companion. They bowed at the waist. He reciprocated with a nod of the head.

"Captain, you've been summoned to the Imperial Hall to stand before the Council of Matriarchs." The man's name was Gan, his wife was on the Council.

Darrin bowed. "Thank you, Sergeant." He hurried to the Imperial Hall.

Not halfway there his stomach growled. He wasn't even to be allowed breakfast before facing the Council. It wasn't right. He gritted his teeth against resentment.

He would miss the freshly baked delights the latest addition to the city's populace had prepared. Just thinking about Valerie's bread made him salivate. What made it worse was the fact that she'd mentioned she would bake something special this morning.

With a huff and a clenched jaw, Darrin arrived at the great doors of the hall. He ran his hand through his hair and straightened his tunic. The guards on either side of the doors admitted him.

He strode in with an air of confidence. That feeling evaporated as soon as he saw his mother's expression. She sat in the lesser seat on the dais.

The Steward stood as he approached. He had never seen her so grave. During the last interrogation, he had received the impression that these women were contemplating a dangerous decision. It seemed they had made up their minds.

As he walked toward the dais, he tried to assess their collective mood. On many faces, he saw smug satisfaction. Some expressions held blatant fear. Still, more of the women seemed resigned to whatever decision had been reached.

His mother's expression troubled him the most. Though she masked it well, she seemed upset. She was ashamed.

When he reached the foot of the dais, he bowed himself to the floor. He sat on his heels and placed his forehead and hands on the cool granite. Closing his eyes, he sent out a silent petition to the Creator. All the while, his stomach twisted in apprehension.

"You may sit comfortably." His mother, Steward Celeniurisa, took her seat.

Darrin sat up straight. Though he did not get any more comfortable than that. He folded his hands in his lap and waited for whatever came.

He focused on the beautiful floor in front of him. Why had he never noticed? It was pale green and white with flecks of gold.

Each piece had been cut with precision. They fit in an ornate design without the smallest gap. It depicted a gathering of green leaves at the foot of a white tree.

"It has been decided that the foreigners pose a threat to the autonomy, indeed the existence, of our people. We've been at war with ourselves and at last, we concede defeat." The great Lady bowed her head.

"We must seal ourselves off from the world once more. This time with no hope of reuniting with the peoples of Frenland or Andolin. May the Creator forgive us." She rested her hands on the arms of the chair.

She met Darrin's gaze. "Shadow, the honor is yours. Cleanse us of foreigners."

Fury immobilized him. At the same time that heat climbed up his neck, he felt his face blanch with indignation. He clenched his fists and launched into a straddle-legged stance.

"I will not kill the Future Queen. I would rather die."

The First Matriarch took to her feet. "Disobedient dog." She glanced toward the back of the room. "Guards."

The Steward raised her hand and everyone silenced.

Darrin tensed in preparation for the fight of his life. They could not do this. Why would they do this?

If Emerald died then all the other deaths were for nothing. His father, his brother, all of his boyhood friends, everyone had died in vain. No. He would not let that be.

"You must change your minds." He looked from the unmoved First Matriarch to the Steward. "Mother, please."

Lady Celeniurisa met her son's gaze with tears on her cheeks. "My son, lest the duty falls to another hand less kind, do as you have been commanded."

Darrin couldn't breathe. The threat was plain. If he did not do this, then someone else would.

There were many who would not grant Emerald or Valerie a merciful death. Some in this room resented the Future Queen. In fact, even he sorrowed over all of the sacrifices that had been made on her behalf.

Darrin bowed his head. His heart quailed within him, but he knew he had to do this. He could not let the task fall to another.

"I will do as you command, great Steward of the West Wind. I ask only one thing, that I am honored with an explanation. Why is the Woman of the Stone, a daughter formed by the hand of the Creator of Heaven and Earth, a threat to our people?"

The First Matriarch strode forward. She kicked him behind the knee, causing him to collapse. "Bow before the Steward and ask no more questions. You will either obey or you will die. No explanation is required."

He flushed with anger and embarrassment. She had kicked him. It was the deepest of insults.

In his culture, one only kicked dogs. If he retaliated, then he would be executed on the spot. Yet, how could he accept this treatment?

"Stand down, Elka." The Steward had not shouted.

She had, however, raised her voice to greater power than Darrin had ever heard. When he looked up at her, she had color in her cheeks and a dangerous flash in her eyes. The First Matriarch paled, bowed, and returned to her place. The room lay silent, every face wary.

"Our people know no limit to shame this day." The Steward stood. "We turn our backs on the Creator as we take this course of action. We do it out of fear. We do it because when the Imperial City was discovered, we learned something about our true nature."

One at a time, she descended the stairs of the dais. "More than four-hundred years have passed since the original betrayal. It took place right here in this city. I'll give a little history first."

The Steward met Darrin's gaze. "The Queen of the Mountain Realm bore no daughters and the King of Andolin bore no sons. Therefore, the two kingdoms agreed to marry their only children in hopes of an heir. The marriage was arranged and soon an heir was born, a male. More children came, all males.

"The aged Queen of the Mountain Realm ascended to the heavens, leaving her son to the mercy of the Council of Matriarchs. Those women ordered Krelor to accuse Dana, his wife, of infidelity with her Shadow. They forced him to abandon her." Celeniurisa looked away from her son.

"Queen Dana, who had ruled in justice and mercy over the people of both lands for half her life, was cast out. The lie was believed throughout the Empire. Everyone despised her.

"However, lest she was destroyed, the old King of Andolin declared a proclamation with a promise. As her father, he prophesied that one-day

Dana's descendant would heal the breach between the nations. The Woman of the Stone would restore prosperity to the people."

The Steward swept out her arms in a wide gesture. "And thus, it was that Dana and her eight sons were given land in the borders between the Mountain Realm and Andolin. She was allowed to survive in order to save the future.

"But you see it was a lie that the Prince of the mountains had told. His wife was faithful to him, she loved him. He betrayed her so his people could have a female heir of his bloodline."

Celeniurisa raised a finger in the air. "Indeed, once he was freed of his wife, he was given to the First Matriarch who bore a daughter. That daughter became the first Steward of the West Wind. That daughter was my ancestress. It is from her that I obtained my position as Steward."

Celeniurisa mounted the dais and faced the people in the hall. "Emerald Stone is indeed the first daughter born to Queen Dana's line in over four-hundred years. She has fulfilled the three challenges of the Ancient Southern King of Andolin. She has danced with the West Wind, found the hidden places, and rewritten the past."

The Steward sat in the lesser chair on the dais. "According to the promise of the Ancient King, the Woman of the Stone will become Empress. That is what we fear, for we cannot stand against Andolin. Nor could we withstand the people of Frenland. Our culture, if not our lives, would be lost forever. Therefore, we choose to hide our faces in shame and destroy the Future Queen."

Silence prevailed in the room as the revelation echoed in Darrin's heart. He was dumbfounded. He'd had it all wrong. Emerald was never to be his Queen only. She was destined to rule the entire Modutan Empire.

Did the citizens of Andolin know this? He shook his head to clear it. Of course, they did, that's why they hated her.

Would they allow a monarch to take power after so many generations of judicial rule? Emerald had a right to be the Empress. But would it truly happen?

"Go now, my son. May your blade be merciful and swift." Sorrow showed in the Steward's posture and gentle tone.

Darrin stood, bowed at the waist, and fled the hall. How could he do this thing? His mind reeled with the onslaught of information. Would his people be destroyed if Emerald lived? Perhaps, it was the Creator's will that they should be obliterated for their treachery.

He couldn't bring himself to go to Emerald first. He would find Valerie. That betrayal would harden him for what he needed to do after.

DARRIN FORMULATED A plan. He would confront Valerie in the stables. So, he hurried to the bottom of the main passageway leading to the tunnels that connected Frenland and Andolin.

He wished there was some way to save her and Emerald. However, he knew they'd be caught if they tried to escape. Furthermore, he didn't dare risk anyone having their way with Emerald. No. He would have to take her life with his own hand.

A horse stuck his nose out of a stall as Darrin approached. Valerie's curious horse, Rumsfahail, was the only animal stabled here. She came down each day after baking to tend him.

Darrin lay in wait in the stall opposite the horse. It wasn't long before he heard footsteps. The General had become a creature of habit in her early retirement.

"Hello, Rumsfahail, my boy. I brought you something special today." Darrin could smell the pastry.

Valerie broke off a piece. "It's your favorite, an apple tart with honey glaze."

The horse whinnied and came to take the pastry from her open palm. He chewed with gusto. She laughed. It was the most innocent gesture Darrin had ever seen from her. She was never this unguarded around people.

Valerie ate the part she had held back. "Pretty good." She petted Rumsfahail's head. "I should've been a baker's wife. We could have made bread all morning and fat babies all afternoon." She giggled. "A baker's dozen of the chubbiest children you have ever seen."

The sparkle left her eyes and she leaned over the gate to hug the great beast. "My father would have liked that. He was a pastry chef, you know."

She entered the stall, closed the gate, and picked up a currycomb. "My father made the cake for Stephan's parents' wedding. It was beautiful. You should've seen it, boy.

"It had a half a dozen layers and at least a hundred yellow roses made of frosting. I was three years old, it's my first memory. Daddy had to redo the roses on the bottom layer three times because I kept taking them."

Valerie rubbed Rumsfahail on the nose with her free hand as she brushed him. "I thought daddy would be mad. But he sat me on his lap and handed me a plate with the most beautiful frosting rose of them all.

"He said, 'I made this one special, just for you, Ree,'" She choked up. "'because I love you, and my little girl deserves a rose of her own. I hope you never forget how delicate and perfect this is because that's how I see you, sweet and perfect, the greatest of my creations.' And then he kissed me on the head and said, 'Don't tell your brother.'" Valerie laughed through her tears.

Darrin hadn't meant to eavesdrop on such a private moment. Since he was studying Frenlandish in his free time, he understood everything she said. He hesitated to intrude.

However, he had to act. If he did not do it soon, then his chance would pass. Without regard for the consequences, he emerged from his hiding place as Valerie uttered the most intimate of pleas.

"Daddy, do you still love me?" There was torment in her whisper.

Darrin stopped but she'd already heard him.

"Shadow?" She recoiled from him and wiped her face.

Her expression darkened upon full recognition. Color rose in her cheeks and anger flashed in her eyes. Darrin vaulted the stall, knife at the ready.

She had no weapon and parried his first strike with the currycomb. Fast, she used the horse to her advantage and evaded his next thrust. Rumsfahail had his great eye on him but Darrin focused on Valerie. He had her trapped.

Darrin realized his mistake too late. Valerie commanded the horse to kick. It took all of his agility to avoid the full impact of the hoof.

As it was, it grazed his hip. The tremendous force of the glancing blow slammed him into the wall. He hit his head and slid to the straw covered floor.

Valerie leaped on him but he was too muddled to stop her. In fact, he barely comprehended what she was doing at all. That is until he felt her hands on his bare hip.

"Stop that." He tried to push her away.

She met his gaze and he tumbled into her deep brown eyes. They were like nothing he could describe. In them, he found no reason to fear. That seemed strange since he had tried to kill her. He rubbed his head.

"I'm assessing the extent of your injuries." She gave her trademark smile. "Was there something else you wanted me to see?" Her gaze shifted to the right of where her attention had been focused.

He caught her hand. "No." Even to him, his voice sounded harsh.

The humor left her expression. "Why? You've had your hands all over me." Her apparent resentment regarding how he'd chosen to 'touch' her when she'd forbidden him to do so, hadn't eased.

He pushed her away as he attempted to stand. "I took no pleasure in it."

The room spun and he reached out to find nothing but air.

Two hands bunched up in his tunic and pulled him out of the way of Rumsfahail's enormous hooves. He had fallen under the horse and decided he'd better hold still until his head cleared. He closed his eyes and braced against a floor. It felt like it was moving.

"Why?" Her tone sounded strange.

He opened his eyes in an effort to understand her. But her expression confused him even more.

"Why, what?" He heaved a sigh.

She growled and took to her feet. Pacing the stall, she muttered under her breath. She ranted in her native tongue things that he could not comprehend at the moment. Somehow, he was sure he was better off not knowing.

When she stopped, he opened his eyes a slit to see if she was still angry with him. She was, so he closed them again. If she retaliated, then he would rather not see it coming.

"Will you be this inept when you attempt to take her life as well?" She spoke his language.

Darrin swallowed against his emotions and turned his head away. He couldn't speak past the lump in his throat. He grabbed fistfuls of straw.

"It has to be done, doesn't it? I knew the Matriarchy would come to this conclusion." She took a breath and let it out. "I've thought of all the ways to escape this city and all of them end in our capture. It can't be done, so this must happen. Emerald must die." Valerie's expression grew grave. "I will do it."

He looked at her and his heart filled with anguish. He knew she would read him well. She already understood he was too cowardly to do this himself.

"How can you?" His voice came out a tortured whisper.

Valerie squared her shoulders. "They view her as a threat. They resent all that has been lost in her defense. They will not be kind. I, at least, can be quick."

Her eyes were so hard. Where did she find the strength? He shook his head, fighting back the tears.

"How?" he asked.

Valerie bent down to take his knife from the straw. "I love her, and she will let me." She headed out the gate, pausing only to give Rumsfahail a farewell caress.

Darrin struggled to his feet and stumbled after her. He couldn't let her complete this gruesome task before he spoke to Emerald. There were too many things left unsaid.

"Wait."

Just then, Sarialla led her white stallion, Lightning, through the stable doors. Exhaustion made her look older than she had a few moons ago. A dozen rebel soldiers led their mighty warhorses behind the Royal Counselor.

Valerie stopped cold. Darrin couldn't see her face. He did, however, see the soldier's reaction to the blade in her hand.

"Stop," Darrin spoke the Frenland tongue but the men did not heed him.

Before he could intercede, they wrestled the knife from Valerie's hand and tackled her to the ground. They subdued her with unnecessary force. She hadn't resisted them.

"Tie her hands and feet." The soldier jabbed his knee with his full weight behind it into her back and wrenched her arms to bind her hands.

"Stop." Darrin ran to her aid but the men drew their weapons and blocked his path.

Sarialla stared open-mouthed until she met Darrin's gaze. "Desist." She shoved the man off of Valerie. "What are you doing? That is my daughter."

She fell on her knees and pulled Valerie into an embrace. Clutching her battered child in her arms, she wept heaving sobs. "I thought I would never see you again." She caressed Valerie's face. "Oh, how I have missed you, Ree."

Valerie remained stiff at first. It was the use of her childhood name that broke through her defenses. Emotion contorted her frame.

"Why did you kill daddy?" Her voice was thick with tears.

Shock registered on Sarialla's face. "I didn't kill your father, sweetheart." She steadied her daughter before pulling the high collar of her cloak down to reveal a hand length scar.

"My brother betrayed me. Salicor is the one who killed your father. Arlon died trying to save you and Byron from him. I'm sorry I couldn't save your father or stop your uncle." She looked away. "I couldn't save your brother either."

Valerie's whole body shuddered. She shook her head. Swallowing a sob, she met her mother's gaze.

"He killed our uncle?"

"Yes." The old woman looked from her daughter to Darrin. "Killed him with Krelor's sword."

Darrin squared his shoulders. The sword had abandoned him, shocked his hand until he dropped it. Its loyalties had shifted to Byron, though it had not saved the man's life. Darrin set his jaw.

Brutal emotions played across Valerie's features. "And Stephan is the King?"

"Yes." Sarialla wept.

Valerie looked at Darrin. "Tell your mother that the Future Queen's brother will defend the people of the West Wind." She spoke in his tongue. "She need not fear being overrun. Stephan does not seek to take Emerald's empire. Be sure to tell the Steward and the Matriarchs that King Stephan would avenge his sister, should any harm come to her."

A slow smile spread across Sarialla's wizened face. "And tell her that King Stephan wields the sword of the ancient Prince."

Darrin nodded. He brushed the hay off of his tunic and discovered his belt undone. He faced away from the ladies to fasten it. His cheeks flushed with heat.

"Ree, what have you done?" Sarialla's voice held a devastating disappointment.

Darrin glanced at Valerie. It surprised him to see her blush even as she looked away in defiance. He didn't know what to say, either.

"Darrin?" Sarialla focused her scrutiny on him.

He opened his mouth to speak, but Valerie beat him to it.

"For once in my life, Mother, I'm innocent."

The women's gaze met before Sarialla kissed her daughter's forehead.

"Let me help you." Sarialla undid Valerie's bonds and assisted her to her feet, plucking straw from her hair. "There you go." She patted her on the shoulder.

Darrin bowed. "I'll be back as soon as I can. Wait for me or for a messenger to usher you up to the city. Keep these men with you at all times." He limped off to meet with his mother.

Chapter Fifty-One

Emerald counted the empty, idle days. Valerie visited her bedchamber often and kept her loneliness in check. The absence of sound made the stone palace feel like a tomb. The white walls closed in.

Emerald tried to leave. However, the guards and the fact she had nothing suitable to wear hemmed her in place. She could have wrapped in a blanket and escaped. Perhaps, she should have. But she couldn't bring herself to do it. Darrin would be scandalized.

So, she paced the floor when Valerie wasn't around. It was impossible to stay in bed. She wanted to go outside.

These people called her their Future Queen, but she felt no different than she had as a slave. Was she a prisoner? Why did they call her their ruler and allow her no freedom?

Valerie's boots sounded on the corridor floor and Emerald paused her deep stretching routine. She'd been exercising often in recent days. Still weak, she couldn't manage it for long, but she couldn't lay in bed all day either.

"Valerie, I'm glad you've come. I need to get out of this room."

Valerie paled. "Emerald, you have company. Cover yourself."

Emerald flushed with heat and looked her friend square in the eyes. "With what? They've given me nothing to wear. I want out of here, Valerie."

Darrin stepped through the doorway with a stern expression on his face. He closed the door behind him. "It does not become." He spoke his language.

The censure made her furious. Perhaps her behavior was inappropriate, but she didn't care. If she didn't get out in the fresh air again soon, then she would go crazy.

She'd been mad once. Would he like to see her that way again? She clenched her jaw and glared at him.

He broke eye-contact first. Anger might have brought color to his neck, but what his gaze fell upon next brought color to his cheeks. He looked away from her and plucked at the sleeve of his gray uniform.

So, her gown was as see-through as she had feared. The sight of her had made him uncomfortable. Well, good. If she had to endure discomfort then he, of all people, should feel it with her.

Valerie blanched and a bluish tint colored her lips. Her throat worked to find words that never came and she avoided Emerald's gaze. Was Valerie ashamed of her?

Emerald stalked over to the bed. She piled up the pillows and climbed in. She sat with the quilt tucked in over her breasts.

"Are you happy?" She spoke to Valerie.

Valerie backed up, bowed, and abandoned the room.

Emerald sat agape. Why had Valerie gone? Darrin must be to blame. She cast the quilt aside and strode over to him.

He lowered his gaze to the floor. The muscles of his jaw worked and his hands curled into fists.

"Are you angry with me, Darrin?" She spoke his language. "I'm here, right here beside you. Yet you act as if I don't exist. Do you hate me so much?"

His silence cut her like a blade. His actions had always defied her comprehension. Irreconcilably, his proximity stirred her body, the clean scent of him drove her to distraction.

Returning to the bed was unthinkable. When a solution presented itself, she acted. Her hands trembled as she undid the buttons of his shirt.

He evaded her to no avail. She grabbed his shoulder and pressed him to the wall. This forced him to look at her, but he shut his eyes instead. He did not fight her.

She put his shirt on over her nightgown. "You may open your eyes."

His eyebrows lifted in surprise as relief eased the tension from his body. He heaved a great sigh.

What had he thought she was doing? "You wouldn't talk to me unless I was clothed. Yours was the only clothing available." She meant it as an apology.

He took a cleansing breath.

What would he have done if she had made advances? His attitude seemed to indicate that she would have been unwelcome. Frightened, by that possibility, she became angry.

A myriad of impulses pulled her in every direction. Why wouldn't he look at her? Why didn't he say something?

"Why have you come to see me, Darrin? What do you want?" Her heart felt like breaking.

He met her gaze. "I've been sent to inquire as to the name you wish to give your son, Princess."

One of her knees buckled but she leaned on the wall to hold herself upright. How could he speak of her son so casually? How could he call her that?

She slapped him.

He recoiled. Anger twisted his features as he retreated. At the door, he paused.

"Please, give me my shirt, Your Highness. The people will not understand if I leave your bedchamber without it."

Emerald reacted as though he had slapped her. "You care more about what other people think than you do about me?"

"I am the son of the Steward." He closed the distance between them and took her by the shoulders. "My life is one of duty." He stepped back and knelt. "I am, and have always been, yours to command." He bowed to the floor.

Emerald tottered on the brink of passing out. Was Darrin the heir of this realm? Had she taken his place as their ruler?

She sank to her knees. Her hand trembled as she lifted his chin. His eyes were so blue.

"Did you ask me to marry you in order to save your crown?"

His jaw fell open. "No, Princess." He bowed his head.

She believed him. Even as relief washed over her, anger clawed within her. Her mind burned with his words.

"Do not call me Princess. Can't you see how much it hurts?" It took all of her courage to admit her weakness.

He looked into her eyes with a searching expression. She opened her soul to him and allowed her feelings to show. His eyes widened.

His gaze shifted to her lips. She didn't hesitate to fulfill his unspoken wish, and he met her halfway. The long-anticipated sensation of his lips dispelled her concerns.

With her eyes closed, she traced her fingers through his hair. He wrapped his arms around her waist, kissing her more deeply. The tip of his tongue touched her lip and she forced him to the floor.

On top of him, she explored his body with her lips. She kissed from his mouth to his ear and from his neck to his chest. She caressed the angry scar on his ribs. At that moment, she realized her peril.

Breathless and unable to trust her own judgment, she backed off of him. She convulsed with trembling. What had she done?

What would he do about it? Would he finish what she had started? Part of her longed for him to do it but another part of her writhed in terror.

His chest heaved. He looked at her. But he didn't move from where she'd lain him.

Was he waiting for her to tell him what to do? Would he obey her? No man could hold back when his body took control. She'd felt him respond to her. How could not trust him?

He sighed and laid his head on the floor. "If you will give me my shirt, then I will go."

Is that what she wanted? She backed further away. A terrible rushing sound roared in her ears. Her fingers fumbled as she undid the buttons of his shirt.

She tossed it to him.

He dressed without looking at her and exercised great care to straighten his apparel. His chest continued to heave for some time as he calmed his breathing. When he looked as he had when he came in, he left.

With the door shut, she threw herself on the bed and burrowed in the covers. Had it almost happened again? What kind of woman had this effect on men? Old feelings of self-loathing fed on her soul.

Whore.

EMERALD HUDDLED IN bed until a knock came at the door.

"Enter." She didn't want guests.

A uniformed mountain woman delivered a roll of parchment to the side of the bed, bowed, and departed.

Emerald stared at the bright blue ribbon that tied it closed. Was the message from Darrin? She slid it under a pillow without opening it.

Hours turned into a day and then two. Still, she kept to her bed. None of the servants would look her in the eye. They must know what she had done. Shame tormented her.

When Valerie finally came to see her, the visit felt different. She stood in the doorway until Emerald beckoned her to sit in the chair beside the bed. Her friend didn't tease or smile. In fact, she looked troubled.

Emerald couldn't meet her gaze. She wanted to cry and she wanted to scream but did nothing. Valerie would say what she had come to say.

"Your Highness, the people of the mountains wish to honor your child with a traditional ceremony. Lady Celeniurisa sent her son to request the name of the boy. However, he came away with no answer.

Darrin would not say what transpired between you but his concern was evident. He asked me to speak with you. Do you have an answer to give to him?

He sent you a letter. I'm not sure what he wrote but he's paced the floor in anticipation of your answer for two days. His anxiety has made everyone nervous. Say something."

Conflicted, Emerald knit her brow. "I've done something terrible, Valerie." With her confession out, she wanted to hide.

Valerie's eyebrows raised. "I knew it." A hint of a smile tipped the corners of her lips. "That man is in love with you. Is he the one you've been pining for? Tell me, just how terrible was it?"

"He's not in love with me. He's just like all the others." Tears washed down her face and she buried her head beneath her pillow.

The chair scraped the floor as Valerie stood. "If he hurt you—"

Emerald threw the pillow at her friend. "He didn't hurt me, but I almost made it happen again." Emerald flipped on her belly and sobbed into the mattress.

Valerie sat with a thud. "What happened, Emerald? What do you think you did wrong?"

"Oh, I attacked him. I couldn't stop myself." She wept harder.

Valerie touched her shoulder. "You tried to kill him, or you threw yourself at him?"

Emerald fought to regain a semblance of composure. "I made him give me his shirt, so I could escape this cursed bed. I wanted to talk to him with some clothes on."

Valerie chuckled and withdrew her hand. "I would like to have seen his reaction." A vindictive smile crossed her face.

"I didn't ask his permission. I think he thought I was trying to seduce him. You should've seen his relief. It was sickening," Emerald said.

Valerie leaned forward. "Only because you wanted him to like it. Even if you hadn't intended it that way. It still hurts to be rejected.

"Even I am rejected from time to time. So, I know how it feels. It hurts, even though I'm not in love with any of my conquests. In fact, I've had no luck at all around here. I'm starting to think there's something wrong with these men, what few of them there are."

Emerald jerked her head up to look at her friend and realized it had been a joke.

"Very funny."

"You take things too seriously. I don't see what's terrible about what you've told me. In fact, if I was in love with the fellow, I would've let him know it in ways that would leave him no doubt." Valerie folded her arms across her chest.

A wry smile lifted one side of Emerald's face. "You and I are quite alike in this."

Valerie burst forward onto her knees at the edge of the bed, her eyes bright with anticipation. "What did you do?"

Emerald blushed and rolled away.

Valerie caught her shoulder and held her in place. "Tell me or I'll go crazy."

How could she admit the way she'd tempted Darrin to rape her? She shook her head. What kind of woman threw herself at men like that? Realization struck and she felt sick because she had been looking at one.

Valerie reacted as if she'd been struck. The muscles of her face tightened and she withdrew her hand. She sat back on her heels as her expression of joy drained away.

"You thought yourself above the desires of the flesh, didn't you? You thought you were better than me. I thought you were too, but this is different. He loves you and you love him. It doesn't have to be tawdry. You don't have to feel dirty."

"I'm not better than you, Valerie. I'm a temptress and a coward. At least, you have the strength to go through with what you start. At the first hint of his feeling the same way, I panicked."

"What happened?" Valerie handed her the pillow.

Emerald adjusted her position under the quilt. She took a deep breath and let it out. The memory caused her to tremble.

"He asked me to marry him once. I don't know if I told you, but he's the one who pulled me from the river after..." Emerald squirmed to find a comfortable position.

Eventually, she lay on her side and looked at Valerie. "He told me he has dedicated his life to my defense. You should see the scars on his body. He's the one who rescued me from your brother's villa."

Valerie snorted and sat in the chair. "He sure takes his time about it. You'd think the man could have hurried a little. What does that make, twice he's let you be raped?"

"Three times." Emerald's voice fell flat. "If you count the first, and each occasion as only once, then it was three times."

She hadn't thought of it this way before. Why did he defend her at all if he allowed these things to happen? Blaming him didn't feel right, however, because he owed her nothing and had sacrificed much.

Why did he do it? Duty? Did he feel nothing else?

Valerie scowled. "You were right to call him a monster."

"No, I wasn't." Emerald looked her friend in the face. "He's just different. His people do things differently.

"I've been foolish to ignore it. I thought I knew him, but I don't know anything about him. I'm not in love with him. How could I be?" Emerald rolled away.

"Well, then get to know him. You haven't said he doesn't know you. Furthermore, it hasn't stopped him from falling in love with you. He knows what he's getting into, so quit making him suffer. Answer his letter." Valerie slapped the bed.

"I can't." Emerald stared at the wall.

"Why, Em-Emerald?"

She rolled over and offered an apologetic smile. Somehow, Valerie always managed to make her feel better.

"I can't read."

Relief and astonishment washed over Valerie's expression. "Is that all?" She slapped the side of the bed.

Emerald pulled the letter from where it had fallen between the mattress and the frame. She touched the silky, blue ribbon that bound the rolled up parchment. At last, she pulled the bow and unrolled the paper. With both hands, she smoothed it flat on the bed to look at it.

"I can't." The words swam before her eyes. "It doesn't make any sense."

Valerie leaned over. "Well, for starters, you have it upside down." She adjusted the paper. "Does that help anything? I only read and write the language of Frenland and this is in your tongue, I think."

Emerald stared at the paper, focused on the letters. She knew her letters, though she'd never been able to write them to Grandmother's satisfaction. She sighed and allowed the parchment to roll together.

"I can't make it out."

"You hold onto that. I'm going to get my mother." Valerie started to leave the room.

"Your mother?" Emerald asked.

"Didn't I tell you?" She flashed an impish grin. "She arrived the day before yesterday."

Emerald sat up in bed. Did this mean that Valerie had made up with Sarialla? She chuckled.

"All right, go get her. And bring me something suitable to wear."

She couldn't wait to see Sarialla. However, she dreaded what her presence meant in regards to Stephan. She hadn't asked anyone about her brother for fear that he had been killed.

Why hadn't Valerie talked about him? Had he won the war? Was Salicor defeated? Was Stephan the King? She dared not ask.

Chapter Fifty-Two

Four guards carried a large wooden wardrobe into Emerald's room. With grunts all around, they set it next to the wall on her left. The men departed, and Valerie and Sarialla walked in. Sarialla rushed forward to kiss Emerald's cheeks.

"It's good to know you are well." The old woman's eyes teared up and her voice quavered. "I owe you everything for what you've done for my children." Her face grew taught. "I apologize for what my son did to you, Emerald." Color blushed her cheeks and deep sadness filled her eyes when she mentioned Byron.

"It is I who owes you many debts of gratitude and none of them can be repaid." Emerald took Sarialla's weathered hand. She found it hard to meet the older woman's gaze. "Do not judge your son too harshly. He protected me for many weeks.

"In a way, it was my fault that it happened. I reached out to comfort him, never suspecting he would take more than I was willing to give. But he is just a man. There are limits to what they can endure.

"I believe he truly loves me. I really don't think he realized what he was doing until it was too late. I have forgiven him." What would Sarialla think of her?

The old woman embraced Emerald, weeping and rocking back and forth. "Oh, Emerald, Byron is dead, killed as he took Salicor's life. I shall never see him again."

Emerald hugged the mother of her friends and let her cry. The news of Byron's death struck hard, but she could not yet weep. He had killed his uncle and rid the world of great evil. He had overcome his fears.

She stroked Sarialla's hair. "I told him about you, of your love for him and how you wanted him still. In the end, the truth broke through the lies. It was that release of emotion that caused him to forget himself and lose control.

"It only took a moment for everything I believed in to be destroyed. You see, I trusted him. I've never trusted any man before. I don't think I will ever trust another." A shudder ran through her.

Sarialla held on tight. "What he did was wrong, and it has made your problems worse. I am sorry. Trust is the crux of your problem with Darrin and always has been.

"You've never trusted him. Perhaps, he's done things to make you question his ability to live up to your expectations?" She pulled back enough to look into Emerald's eyes.

"Darrin has done nothing I can reproach him with, not really. There are too many unanswered questions to make a sound judgment. The fact is, I don't understand him.

"I don't understand any of these people. It would help if they would communicate with me. But they won't even look at me." Emerald clenched her fists, though she held back most of her unwieldy frustration.

Sarialla smiled and kissed her forehead.

"It is their way. As their Princess, you are unapproachable, godlike. They serve you with deference.

"They do not meet your gaze. That is a gesture of familiarity reserved only for those who have pleased you. They believe you will grant the privilege as a reward for their dedication."

Emerald's eyes widened. "I had no idea."

"Trust me, it's complicated. I haven't figured it all out yet. However, I am fortunate to be low enough in status to have peers and betters as well as underlings. My peers have taught me much in a short time." Sarialla patted Emerald's shoulder as she arose from the side of the bed.

"So, you're saying I have no peers and no betters in this society? What of the Lady Celeniurisa and her son? Aren't they more important than I?" Emerald had trouble believing they could possibly view her as godlike.

"You are the Woman of the Stone, heir of the Ancient Queen and King. You were formed by the hand of the Creator. You have no equal," Sarialla said.

"I thought I needed to do something before I could be made a ruler here. I'm not sure what I'm supposed to do and I'm not sure I want to try. I need people to be honest with me. That's what I like about Valerie. She never hides her feelings." Emerald smiled at her friend.

"You can count on me for that." Valerie averted her gaze.

Emerald's expression softened into one of true affection. "Your honesty saved my life. I hold your friendship dear. Don't value your gifts so cheaply."

Valerie nodded and wiped a tear.

Sarialla took Valerie's hand and then turned to Emerald. "I've been told that you have passed the three tests. They say you have proven yourself worthy of the crown through incredible feats of bravery, strength, and vision. Nothing more has been explained to me except that the matter is most sacred. The details can only be revealed during a special ceremony to be held at your coronation as the Queen."

Emerald shook her head. "I don't understand. But I guess I'll have to wait to find out with the rest of you. I assure you though, I have not sought to rule the Mountain Realm. If Darrin is the heir, then he should rule, not me."

Sarialla shook her head. "Ah, but that's not how it works with the people of the West Wind. This is a matriarchal society. The men are second class citizens here. They do not rule. They serve as commanded, placing duty before all else.

"The Lady Celeniurisa has high status as the Steward, but her son is a simple Guardian. Though he is the Captain of the Royal Guard, without your permission he has never had the right to speak to you or even look you in the eyes. His mother is quite displeased to know that he has broken these unbendable rules." Sarialla winked.

"Incredible." Emerald arched an eyebrow. "He never told me any of this. Though, from what you have said, he was more honest than he had permission to be. Not as honest as I would have liked, but I'm starting to understand the dilemma. I only wish I had known sooner. It could have saved us both a great deal of misunderstanding."

Emerald frowned as she remembered her actions toward Darrin the last time they had met. His actions made more sense now. But hers brought fresh shame and remained incomprehensible.

She had been brazen. That wasn't like her. Yet she was guilty of every touch. The memory brought heat to her cheeks.

"You say I speak the truth?" Valerie glanced at her mother before she met Emerald's gaze. "Then let me tell you the truth."

She walked to the other side of Emerald's bed. "I haven't felt the need to bed a man since I came here. You were right about me. I did it to desensitize myself for when my uncle did his worst." Her hands fluttered and she clasped them behind her back.

Tears slid down Sarialla's face.

"What I haven't told you is what Byron said about the night he raped you. He said it was the worst thing he had ever done because he stole your innocence. He knew you would blame yourself.

"He wanted me to tell you that he only stopped thinking about your wellbeing for a moment. But that moment couldn't be undone. He told me that he was crossing the threshold when you started to scream.

"He withdrew immediately, but you wouldn't stop screaming. Your terror was something he had never seen before. I think you know he has felt his share of it. But this was different, worse somehow.

"You were barely breathing and lost consciousness. It was then that he noticed a stranger in the room. A dark-haired man fought with him until neither of them had the strength to fight anymore. The man went to your side, covered you, and took you away." Valerie glanced at Emerald before focusing on the floor and continuing the tale.

"Of course, the man who rescued you was Darrin. He spared Byron's life out of a belief that you were in love with my brother. Darrin accepted no help and brought you here.

"I learned these things when I met up with Byron. He begged me to come to you and try to explain. He wanted both of us to be safe. He did love you." Valerie looked her in the eyes.

Emerald tried to sort out her thoughts and feelings. Byron had cared. He hadn't finished what he had started because he hadn't meant to hurt her.

Knowing this changed things. The struggle between who she thought she was and who she really was shifted in the right direction again. The last few months had confused her until she hadn't recognized herself anymore. But for the first time since her climb over the mountains, she felt at peace with her identity.

"Did you need me to read something?" Sarialla's voice was gentle.

Emerald gave herself a mental shake. Yes, what had Darrin written in his letter? Suddenly, she had a burning desire to know. She handed the important missive to the Sage.

Sarialla unrolled the parchment on the bed and focused on the crisp handwriting. She read it in the Andolin tongue it had been written in.

"Esteemed High Ruler of the Mountain Realm, your servant, Darrin of Wolfe, Captain of the Royal Guard, has need to thank Your Grace for the eloquent expression of feelings concerning him. As is appropriate for one of his station, he reciprocates your affections and places himself at your command in all things. Should it please Her Royal Highness to grant him the honor of courtship, he would be most grateful. Within the bounds of propriety, her servant, Darrin of Wolfe would ask an audience with a chaperone in attendance to discuss the terms of courtship. Respectfully, Darrin of Wolfe"

Sarialla translated for Valerie.

Emerald remained lost in contemplation. His version of her shameful actions felt like a kindness. His mention of a chaperone rang as censure. By placing himself at her command, he admitted he would do whatever she asked. She understood too much of his modesty to believe that he wanted her to take advantage of his helpless social standing.

In fact, knowing more about his culture colored every interaction she'd ever had with the man in a different light. She had feared him because he was a man and therefore powerful. She had never realized that he placed himself far beneath her, so much so that he felt he had no right to speak to her.

From the beginning, she had been cruel and expected nothing but cruelty in return. It was a terrible mistake. She had treated a tenderhearted servant like an enemy.

Darrin had watched over her in good faith. Had he seen her in Byron's bed? What must he think of her?

Oh, how she must have hurt him. Yet he had come to her aid. He had rescued her again. For her sake, he had spared Byron's life, even though he had wanted to kill him.

Each and every memory she had of Darrin altered in meaning. Each of her actions condemned her and lifted him up. How could she ever be worthy of such a man? Uncertain as she was, she felt she must try. She wanted to make him proud of her.

Sarialla and Valerie whispered by the wardrobe about the dresses hanging there. She smiled to see the two of them. It was nothing short of a miracle that they had healed the breach between them.

Emerald vowed to follow their example. She would humble herself. She would learn to trust Darrin. She would study his culture. Most importantly, she would discover his genuine feelings and accept them, no matter what the consequences.

It wouldn't do for him to continue giving for duty's sake. She couldn't trespass on his kindness or tread on his tender sensibilities any longer. He deserved better. He expected more from her, and she would not disappoint him again.

She cleared her throat and the two women looked her way. "Thank you for granting me time to think. I have made up my mind concerning a certain Captain of the Guard. I'd like to accept his offer and grant his request for courtship.

"I would set the meeting he described as soon as he is able to choose a chaperone. I request that the chaperone provide a thorough explanation of the rules of courtship at the first meeting. Since I would like to avoid making any further blunders. Sarialla, will you write this letter for me?"

"It would be my honor, Your Highness." Sarialla inclined her head.

Emerald looked at Valerie. "Do you think it would be possible for me to have a bath? I'd like to be presentable when I meet with the Captain."

Valerie flashed a wicked smile that made Emerald blush. However, the wink that followed took the sting out of it. "Of course, I will, My Lady. When we return from our errands, we'll show you what we've discovered for your rendezvous with Darrin. Give me your word you won't peek while we're gone. Promise me or you will not get hot water."

Emerald laughed. "I promise."

EMERALD'S HAIR FLOWED in waves of curls to her hips, unbraided and held back with golden combs. She wore a flowing silk dress the exact color of her emerald eyes. Anticipation caused her to hurry.

Alone, she walked to the great hall of the palace. She had still not been outside to obtain her breath of fresh air. Perhaps Darrin would be allowed to take her on her first walk around the grounds.

She saw him. The shine on his boots matched his glossy black hair. He looked well and wore a blue tunic and gray leggings.

Sarialla had explained the customary greeting and farewell gesture exchanged by courting couples. Emerald had seen it depicted in the quartz statue of the Ancient Prince and Dana the Stonehearted in the dusty city inside the mountains. It would delight her to tell Darrin of that beautiful place. Perhaps, one day, they would visit it together.

She took steady steps and measured her breathing. Doing this right held the highest importance. With the last step, she extended her palm to meet Darrin's. They rotated their wrists and leaned forward to kiss the back of the other's hand.

Emerald breathed in the scent of his skin, giddy with a joyful thrill. The heat of him radiated with sudden intensity. Embarrassed that she'd lingered so long, she stepped back and let her hand drop.

She climbed the steps to take her seat on the dais. Darrin and the chaperone stood at the foot of the platform. Even when seated, her head remained far higher than the two of them.

She preferred it otherwise, but she had finished disregarding the rules. If she hoped to win him, then she would do it according to the customs of his people. At last, she would show some modesty.

The chaperone recited the proprieties of conduct to be observed by the courting parties. The tedious formalities of the explanation tried her patience. It surprised her, however, to discover that she was required to initiate each phase of the process. If at any point she wished to withdraw, then all she needed to do was bow and walk away. No further contact would be initiated by the under party.

The next step of the courtship process was, under normal circumstances, the first step. But in this case, the additional meeting to proclaim the rules had been deemed appropriate. Emerald was required to formally request permission to court the under party. A meeting with Darrin's mother had already been scheduled and should she be late it would be taken as a great offense.

There were many other rules. The courtship process took a number of moons to complete. Somehow, Emerald found the timeframe reassuring.

She would have ample opportunity to acquaint herself with the man she loved. By the time the courtship culminated, there would be no mistaking his feelings for her. She wanted him to love her, but she needed to earn his respect.

The chaperone finished his speech. He knelt, bowed his head to the floor three times, and went to stand behind Darrin. Astonishing.

She descended the dais in order to exchange the formal gesture, this time in farewell. Gazing into Darrin's eyes was a revelation. His touch told her there was no mistake. The caress of his lips on her hand caused warmth to pulse through her body.

They parted as was appropriate. He departed the hall with the chaperone. Emerald felt as if her feet no longer touched the floor. He loved her.

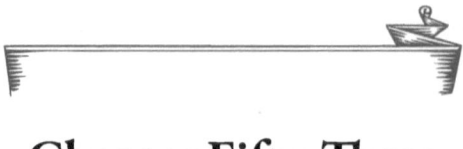

Chapter Fifty-Three

Squeezing the bridge of his nose, Stephan tried to ignore a headache. The court had emptied. It had been a long day involving an endless stream of petitioners. Each one had leveled accusations against someone who had wronged them.

Every day was like this. Unfortunately, today wasn't over yet. Enough evidence and testimony had been heard for him to pass judgment on another man today. This man wasn't the first and he wouldn't be the last but he would soon meet the Creator for his crimes.

Stephan stood up from his seat on the throne with a sigh. He stretched his back and looked out the high windows at the fading sun. Light bathed his scarred head and face.

Something in him had changed. He knew others saw it. Helen had mentioned it, afraid on his behalf. But he couldn't comfort her any more than he could console himself.

He looked at his right hand and scowled. The ink on his fingers might as well have been blood. He had issued orders for the capture of more than a dozen men and one woman today.

He clenched his hand into a fist. It was a good thing Sarialla wasn't here. Testimony of her daughter's cruelty and the suffering that had traveled in her wake had been described in damning detail.

He'd been forced to order her capture. He knew Valerie would not come easily. More than likely, he had ordered her execution.

An unhealthy laugh escaped him. What a coward he was to hope she would fight to the death and not be brought to face justice by his hand. At the same time, it seemed masochistic to cling to the desire to see her again.

Even after hearing the atrocities she had committed, he still had feelings for her. His shoulders slumped and he dropped his chin to his chest. He felt sick.

How could he execute the woman he loved? How could he kill her? Especially when he had discovered first hand that she too had suffered unnamed atrocities at Salicor's hand?

"Sire, it's time." The soft words of his adjutant echoed in the vast hall.

Stephan looked up, squared his shoulders, and walked stone-faced from the hall. He made deliberate progress toward the bloody block that served as the executioner's place of work. A crowd had already gathered.

The guillotine waited at the ready. The guards forced the condemned man to his knees. The look in his eyes wrung compassion from Stephan until he remembered the criminal's heinous crimes. Clenching his jaw, Stephan closed the distance between his hand and the lever. He pulled it with a solid stroke.

EMERALD WAS REQUIRED to wear a traditional costume at the formal meeting with Darrin's mother. It was a painstaking process. Female servants fanned her to prevent her from sweating.

First came a slip to keep the body from chafing under the stiff material of the dress. Then came a corset, followed by the dress. The corset lifted the bosom, thereby enhancing what little these women had in the way of breasts.

In Emerald's case, it worked all too well. She flushed with embarrassment at the prominence of her display. Next came the intricate slippers. They appeared delicate. But must have been designed for appearances only with no regard for comfort.

Each article of the formal dress insured the maximization of the wearer's poise and beauty. Emerald found it impossible to slouch. Furthermore, she could not take more than a shallow breath, lest the fabric chafe to the point of drawing blood.

When the dress settled over her, the sound of the crisp fabric reminded her of the rustling of leaves. She would have preferred the color of the dress matched the leaves it sounded like, but it was red. This shade of red was apparently reserved for Royalty and signified her status.

The servants tied the fasteners. Emerald blushed to see her bosoms protruding with such prominence. There was a great deal of fabric and yet the tops of her breasts were exposed.

She felt half naked. The final touch, a wrap of the same stiff fabric covered her bare shoulders and lent some modesty to her chest. She attempted to sigh in relief but stopped, because the corset would not allow such a deep breath.

The knock at her chamber door announced that it was time to proceed to the Imperial Hall. The servants continued to fan her until she reached the doorway that she must enter in order to meet her future mother in law. She trembled, overwhelmed with doubt. Her lips and fingertips tingled and tiny stars floated in her vision.

Her last spark of dignity found the air to ignite hope. She rallied her courage. It would not due to faint before the Lady of the Mountains. At that moment, the color red did not feel regal. It did seem fitting that she should wear the brazen color, however.

Her confidence collapsed as a feeling of wretchedness swept over her. She could not command her feet to take her into the hall. She stood on the threshold paralyzed by fear.

She knew herself to be unworthy of Darrin's love. How could any mother give her child to such a wanton? Just as Emerald would have fled, the servants swept open the doors of the hall and ushered her in.

The Lady Celeniurisa stood in the light that came through a high, quartz ceiling. Emerald's breath caught at her beauty; her silky black hair flowed to the floor. She looked comfortable in her formal dress of gold.

Emerald crossed the distance between them. The fabric of her dress crackled like a lightning storm as she walked. Everything about the costume induced awe.

She mounted the dais and sat on the throne. The Lady had been provided with a seat as well, though lower and less ornate. Celeniurisa sat on the edge of her chair.

"Greetings Lady Celeniurisa, Steward of the West Wind. I am Emerald Stone, Future Queen and..." She swallowed the words.

Her tears could not be held back. She looked away from the woman in an effort to control her emotions. She could not accept this definition of herself.

The Lady made no movement, her gaze had fixed to the right of Emerald's shoulder. At that moment Emerald felt like a foolish child. How could she ask for this woman's son?

As the Queen, Emerald would be taking everything else from the Lady. It seemed ungrateful to ask for Darrin as well. He was the Steward's only child.

Another realization steeled Emerald's courage at the last possible moment. She remembered the look in Darrin's eyes when she had bid him the formal farewell. He loved her.

She knelt on the floor at the Lady's feet, sat on her heels in a formal way, and bowed her head. "I have come to ask your permission to court your son. I find I cannot ask you until I confess the kind of woman I truly am. I am…a whore, had by many men. I don't deserve your son, though I love him."

She looked into the Lady's eyes. "I love him more than life itself and I will be faithful to him. I will not allow him to place himself in danger for my sake.

"If you will grant my wish, then I will bear as many children for him as I am able. I will raise his little ones in modesty and virtue. You have my solemn vow."

Tears traced the delicate cheeks of the Lady Celeniurisa. They were the only sign of what she thought or how she must feel. She raised her hand onto her lap, it held a dagger.

Emerald gasped. It was the one she had lost in the crystal pool at the waterfall. It was his dagger, Allan, the man who had come so close to destroying her. The weapon struck fear in her. But it seemed fitting she should die by its sting and at the hands of this Lady.

Emerald released the drape around her shoulders. It fell to expose her neck to the blade. She bowed her head and waited for the feel of cold metal against her skin.

When it never came, she looked into the Lady's face. She recognized raw emotion. The blade sat in her lap, but the Lady did not wield it. Just then Emerald remembered she was required to grant permission for others to speak. She reached out to take hold of the Lady's slender fingers.

"My Lady, tell me what is in your heart."

A torrent of tears flooded from the Steward. "Princess, you are a precious gem. It honors me that you have come for Darrin. He has told me much about you. I know you are no whore.

"Though your passions run high, you have never given yourself to the men who hurt you. You have been victimized, and your suffering grieves me. I weep for you and long to make right what my eldest son has done."

She held up the dagger. "This blade belonged to my son, Allan. He grew up a rebellious boy and became an ambitious and cruel man. Allan wished to change the laws of our people and seal his posterity to the throne." The Lady reached out but hesitated.

Emerald grasped the Lady's hand and pressed it to her face. This Lady was a mother. Closing her eyes, she reveled in the softness of the skin against her cheek.

"In the past, I banished all such dissenters. But before I could banish Allan, he joined them of his own free will. I never imagined the havoc they would rein on the unsuspecting farmers of the Danalan. I never thought my son would seek to destroy you." Her voice quavered.

Emerald leaned forward to hug the Lady around the middle. She buried her face in the golden gown. Allan's dagger fell to the floor with a clatter, but neither woman reached for it. Their tears rained.

"You could not know what he would do." A tremor ran through Emerald's body. She hugged the Lady tighter in hopes of driving away the memory of what Allan Wolfe had done.

"No, Princess. I am to blame. My foolish act caused all of your pain. If I had executed the traitors, then you would have grown up safe and happy." The Lady shifted uncomfortably. "With regret, I have another confession."

Emerald sat back on her heels to appraise the Lady's expression. The Steward avoided her gaze.

"I delivered your son, Princess. It is I who could not save him. He died because I had no skill to make him breathe. I am so sorry." The Lady gritted her teeth.

This news struck Emerald. She was still processing the idea that Darrin's brother had raped her and that she had killed the Steward's eldest son. The pain she felt for the loss of her own son was still fresh in her heart.

She had not been able to mourn for him yet. Her memories of him were precious. This kind Lady had given her that gift. It was this woman who had saved her life when death loomed to take her.

"My Lady, you may meet my gaze," Emerald said.

The Lady obeyed and her remorse showed in their dark blue depths.

Emerald took her hand. "You gave me a great gift. You delivered my son alive and placed him in my arms. He looked at me and I knew him. I can never repay you for that treasure of time with him, and yet you have given me more.

"You saved my life when I did not expect to live. It was you, I think, who tended me in hopes I would recover. And when I rejected your help, you found another way to make me live. You brought my dearest friend to help me as only Valerie could, and because of that I am alive today."

The Lady swiped away her tears. "You owe me nothing, Princess."

"I owe you everything. Yet I must ask for more. I took your eldest son's life and now I am asking for your remaining child's hand in marriage.

"Use your best judgment to make this decision concerning Darrin. I will not influence you. There will be no reprisals if you choose to deny my request." Emerald bowed her head to await the Lady's decision.

"Emerald Stone, I welcome you as a daughter. I pledge to act as becomes a mother to her daughter and a subject to her ruler. You survived tortures I cannot imagine. I am proud that you have chosen Darrin as your mate. When you wed, I am certain you will bring each other joy. The love you share will unite the two nations and build a future for our people.

"Princess, you are the blessing we have sought for four-hundred years. You have undone the selfish, cruel acts of the past and have given your all in the effort. For this, I thank you." The Lady bowed her head.

What would it be like to have her as a mother?

Chapter Fifty-Four

The next day, Emerald strode into the Imperial Hall with a smile on her face. Darrin waited for her. She greeted him in the formal gesture, unable to suppress her joy.

The chaperone stepped forward from his position behind Darrin, giving her pause. She had dressed for the occasion and wore a warm, white gown of wool. Darrin wore a high collared gray tunic.

Today would be their first walking out together. She still had never left the palace. Never in her life had she ached to feel the sun on her face or the wind in her hair this much.

It felt right that Darrin should be her guide. She was not permitted to touch him except for the formal gesture. But she walked beside him now, elated to be near him. Their eyes met in a furtive glance and they both smiled.

Emerald could not hold her tongue any longer. This opportunity marked the first chance for them to speak to one another freely. However, she must grant him permission.

"Captain Darrin Wolfe of the Royal Guard, I hereby grant you leave to speak your mind. I extend that privilege for all time." It was a high honor, but a small payment for what he had done for her.

In truth, it was a selfish gift. Her greatest desire was to hear his voice and know his thoughts. She longed for the intimacy of the communication they had shared at Stone Castle. He had been her first confidante and she had missed him.

"I'm deeply honored." His emotions made his voice low. "The gracious nature Your Highness has demonstrated with this act of kindness moves me."

Tears shone in his eyes. "In gratitude for this wondrous gift, I vow to hold our communications sacred. From this time forward, you will always know my mind."

She wanted to hug him. He had fulfilled her fondest wish. With the formalities exchanged, their communication could be as informal as they desired. Though, the bounds of propriety must still be observed as far as touching was concerned.

They walked toward the ornate doors of the palace. The servants pushed them open on silent hinges. Out on the landing, two figures reflected the sunlight through their quartz hearts.

Emerald's breath caught in her throat. It was them, Prince Krelor and Dana the Stonehearted, captured for eternity by the hand of a master sculptor. Her gaze swept past the figures to the city beyond. The wonder of the sparkling surfaces blinded her, but she could not look away.

"I didn't know we were in this ancient city." She looked at Darrin. "How did you find it? I never had the chance to tell you."

His smile vanished and he ducked his chin. "I'm your Shadow. I have followed your footsteps since I was twelve years old. What you see, I see. Only your visions have been your own."

The declaration amazed her. She knew he had been her protector. He had shown her the wounds he had suffered in her service.

She had not, however, considered that he could have followed her here. It could not be true. Yet, he had found her in Frenland.

"I searched high and low for your people. I don't understand how you could have gone undetected? I am quite good at knowing my surroundings. Yet here we stand in this marvel of man and the Creator." She swept out her arm to indicate the shining city within the body of the mountain.

He continued to avoid her gaze. "I told you once that many others have tried to be your Royal Shadow. It's a position of honor most sacred. No other has been successful. Indeed, you do have a gift for sensing the presence of others. Even as a child, you knew you were being watched."

He led her into the city. A few people could be seen bustling about their business. The people they encountered, bowed to the ground in obeisance until they passed.

Emerald tried to ignore it because the custom seemed so strange. She deemed herself unworthy of it. Though she accepted the honor it implied with what grace she could.

"How then did you succeed when others had failed? Twelve seems full young to receive such an honor as you describe it. How did you become the Shadow?" Walking felt good, but she soon tired.

If only she had been given work to do, then she would be her old self again by now. Unfortunately, her hands had been granted little relief over the past weeks. Though of late her mind had been much employed with lessons from Sarialla.

Darrin stopped beside a sparkling fountain. The rim served as a bench. He put a foot on it as he gazed into the water. Emerald sat and observed him compose his thoughts.

"It was a simple thing that made it possible for me to do the job." A frown distorted his face. "You never noticed me at all. I could be three paces behind you and if I didn't make a sound, then you never realized I was there."

She wondered what it must have been like for him to go unnoticed. He'd been so close that it was like he was a part of her. Her eyes went wide.

"You're my match. We are two halves that make a whole." She stood and looked him in the eyes.

He tilted his head in apparent confusion, though his expression brightened at her words.

"I've seen the dead." Emerald frowned. "Well, not so much as seen them, but felt them. Each person has a unique spirit. With you, I feel peace. You are like me and I am like you.

"I think that's why I'm not troubled by your presence. That's why I never realized you were there. Oh, Darrin." She reached out to embrace him, but the chaperone stepped forward and she stopped.

"I had never thought of it like that." Darrin bowed his head. "I felt like I was nothing to you. I believed you took no more thought for me than for your true shadow. It has been difficult to keep my mind on my duty with such a beautiful woman at the center of my work." He blushed.

"Oh." Emerald clapped her hand over her mouth. "I can only imagine. In my defense, I rely on my senses to be certain no one was around because

I enjoy my privacy. If I had known you were there, then I would never have...." She regretted so many things.

His rueful smile expressed with eloquence the afflictions he had borne. Gazing into his eyes, she recognized within him a mirror image of the wound she carried. How could he have suffered so much for something that hadn't happened to him? She searched for an explanation.

"I share your pain, Emerald. What my brother did to you, in a way, he did to me. I felt it." Darrin brought his clenched fist to his chest. "But I couldn't comprehend it.

"You say you have been cruel. Well, you have been as cruel to me as you have been to yourself. I haven't suffered as you have. But seeing the effects of those events on you has caused me almost as much pain." He looked deep into her eyes.

She saw him as if for the first time.

"I failed." He shied away. "I could not protect you from harm. I could not always be with you, because I had other duties that sometimes drew me away. Returning from my father's funeral to find you changed broke my heart and filled me with rage." His spine curled inward with tension as he clenched his fists.

"The first time you were hurt destroyed the gentle girl I served. I often wondered where that girl had gone and why. I didn't realize what had happened until I slept in your castle last spring.

"I heard the terror of your screams as your nightmares replayed the horrors you had lived. It wasn't unexpected. I had seen your wounds at the river. There was so much blood.

"However, the children reacted as if your cries occurred often. It was then that I realized what had happened long ago." He gazed across the city.

She considered saying something here but held her tongue. He wasn't wrong. Somehow, seeing it all through his eyes, lessened the hold the memories had on her.

Darrin rubbed his face. "I never imagined that Allan was to blame until I found the dagger you lost at the waterfall. The realization was more than I could handle. For a while, I didn't recognize or comprehend myself.

In the end, I wept for you. I mourned to know that one who should have protected you had chosen to destroy you instead. The knowledge felt like a noose around my neck."

Heat warmed her skin. "You were the one who found the dagger? Have you discovered the marks he left in my flesh as well?" Fury caused her to grind her teeth. "I looked for you. All that time you were right there? Why did you hide from me?"

He stared into the water fountain. "I was a coward." His jaw bunched. "I feared you would order me into your bed. You had refused to marry me, so I was certain you would tire of me eventually and cast me off."

Her jaw gaped. How could he think she would do anything like that? She dared not speak for the angry things she would say.

"I had failed you at the river." He took two paces away with his back toward her. "Furthermore, I had proved I was not the man I thought I was at the waterfall. I did not dare to face you.

"If I had been there the day my brother had raped you, then I could have prevented it. If I had been with you like I should've been on the day the Carpenters attacked you, then I could have stopped them. I arrived too late."

He bunched his hands in his hair. "I arrived in time to see them toss you in the river. One moment longer and I could never have found you. I thought you were dead.

"Your eyes were open and you drifted, listless in the water. It was my worst fear come true. But then you looked at me." He met her gaze.

"I remember it. You outshined the moon in wonder." She hoped her words soothed him, though his recollections hurt her.

His lip trembled. "I carried you out of the water and laid you on the shore. You were broken and bleeding."

His voice cracked. "You were not breathing, at first, but soon coughed and fought for life. I pulled your trousers up over your bruised hips. But I could not make your torn shirt stay closed." He put the back of his hand to his mouth.

She willed him the strength to purge his soul. He needed to shed the burden of his guilt. His point of view added sorrow to the events, but the sharing of the burden somehow lightened it as well.

"You were alive, but there was no time to do anything except the one thing I was forbidden to do. I took you home. I had already shown myself to you and what I saw in your eyes made me want to meet you even more. I needed you to live." His expression communicated everything to her.

She blushed and walked back to sit by the fountain. What had he seen in her eyes? She remembered feeling wonder bordering on awe at the sight of him. Looking at his face was like a vision. Had she dreamed of him before? She snapped her head up to look at him.

"I dreamed of you when I was a child. We were both children in my vision and so innocent. We held hands and ran through the woods in springtime. The colors were vivid, but none as clear as the blue of your eyes." She shook her head without breaking eye contact.

"I had forgotten the dream. But when I saw your eyes, part of me remembered the peace I had felt in that vision. I'm sorry I ignored my impulse to trust you. It was a terrible mistake." She looked at her hands in her lap. "You're right about my cruelty. I've treated no other person in the world as harshly as I have you."

A rueful smile returned to his face. "Except yourself. Emerald, we both made mistakes. However, all of mine were made in pride. Yours were committed without understanding."

"No. I was cruel on purpose because of what you made me feel. I feared those feelings more than anything. If I loved you, then I would need to trust you. I could not do that.

"I still have trouble with that. I overcame my fears only once. But that ended badly." She looked away.

"You were betrayed, by Byron, and by me."

She snapped around to meet his gaze. "What are you saying?"

He evaded eye contact. His fists clenched as rage flamed in his eyes. His breathing became ragged. Without warning, he rushed at her, leaving just enough space between them to keep the chaperone at bay.

"I watched you lie in his bed night after night. I saw you bathe with him and touch him. I saw his response to you. But worse than that, I saw your reaction to him." Darrin shook.

Scalding tears of wretched shame fell from her eyes. "I prayed every day that you would come for me. But I never dreamed you saw those things. I stayed with Byron because I had to, not because I was in love with him. I'm sorry it seemed otherwise."

She stood to face the man she did love. "You were always in my heart. You filled my dreams." Heat rose in her cheeks and she averted her gaze. "The wonderful scent of you that morning I awoke in your bed is still fresh in my memory. When I looked at your sleeping face, I didn't want to leave your side. But I couldn't face my feelings." She slowly shook her head. "I did not know how."

He watched her for a long time before he let go of the breath he held. "I thought you wanted Byron. I couldn't bear to see it anymore. That's when he did it, while I wasn't close enough to stop him. He did what he had promised he would never do. That is why I came too late." Darrin's fists shook.

A shudder ran along Emerald's spine. "You spared his life for my sake. He told Valerie, what you did and what you said. He was truly sorry."

Darrin shook his head. "It isn't enough. He deserved to die. But I couldn't kill him.

"I understand that he found the courage to defeat his uncle because you wanted it. His act ended the war. Prince Stephan would not have been victorious without Byron's sacrifice. But it isn't enough." Darrin's eyes darted this way and that.

One question filled her mind. "I have not asked about my brother." She stood and took a few steps around the fountain, fearful of the answer. "When Sarialla came, I hoped he would be with her, but he wasn't. She never mentioned him. Does it not seem strange that no one would tell me how he fared?"

Darrin took a step closer. "He lives, Emerald. He is setting the Kingdom of Frenland in order. He sent a request with Sarialla to ask that we keep his plans a secret. But he intends to attend your coronation ceremony next moon.

"He asked my mother for permission to enter the mountains when it came time. She granted it gladly but felt some misgivings about not telling you. I see we have hurt you and I'm sorry." He moved toward her with his hand extended though he stopped short of touching her.

She longed to have him hold her. "Your words are a relief. I couldn't face another loss. Not so close to the death of my son."

He stiffened and drew his hands behind his back.

"I don't blame you for anything, Darrin. I blame myself. In the tunnels, I didn't realize I was ill. I just thought I was tired and I was too proud to beg you to stop.

"In the high grass, I had mistaken you for Byron. I had taken out my anger on you. You had a right to be unhappy with me.

"It confused me, though, because I sensed your disappointment. I thought you blamed me for letting it happen again. It was my fault." She met his gaze.

"No." Darrin's brows crashed together. "I'm the one who made mistakes. I am angry with you, and with myself. But how can you think you were responsible for Byron's actions?"

Heat radiated from her neck and she took off at a steady pace. Darrin walked beside her through the statuary of a rock garden. Neither one of them stopped to admire its beauty.

"I shouldn't have been in his bed, Darrin. I should not have let it happen. I should have fought him. I should have stopped him." She clenched her jaw as she thought back on that last time in Byron's bed.

"He didn't listen to me. I told him to stop. I believed he would stop before it was too late. But he didn't." Indignation brought more tears and she wiped them with determined strokes of her hand.

"He betrayed your trust, Emerald. Being sorry for what he did does not change the choice he made or the consequences."

The echo of her greatest fear thudded in her ears. "Did the baby die, because I didn't stop Byron? Did his entering my body somehow harm the child within me? Did I kill my son?"

Darrin's hand hesitated to take her arm. He glanced at the chaperone. The man stood a respectful distance away, staring at the ground.

"No. I don't think so." Darrin took her in his arms. "There was no blood. He hadn't tried to hurt you."

She trembled at the feel of him against the length of her body. "Valerie told me that Byron said he withdrew as soon as I screamed. What does that mean? Surely, it wasn't good for the baby."

Darrin pressed her head to his shoulder. "It means, he didn't go through with it. Trauma to the mother is never good for an unborn child. But I think it was the fever that did the real damage. You burned so hot it scalded me to touch you. I've never been so afraid."

She lifted her head from his shoulder. "I am to blame. I should have found somewhere else to go. There had to be some other way to survive. Instead, I chose to be in that bed. I killed my son."

Darrin took her by the arms. "No, Emerald. The action you have described doesn't harm an unborn baby. In fact, men are permitted to go to their wives while they are with child. I've heard the men joke about how often they are invited in during that time."

"I don't understand." Emerald controlled her sobs.

Darrin's cheeks reddened and he avoided her gaze. "It seems that a woman's need sometimes heightens during pregnancy. As her body changes, she may grow weak, but her ardor can increase. I know because I asked my mother. I didn't understand your actions and confided in her for an answer to ease my torment."

She blinked back her disbelief. "Then I did not kill my child?"

Darrin radiated heat. "No, and neither did Byron. I alone am to blame for the little one's death."

She swiped at her tears and sniffed her nose. "I thought we had already been through that. Has anyone ever accused you of being stubborn?" The joke had worked with Valerie, and she hoped it would ease Darrin's mood now.

"I know I'm stubborn. But I'm not wrong." His frown deepened.

She locked eyes with him. "We all do things we regret. It was a simple mistake. You have to forgive yourself." She touched his cheek.

He closed his eyes and tears splashed on his face. He squared his shoulders and opened his mouth to speak.

She cut him off. "Then you would let this come between us. You would divide us with the child's death and never trust me again?" Her breath came quicker.

He backed away and started to bow.

"No. Darrin, please. You can't do this. I'm begging you, don't give up on me." She reached after him.

He didn't look at her but stopped backing away. "Then tell me his name. Let us honor him."

She gasped, recoiling as if he had struck her. "I don't know his name."

Darrin's face contorted. "What do you mean you don't know your own son's name?"

Darrin's gaze held her as if on a knife's edge.

"If it were up to me, then I would name him Ethan, after my father." She swallowed back a sob.

Darrin's jaw clenched. "Whose decision is it Emerald, if not yours?"

She broke eye contact. "His father's, it is his father's choice. I promised Roger he could have his child." She curled into herself for the shame of it.

"Why?" Darrin menaced over her.

"Because he asked me." Her shoulders hunched and she clutched her hands around her middle. "Because I didn't want the child and he did. I thought it was the only way."

She slowly shook her head, unable to look at Darrin. "It took me a long time to overcome my hatred for my son. I don't know how I could blame an innocent baby for what had happened at his conception. But I did. It doesn't make sense when I say it like that."

She stole a glance at the man she loved. "I can't begin to explain to you the fear I felt when I considered the weakness brought on by carrying a child."

Darrin's expression was livid.

Desperation ripped the words from her. "Weakness meant it would happen again. It meant men would have power over me."

She abhorred telling him these things. "My body was betraying me with feelings I had never experienced. I had no idea what to do. Everyone depends on me to fulfill my destiny as Woman of the Stone. I had a mission to complete and a child did not fit into those plans."

She tried to capture his gaze to no avail. What would he say? She prayed he would forgive her.

"Why marry me? You have what you came for. Why risk your precious life bearing my children?" His voice held the deepest kind of resentment.

All of the blood drained from her face. "I don't want to be your ruler. I want to be your wife. Giving you children would be an honor.

"To be sure, I'm not without fear concerning the act that produces children. However, I'm willing to endure it in order to be with you." She did not waver.

"Endure it? As if I would force you." His voice shook. "If only you had loved your son, Emerald. Then I could still hope that you truly love me. But no mother could give her son to a rapist. I will not marry a woman capable of that." He bowed and walked away.

Chapter Fifty-Five

Emerald sank to her knees. Darrin was right and yet so very wrong at the same time. She had despised her unborn child at first but in the end, had truly loved him. Tears streamed down her cheeks.

The chaperone knelt and bowed his head to the ground with the palm of his right hand stretched forward. It signaled a request for permission to speak. She took a moment to regain control of her voice.

"You may speak, chaperone." She didn't even know his name.

"Princess, Captain Wolfe has no right to withdraw from his courtship contract. The Steward has given him unconditionally. You alone possess the power to reject him. He cannot withdraw. The penalty is death."

"No." Her stomach lurched. "Please, I will not allow him to die. No, chaperone, he will live and I will go."

She ran away but running did not bring freedom. Her legs burned with the exertion. The exercise and her tears left her gasping for breath, though she kept going.

As she neared the edge of the city, she was drawn toward a building. It had two silver doors and a shrine in front. She did a double take as she realized it was a display of homage.

Its focal point was a bright copper broadsword. A long lock of curly, auburn hair was tied to the hilt. Numerous small gifts sat placed around it.

Stunned, she stopped to look at the newly forged weapon. Unadorned, the sword had no name etched on the double-edged blade. Was this how the people of the West Wind had honored her child? Was this all that remained of him? Her tears started afresh.

She touched the blade. It felt warm. She took the hilt in her hand and a feeling of love rushed through her arm and into her heart. She collapsed to the floor at the foot of the shrine, keening for her lost boy.

"What have I done?"

The baby had died. Darrin didn't want her. She couldn't prove to anyone how much she had grown to love the child. She caressed the blade where her boy's name should lay.

"I did love you, son, just not enough to think of you first."

Even Valerie had proven to have more of a female heart. Valerie had loved her daughter more than anything. She would never have given Lily up, especially to a rapist.

With this understanding, Emerald could not fault Darrin. He didn't trust her. He didn't want to marry her. Who could build a future with someone so broken?

Darkness welled inside her like toxic ooze. It threatened to overwhelm her. She clutched the hilt of the sword, but in her mind, she clutched a blood-soaked stone.

The stone held her bound to a long-ago day. She shook her head and tried not to remember it. But everything was wrong now and she could not deny that her life lay in ruins. She fell to her side as the destructive influence overpowered her hope of ever being happy.

"Not now."

She curled into a ball, unable to resist the evil that enveloped her. She could not look at the blood covered stone. She could not see what she carried within herself.

For six years, she had always run away from what had happened that day. Faced with annihilation from within, she forced herself to look at the bloody thing she had held for so long. Her breath caught in her throat.

A vision of the past came to her mind's eye. Allan was on top of her. Grandmother's severed head lay staring at her. It hurt beyond words to remember her lifeless eyes.

Allan had beheaded Estelle Stone. That was why the air had sprayed with blood. Defeated as she had been, Estelle had not left Emerald alone during the assault. Her spirit lingered through it all, prompting her to take courage.

Estelle Stone's skull was the stone Emerald had used to slay Allan. It wasn't a rock at all that she carried within herself. It was her grandmother's sacrifice; it was her love.

"Grandmother." The darkness within Emerald fled from the warm light of the revelation.

Grandmother had loved her so much that she had sacrificed her own life to save her. She had stayed with her and lent her very body in her defense. It was Grandmother's greatest wish to help Emerald endure the thing she had foreseen. She had succeeded.

Understanding this set Emerald free. Free from the past and the terror it held. Free from Allan and the terrible action she had been forced to take in order to survive.

Grandmother's desire for her to live somehow made it all right that she had done so. The guilt she had concealed for so long disappeared. In that moment the wound she carried closed. Now, she could heal.

She opened her eyes and stood with the sword of her son in her hands. She was done weeping. She sorrowed over Darrin, but he had made his choice and she would respect it.

The sunset shone red inside the crystal city. She walked the downward sloping street to a cavern that undoubtedly led to the passageway under the mountain. However, as she was about to enter it, a gong sounded.

Alarmed by the sound, she glanced toward the palace in time to see white-clad figures flood the city from the upper entrance. West Wind Guards ran past her. It didn't matter however because she no longer cared about her duty as the Future Queen.

With her back turned to them, she descended into the tunnel. The smell of horses drew her to the stables. Dusty poked his head out of his stall and whinnied. A smile spread across her face even as a lump formed in her throat.

"You are a welcome sight, boy." She stroked his neck. "Let's go home."

Don't miss out!

Visit the website below and you can sign up to receive emails whenever S.V. Farnsworth publishes a new book. There's no charge and no obligation.

https://books2read.com/r/B-A-LKBI-OEMY

BOOKS 2 READ

Connecting independent readers to independent writers.

Did you love *Woman of the Stone*? Then you should read *Monarch in the Flames*[1] by S.V. Farnsworth!

Emerald Stone returns from her quest to find everything she took for granted in Danalan hanging in the balance. She must make an impossible decision in order to regain some of what she has lost. In the process, she will become the best version of herself by facing challenges she is newly prepared to overcome.

Read more at https://mailchi.mp/79a2e6d8a775/svfarnsworth-author.

Also by S.V. Farnsworth

Modutan Empire
Woman of the Stone
Monarch in the Flames

Watch for more at https://mailchi.mp/79a2e6d8a775/svfarnsworth-author.

About the Author

S.V. Farnsworth is a linguist librarian who has spent time in Asia. Issues with grit give her multicultural novels the traction to move you.

She is currently writing book two in the Modutan Empire Series, an epic fantasy with appeal to readers who connect with #MeToo concerns and admire strong female characters.

She graduated with a B.S. from SUU in 2002. She recently completed advanced writing courses at MSSU and frequently takes classes and attends workshops on writing.

She belongs to the Ozarks Writers League. She is serving a second year as president of the board for the Joplin Writers' Guild, successfully coordinated the July 2019 writing conference, and is editing the guild's 2019 anthology.

Follow her writing by subscribing to her newsletter!

Read more at https://mailchi.mp/79a2e6d8a775/svfarnsworth-author.

www.ingramcontent.com/pod-product-compliance
Lightning Source LLC
Chambersburg PA
CBHW051558100726
47898CB00001B/142